For my dear friend Dana

# Me and Mr Darcy

# Me and Mr Darcy

# ALEXANDRA POTTER

**LARGE PRINT**

Oxford

First published in Great Britain 2007
by
Hodder & Stoughton, a division of Hodder Headline

Published in Large Print 2007 by ISIS Publishing Ltd.,
7 Centremead, Osney Mead, Oxford OX2 0ES
by arrangement with
Hodder & Stoughton, a division of Hodder Headline

**British Library Cataloguing in Publication Data**
Potter, Alexandra
    Me and Mr Darcy. – Large print ed.
    1. Austen, Jane, 1775–1817 – Characters – Fiction
    2. Vacations – England – Hampshire – Fiction
    3. Bus travel – England – Hampshire – Fiction
    4. Literary landmarks – England – Hampshire
    – Fiction
    5. Hampshire (England) – Social life and
    customs – Fiction
    6. Love stories
    7. Large type books
    I. Title
    823.9'14 [F]

    ISBN 978–0–7531–7954–3 (hb)
    ISBN 978–0–7531–7955–0 (pb)

Printed and bound in Great Britain by
T. J. International Ltd., Padstow, Cornwall

# Acknowledgements

First and foremost I'd like to say a big, big thank you to everyone at Hodder for all their support and enthusiasm for this book, especially Sara Kinsella, who's quite simply the best editor a girl can have. Thanks also to Isobel Akenhead for all her hard work and Alice Wright for her beautiful covers. I'm also very grateful to my wonderful agent, Stephanie Cabot, for her continued belief in me as a writer and for not telling me I was crazy when I told her about this idea!

As always I couldn't have done this without the love and support of my mum and dad. What can I say? You've done me proud as usual! And a big hug to my big sister, Kelly, for a wonderful Christmas in Alamos (thanks to you too, Stevie!), flying to London to put together IKEA furniture in my new flat (now that's love for you) and for being not just a wonderful sister, but a really brilliant friend too.

Talking of friends, I'm very lucky to have such wonderful ones. None more than Dana, who spent the whole of last year patiently listening to me talking about Mr Darcy, being a constant source of kindness and encouragement and — true to her nickname of Wrong Way Schmalenberg — leading me down the wrong path, so I could find the right one! A special mention also to Kathleen for being a great roommate and brainstorming with me during our time together at

Electric Avenue, Lynnette for her continued friendship and support, Beatrice for our weekend hikes and G&Ts and Jamie for always being so kind and enthusiastic about my writing. Thanks also to Melissa for being a truly special friend.

And finally to Barney, my ever loyal companion during those long hours at the keyboard. Big kiss, buddy. Here's to the next one!

To you I shall say, as I have often said before,
"Do not be in a hurry, the right man will come at last."
*Jane Austen*

# CHAPTER
# ONE

It is a truth universally acknowledged that a single girl in possession of her right mind must be in want of a decent man. *There's just one problem . . .*

". . . so we had a drink each and shared a pizza, but you asked for two extra toppings on your half, which means you owe . . . Hang on a minute, I've got a calculator on my BlackBerry . . ."

Sitting in a little Italian restaurant in Manhattan's Lower East Side, I stare across the checked tablecloth and watch, dumb-founded, as my date pulls out his CrackBerry and proceeds to cheerfully divvy up the bill.

*. . . where on earth do you find a decent man these days?*

I'm having dinner with John, a thirty-something architect I met briefly at a friend's birthday party last weekend. He seemed nice enough when he asked for my number — nice enough to share a pizza with on a Tuesday evening after work, anyway — but now, watching him hunched over the table, number-crunching, I'm fast realising I've made a mistake.

". . . an extra seven dollars seventy-five cents, and that includes tax and tip," he declares triumphantly, and shows me the screen to prove it.

A very big mistake.

To be honest, I blame Mr Darcy.

I was just twelve years old when I first read *Pride and Prejudice* and I fell for him right from the start. Forget fresh-faced Joey from New Kids on the Block or leather-clad Michael Hutchence from INXS — whose posters I had tacked to my wall — Mr Darcy was my first love. Devastatingly handsome, mysterious, smouldering and a total romantic, he set the bar for all my future boyfriends. Snuggled under the bedcovers with my flashlight, I couldn't wait to grow up so I could find a man like him.

But now I have grown up. And here I am, still looking.

Digging out a twenty-dollar bill from my pocket, I pass it to John.

"Have you got the seventy-five cents?" he prompts, his hand still outstretched.

*You have got to be kidding.*

Except he's not.

"Oh . . . um . . . sure," I mutter, and begin rooting around in my change purse.

Don't get me wrong. I'm not Renée Zellweger. I don't *need* a man to complete me. I have a career, I pay my own rent, I have a set of power tools and I know how to use them. And as for the other thing, well, that's what battery-operated toys were invented for.

I hand John the seventy-five cents. Then watch in disbelief as he proceeds to count it.

Still, that doesn't stop me hankering after a bit of that good-old fashioned romance I'm always reading about in books. Or daydreaming about meeting someone who could sweep me off my Uggs and set my pulse racing. A dark, handsome, *faithful* man, with impeccable manners, brooding good looks, witty conversation and one of those big, broad, manly chests you can rest your head upon . . .

Instead, in the last twelve months I've been on one disastrous date after another. Now, OK, I know everyone has a bad-date story to tell. It's completely normal. Who hasn't been out with Creepy Guy/Mr Nothing in Common With/The Forty-something Fuck-up (delete as applicable, or in my case, don't delete any of them)? It's just part of being single. It has to happen once. And twice is bad luck. *But a whole string of them?*

For example, here are a few off the top of my head:

1. Bart had "issues with intimacy". Translated, this meant he wouldn't hold my hand as it was "too intimate", but it was perfectly OK to ask me back to his to watch a porn movie on our first date.
2. Aaron wore white cowboy boots. Which is bad enough. But after cancelling on me at the last minute, telling me that he had to work late, I

spotted the boots glowing in the darkness of the movie theatre that night. Scroll up and there was Aaron on the back row with his tongue down another girl's throat.

3. Then there was Daniel, the nice Jewish banker who invited me over for a home-cooked dinner. Unfortunately, he "forgot" to tell me it was his mother doing the cooking. Sorry, did I say mother? I mean, *smother*. Five courses and three hours of listening to how fabulous Daniel was later, I managed to escape before she got out the baby photos.

4. And now there's John, otherwise known as Mr Chivalrous . . .

"So, how about we do this again?" he's asking me now as we're leaving the restaurant.

"Oh —" I open my mouth to reply but instead give a muffled yelp as John lets the door swing back in my face. I just manage to stop it with my elbow. Not that he notices — he's already on the sidewalk lighting up a cigarette.

Rubbing my bruised elbow, I join him outside. After the warmth of the restaurant the cold hits me immediately. It's December in New York and it's way below zero.

"What are you doing Friday?" he persists, raising his eyebrows and taking a drag of his cigarette.

Oh, hell, what do I say now?

I falter. Come on, Emily. You're both adults. It will be fine. Just be honest and tell him.

Tell him what? pipes up a little voice inside me. That you'd rather stick pins in your eyeballs than go on another date with him?

"Erm, well, actually —" I say in a constricted voice and then stop mid-sentence as he blows smoke in my face. "I'm kind of busy," I splutter.

Busy being too busy to go out with a complete dickhead like you, pipes up that voice again. Only this time it's yelling.

"Too many parties, huh?"

Trust me, I so want to be honest. Why let him off the hook with an excuse? Why protect his feelings? What about those of the next poor, unsuspecting girl he's going to date? It's my duty to tell him. I mean, not only is he cheap and rude, but he has hair plugs.

That's right. *Hair plugs.*

I glance at them now. Under the street lamp, you can see the neat little rows dotted across his shiny scalp. Tiny seedlings of hair planted in a desperate attempt to disguise his receding hairline. Despite my feelings, sympathy tugs. Oh, c'mon, don't be so mean, Emily. He deserves understanding and kindness, not judgement and derision.

Swallowing my annoyance, I force a smile. "Yeah, 'fraid so." I nod, rolling my eyes in a "Phew, I'm exhausted from all this crazy partying" kind of way. Honestly, I should be an Academy Award-winning actress, not the manager of a quirky little bookstore in SoHo.

In truth I've been to one party. It was at the Orthodontists' Society and I had a cold. I spent the whole evening popping Sudafed and discussing my cross-bite, and I was in bed by nine thirty. The excitement nearly killed me.

"But it was nice meeting you," I add warmly.

"You too."

John appears to visibly relax and I feel a warm, virtuous glow envelop me. See. Look what a difference a few kind words can have. Now I feel really good about myself. Saint Emily. Hmm, it's got quite a ring to it.

Buoyed up by my success, I continue: "And the plugs are amazing."

"*Plugs?*" John looks at me blankly.

Shit. *Did I really just say that?*

"Er ... I meant to say pizza. The *pizza* was amazing," I fluster, blushing beetroot and trying not to look at his hairline, which of course my eyes are now drawn to with some kind of magnetic force.

Argghh. Look away, Emily. Look away.

There's an excruciating pause. We both try to pretend we're not aware of it. Me by picking my cuticles. Him by surreptitiously patting his hair and checking out his reflection in the restaurant window when he thinks I'm not looking. Guilt overwhelms me. Now I feel like a *really* bad person. Maybe I should apologise. Maybe I should —

In one seamless move, John takes a final drag of his cigarette, grinds it out under his foot and lunges for me.

Oh, God. This isn't happening. This can't be happening.

6

*It's happening.*

For a split second I freeze. Everything seems to go into slow motion. I watch him looming towards me, eyes closed, mouth open, tongue sticking out, and realise he's misinterpreted kindness for a come-on. Fortunately (or should that be unfortunately?), I've been on enough bad dates in the last year to keep my reflexes sharp, and at the last moment I come to and manage to swerve just in time.

His lips crash-land on the side of my face and he plants a sloppy kiss on my ear. Eugghhh. I pull away sharply. Even so, it's a bit of a struggle as he has his hand wrapped round my waist like a vice.

We spring apart and face each other on the sidewalk.

"Well, in that case, I think I'll grab a cab home," he says curtly, stuffing his hands into the pockets of his pleated pants.

"Yeah, me too," I reply shakily, wiping my spit-soaked ear with my sleeve.

Silence. We both stand on the kerbside trying to hail a cab. Finally, after a painful few minutes, I see the familiar sight of a yellow cab with its light on. It pulls up and I heave a sigh of relief and reach for the door handle, but John beats me to it. I'm pleasantly surprised. At last! A bit of chivalry.

Heartened, I soften and throw him my first real smile of the evening as he tugs open the door. Perhaps I've misjudged him. Perhaps he's not so bad after all.

Without hesitation, he jumps inside and slams the door.

"Well, thanks for a great evening," he says, sticking his head out of the window. "Happy Holidays!"

"Hey!" I yell, suddenly finding my voice. "Hey, you've stolen my —"

But the cab takes off down the street with a screeching of tyres.

Abandoned on the slushy sidewalk, I watch the tail-lights disappear into the traffic and, despite my anger, I suddenly feel myself crumple inside. Unexpectedly my eyes prick with tears and I blink them back furiously. Honestly, what's got into me? I'm being ridiculous. The man was a total moron. I'm not upset. I'm fine, totally fine. And sniffing determinedly, I stuff my hands in my pockets and head off in the direction of the subway.

"You should have called the cops."

It's the next morning and I'm at work at McKenzie's, a small, family-owned bookstore, where I'm the manager. I look up at Stella, my assistant, who's standing on a stepladder stacking books.

"Why? For stealing the first cab?" Smiling resignedly, I pass her more titles. "Please, Officer, my date stole the first cab. He's not a gentleman. Arrest him."

"No, not for that," she retorts, putting one hand on her hip and pulling a horrified expression. "*For wearing pleated pants!*"

Stella and I met when she came in for an interview and bowled me over with her extensive knowledge of literature. At least, that's what I'd been expecting after reading her impressive CV. However, five minutes into the interview it became apparent that works of fiction weren't just limited to the bookshelves. Having just graduated from fashion college, Stella didn't have the first clue about books, thought a thesaurus was a dinosaur and finally confessed that the only thing she ever read was her horoscope.

"Well, at least she was honest, and honesty is very important," I'd pointed out to Mr McKenzie, the owner, as justification for hiring her.

To tell the truth, it had been a case of the lesser of several evils. With her bubblegum-pink hair and bizarre asymmetrical outfit that, to a fashion flunky like me, looked frighteningly fashionable, Stella had seemed like she'd be a lot more interesting to work with than some of the other applicants — such as Belinda, a self-confessed "Internet geek" who spent every evening on her sofa updating her blog on MySpace, or Patrick, who was nearly forty, still lived at home with his parents and "adored modern jazz".

Exactly. Like I had a choice.

Three years and an entire rainbow of hair colours later, we're the best of friends, and although professionally speaking I'm her boss, most of the time it doesn't feel like that. Probably because when I give orders Stella ignores them.

"But seriously, Emily, you should have punched this John guy's lights out," she continues, vigorously shoving a fistful of books on the shelf. "If he'd stolen my cab I would have killed him."

"I don't doubt it." I nod. Behind all those wacky outfits and perfect accessories lies the fierceness of a

Rottweiler. In fact, Stella once nearly killed an ex-boyfriend by squirting pepper spray at him during an argument over who should win *Survivor*. It triggered an asthma attack and he had to spend the night in the emergency room.

"So, what are you going to do now?"

"Delete his numbers." I shrug, ripping the tape off a fresh cardboard box.

From the top of the stepladder Stella throws me a sympathetic look. "Oh, fuck. I'm sorry, Em, that sucks."

"Hey, I'm over it," I say, doing my best to sound casual. "Don't worry, I'm not upset over last night. More resigned."

I'm trying to put a brave face on things, but to tell the truth, last night really got to me. It wasn't John that upset me — he was just the straw that broke the proverbial camel's back. Or to put it another way, the date that broke me. Because that's it. I've decided. No more disappointment, dashed hopes and disastrous dates. I'm done.

"You know, I have a friend who's got this really hot brother that's just broken up with his girlfriend . . ."

"Thanks, but no thanks." I shake my head determinedly.

"But he's really great," persists Stella.

"If he's that great, why did they break up?"

With the palm of her hand, Stella rubs her nose in concentration, her chunky wooden bracelets clanking loudly. According to Stella, ethnic is the new boho.

"Hmm, I'm not exactly sure. I think it might have been something to do with his drinking . . ."

I shoot her an incredulous look. "You're trying to fix me up with an *alcoholic*?" I gasp indignantly.

"*Was*," she retorts defensively. "He's AA."

"Well, then he's not allowed to date anyway," I say firmly. "It's part of the twelve steps or something."

Stella looks suitably chastised. Chewing the purple nail polish from her fingernails, she waits mutely at the top of the ladder as I resume unpacking the paperbacks, peeling off the plastic wrapping and piling them up on the floor.

It's still early and the shop is empty. For a few moments we work together without speaking, until the silence is interrupted by the tinkle of the doorbell. I glance over and see a customer entering. A woman, wrapped up in furs. She catches my eye and smiles, before heading into the biography section.

"Why aren't men today like the men in books?" I continue, unpacking a pile of classics. "Seriously, Stella, I've had enough of modern-day love," I say firmly. "And I'm sick of modern-day men. From now on I'm going to stick with the men in here." I pause over a copy of Jane Austen's *Pride and Prejudice*, fingering the cover affectionately. "Just imagine being in a world where men didn't steal your cab, cheat on you or have an addiction to Internet porn, but were chivalrous, devoted and honourable. And strode across fields in breeches and white shirts clinging to their chests . . . yum . . ."

Absently flicking open the novel, I plunge straight into a sexually charged scene between Elizabeth Bennet and Mr Darcy. God, I love this bit. I lean against the bookshelf and continue reading.

"I mean, why can't *I* go out on a date with Mr Darcy?" I sigh wistfully. Pressing the open book to my chest, I gaze off into the middle distance.

"Oh, is he the cute guy who works at the Mac store?" pipes up Stella from the ladder.

I look up at her. Surely I didn't hear that right.

"Because I can try to get his number for you . . ."

"Stella!" I cry in disbelief. I knew her grasp of literature was slim, but this is unbelievable. Surely she's seen the movie at least. "Are you telling me you *don't know* who Mr Darcy is?"

She looks at me warily.

"He's not the guy that works at the Mac store?" she asks tentatively.

"No!" I gasp impatiently. "He's the sexiest, most romantic man you can imagine. Not only is he respectful and knows how to treat a woman, but he's this dark, brooding hero who's incredibly dashing and has all this repressed passion that's just waiting to be unleashed . . ."

"Jeez, he sounds like a female wet dream," she giggles.

I throw her a sobering look.

"So, where do we find this Mr Darcy?" she asks in a subdued voice. "I wouldn't mind meeting him myself."

12

Picking up a copy of *Pride and Prejudice*, I waggle it at her like a prosecution lawyer with a piece of evidence.

Puzzled, Stella narrows her eyes and peers at me for a moment, trying to work it out. Then suddenly it registers.

"*A book?*" she gasps in disbelief. "This amazing man you're raving on about is a character in a *book?*" For a moment she glares at me, wide-eyed, then she stomps down the ladder and snatches the paperback from my hand. "I'll tell you why you can't go on a date with Mr frigging Darcy," she scolds. "Because it's fiction." Climbing back up the ladder, she holds the novel out of my reach. "He's not real. Honestly, Emily. Sometimes you can be such a hopeless romantic."

She says it with such pity it's as if I'm suffering from a terminal illness.

"What's wrong with being a hopeless romantic?" I demand defensively.

"Nothing." She shrugs, plopping herself down at the top of the stepladder and hugging her bony knees to her chest. "But I'm afraid you're going to have to face facts. You need to live in the real world. This is New York in the noughties, not the pages of —" breaking off, she glances at the blurb on the back of the book "— a nineteenth-century novel set in the English countryside."

Then Stella descends the ladder, grabs the rest of the pile of *Pride and Prejudice* and stuffs them unceremoniously on the shelf behind her. "Repeat after me, Em: *Mr Darcy does not exist.*"

# CHAPTER
# TWO

The rest of the morning slips away in a frenzy of
Christmas shoppers. Most of the bookstores these days
are the large generic ones with in-house coffee chains,
more interested in 3-for-2 promotions, sales figures and
attracting people to buy overpriced non-fat lattes, but
McKenzie's is different.

Small and owned by the same family for three
generations, we're tucked down a side street and
squashed in between a milliner's and an Italian bakery.
Most people walk straight past us, too busy looking at
all the weird and wonderful hats in the neighbouring
window or dashing next door to order a toasted
ciabatta sandwich. They don't notice the old mahogany
door with the original stencilled glass, through which
the sun shines of a late afternoon, creating patterns of
light on the polished wooden floor. But for those
passers-by who do happen upon us, either by chance or
through recommendation, their first time is never their
last.

I always think stepping through that door is a bit like
stepping through the wardrobe and into Narnia.
Outside is the hectic buzz of everyday New York, but as

the bell chimes to greet your arrival, you leave reality behind and enter a world of your imagination.

McKenzie's is only a small shop but it's brimming with an eclectic mix of reading material. The walls are lined with floor-to-ceiling bookshelves where bestselling paperbacks rub spines with first editions, specialist titles and rare publications, while in the middle of the floor is a large trestle table laden with sumptuously photographed coffee-table books.

My favourite spot is over by the window. There, next to magazine racks filled with publications from all around the world, is an old leather button-back sofa. Worn and sagging in the middle, over the years it's where thousands of customers have escaped their everyday lives for the few moments it takes to read the first chapter of the latest suspense thriller or be moved by a single verse of beautiful poetry.

I've worked here ever since college, and for someone who loves nothing more than curling up with a good book, it's my dream job. My parents joke that I was predestined from birth to end up here, that books are in my blood. My parents are academics — my mom teaches English, and my dad art history — and they're both total bookworms.

Growing up, there was no TV in our house. Instead, my brother and I were told to use our imaginations and were given books. According to my parents, I learned to read when I was only two and half years old. When all the other toddlers were going to the park to play on the swings, my mom and dad were taking me on trips to the public library.

Apparently, my first words were "Please be quiet."

However, Mr McKenzie is getting old, and with his only son a doctor and not interested in taking over the business, there's been talk of him selling up. Six months ago he had an offer from one of the big coffee chains, who wanted to replace the stencilled glass with their logo, lay a cement floor and put fake books on the mahogany bookshelves. He turned it down, said over his dead body. But even so, I've got a feeling my days here are numbered. Not that I'm bothered about myself — I can always get another job — but there'll never be another bookstore like McKenzie's. Once it's gone, it's gone for ever.

Handing a customer his change, I turn to the person next in line and see there isn't anyone. I heave a sigh of relief. Thank God. Stella's still out at lunch and the run-up to Christmas is always manic. Everyone's on the hunt for the perfect gift. This is the time of year that most people head to the table first, under the illusion that bigger is always better and only a large, expensive coffee-table book will suffice. True, they make an impact, but invariably these volumes of glossy photographs are flicked through once and then left to gather dust, whereas a much-loved paperback will be enjoyed on the subway, in the bathtub and under the bedcovers, and loaned to friends and family to be read time and time again.

Nobody will ever forget *Wuthering Heights*, but who's going to remember *The History of the Romanian Trapeze Artists?* I muse, noticing a figure over by the trestle table. Short and stocky with hair almost a whitish-grey, he's leafing through the large hardback book. I walk up to him. He's deep in concentration.

"Is that for Stella?" I ask, peering over his shoulder.

He jumps. "Hey, Em, how are you?" he gasps, his boyish face breaking into a grin.

"Oh, you know." I smile as he gives me a kiss on each cheek, sprinkling me with the flour that has coated his jet-black hair, making it appear white. "How are you, Freddy?"

Freddy is Stella's husband, but theirs is only a green-card marriage. They met two years ago when she went into the bakery next door to buy sandwiches for lunch and they've been great friends ever since. Freddy's Italian, and when his visa ran out, Stella offered to marry him. In return she gets to live cheaply in his little apartment above the bakery. It sounds like the perfect arrangement, and it is. Apart from one little fact: Freddy's obviously hopelessly in love with her — and the only person who doesn't notice is Stella.

"So, what do you think?" he's asking, gesturing to the book. "For Christmas."

I wrinkle up my nose. "Stella might work in a bookstore, but I don't think I've ever actually seen her read a book."

"Hmmm, I guess you're right . . ." He nods, frowning. "But she could look at the photos," he suggests brightly.

"Have you ever seen her look at a photo that wasn't fashion photography?" I ask, raising my eyebrows.

Freddy slumps and lets out a deep sigh. "I give up. I'm useless. I can't even buy her a gift."

He looks so woebegone my heart goes out to him. "Look, can I make a suggestion?"

"Sure." He nods dolefully.

"Let me do a bit of detective work for you, find out what she'd really like." I squeeze his arm. "And I promise it won't be *Romanian Trapeze Artists*." I smile, gently easing the book out of his hands. "Not that I'm saying it's not a great book," I add, in loyalty to the store. "But just not for Stella."

Freddy shoots me a grateful look, and after saying our good-byes he leaves the store. On his way out he nearly collides with Stella, who appears back from lunch, her face flushed with excitement.

"Hey, Freddy," she says distractedly. Sweeping right past him and over to me, she announces, "Have I got a surprise for you!"

Over her shoulder I can see Freddy. Pausing momentarily in the doorway, he's looking at Stella. His expression says it all.

"You are going to *love* this."

As he disappears into the street, I turn back to Stella.

"Love what?" I murmur. Plonking myself down on to the little wheelie stool behind the counter, I slide over to the computer. I know Stella well enough by now to know that whenever she thinks I'm going to love something, I invariably don't.

I begin checking work e-mails. The shop has finally emptied, apart from the woman still over in the

18

biography section, and it's a good opportunity to make a start on all the last-minute Christmas orders.

"I know what you're going to do!" Stella continues, oblivious in her enthusiasm. Unknotting her stripy scarf, she skips round the counter and stands next to me, panting breathlessly at my side, not unlike my parents' Labrador when there's food around.

"About what?" I continue typing.

"About all these *terrible* dates you keep going on," she gushes.

"Thanks for reminding me, but I'm not dating any more."

Stella waves her fingerless-gloved hand dismissively. "You're going to cheer yourself up and come with me and a bunch of girlies," she continues excitedly.

There's a pregnant pause as she waits for me to ask where exactly it is I'm supposed to be going with her and a bunch of girlies — no doubt with an equal sum of excitement to hers — but I can only manage a half-hearted "Hmmm."

Which isn't enough for Stella, who whoops, "Em, you're going to Mexico!" in the kind of voice quiz-show hosts use on their poor, unsuspecting contestants.

I turn away from the monitor to stare at her. "Stella, what in God's name are you talking about?"

"For New Year!" she gasps, plonking herself down on the counter. I throw her an authoritative look, but as usual she ignores me. Crossing her legs, she yanks up her fishnets and continues: "My friend Beatrice who lives in London just called. She's booked this trip to Cancún in Mexico. Two people have dropped out at the

**19**

last minute, which means there's two spaces left." She grins excitedly. "Me," she announces, pressing her thumb against her chest. "And *you*." With a flourish, she points her finger at me. "We just have to buy our own flights from New York."

"And who's going to be working here while we're both swanning off to Mexico?" I mutter dismissively. Honestly, Stella has no clue what it's like to be a manager. She thinks a store runs itself.

"It's all sorted," she says triumphantly. "Mr McKenzie's already offered."

"As in Mr McKenzie the owner?" I look up with surprise. "You mean you've already asked him?"

"I called him earlier. He said he'd be only too happy to look after things while we're away. To be honest, he seemed rather delighted to be asked," she confides happily. "Says it will do him good to get out from under his wife's feet for a change." Stella pops some bubblegum into her mouth and starts chewing.

Taken aback, I stare at her. I don't know whether to be happy that, for the first time in five years, I don't have to work the week between Christmas and New Year, or annoyed that Stella's gone right over my head. I go for the first option.

"Oh, OK." I nod, for want of something to say.

"Awesome," whoops Stella, blowing out a big purple bubble and popping it with her tongue. "It's gonna be fab. Apparently, it's one of these package holidays for adult singles — it's called Club 18–30."

Oh, no.

I get a sudden sinking dread. I'm always flicking through the British mags we sell in the store, so I know all about these types of vacation. Enough to know they're my idea of hell.

"Club 18–30?" I repeat, surprised just the words themselves don't create a gag reflex.

"Uh-huh." She beams proudly. "Great, huh?"

Now wait just one moment. Did she actually say the word *great*?

"Well, the thing is —" I begin, quickly trying to think of an excuse.

But she doesn't let me finish. "Oh, fuck!" she gasps, clamping her hand over her mouth. "I didn't think."

Now what?

"I'm so tactless." Laying a consoling hand on my shoulder, she says in a hushed voice, "I didn't think about the age issue." There's a pause and then she whispers consolingly, "You're not under thirty, are you?"

I pull away crossly. "Excuse me, but I'm twenty-nine!" I admonish, putting my hands to my face as if suddenly expecting it to have sagged down by my knees since I last looked in the mirror.

Honestly. I love Stella and I know she means well, but sometimes I wonder what's going on in that (currently) platinum-blonde head of hers. First she tries fixing me up with an alcoholic, and now she's telling me I'm old.

"I'm only two years older than you," I add defensively.

Stella winces. "Oops, sorry, I didn't mean . . . I just meant . . . Well, you know what I'm like with numbers and shit and . . . you're ageless, Em," she finishes brightly, smiling at me with that pink-cheeked, perky-eyed, twenty-seven-year-old face of hers.

"And you're about to be out of a job if you keep going," I warn grumpily.

"Oh, come on, Em, it's just what you need."

Stella's enthusiasm is like a bulletproof vest. I swear it's impenetrable.

I swivel my stool to face her fully. "Stella, believe me, it's the last thing I need."

"It's all-inclusive," she adds, winking.

I don't even want to begin to imagine what she's referring to. Fortunately, I don't have to as we're interrupted by a customer.

"Excuse me, but I'd like to take this, please."

I look up and realise it's the woman from the biography section. Gosh, is she still here? I thought she'd already left.

"Did you find everything you were looking for?" I ask, regarding her curiously. Wearing a fur hat, delicate drop earrings and a heavy, flowery scent, she has a quaint, slightly old-fashioned air about her. You'd think she'd just stepped off the set of a Merchant Ivory film and not the streets of Manhattan.

"Yes, thank you," she replies in an English accent. Without looking up she slides a slim, leather-bound volume on to the glass countertop.

I pick it up and glance at the title. "*The Private Letters of Jane Austen*" is embossed in gold lettering.

Funny, I don't remember ever seeing this book before. I turn it over, but there's no barcode on the back, just a handwritten sticker. It's not my handwriting. The book must have been sitting unnoticed on the shelves for years, I ponder, ringing up the purchase.

"Here. Why don't you take a look at the resort?" Reappearing from the back, Stella plops a glossy brochure next to the cash register. Out of the corner of my eye I see a close-up shot of busty girls in bikinis shrieking with their arms above their heads as they ride an inflatable banana. The words "FUN!FUN!FUN!" are emblazoned across it in acid-yellow.

"I'm afraid you're going to have to count me out," I reply, without even picking it up.

"But why? It's a really good deal, it'll be fun. Think of all that sun, sea, sand . . ." Glancing at the customer, Stella lowers her voice, leans towards me and whispers in my ear, "*Sex!*"

A vision of dancing around in a foam-filled nightclub in a beaded wristband with a spotty-faced eighteen-year-old and a pina colada stuffed full of brightly coloured umbrellas fills me with dread.

"I am," I murmur, handing the English lady her receipt and brown paper bag with "McKenzie's" printed on the side. She dips her head politely, her face still hidden by her gigantic fur hat, and then turns and walks away.

"I mean, look at this guy. He's gorgeous."

I turn my attention back to Stella, who's poring over the brochure.

"I'm not going," I say firmly.

"Oh, Em . . ." she whines.

"No." I shake my head resolutely and move back over to the computer. I resume checking e-mails: books on order . . . promotional offers . . .

"So what are you going to do? Are your parents going to be home this year?"

My parents live upstate but they haven't spent Christmas and New Year at home since I graduated from college. Last year it was a safari in Botswana. The year before it was two weeks on a houseboat in India. And before that . . . God, I've lost track, but it was somewhere cell phones don't work.

"Spending your inheritance" is how they laughingly describe these trips, and I'm really pleased for them. They're born-again hippies with money. They wear Birkenstocks, drive a Prius and eat organic — Dad even took up yoga until he put his back out — and every year they disappear without so much as a Christmas card.

"No, this year they're going to Thailand on some meditation retreat." I shrug. "But I've been invited to my auntie Jean's for dinner on Christmas Day."

Admittedly I used to get a bit upset when all my friends were going to spend the vacation at home, with the tree and turkey and everything, but I've got used to it now. Usually I go stay with my brother, Pete, in Brooklyn, but six months ago he met Marlena, an actress, so this year they've decided to visit her parents in Florida for New Year. Which is fine. I'll probably stay home this year and curl up with a glass of wine and a good book. New Year's Eve is always a huge anticlimax anyway, isn't it?

"But what about New Year's Eve?" asks Stella, not looking up from her brochure.

Saying that, I'd prefer not to admit my plans to the girl who thinks staying in on just a *regular* Friday night is a fate worse than death.

I pause, and at that moment I notice something on the counter. It's a flyer. That's weird. I didn't see it before. I wonder who left it? Curious, I reach over and pick it up. It's a photograph of stunning countryside over which, in black lettering, reads:

## SPECIALIST TOURS FOR LITERATURE LOVERS.
Spend a week with Mr Darcy. Explore the world of Jane Austen and *Pride and Prejudice* in the English countryside.

"I'm going to England," I blurt.

As soon as the words come out of my mouth, I want to stuff them back in again. Oh, shit. Why did I go and say that?

"You are?" Stella rounds on me, her eyes wide with astonishment. "When?"

Oh, double shit. I have no frigging idea.

Anxiously I glance at the flyer. There's a website address and so, pretending to be still busy checking e-mails, I quickly type it into the computer. Thank God for DSL. A box immediately opens.

"Um . . ." I try to act all casual while quickly scrolling down through the information surrounding the tour. I'm just going to have to bluff it. "Soon . . ." I hedge, playing for time. Oh, sweet Jesus, where are the damn dates? They must be here somewhere. Trying to stay cool, calm and collected, I smooth back my hair and keep scrolling, my eyes scanning furiously. I can feel Stella's eyes burning a hole in the side of my head.

OK. No need to panic, Emily.

An image of the inflatable banana pops into my head.

I panic.

Then I see them. Written in fine type at the bottom are all the various dates for tours. At last! Spotting one that coincides with the vacation to Cancún, I click on it. Well, you never know, they might have a cancellation over New Year. Surreptitiously I cross the fingers of my left hand underneath the counter. And anyway, it's not as if I'm actually going, I'm just pretending.

I do a double-take as "ONE SEAT LEFT" pops up on the screen and stare at the words in astonishment.

"How soon?" challenges Stella.

Then again, it might be rather fun. England for New Year. I can just imagine it now. All those cute little villages, cosy British pubs with open fires and bursting with history.

*And not an inflatable banana in sight.*

I move the mouse to "BOOK NOW" and click.

"Next week."

# CHAPTER
# THREE

A week later, having spent a quiet Christmas Day at my auntie Jean's, I'm back at my flat packing for my trip. It's December 27 and my flight leaves in a few hours. Stella's sitting on my sofa bed eating her way through a tub of hummus and watching me trying to squeeze more books into my holdall. No matter that I'm only going for a week, I have to be prepared. Obviously I've had to pack all six of the Austen novels, which takes up a fair amount of room, although I've left out *Pride and Prejudice* to take in my hand luggage as I want to read it again.

Then of course there's the contemporary stuff, like this book by a new writer that's been number one on the *New York Times* bestseller list for the last six weeks that I've been dying to read.

"You're going to spend the holidays in England. In the freezing cold. With some Jane Austen book club?" asks Stella, interrupting my thought process.

"It's not a book club, it's a specialist tour. And it's for literature lovers," I correct primly, quoting the flyer.

Scooping up a blob of hummus on the end of a baby carrot, Stella looks at me with undisguised despair. She's come over with the excuse of borrowing my flat-irons, which I've never used and are still in their box, to take to Mexico. But now, nearly a whole tub of hummus later, I realise it's all been a ruse — she's here to try and get me to change my mind.

And she'll stop at nothing.

"You know what that means, don't you?" she continues, munching loudly, her chin resting on her black Lycra-clad knees.

Reluctantly turning away from a pile of paperbacks on my bedside table, I make a start on my sock drawer. "No, but I'm sure you're going to tell me," I say stiffly, bundling socks into little balls.

"Kooks," she says matter-of-factly, throwing me a look.

I pause mid-sock-ball. "What do you mean, *kooks*?"

"You know. Weirdos. Misfits. *Old people.*"

Aghast, I stare at Stella. "I can't believe you just said that."

Oh, OK, so I'm not really shocked, but being her boss I have to at least *appear* to take the moral high ground here.

"Well, think about it. What kind of people want to spend the vacations with a bunch of strangers, talking about books?"

"*I do*," I gasp, offended.

Stella throws me a look of pity.

"I happen to like books. I'm the manager of a bookstore, remember? Does that make me a kook?" I ask haughtily.

Stella scrapes another baby carrot round the sides of the plastic tub to get the last of the hummus. "No. You were a kook anyway." She smiles, licking off the excess.

Throwing a velvet cushion at her, I turn back to my bookshelves to make sure I haven't forgotten anything.

"Forgive me if I'm being stupid, but are you actually going to take any *clothes* on this trip?" asks Stella after a moment.

"Of course," I reply indignantly. "I just haven't gotten round to that bit yet."

Actually, to tell the truth, I haven't really given the clothes bit much thought. After all, I'm only away for a week.

"And it's not as if I'm going to need that much," I point out in my defence.

"But you're going to need *some*."

I turn round to see Stella eyeing my little holdall with suspicion.

"I don't see any in here yet, and it's already quite full," she continues doubtfully, before suddenly flashing me a smile, "Don't tell me! You're planning a trip to Topshop the moment you arrive."

"What's Topshop?

Stella looks at me in disbelief. "*What's Topshop!*" she cries. "Topshop is my holy land."

I look at her blankly.

"Never mind, you wouldn't understand," she sighs, shaking her head. "Clothes are obviously not a priority." She looks pointedly back at my holdall.

"OK, OK, point taken," I say huffily. "Maybe I need to bring a bigger bag." Reaching under my bed, I tug out my old suitcase on wheels and flip it open. "See. Plenty of room." Hastily I decant my books into it and turn to my closet.

I tug out a couple of sweaters. One is pink mohair with glittery bits round the cuffs and is sort of my fun sweater — you know, for having a snowball fight or something. Not that I've had a snowball fight since I was about ten, but it was featured in a magazine in one of those photo shoots where the models are rosy-cheeked and twinkly-eyed, and wearing mini-skirts and stripy tights. A look I've never managed to achieve, being a total fashion flunky. Every season I think about it — for about five minutes — and then put on my old jeans I've had for years.

My other sweater's a black cashmere turtle neck. I bought it in DKNY one January as part of my resolution to be more stylish after Stella, with typical subtlety, had pointed out that "Books might be your passion, but you can't fuck a paperback." Even in the sale it set me back a fortune. I thought it would make me look smart and elegant, but to tell the truth I feel really boring in it. Like I'm an accountant or something.

I hold up both sweaters for Stella's opinion. "Pink or black?"

She peers at them with a disapproving fashionista's eye. "Definitely the pink," she says after a moment.

"But the other one's cashmere," I point out.

"So?" Stella shrugs.

Being a couple of years younger than me, Stella has not yet reached the age when you read *Vogue* at the hairdresser's and crave to be one of those celebrities who, when interviewed about what essentials they buy for their winter wardrobe, reply casually, "Cashmere in bulk." She's still happy with an acrylic mix.

"It's boring." She yawns dismissively.

I stuff both in my suitcase. She's right — the pink is much nicer — but I have to bring the black with me to justify spending that much. Even if it just passes back and forth across the Atlantic without even leaving my suitcase I'll feel better. And I might wear it.

No, you won't, Emily. You've had it for three years and you've never worn it. It makes you look like Auntie Jean.

Oh, shut up.

Turning back to my closet, I try deciding what else to take. God, I hate packing. I'm crap at it. I have no idea what to take.

Giving up with any pretence of choosing, I chuck in lots of basic stuff — T-shirts, jeans, sweatshirts — then try to zip it up. But the zipper won't budge. Seeing my plight, Stella untangles her legs from beneath her and joins me. Together we bump up and down on the lid, wiggling our butts and grunting a lot. Finally I zip it up. Just.

"Right, that's it. All done." I stand back and look at it with satisfaction. "What about you? Have you packed already?" Stella's flight to Mexico this evening too, but she's apt to leave things to the last minute.

"Yep. I did a major splurge at this really hip new store in Greenwich Village," she enthuses, idly looking through all the bottles of nail polish on my dresser. "And then I found these amazing sarongs in Chinatown. I'm taking a different one for every day that I'm going, to just throw on over my bikini and Havaianas." Unscrewing a lid, she paints a thumbnail, holds it to the light, then wrinkles up her nose in distaste and screws the lid back on. "I've got my whole look planned. It's a sort of fusion between Miami Beach and the East."

"But you're going to Mexico," I point out, puzzled.

"Honestly, Em, it's a fashion term," she gasps, shaking her head in despair. "Oh, and of course I've packed condoms," she adds nonchalantly, in the way people always do when they're dying for you to ask them about it. Usually I'd ignore it, but this time I *am* dying to know.

"Condoms?" I repeat, slightly shocked. "But what about Freddy?"

"What about him?" she says innocently, picking up a copy of *The Time Traveller's Wife* from my dresser and leafing through it. Trust me, if ever there was suspicious behaviour, this is it.

"I thought something might be happening between you two."

"Why, because we're married?" she teases. "You know that was purely so he could get his papers. He's adorable and I love him to bits, but he's *so* not the right guy for me," she says decisively. "And I'm *so* not the right girl for him."

"Why not?" I persist.

"We're complete opposites," she says simply. "I'm a vegetarian, he eats salami for breakfast. I'm untidy, he's a neat freak. I like to stay up late, he's in bed by nine thirty every night as he has to be at the bakery for four a.m. We'd drive each other crazy if we were really a couple." She fidgets with her wooden bangles, rolling them up and down her forearm in agitation. "Look, Freddy's the sweetest person in the whole world, and he'll make someone a wonderful boyfriend, but not me."

Grabbing my big, fluffy, mohair scarf, I turn to face her. "Well, I think you'd make a great couple," I persist.

"Oh, Em . . ." Stella shakes her head pityingly. "Get real."

"I am real," I reply indignantly.

"No, you're not, you're a romantic," she dismisses.

That's the second time Stella's called me a romantic this week, and it's beginning to grate.

"I'm also a realist," I point out righteously.

Stella throws me a look that says *purlease*.

"I am," I repeat feebly.

"And this from the girl who wants to date Mr Darcy."

Feeling my cheeks burning, I stalk over to my hand luggage to start packing that.

"Who, might I add, you told me was fabulously wealthy," adds Stella, picking up my brand-new copy of *Pride and Prejudice*, which I bought to take with me on this trip. My old one has been read so many times it's falling apart. "I mean, c'mon. Let's be honest. That Elizabeth Bennet was only interested in Mr Darcy because he was an aristocrat and had that big fuck-off estate wherever it was . . ."

"Pemberley in Derbyshire," I prompt. Earlier I gave Stella a little potted synopsis of the novel, though I don't remember it sounding like this.

". . . trust me, she would never have even looked at him if he'd lived in a tiny apartment above a bakery." Sighing, she puts down my book and absently picks up my itinerary. "Ooh, look, you're going to a New Year's Eve ball," she says, perking up. "*Groovy.*"

"I know, great, huh?" I smile, relieved to be changing the subject. Padding into my tiny bathroom, I open my cabinet and begin haphazardly chucking stuff into a sponge bag.

"So what are you going to wear?"

"Wear?" I pause mid-chuck, feeling my frisson of excitement disintegrating at the thought of being hauled in front of the fashion police.

"Please tell me you have a dress," hollers Stella sternly.

I shut the door of the bathroom cabinet and look at my reflection in the mirror: *shit*

"Of course I have a dress," I say defensively, emerging from the bathroom. "Honestly, what do you think I'm going to wear? T-shirt and jeans?"

By the look on her face that's a yes.

She narrows her eyes. "Well . . . where is it?"

"In my suit bag." I gesture to the black vinyl bag hanging on my closet.

"Can I see it?" she asks, reaching for the zipper.

"Not really. It's all packed," I say, hastily making an excuse. "In tissue paper," I add.

Good thinking. Tissue paper makes it sound as if it's from a really expensive boutique.

Stella looks suitably impressed, but still suspicious. "Describe it," she demands, folding her arms.

34

"Erm . . . well, it's . . ." I falter as I think about my shopping trip a couple of days ago on a mission to find something. And how I flailed around in H&M with armfuls of dresses, feeling overwhelmed and desperate, until finally I just went for the most — "Festive," I say vaguely.

"*Festive?*"

"And fun," I add hopefully.

"*Festive and fun?*" she gasps in disbelief. "Emily, are we talking about a dress here or a novelty blow-up Santa?"

I make a last-ditch attempt. "It has sequins," I venture doubtfully.

Stella's face collapses. She looks distraught, standing there in her vintage pussybow blouse and asymmetrical skirt from a boutique that's so intimidating I daren't even peer in the window.

"Festive is not fun, Emily, it's a fashion *nightmare*," she's shrieking, clutching her temples. "Festive has zero style. All those boring little black dresses, sequinned scarves and sparkly eyeshadow." She gives a little shudder and suddenly I remember.

Oh, no. Please don't let her see my new —

"What's this?"

Too late.

Pouncing on my new sparkly eyeshadow that I bought in the same desperate shopping trip, Stella sweeps a shimmery stripe across her eyelid, then stands back and peers at herself.

"Iridescent Frost?" she accuses.

I knew I should have bought matt. I *knew* it.

"So, back to Freddy. There's definitely no chance of romance?" I ask, trying to distract her before it gets worse and she discovers the sequinned scarf I bought on a whim at the weekend.

Thankfully it works.

"Absolutely not," she gasps and flops down on to my white cotton comforter. "I may be married, but I'm very much single. And I need my best friend." Pouting, she rolls over on to her stomach and props herself up on her elbows. "Are you sure I can't persuade you to ditch the old folks on the minibus and come have some fun in Mexico instead? There's still one space left." She pretends to whimper.

"It's a luxury tour bus," I correct her. "And no thanks." I shake my head. "I know you find this hard to believe, Stella, but I *want* to go on this tour." It's true. Now I've had the chance to think about it, I'm really looking forward to it. "I've always wanted to go to England, ever since I read Jane Austen, and now's my opportunity."

"Well, the British men can be pretty cute," concedes Stella, completely missing my point. "Just look at Daniel Craig."

"I'm not going for the men," I gasp impatiently, attempting to stuff *The Time Traveller's Wife* through a tiny gap in the zipper of my suitcase.

"Not even James Bond?" she sighs dreamily. Then seeing me struggling, snaps, "Jesus, Em. Haven't you got enough books already?"

"Some people pack too many clothes, with me it's books," I say coolly, in an attempt to justify myself.

Hoisting herself up from my bed, Stella shoots me a look that says she's not buying it.

"I never know what I'm going to want to curl up in bed with." I shrug.

"How about trying a man?" she retorts, tugging on her scarf and mittens.

Now it's my turn to shoot her a look.

"Seriously, Em, how long has it been since you actually . . .?"

"I've told you. The only men I'm interested in are in here . . ." I grab my copy of *Pride and Prejudice* and slap it on the top of my suitcase.

"OK, OK, I won't say another word." She holds up her mittened hands in surrender. "Anyway, I'd better go. I've got a plane to catch?"

I nod. "Shame we're flying from different airports or we could have shared a cab."

We both look at each and I realise it's time to say goodbye.

"Well, toodle-pops," trills Stella in an appalling attempt at a British accent.

"I think it's toodle-*pip*," I grimace, laughing.

"Oh, well, whatever it is those crazy Brits say." She shrugs, and then her face softens. "You look after yourself and have a good time, OK?" Throwing her arms round me, she gives me a hug. "Promise?" she asks, uncharacteristically emotional.

I squeeze her tightly. "Promise."

For a brief moment I feel a twinge of doubt about spending New Year's alone and not with Stella and her friends, but just as briefly I dismiss it. I'm a big girl. I'll be fine. "Now, make sure you call me from Mexico, let me know how the margaritas are, won't you?"

"Definitely." She nods, throwing me that famous Stella grin. Releasing the latch, she tugs open the door. "Oh, and by the way . . ." she pauses in the doorway ". . . this eyeshadow is awesome." And winking at me, she disappears into the hallway.

# CHAPTER
# FOUR

Fast-forward eleven hours and I'm standing in the immigration line at Heathrow Airport, jet-lagged but excited. I feel a whoosh of exhilaration. Even now I can't believe it's actually happening, that I'm actually here in England. *England!*

"Next!"

Stifling a hippo-sized yawn, I look up to see I'm being waved forward by one of the officials, a grim-faced, middle-aged woman with short, frizzy hair and glasses.

"How long do you intend to spend in the United Kingdom?" she demands in a clipped voice as I approach the counter.

"A week," I reply, giving her a friendly smile.

It has absolutely zero effect. Taking my passport, she studies it gravely and begins tapping furiously into her keyboard.

"And what is your purpose for visiting?"

"I'm here on a tour," I reply eagerly.

Without looking up, the immigration officer pushes up her glasses and continues tap-tapping, her lips tightly pursed.

My excitement wobbles. Her silence is beginning to make me a bit nervous. As if I've done something wrong somehow. A flashback of being caught shoplifting pops into my head and I feel a beat of worry. Oh, God, don't say I've got some kind of criminal record and they've found it on an international database. OK, so I was only eleven and it was Barbie clothes, but still. *I have a history.*

With my front teeth I begin chewing the flaky bits off my lips, which I only ever do when I'm nervous, and which I shouldn't do as they always start bleeding.

They start bleeding.

"What kind of tour?" asks the officer, breaking off momentarily to flick through my passport. She grimaces at my picture — which isn't *that* bad — then resumes her work at the keyboard. What on earth is she typing? An essay? *A police report?*

My stomach nosedives.

"It's a specialist tour for literature lovers," I croak, my voice coming out all funny and high-pitched. Clearing my throat, I swallow a few times. "A week in the English countryside to explore the world of Jane Austen and *Pride and Prejudice*," I add weakly.

As if she cares, I think anxiously.

"*Pride and Prejudice?*" she repeats sharply, without looking up. Her fingers freeze on the keys. "Did you just say *Pride and Prejudice?*"

My immigration officer seems galvanised by this news.

"Um, yes." I nod, uncertainly.

40

She looks up, her face flushed with excitement. "Oh, my giddy aunt, I can't believe it! I *love Pride and Prejudice!*" she shrieks loudly. Clutching at her polyester chest, she throws me a dazzling smile. "I just saw the film adaptation with Keira Knightley on DVD. Wasn't it wonderful?"

I'm completely taken aback by her transformation. "Erm, yes . . ." I stammer.

Leaning back in her chair, she loosens the top button of her blouse and begins fanning herself with my passport. "And that Mr Darcy." Rolling her eyes, she shoots me a lustful look. "Sex on a stick!" Leaning forwards, she winks conspiratorially. "I tell you what, I wouldn't kick him out of bed," she whispers, and giggles girlishly.

I stare, dumbfounded. I know Mr Darcy has an effect on women, but this is incredible.

Several minutes later we're on first-name terms and Beryl is telling me all about her recent divorce from her husband, Len, her decision to work over the Christmas period and how much she wished she'd heard about the tour . . .

". . . because it sounds marvellous, love." She smiles warmly, handing back my passport. "I'd rather be spending the festive season with Mr Darcy than a load of asylum seekers, I can tell you. Maybe next year, eh?"

"If you want, I'll let you know how it is," I offer pleasantly.

"Ooh, would you do that?" Beryl smiles, and scribbles something on a piece of paper. "Here's my e-mail address."

As I take it from her she squeezes my hand earnestly. "Have a great trip."

"Thanks, Beryl." I smile, slipping my passport into my pocket.

Waving goodbye, I grab my wheelie suitcase and pass through immigration with ease, then pause at the exit to look back. Just in time to hear Beryl bark, "Next," and see her smile morph into that scarily grim expression as she summons another nervous passenger. "How long do you intend to spend in the United Kingdom?"

I smile to myself. Thanks a lot, Mr D.

Walking through the arrivals gate, I'm greeted by crowds of people leaning over the barriers waiting for their loved ones to appear off their flights. The place reeks of festive excitement. Strung with Christmas decorations, carols are being piped over the speakers and tinsel and lights are everywhere. A buzz of English accents hums around me, and my ears home in on pieces of conversation, like a radio being tuned in, picking up the different stations.

"Oooh, sweetheart, you look smashing with that suntan. Doesn't she look smashing with that suntan, David? It's been brass monkeys here . . ."

". . . you snogged how many blokes in Bali . . .?"

". . . what on earth do you mean, his plane's delayed, darling? Crikey! We're supposed to be at the registry office in less than an hour . . ."

". . . so what was Goa like? Did you go to any of those beach raves . . .?"

"... we're taping *Coronation Street,* so as soon as we get home I'll put the kettle on. I bet you're gagging for a nice cup of tea after all that foreign muck ..."

*Snogged? Blokes? Crikey? Gagging? Brass monkeys?* What on earth are they talking about? Marvelling at all these weird and wonderful words, I weave my way through the crowds. Apparently, someone is going to be here to meet me, but I don't know how I'm supposed to recognise them ...

"Emily Albright?"

In the middle of the scrum of people, I spot a tiny, bird-like figure in a tweed suit holding up a sign with my name on it. I rush over, wheeling my trolley with my luggage behind me.

"Hi," I say politely. "Nice to meet you."

The woman with the sign throws me a lively smile and extends her hand. "Miss Steane. Your tour guide. A pleasure to meet you, too," she replies jovially, her hazel eyes twinkling.

Something about her makes me falter. She seems really familiar. Have I met her before? For a moment I try to place her. Her face is freshly scrubbed and her hair is pinned up in a no-nonsense fashion. Yet, despite her frumpy appearance, she's probably only the same age as the forty-something women I see on the streets of Manhattan, groomed to within an inch of their expensive honey-blonde highlights.

I smile, giving up on wracking my memory. Nope, it's impossible. She probably just reminds me of someone off TV or something, I decide, going to shake hands.

"We're delighted to have you on board our Jane Austen tour."

"Why, thank you." I nod as she grips my hand and pumps it vigorously up and down.

For such a petite woman, Miss Steane has an unexpectedly firm handshake.

"I'm sure you're going to find the next few days truly fascinating," she continues.

"Great, thanks."

"You'll discover a whole new world."

"Um . . . wow . . . thanks," I say, trying to sound casual.

*She still hasn't let go of my hand.*

"And as your guide I'm here to make sure it's an experience you'll never forget," she intones earnestly, fixing me with her bright hazel eyes.

Wow, she's certainly very enthusiastic about her job, isn't she?

"Fab." I nod, smiling harder.

She beams broadly. "Splendid!"

Finally releasing my fingers, she deftly snaps the sign to her clipboard and tucks it under her arm. "Now, if you'd like to follow me . . ." And I've barely had time to register before she's taken off across the airport and is disappearing in a blur of tweed into the automatic twirling doors.

For a moment I watch her. Seriously, she really does look very familiar. I wonder if — Oh, God, Emily, you're being ridiculous. You've never met this woman in your life. And pushing it from my mind, I grab my wayward trolley and race after her.

I'm loving England.

OK, so I've only been here an hour, and we're still only in the parking lot, but I'm already won over. For a start, everyone's just so polite. They keep saying sorry, even when it's *me* who bangs my trolley into *their* legs. Plus, there are all these orderly lines — sorry, I should say "queues" — for cabs, tickets, the washrooms, you name it, and everyone is waiting quietly and patiently. Which would *never* happen back in the States, they'd be kicking up a fuss and loudly complaining.

Plus, everything just seems so *cool*. Stella's always telling me that New York is the fashion capital of the world, but everyone looks so stylish here. *Everything* does. Like, for example, the money. I just love how it's all different sizes and has the Queen's head on it. Dollars are so boring and green, and just so *samey* in comparison.

And what about the black cabs? Our yellow ones barely fit two people in the back, and my knees are always banging up against the driver's seat, but I just saw a whole family climb inside one of the black ones a moment ago. *And* with all their luggage. It was incredible.

Stepping on to a pedestrian crossing, I look the wrong way and nearly get myself run over by the aforementioned cab. (Repeat after me, Emily: look right, not left; look right, not left.)

"Watch where you're going, luv," yells the burly cab driver as he screeches to a halt.

My God, did you hear his accent? Is that real Cockney? Throwing him an apologetic smile, I scoot to the other side. Because I love it. It's like something out of *Lock, Stock and Two Smoking Barrels.* Which is kind of apt, as I would *kill* for that accent.

"We're parked over there," Miss Steane is trilling as we hurry across the parking lot. "It's the blue-and-white one at the end." She gestures over to a large tourbus and I feel a beat of pleasure. It looks really swanky. The type that has air-conditioning and a luxury bathroom.

See, I knew it wasn't going to be a battered old minibus or anything, I think righteously, remembering back to Stella's negative comments last night.

With a whoosh of air pressure the automatic doors swing open and Miss Steane hops up the steps.

"Leave your luggage right there, dear," she instructs, turning from the top step and peering down at me. "Ernie will take care of it and pop it in the hold." She gestures to the driver, who's sitting behind the steering wheel, his peaked cap resting on the dash, a newspaper spread out in front of him. He pauses from eating his breakfast, which, by the delicious smell of things, is a fried bacon sandwich, and looks up.

"Be careful, it's rather heavy . . ." I begin guiltily. Perhaps I shouldn't have brought *quite* so many books.

"Don't worry." He winks and pretends to flex a bicep.

I laugh and, pushing down the little handle on the suitcase, leave it on the asphalt and clamber eagerly up the stairs.

"It's a full house, so I'm afraid there's only a couple of seats left," chimes my tour guide. "There seems to be a space next to Maeve."

I smile happily. I am *so* pleased I didn't listen to Stella. I *knew* this would be a great trip.

I turn to head down the bus.

Which is when my smile freezes.

In front of me is a sea of curly grey heads. A whole vista of them. Stretching out as far as the eye can see, all the way to the horizon that is the luxury bathroom. It's like being on a senior citizens' outing.

All of a sudden someone presses "play" on my cerebral tape recorder and Stella's voice begins replaying in my head: *Kooks and old people. Kooks and old people . . .*

"Over here . . ."

An Irish accent interrupts my thoughts and I look up to see an arm near the back of the bus waving at me above the headrests. Still reeling, I smile dazedly and walk the plank to my seat.

"Excuse the ploughman's . . ."

Almost hidden behind the seat is a small woman with short, grey hair and oversized reading glasses. Tucking her pleated polyester skirt underneath her legs, she pauses from eating a hunk of cheese and smiles up at me timidly. "They didn't have anything to eat on the flight over from Dublin," she adds apologetically, trying to cover her mouth with her napkin while standing up at the same time and spilling crumbs everywhere. "Oh, now look what I've done . . . Look at the mess I'm making . . . Sorry . . ."

I stare at her blankly. I'm experiencing a moment of sheer panic. Oh, shit. What have I done? What am I *going* to do? For a whole week. With a bunch of senior citizens?

As she fusses around me I shuffle past her and into my seat.

"What about you? Where did you fly in from?"

"New York," I reply, trying not to think of the buzzing metropolis I've left behind in favour of this.

I catch myself. Oh, for Godsakes, Emily, pull yourself together. It's going to be just fine. You're not going clubbing with them, you're going on a book tour.

"Oooh, the Big Apple?" There's a lot of murmuring and several curly grey heads appear in the aisle to look at me.

"So you're an American?" asks one.

"Yes, that's right." I nod.

"How exciting," smiles another. "*An American.*" She says it as if I'm a species from outer space.

Lots of knowing glances fly around me.

"Overpaid, oversexed and over here," booms a large, striking woman, her head popping above the parapet of the headrest in front of me. Unlike the others, she has dyed black hair, cut into a strikingly severe Cleopatra bob and is wearing a lot of dark-red lipstick. It suits her, despite her seventy-something years.

"Excuse me?"

"That's what they used to say about the Yanks during the war," she remarks, her dark, inquisitive eyes shining brightly beneath her fake eyelashes and painted-on eyebrows. "And I should know, I married one."

Hoots of laughter fly around the coach.

She extends a plump hand laden down with diamonds the size of knuckle-dusters. "Rose Bierman."

"Emily Albright."

Her handshake is firm and unwavering, and I get the distinct impression she's sizing me up. How funny, and there was I thinking *I* was the one sizing *her* up.

Ten minutes later we still haven't moved. There's one empty seat left and we're waiting for the last person to arrive. Apparently, they're travelling from Central London so they should be here any minute.

A hum of chatter fills the air, which is already heavy with a cloying cocktail of perfumes. Impatiently I glance at my watch — how much longer? I glance around me, expecting a coach full of discontent, but everyone else seems happy sharing packets of cookies called, strangely, "custard creams", whatever they are, swapping photos of grandchildren and comparing wardrobes from some place called M&S. A couple of passengers have even nodded off, I notice, looking at them now, heads rolled back, mouths open, snoring quietly.

"Um . . . would you care for a midget gem?" asks Maeve shyly, shaking a bag at me.

"No, I'm fine, thank you." I smile, not having a clue what a midget gem actually is but refusing anyway. I turn to gaze out of the window. Where on earth is this person? What are they doing? I've come all the way from New York and I've managed to be on time. What's taking them so long?

Agitatedly I press my cheek against the glass to see further across the parking lot, my eyes desperately scanning back and forth for signs of a woman of pensionable age. But it's empty. No short, curly, grey perms. No lilac sweaters from this strange place called M&S. Nothing. Just puddles from where it's started to rain.

I flop back into my seat. Normally it wouldn't bother me so much, but I've just flown across the Atlantic and I'm exhausted. All I want to do is get to the hotel and freshen up. However, knowing there's not much I can do, I dig out my copy of *Pride and Prejudice*. Yawning, I turn back the earmarked corner of my page and continue reading where I left off. It's the bit about Mr Darcy at the ball . . .

> He was looked at with great admiration for about half the evening, till his manners gave a disgust which turned the tide of his popularity; for he was discovered to be proud, to be above his company, and above being pleased; and not all his large estate in Derbyshire could then save him from having a most forbidding, disagreeable countenance, and being unworthy to be compared with his friend.

A male voice talking loudly on the other side of my window distracts me. I glance outside to see a man clambering out of a tiny red Renault with a briefcase, laptop bag and a large holdall. He's a big guy, unshaven and unkempt, with his shirt tails sticking out of baggy chinos, exposing a little bit of a belly as he leans back into the car.

The driver, meanwhile, is an immaculate blonde in a tight black turtle neck and red lipstick. She's staring blankly through the windshield, ignoring him while he yells something I can't quite hear. Hmm, I wonder what they're rowing about. Intrigued, I watch them for a moment, before remembering it's rude to stare and turning back to my book.

His character was decided. He was the proudest, most disagreeable man in the world, and every body hoped that he would never come there again.

Outside, there's the sound of a car door slamming with enough force to take it off its hinges. I'm half tempted to look up, but I ignore it. I can hear the woman now, but I can't tell what she's saying as she's screaming in French.

And I'm reading the same line over and over again.

I give in to my curiosity and look out of the window, just in time to see the Renault reversing at full pelt, its gears whining painfully. With a sharp twist it swerves, brakes, then shoots forward and races out of the parking lot.

Jesus. What happened there? I wonder.

I glance back at the guy. He's just standing there, leather holdall and briefcase on the ground, laptop bag slung over his slouched shoulder, battered old corduroy jacket flapping in the wind. Raking his fingers through his messy blond hair, he stares after the Renault as if he

**51**

can't quite believe he's been dumped in the middle of the parking lot — and in the rain. He cuts a sorry-looking figure and I feel a pang of sympathy for him.

Though he was shouting at a woman, I remind myself. He catches me staring at him and I glance away sharply. He probably deserves it.

Drama over, I turn back to my book, but no sooner have I found my place on the page than I hear the automatic doors of the tour bus swish open and then there's a round of applause. Hallelujah. The last person must have arrived.

I hear Maeve clicking her tongue. "Nosy things. What's all the fuss about?" she tuts quietly.

And this from a woman who's got her head stuck out at a right angle into the aisle.

I continue reading. Maeve's obviously from some sleepy little country village in Ireland where nothing happens. This is probably the most exciting thing to happen to her in a long time. Unlike me, living in the daily hustle and bustle of New York, the city that never sleeps. I see way more exciting stuff than this every day so it's really no big deal for me.

Oh, who are you kidding, Emily? City that never sleeps? Hustle and bustle? You're as curious as Maeve.

Grabbing the headrest in front of me, I hoist myself up from my seat to get a good look at the little old lady. Except it's not a little old lady.

*It's him.* The guy from the Renault.

Something stirs and if I didn't know better I'd think it was excitement. Surely he's not . . .? I mean, he can't be . . . There's no way he's the person we're waiting for, right?

*Wrong.* Engaged in a conversation with Miss Steane, our tour guide, who's tapping her watch and frowning, he's talking nineteen to the dozen, gesticulating widely, while trying to tuck in his shirt, which refuses to stay in his chinos.

Then all at once he seems to notice Ernie, our driver, and stops mid-sentence to throw him a furious glower. Jeez, Louise, this guy *is* in a bad mood. And now he's turning and thundering down the aisle, bashing people left and right with his laptop bag and briefcase as he heads towards the back of the coach. Suddenly he looks right at me and I smile politely.

He responds with a filthy scowl.

*What the . . . ?*

I feel a slap of indignation. What an asshole! And there was me just trying to be nice to him. Infuriated, I respond by glaring right back. Then he strides past me to the back of the tour bus and flings himself into the empty seat. Bristling, I sit back down. The driver starts up the engine and, as we begin to pull out of the parking lot, I make up my mind to ignore him.

*Even if he is a handsome stranger*, pipes up a voice inside me.

For a millisecond I waver; but it's just a millisecond. So what if he is? That doesn't change anything. He's *still* an asshole, and I'm *still* going to ignore him. Completely and utterly. For the whole week. Just you watch me.

# CHAPTER
# FIVE

I must have dozed off because the next thing I know I'm waking up to discover we've pulled off the freeway — sorry, correction: motorway — and are now winding our way through the Hampshire countryside on some of the narrowest roads I've ever seen. Outside, a blur of hedges fly past, a vivid band of green against the blank, grey expanse of sky. It's still drizzling and raindrops are weaving their way down the windowpanes, making everything look like a watercolour painting that's gone all streaky.

"This is the countryside that Jane Austen would have known growing up . . ." our tour guide's voice is chatting away over the microphone ". . . and which featured in many of her novels."

There's a buzz as people stop what they're doing to look out of the windows. We're entering a small village now. Rows of skinny red-brick houses line the tiny streets, their crisscross leaded windows glittering as we pass by. I stare at them, feeling a tingle of excitement. It's just like I imagined. Over there, there's even a village green with a duck pond and real ducks and everything.

I watch them bobbing contentedly, dipping their beaks into the water and raising their feathered bottoms comically into the air. I smile to myself, reminded of the ones in Central Park. Ducks, it would appear, like to stick their butts in the air whether they're English *or* American.

But now they're behind us, and as we manoeuvre round a tight corner I see a traditional English pub up ahead. Oh, my God, is that a real thatched roof? And does that sign actually read "Ye Olde" something or other?

I squash my nose against the window in disbelief. I feel as if I've fallen asleep and woken up two hundred years ago. There's not a Hummer or a Mac store, or even a Starbucks in sight. Just cobbled streets, a village church and real fires, I marvel, watching the smoke spiralling up from the chimney pots. It really is like being on a movie set. It's hard to believe it's not just a façade for tourists and as soon as we drive through it will be taken down and flat-packed until the next tour bus runs through.

"And now ladies *and gentleman* . . ." Miss Steane's voice interrupts my daydream and I turn away from the window.

Gentleman? Hardly, I think dryly, remembering the obscenities this "gentleman" yelled earlier. I flick my eyes back over my shoulder at the culprit in question. Mid-yawn, he catches me staring and sticks out his tongue.

How old is he? *Five?*

Irritated, I pretend to be looking at something behind him, but seeing as he's on the back row and behind him it's the washroom, I'm pretty much busted. Still, I'm way too proud to let him think he's caught me, so I continue to gaze at the green "VACANT" sign as if it's the most interesting thing I've ever seen until Miss Steane rescues me by chiming,

"This is the Old Priory, where we'll be staying for two nights, before continuing our journey to Bath."

Gratefully I turn back to the view out of the window and —

*Holy shit.*

Turning left into a pair of impressive wrought-iron gates, there's the delicious sound of gravel crunching under the tyres as we slowly make our way up the broad, sweeping driveway. Just this is enough to set the wings of my anticipation fluttering. I've always thought you can tell instantly, just by the driveway alone, whether or not you're going to love a place. *And I'm going to love this place.*

Big, bold and beautiful, it stands at the top of the driveway to greet us like something torn from the pages of *Pride and Prejudice* — the kind of place I always imagined Netherfield Park, home of Mr Bingley, to be. I gaze at it in awe. Set in beautiful grounds, with ivy-covered walls, an imposing entrance and rambling outbuildings, it's everything I dreamt it was going to be and more.

The tour bus pulls up outside the hotel and the next half-hour is spent disembarking, collecting luggage and checking in, while our tour guide flaps around us with

56

her clipboard like a tweed butterfly. The hotel is even more spectacular from the inside: wood-panelled hallway, sweeping staircase, hunting pictures, portraits of bygone ancestors, stone-flagged floors . . . Everything reeks of history.

"You're in room twenty-eight," instructs Miss Steane, standing behind the front desk a few minutes later. Behind her is a large board filled with differently numbered keys, and handing me a small brass one, she ticks me off her list, seemingly oblivious to George, the general manager, who is standing next to her looking rather redundant.

"It's on the second floor," George is now adding timorously. "Turn right and it's all the way to the end of the corridor."

"Great. Thanks." I nod, reaching for the retracting handle on my wheelie suitcase. "Which way's the elevator?"

There's a pause.

"The elevator?" repeats George, twiddling his cufflinks uncertainly. I notice a few glances flying around me and I twig.

Oh, God, Emily, don't be so stupid. Of course there isn't a goddamn elevator. This place is hundreds of years old.

But just as I'm about to correct myself, I hear a derisive snort behind me and someone mutters, "Americans, huh?"

I stiffen. I know immediately who that someone is, even before I twirl round and see him leaning up against the desk, arms folded, picking his teeth with a matchstick: Mr Asshole. I glare at him challengingly.

"Have you got a problem?" I demand, trying to appear ballsy and confident and not like the complete idiot I really feel. Unfortunately, my voice doesn't play along and betrays me by coming out all shrill and nasal. I sound petulant, rather than nonchalant. I feel my face burning up, and curling my hand tightly round the handle of my suitcase, I dig my nails into my palm.

But Mr Asshole doesn't react. Instead, he fixes me with his heavy-lidded eyes and adopts a bemused expression. "No," he replies casually, taking the matchstick out of his mouth. For a moment he studies it as he twirls it between finger and thumb, then flicks his gaze back to me. "But it appears that you have." The corners of his mouth turn up in smug amusement.

"Really?" I return the smile with as much sarcasm as I can muster. "And what might that be?"

*Apart from you, you arrogant little shit.*

We eyeball each other. Which is when I'm suddenly aware that it's all gone very quiet. Everyone has stopped what they're doing at the front desk and are now watching us like spectators at a boxing match.

*Ding, ding.* Round two.

"This isn't Macy's, you know." He smirks.

"Now you tell me," I reply dryly.

"This building happens to be over four hundred and fifty years old."

"I know that."

"And you want to take the elevator?"

My cheeks are on fire. "Well, no, obviously. I wasn't thinking. I'm a bit jet-lagged, that's all —"

"Perhaps you'd like me to ask if there's an *escalator* instead," he interrupts, his faded blue eyes twinkling.

"Thank you, but that won't be necessary," I say stiffly, and grabbing my suitcase, I head for the staircase and begin bumping up the stairs.

George rushes to help me. "Now then, miss, let me do that, I can easily —"

"I'm fine, honestly, I can manage," I insist, grasping on to the handrail and tugging the suitcase up behind me, trying not to grunt. Jesus Christ, it weighs a ton. What the hell's in here? *That freaking black sweater you're never gonna wear*, I tell myself crossly. I curse the black sweater. Thump, bang, thump. Because it's all that black sweater's fault. Bang, thump, bang. If it wasn't for that black sweater, I wouldn't have even thought about taking an elevator.

Thump, bang, thump. *Ouch!*

Banging my legs on the corner of my suitcase, I wince with pain and bend down to rub my throbbing shin. Then catching Mr Asshole staring at me from the bottom of the staircase, I pretend I can't feel a thing and continue climbing. Until, finally reaching the top, I hoist my suitcase on to the landing and flounce off down the corridor.

Lunch is being served in the Elizabethan dining room and so I quickly freshen up in my room. Dark and chintzy, it has a real four-poster bed, over which is hung a watercolour of a hunting scene (they seem to be very

**59**

popular, they're all over the hotel) and in the corner stands a big old wooden closet.

Having lived for as long as I can remember with birch-veneer flat-pack from IKEA, it's a bit of a shock. Real furniture! And stuff that looks like it belongs in a museum, I think in amazement, running the flat of my hand across the door of the closet and feeling the centuries-old smoothness of the wood.

I'm interrupted by the jingly chime of my cell phone ringing. Grabbing my bag from my bedspread, I flounder around inside, trying to find it before it rings off. It can only be one person.

"*Buenos dias.*"

"Stella!" I yell, grinning. Being independent, impulsive and all those strong adjectives is all very well, but there's nothing better than getting a call from your best friend when you're in strange surroundings. "It's great to hear from you. What are you up to?"

"Getting drunk," she laughs down the crackly line. "It's the early hours of the morning here, and we've just arrived but I'm managing to keep awake with the help of tequila." She breaks off to take a loud slurp, and in the background I can hear the vibrant mix of music and laughter. "So, how is everything?"

"Great," I reply enthusiastically, trying not to think about my run-in with the English guy downstairs. "How about you?"

"Fabulous. White sand, eighty degrees, lots of men and the best margaritas ever. This is my . . . Um, I've lost count," she laughs, drunkenly. "So, tell me. What's happening over there?"

"Well, we just checked into this really amazing hotel . . ." spying the view from the window I let out a gasp ". . . and it's in the middle of all this gorgeous countryside," I continue, looking out at the wide, flat fields dotted with nothing but sheep and crossed with stone walls. It's like a giant chessboard.

"Mmmm, really?" murmurs Stella on the end of the line.

"And they've got all this amazing old antique furniture." Flopping down on to the flowery bedspread, I prop myself up by my elbows.

"Mmmm, really?"

I can tell Stella's not listening. Antique furniture probably isn't high on her list of interests right now. If ever. "Anyway, it's lunchtime here so we're going to grab something to eat and then it's sightseeing this afternoon," I say, changing the subject quickly.

"So did you meet your Mr Darcy yet?" she teases.

"Ha, ha, very funny," I reply. Leaning over the side of the bed, I dig out my toiletries bag and slick on some deodorant. "No, I met an asshole instead."

"Is he cute?"

"He's a pain in the ass."

"But cute?" she persists.

I think about him for a moment, with his old corduroy jacket, shirt that's buttoned up the wrong way, and under which I'm pretty sure love handles are lurking, and his messy hair that needs a good cut.

"No, you definitely wouldn't describe him as cute," I answer firmly.

"Huh? Assholes are usually cute," tuts Stella, sounding surprised. "Oh, well, that's a shame. A holiday romance might have been fun."

"*Fun?*" I shudder at the thought of having any kind of romance with Mr Asshole. "No thanks. And anyway, I'm off men. I want to spend this vacation catching up on all my reading."

"I think you should keep an open mind. Just because you had a few bad dates . . ."

"A few?"

"Oh, come on, Emily. Live for the moment. Haven't you read *The Power of Now?*"

Hang on a minute. Did she just say what I thought she just said? In all the time I've known Stella I've only ever seen her read her horoscope and the laundry instructions on her clothes. "No, I haven't. Is it good?" I ask, impressed.

"Well, I haven't actually read it myself," she confesses. "But I've met this guy who's been telling me all about it. About how we have to stop projecting into the future all the time and not worry about what's going to happen."

"What guy?" I ask suspiciously. Not projecting into the future and living for the moment translated into man-speak sounds like a ruse to get Stella into bed.

"His name's Scott," she announces happily. "Do you want to say hi?"

"No, it's OK," I say quickly. One of my pet hates is when a girlfriend puts some random man they've just met on the phone. OK, so they're in a darkened bar, intoxicated by alcohol and male attention, and I can see

62

how it might seem a fun thing to do — *sort of* — but fun for who exactly? Never you. Nine times out of ten you're usually at home, in your baggy old sweat pants, doing your hand-washing. Literally scrubbing your gussets with a nailbrush. The last thing you want to do is have a stilted, awkward conversation with a stranger whom you've never met and with whom you have absolutely *nothing* in common.

Apart from your friend, who he wants to sleep with.

"Aww, go on, he's right here . . ."

"No, honestly —"

It's too late. I can hear the phone being passed over. My heart plummets. Oh, no. *Please no.*

"Yo," demands a male voice on the other end of the line.

"Oh, hi." I wince. "I'm Emily."

"Scott," grunts the reply.

There's an awkward pause. I grope around for something to say.

"Um, so what do you do, Scott?" I ask stiffly. God, I sound like Stella's mother.

"I party," he laughs raucously.

I wince and persevere.

"So, are you having a good time?"

Honestly, why don't I just add "*dear*" and go the whole hog?

"Yeah, it's totally wicked, and your friend Stella is rockin'."

OK, I'm not going to judge. "Wicked" and "rocking" are perfectly good adjectives.

"Boy, does she lurve to *par-taayyyy*," he whoops.

I take it all back. I'm judging. And Scott is guilty of being a total moron.

"Um . . . will you pass me back to Stella?" I say, only I have to shout loudly as he's now pretending to howl like a dog.

Thankfully I hear the rustle of the phone and then, "Em?"

It's Stella, back on the phone. Part of me is relieved, but the other part knows what's coming next: the appraisal.

"So what did you think?" she whispers.

"It's difficult to tell, on the phone," I say, trying to be tactful.

"He's really successful. He owns an advertising agency," she confides. "And he's really handsome."

"I'm sure he is," I agree. Who isn't after a night of margaritas? I once kissed my own reflection in the mirror of the ladies.

"He's such great fun, Emily. He's really crazy and he makes me laugh. I've only known him a couple of hours. I feel like we're really connecting."

Oh, shit. This sounds dangerous. I try jolting her back to reality. "So, have you heard from Freddy?" I ask hopefully.

"Yeah, he's already sent me about ten text messages asking if I arrived safely, how's the hotel, if I was OK . . ."

"Aw, he's so sweet," I say fondly. "You're lucky. Freddy really cares about you."

"Well, I wish he didn't, he drives me crazy," grumbles Stella. "I wish he'd leave me alone to enjoy my vacation."

"You say that, but I bet you'd really miss him if he did."

"I bet I wouldn't."

"OK, have it your way," I surrender. "But you want to be careful what you wish for . . ."

My warning is drowned out by drunken giggling. I feel a wave of irritation. Has she heard a word I just said? I listen for a few moments. God, no. That's not the sound of her and Scott kissing, is it?

"Erm, Stella . . .?" I say tentatively.

"Umm, yeah?" she says distractedly.

Oh, hell. That *is* the sound of them kissing.

"You know, perhaps I should talk to you later."

"Sure," she replies, not protesting. "Have fun at your museum."

God, that makes me sound like a total dork, doesn't it?

"It's not actually a museum, it's where Jane Austen . . ." I begin, but my voice trails off as I hear what sounds like Stella groaning on the end of the line. Oh, Lord. I feel as if I've rung some kind of adult sex line. "OK, well . . . um . . . take care."

"Mmmm, yeah . . . bye."

Hanging up with relief, I glance at my watch. I'm running late as usual, and rubbing on some lip gloss, I grab my coat and sling my old tote bag over my shoulder. Bobbing my head so as not to bang it on the low doorframe, I twist the little brass key in the lock and head down the darkened hallway. Catching sight of my reflection in the mirror at the top of the stairs, I pause. My hair's gone all limp and the front bits are all static-electric from my mohair scarf. I blow them off my face, only for them to cling straight back on again.

I grimace. Sometimes I hate having long hair. All that hassle of combing out tangles in the shower and blocking up the plughole and having to scoop it out with your fingers. Not to mention the expense of all the leave-in conditioners, serums and hot-oil treatments. I swear I have a cupboard full of them and my hair still looks exactly the same: shoulder-length, darkish brown and with enough split-ends to start a stylist tutting like a metronome. To be quite honest, I don't know why I don't just cut it all off. Actually, now I think about it, I do.

Two words: *Sienna* and *Miller*.

Not that it matters what my hair looks like, of course. Nobody knows me here so it's not as if I need to make an effort or anything. But I suppose it wouldn't do any harm to tip my head upside down and do a bit of volumising with my fingers like this, and then throw my hair back and —

"Erm, excuse me."

I hear a voice behind me at exactly the same moment I catch sight of myself in the mirror. Which is when I see three things:

1. My hair has smeared my lip gloss across my face, making me look like a Jackson Pollock painting.
2. The blood has rushed to my head, making the

veins around my eyes bulge and my face turn scarlet.

3. Mr Asshole is right behind my left shoulder.

Jesus. How long has he been standing there?

Embarrassed at being caught doing my hair-commercial head-toss, I feel two spots of colour burning on my cheeks. I turn round and, with as much nonchalance as I can muster, rub the lip gloss off my cheeks while saying casually, "Yes? Can I help you with something?"

He has one eye squeezed shut and is rubbing the corner of it with his forefinger. "You could start by not flicking your hair in my face," he complains.

"Oh, sorry —" I begin, but he interrupts.

"Yeah, well, you need to look what you're bloody well doing. You nearly took my eye out," he snaps.

I feel a flash of annoyance.

"Only nearly? Damn. I'm usually a good aim," I reply before I can stop myself. Well, honestly, he's so patronising — he needs a taste of his own medicine.

"In that case, I'm glad you're only in possession of your hair and not a firearm," he retorts dryly and strides off down the stairs, shoelaces flapping.

Right. OK. Well, that told him, didn't it?

For a moment I watch his retreating figure, trying to think of a suitable comeback, then give up. And feeling disgruntled, I follow him downstairs.

# CHAPTER
# SIX

"He's a journalist?"

"From the *Daily Times*?"

"And he wants to interview *us*?"

As I walk into the wood-panelled dining room a commotion greets me. A medley of voices, each one rising higher and higher up the scale as they shout questions over one another. I pick out Rose's distinctive tones, but the loudest voice is coming from a tiny Indian lady called Rupinda. Wearing a turquoise-blue sari embroidered with silver peacocks, she's sitting at the table waving a soup spoon like a conductor's baton and demanding, "What he want to ask me, hey? What he want to ask me?" over and over like a cockatoo.

Curious as to what's going on, I look for a place to sit, but as I'm late they all seem to be taken already. I hover awkwardly, feeling like a child on her first day at school, when Rose rescues me.

"*Em-i-lee*, darling, over here," she booms, waving me over to the table nearest the fireplace with those huge glittering rocks of hers on her fingers.

I smile gratefully and, squeezing myself in between the tables, plop myself down next to her. Immediately a waiter swoops on me with a silver tureen of soup and begins ladling it into my bowl.

"Cream of cauliflower. Lukewarm and rather hideous," Rose criticises, seemingly unaware of the waiter at her elbow as she takes a large slurp from her own bowl.

She's applied even more make-up, and despite it being only lunchtime, I notice she's changed into a black chiffon top, the beaded sleeves of which are trailing in the aforementioned soup. However, she seems not to notice and so I don't mention anything. To be honest, I'm rather afraid to. Despite her seventy-something years, Rose is more than a little intimidating.

"So, what do you think of all this interview nonsense?" she asks, breaking off to butter a bread roll.

"I don't know anything about it," I reply, watching with fascination as she cuts thick, creamy slices of butter, lays them on top of the bread as if they're pieces of cheese and then, picking up the silver salt-shaker, sprinkles them with a dusting of salt. "Why, what's going on?"

"They're writing an article about us," whispers Maeve, looking worried. "Apparently, we have to give interviews."

"When I was in the theatre, I was always having articles written about me," says Rose. "I have scrapbooks filled with press cuttings."

"You were an actress?" I ask interestedly.

"Not just an actress. A leading lady," she corrects mindfully. "I played opposite them all, Gielgud, Olivier, McKellen . . ." Taking a mouthful of bread, she waves her arm flamboyantly. "I had the pick of the crop."

"So you're famous?" gasps Maeve in a hushed voice, visibly impressed.

"Well, I wouldn't say that," refutes Rose, lowering her eyelashes and batting them in an attempt at a modicum of modesty. "But in my youth the stage door would be crowded with autograph-hunters." She pauses for effect, puffed up by Maeve's wide-eyed admiration. "But time passes, and I'm afraid the public have a terrible memory," she adds. "I doubt anyone remembers me now. *C'est la vie.*" She laughs carelessly and dives for another bread roll, but I get the distinct impression that although Rose might no longer be on the stage, she's still very much acting.

"So who's writing an article about us?" I ask, changing the subject.

Taking a hungry bite, Rose gestures with the piece of leftover crust. "Ask that young chap, he knows."

As soon as she says "young chap" I feel a clunk of inevitability. In fact, to tell the truth, as soon as I walked in and heard the word "he" I had a feeling who they meant. My eyes flick towards the end of the table, where Rose is pointing.

"So he's a journalist, huh?" I shrug, disinterested. Whoopy-doo. Like I care.

I continue eating my soup. I can hear him talking, feel everyone's eyes upon him, but I'm just going to ignore him. He can't exactly be here to report anything very interesting anyway, can he?

OK, so I can hear snippets of what he's saying and it does sound *vaguely* interesting, but I'm not going to listen. He's so arrogant I wouldn't give him the satisfaction. Besides, I'm too busy focusing on my soup. My lovely cauliflower soup. Despite what Rose thinks, it's actually rather delicious, sort of spicy with a hint of —

Oh, for Godsakes, Emily, talk about my lady doth protest too much. Quit the excuses and listen.

". . . and so I think our readers will be interested in hearing what you've got to say." Sleeves rolled up to reveal his hairy forearms, he's dragging heavily on a cigarette as he fields questions from the women clustering round him.

"But why us?" exclaims one in a lilac turtle neck, clutching her ribbed woollen chest and looking at him beseechingly. If she was thirty years younger I'd swear she was flirting. On second thoughts, she *is* flirting, I realise, feeling vaguely shocked.

"Who better equipped to answer my questions?" he fires back unwaveringly. Folding one leg across the other, he hugs his ankle and eyes his captive audience. "Recently a poll by the Orange Prize for Fiction asked nearly two thousand women over three generations who their dream date would be . . ." taking a breath, he drags on his cigarette ". . . and one man got more votes than any other . . ."

Well, I know who gets my vote, I think dreamily.

". . . Mr Darcy."

I feel a jolt of surprise. Did he just say what I think he said? I lean forward in my seat to try to hear better. Just curious of course.

"And so my paper thought it would make a great idea for a story if I came along on this tour and spent a week with die-hard fans to discover just why this fictional hero has such a hold over women today. What is it about Mr Darcy that women love so much?"

"He's enigmatic," calls out a smartly dressed woman with a Hermès silk scarf knotted round her neck.

"And noble," announces another, pausing from sipping her soup to stare wistfully into the middle distance.

"He's honourable," adds Maeve timidly, seeming almost scared of her own voice. "In those days men knew how to treat a woman."

There's a lot of murmuring and nodding of heads.

"Enigmatic? Noble? Honourable?" mocks Rose, throwing down her napkin. "Ladies, please! I can appreciate his finer qualities, but did nobody *see* the BBC adaptation?" Her dark eyes are flashing and her shiny black bob swings backwards and forwards. "The one when he came out of the lake in that white shirt looking devastatingly handsome," she continues pointedly, looking around the room for a reaction.

Immediately there's a rowdy response of agreement and a lecherous cry of "*Phwoar*", which, when I turn round, I am taken aback to see came from Rupinda. *Jeez*. And she looks the picture of elegance in her embroidered sari.

"Mmm, I love Colin Firth," yells out someone.

"Oooh, me too," agrees another.

"But he was just playing Mr Darcy, ladies," interrupts Miss Steane, entering the room, clipboard in hand. "Remember, Mr Firth was just an actor, he is not the real Mr Darcy."

"And who is the *real* Mr Darcy?"

All eyes turn to the journalist. He's looking at Miss Steane, his thick blond eyebrows pitched with interest. He stubs out his cigarette on the side plate he's been using as an ashtray, leans back in his chair and folds his arms behind his head.

"That's for you to find out, Mr Hargreaves," she replies curtly.

"Please call me Spike," he replies in deference, but she's already addressing the dining room.

"Now, just to remind everyone, we'll be departing *promptly* after lunch." Turning to leave, she glances at Spike and nods her head. "Mr Hargreaves," she says politely but firmly, and strides off across the swirly carpet.

Watching from across the other side of the room, I'm absorbing this information. So Spike's here to write a story about us, huh?

"Your soup's going cold." Abruptly I turn to see Rose gesturing to my bowl and grumbling, "Best eat that up, my dear. The main course is bound to be even *more* dreadful."

Well, if he thinks I'm going to answer his stupid questions, he can think again. And turning my attention back to my soup, I take a hungry mouthful.

Thirty minutes later lunch is over and we're back on the tour bus driving through country lanes on our way to the first stop on our itinerary. I, however, am engrossed in the world of Elizabeth Bennet and Mr Darcy. With my book open on my lap, I'm at the bit where they first meet and Mr Darcy sees Elizabeth.

"Which do you mean?" and turning round, he looked for a moment at Elizabeth, till catching her eye, he withdrew his own and coldly said, "She is tolerable; but not handsome enough to tempt *me*."

God, imagine being described as "tolerable". How insulting. I'd die.

I turn the page and suddenly my bladder twinges. I try ignoring it. I love this part.

Crossing my legs tightly, I focus back on the page.

Like an insistent child, my bladder twinges again.

It's no good, I'm going to have to go for a pee.

Turning over the corner of my page, I tuck the book down the side of my seat and stand up.

"The first stop on our tour is Chawton Manor," announces our tour guide, standing at the front of the coach, microphone in one hand, clipboard in the other. "Home to Jane Austen in the latter part of her life . . ."

The microphone fizzes and whines with interference, making it difficult for us to hear, but instead of abandoning her speech, Miss Steane simply ups the vocal ante and firmly proceeds. I have a feeling that nothing would stop our tour guide, short of a ten-ton truck, and then she would probably emerge victorious with only a few hairs out of place, and perhaps a small snag in her thick woollen tights.

". . . where she wrote and revised many of her novels, including everybody's favourite, *Pride and Prejudice*."

Making my way down the aisle, I head towards the bathroom. Out of the corner of my eye I can see the top of Spike What's-his-name's head looming, as he's sitting right at the back. Tufts of blond hair are popping up over the tartan upholstery, and as I near him, his arm rises upwards in a stretch, then begins scratching his scalp in a lazy, absent-minded way. Classic telephone behaviour, I note. It's the same with every man I know. It's either the scalp, the belly or the you-know-whats.

"Yeah . . . yeah . . . Absolutely . . ."

Told you.

Reaching for the handle on the bathroom door, I glance sideways and there he is. Head turned towards the window, cell phone wedged up against his ear, chatting away. Fortunately, he doesn't see me, so we don't have to go through the pretence of that awkward silent hi-nod-wave-of-recognition thingy, and I quickly close the door behind me.

Now, then.

Once inside, I'm pleased to find it all looks pretty clean. I take a cautious inhalation. And it smells fine, too. I'm relieved. Stella calls me a hygiene freak, but I don't know why. OK, so I carry a little bottle of sanitiser in my bag, but that doesn't make me Howard Hughes. Plus, I admit I wash bags of pre-washed salad, but I'm just being careful. And yes, it's true, I won't eat those little mints they have in a bowl in restaurants, but that's because I once read an article about how they'd put one under a microscope. Do you have any idea how many traces of urine they found on a single mint?

Hundreds — *thousands even* — of tiny little bits of pee.

75

Ugghh.

I look down at the toilet and that's when I notice someone has dribbled on the seat. Oh, God. Yuk. I reach for a piece of toilet paper, but that's when I notice something else — there isn't any, just an empty cardboard tube rattling on the holder.

Damn.

Suddenly a long-ago story of my mom visiting France comes flashing back to me. Forget stories of Parisian style, St Tropez sunshine and sophisticated sidewalk cafés. All my mother could talk about was the hole in the floor and how she'd had to squat over it. Seriously. And in her stilettos. She's never been the same since. She blames it on the menopause, but I reckon it was that trip. She was so traumatised she's been having hot flushes ever since.

Thankfully I am made of stronger stuff than my mother and so I peel down my jeans and sort of hover. Actually, this is a really good workout for my outer thighs, I realise, as I start peeing. They should put it in *Allure* or *Shape*, or one of those health and fitness magazines as a top tip:

For buns of steel, forget lunges at the gym. Instead, go to a public washroom and squat over the seat for a count of 10. Repeat three times daily.

". . . believe me I want to bloody kill my editor . . ."
Outside, I can hear someone talking.
". . . all the other journalists are married with children, which left muggins here . . ."

*Muggins?* Who the hell is Muggins? Intrigued, I try listening closer. It's definitely a male voice, so I guess that can only mean —

Shit.

Suddenly, in mid-flow, I realise two things:

1. It's Spike who I can hear on the phone.
2. If I can hear him, *he can hear me.*

Cue pelvic-floor muscles.

I stop mid-pee.

Impressive.

Silently I thank God for *Cosmo* and all those articles about doing your Kegel exercises.

Now I can hear much better.

". . . right now I should be spending Christmas and New Year in the Alps with my hot French girlfriend . . ."

My interest is sparked. So that's who the blonde was in the car? Well, that would explain the Renault and the *terrible* driving.

". . . I'm so pissed off. I can't believe it. It was all arranged. Two weeks of sex and snowboarding . . ."

He snowboards? Admiration stirs. I never had him down as the sporty type, all those cigarettes and his beer gut made me presume he was unathletic. I adjust my position. My thighs are beginning to ache. Though, I'm proud to admit, my pelvic floor is holding up pretty damn well.

". . . I tell you, right at this moment there's no one I hate more than Mr bloody Darcy . . ."

*What?* Hearing him insult Mr Darcy, indignation bites. How dare he? Darcy's much more of a man than he'll ever be, I think protectively.

". . . it's all his bloody fault. If it wasn't for him, I wouldn't be on a coach full of old women. I swear, forget 18-30, this is like Club 60-80 . . ."

My ears prick up. He's talking about the tour. And not very favourably either, I muse, absently wondering if he's going to mention me.

". . . there's just one girl my age . . ."

Oh, wow, he *is* talking about me. Feeling a curious surge of anticipation, I try leaning a little closer. Not so easy when you're hovering over a toilet with your G-string stretched round your knees. I steady myself on the door handle. I wonder what he's going to say?

There's a pause. I can hear him laughing at something the other person just said, and holding my breath, I wait expectantly. Every second is beginning to feel like an eternity. Not only are my thigh muscles burning but my pelvic floor feels like a dam about to burst. Hold on, just hold on. I grit my teeth, and clench.

". . . no way. She's not my type . . . She seems pretty dull . . . average-looking . . ."

*Oh.*

Reality slaps me cold in the face. I wasn't expecting that. I was sort of presuming he was going to say something nice, though I don't know why — it's not as if *I* like *him*, it's just . . . My thoughts trail off lamely. God, I feel like a bit of an idiot now. Trust me to get it totally wrong. I mean, not that it matters — he's an

78

asshole anyway — I just wasn't expecting him to be so, well, *hurtful* . . .

Suddenly, much to my astonishment, my nose goes all tingly and I feel my eyes start welling up. Horrified, I sniff the tears back at once. Gosh, I'm being ridiculous. What on earth am I getting all emotional about? I'm not upset, I'm — OK, so I'm upset.

For like a second.

". . . and even worse . . . she's *American* . . ."

Then I'm furious.

Right, that does it. Plonking myself down on the seat, I finish with not a care for who hears me, or for the fact I'm sitting in someone else's dribble. I'm not going to have some snotty-nosed Brit think he's better than me because he's got a cute accent, a country full of old buildings and Ricky Gervais. We've got Madonna, the city of Manhattan and Abercrombie & Fitch, I think defiantly, as I wash my hands and emerge from the bathroom.

OK, so Madonna might be *masquerading* as a Brit, but she's still American.

As I slam the door loudly behind me Mr Spike-arrogant-Hargreaves looks up. He's still on the phone and I throw him my scary face before stomping back to my seat and snatching up my book. Now, where was I? Oh, yeah, the bit where Elizabeth Bennet is being described as "tolerable" by Mr Darcy.

In my mind I hear Spike's voice again: "*pretty dull . . . average-looking*". Now I know how Elizabeth Bennet feels, I realise, feeling a new and powerful identification with Jane Austen's heroine.

"But I can assure you," she [Mrs Bennet] added, "that Lizzy does not lose much by not suiting *his* fancy; for he is a most disagreeable, horrid man, not at all worth pleasing. So high and so conceited that there was no enduring him! He walked here, and he walked there, fancying himself so very great!"

Honestly, I couldn't have put it better myself. Who cares what Spike thinks? He's so conceited and full of himself I'm glad he doesn't like me. If he did he'd only be trying to hang out with me the whole time. How horrible would that be?

And feeling completely self-righteous, I throw myself back in my seat and turn the page.

Quite frankly, as far as I'm concerned, I've had a lucky escape.

# CHAPTER
# SEVEN

It's like stepping back in time.

"Jane Austen lived here during the last eight years of her life and this is regarded by many to be her literary home . . ."

Our tour guide is chuntering away as she leads us through the seventeenth-century red-brick house which has been turned into a museum, and although I'm trying to focus, my attention keeps drifting.

Gazing around the tastefully decorated rooms of Chawton Manor, filled with original Regency furniture, the twenty-first century seems to have slipped away. Gone is the noise, bustle and frantic pace of modern-day life where you have to run just to keep up. It's as if someone hit "Mute" and everything's slowed right down. I've entered this peaceful, contemplative world of writing letters with feather quills and Indian ink, reading quietly in button-back chairs and playing the harpsichord after dinner.

I stare at the harpsichord now, picturing myself sitting upright in my corset, tinkling on the keys. Actually, I can only play "Chopsticks", despite years of piano lessons, so I'd probably be reading instead. Poetry maybe, or something romantic in Latin. Not that I can read Latin, but I'm sure it would be different if I'd lived then.

I mean, everything would be so different, wouldn't it? There'd be no listening to the new Killers album on my iPod, no surfing the Internet and Googling that new man I've just met, no ordering Indian takeout and eating spicy shrimp bhuna while watching the first series of *Lost* on DVD . . .

OK, now that might be tough. I pause for a moment to reflect on a world without Matthew Fox. But you can't miss what you've never had, and think how wonderful it would be to spend your evenings doing something mentally stimulating, instead of slobbing in front of the TV. Like writing a letter to a distant cousin, or discussing the merits of Shakespeare, or doing some needlepoint.

Oh all right — so perhaps the needlepoint might get a *little* boring after a while. I mean, sewing "Home Sweet Home" probably isn't *that* stimulating, but I'm sure you can embroider whatever you want. Like, for example, Coldplay lyrics on to a pillowcase, or a picture of Frida Kahlo on to a dish towel . . . Actually, you know what? That's probably really hard. Especially if, like me, you're not that good at art, and you can't even sew on a button without pricking your finger and making it bleed, but I'm sure you could think of something.

I'm only drawing a blank at the moment because of the jet lag.

". . . and ahead of us we have the dining parlour, where she would spend her mornings writing, and the 'creaking door', which would alert her to visitors . . ."

82

Zoning back in to our tour guide's commentary, I see she's now moving through the vestibule and into a room at the front of the house. Gathered loosely into a group, we obediently shuffle along behind her, our footsteps echoing on the polished honey-coloured floorboards. I glance down at them now, at the thick, battle-scarred varnish beneath the crêpe soles of my boots. Gosh, it's so amazing to think that Jane Austen once walked around this house, and on these very floorboards. She probably stood in this very spot, I tell myself, pausing by one of the many windows to gaze out across the neatly planted garden, which is being slowly drenched. It's raining pretty hard now and it's getting dark. It almost looks like there's going to be a storm.

". . . and as you can see, we have photocopies of some of Jane's letters displayed on the walls, and a copy of Cassandra's portrait of Jane in 1810 hangs over the fireplace . . ."

Turning away from the window, I follow the group into the parlour and stand on tiptoe to see over everyone's shoulders. Despite being quite tall, it's difficult to see. Older women, I'm discovering, don't swap their high heels for comfy flats and crêpe-soled Hush Puppies once they hit sixty — something that I've been led to believe. On the contrary, Rose is wearing a pair of killer black stiletto boots with three-inch heels, and Maeve's tramping around in a pair of vintage brown leather boots, not unlike the ones Lindsay Lohan was wearing in Stella's copy of *Elle*.

In fact, the only person wearing comfy flats with crêpe soles is me.

Dismissing the worrying thought that I've been out-fashioned by women old enough to be my grandmother, while simultaneously wishing I'd taken more style advice from Stella rather than hooting with laughter every time she came to work in a wacky new outfit, I peer over the roped area to where Miss Steane is pointing.

". . . by the window is the original table where she revised *Pride and Prejudice* and created the Mr Darcy we know and love today," she declares, getting rather carried away. "And we also have an example of the type of feather quill she would have used to bring him to life. Or could it be, perhaps, *the very one!*"

Wow. I stare at the little round wooden table for a moment, absorbing its significance. Just think, that's where it all happened. Pretty incredible.

"Amazing, huh?" mutters a voice close to my ear.

I jump. Spike, the journalist, is standing next to me. Seeing him again is like a trigger.

"*pretty dull . . . average-looking*".

The effect of his words hasn't dulled. They sting just as hard as when I heard them. I throw him the most withering look I can summon up. I call it my "shit-on-my-shoe" look, and I have to say, it's pretty effective. I once did it to myself in the bathroom mirror, just to see, and boy, it even made me feel like shit.

Satisfied, I turn away. Well, that's the last you're going to be hearing from him, Emily Albright.

"To think she wrote all her stuff longhand, and with a feather quill. It's bloody unbelievable, isn't it? I mean, crikey, I write all my articles on my laptop and it still takes me for ever," he chuckles to himself.

Er, hello, is that dumb-ass still talking to me? Doesn't he realise I'm *blanking* him? The group is shuffling around the parlour, looking at the various objects of historical interest and reading the plastic-covered information that goes with them. Moving sideways, I stare determinedly ahead. *I will not make eye contact. I will not make eye contact.*

"Just imagine not being able to hit the delete key."

I wish *I* could hit the frigging delete key. That way, I could delete you, I curse silently.

Anger now, Emily, warns a little voice.

I quickly compose myself. I'm not angry. I'm not angry at all. I really couldn't care less what he said about me.

"So, you're a big Jane Austen fan, huh?" he persists obliviously.

Right, that's it. I've had enough.

"Listen, buddy, I couldn't care less about you, your laptop or your stupid newspaper article," I snap, rounding on him. "So why don't you go hassle someone else with your questions and leave me alone?"

OK, I take it back. I'm angry. And I've made eye contact. Fuck.

"Whoah." He throws up his hands in mock surrender. "Who rattled your cage?"

He pretends to back off, his hands still up in the air, a sardonic look on his face. God, that man is so unbearable, I fume.

Finally he turns away and begins excusing his way through the group, his spiral notebook in one hand, a Dictaphone in the other. I stare after him for a moment and notice how the hem of his corduroy jacket is coming unstitched and the way his jeans are so old they've worn away by the back pocket and you can see a flash of boxer-short material beneath.

Huh. And I thought British men were supposed to be all smart and stylish. Or at least foppish like Hugh Grant. I mean, just look at him. This guy is such a mess.

Feeling irritated, I turn and focus on a pair of Victorian buckled shoes in a glass case.

Cute, though, I think begrudgingly.

Forty minutes later we're still slowly making our way around the house. So far we've seen the drawing room, the dining parlour, where Jane wrote on the small round table, and been upstairs to the bedrooms to look at the patchwork quilt she made with her mother. Hers was obviously not the life of disastrous dates, vodka martinis and Sunday mornings spent in bed with a hangover, I reflect, thinking about how different my own life is. But at least we do have one thing in common — books.

Entering one of the rooms, I see a showcase that houses an interesting collection of books. My eyes flit across the embossed spines, reading the various titles. Like myself, Jane was obviously a huge fan of reading, I reflect happily, feeling a bond with the author.

She also died single, reminds a little voice inside me.

Right, OK.

Turning away from the showcase, I look at the other members of the group. Absorbed in their pamphlets and brochures, they're stopping and staring at various points of interest. Maeve is bent over a showcase of family silver, while Rose is peering at some jewellery and brooches and fanning herself with a copy of *Sense and Sensibility*.

I stifle a yawn. Gosh, my jet lag is really bad. I could do with a little nap.

"And so, moving on to the admiral's room. Here you will find memorabilia of her two sailor brothers, Francis and Charles, both of whom had distinguished careers in the Royal Navy . . ."

Hmm, that doesn't sound very interesting. I glance at my watch. The museum is about to close, so it wouldn't hurt if I skipped this bit. Maybe I should go for a little walkabout. Go outside and get a bit of fresh air to try and wake myself. I glance out of the window. It's still raining, but I think I saw some umbrellas at the entrance when we came in.

I hang back as Miss Steane leads the rest of the tour through a doorway, and when I'm sure no one's looking, I slip quietly out of the room.

I wander into the narrow hallway and go downstairs, looking for the exit. I'm sure we came in this way, but then again, there's no one worse for directions then me. I turn a corner, then another. It's strange — the house isn't very big at all, in fact it's quite small, but I've lost my bearings. No, it's not this way, I realise, seeing the gift shop ahead and retracing my steps.

Doubling back on myself, I turn a corner. Ahead of me I see a door has fallen closed. Aha, that must be it. Pushing open the door, I walk inside, only to recognise it's the dining parlour where I was earlier. Damn, it must be the other way. Stifling a yawn, I wander inside anyway. It's nice and quiet in here. Maybe I can sit down for a little while. Close my eyes for a moment.

Feeling a wave of jet lag, I glance woozily around the room. There's a wooden chair but it's the one Jane Austen used to write at her table and it's sectioned off to the public by a plastic barrier. Of course I can't sit there. I don't know if it's the real thing, but it *looks* like an antique. It's, like, two hundred years old or something.

Then again I am really exhausted.

I eye it for a moment. I've never been one to break rules, but saying that, there's no one here and it would be just for a few minutes. I mean, it wouldn't do any harm, I'd be super careful . . .

Stepping over the plastic barrier, I sink down on to the wooden chair gratefully. Ahhh, that's better. I lean back and rest my head against the wooden frame. In my head I hear Miss Steane's words: "*By the window is the original table where she revised* Pride and Prejudice *and created the Mr Darcy we know and love today. And we also have an example of the type of feather quill she would have used to bring him to life. Or could it be, perhaps, the very one!*"

I look at the small polished table in front of me. In the corner there's a bottle of ink against which is propped a quill. Of course I can't touch it. You're absolutely not allowed to touch any of the items: there's signs everywhere telling you so in no uncertain terms. I'd really get into trouble.

Saying that, there's nothing worse than a sign saying "Don't touch" for making you want to touch something, is there?

I pick up the quill. If I was expecting something spooky to happen, I'm disappointed, and for a moment I just hold it in my fingers to get the feel of it. It's probably a reproduction anyway, but even so, it's still fascinating to think Jane Austen wrote a whole book with a pen like this. I mean, can you imagine? *A whole book?*

I glance at the ink bottle, an idea stirring. Honestly, this is so completely unlike me to be even contemplating this, but how *cool* would it be to write something? Anything. Just my name even. Of course I can't.

*But of course I know I'm going to.*

Unscrewing the lid, I dip the nib, and using the back of a piece of paper that was in my pamphlet, I press it carefully against the blank page and write *Emily*, then with small, scratchy strokes, add *& Mr Darcy*. I smile sheepishly at myself. Look at me. It's like I'm thirteen years old again and back at school. And just for the hell of it I begin doodling *Emily Darcy, Mr & Mrs Darcy, Emily 4 Darcy* and a little love-heart with two arrows through it.

My smile turns into a wide yawn and I stop to let it out. Oh, wow, I really am dog-tired. Putting down the quill, I rub my watering eyes. It feels as if I've got lead weights plonked on top of my eyelids. The waves of jet lag are coming thick and fast now. I'm going to have to close my eyes. Just for a moment . . .

"Ahem."

I must have dropped off, because the next thing I'm jolted awake by someone coughing. I open my eyes to see a man over by the fireplace. Tall and broad, he has thick black hair curling over his collar and dark eyebrows that look like two smudges of charcoal. They're pitched together in curiosity.

"Hello, can I help you?" he says.

"Uh . . .?" Still half asleep, I prop myself upright and blearily survey my surroundings, taking a moment to register. Uh, where am I?

Then it hits me. Oh, shit.

Hastily I jump up from the chair. *Shit, shit and double shit.* Trust me to fall asleep and get caught.

"I . . . um . . ." Suddenly I realise I've drooled on my chin. Oh, God, how embarrassing. My cheeks burning, I wipe my chin with my sleeve. "Sorry . . . I . . . um . . . was just resting for a moment . . ." I trail off uncertainly as the stranger crosses the room and I suddenly notice his odd clothes. He's wearing a frock coat, breeches and a white shirt with this funny high-necked collar and some kind of cravat. I glance down at his feet. And what's with the riding boots?

Puzzled, I watch him as he strides confidently around the large dining table in the middle of the room. That's funny. It's set for dinner, but I don't remember candles being lit.

"Are you lost?" His voice is deep and softly spoken. Replacing a slim volume into the showcase in the corner, he turns to face me.

"Um . . ." I falter. Up close I can't help noticing he has one of those sexy clefts in his chin that movie stars always have. I don't think I've *seen* a man with one of those in real life. "Well, I wouldn't say I was lost exactly," I begin. "I'm actually here with a tour . . ."

"A tour?" he repeats, furrowing his brow.

I nod. "Yeah, but I just wanted to get some air . . ." I explain, gesturing outside ". . . but it's raining."

Only it's not raining. Looking out of the window, I'm surprised to see that instead of gloomy grey skies, it's bright outside. Shafts of winter sunshine are bouncing in through the panes of mullioned glass and shining on the walls, brightening up the wallpaper.

Wallpaper that had seemed so faded and old earlier, but now looks much more vibrant and colourful, as if it was only decorated yesterday . . . And it's much warmer, I realise, remembering how chilly it was in here before.

Then I spot a fire burning in the grate. I could have sworn it wasn't lit before.

"Someone's lit a fire," I point out, somewhat obviously. Or am I wrong? Was it lit before? To be honest, I can't remember. I'm feeling so muddled. I'm vaguely aware of my forehead throbbing, and I press my fingertips to my temples. It must be the jet lag. My head feels thick and woolly, as if it's packed with cotton balls. I'm not thinking straight. Quickly, I pull myself together.

"Yes, I asked the housekeeper." He nods, his face impassive. "It gets rather cold in here towards late afternoon."

"I can imagine," I reply, briskly unfurling my scarf from round my neck and beginning to fold it up. I'm in mid-fold when it registers. Did he just say *he* instructed the housekeeper? As in this is *his* house?

Realisation dawns. Oh, shit. Trust me. He's probably the owner of Chawton Manor. Aren't all the big stately homes and historical houses still privately owned and just opened up to the public to pay for the upkeep or something? God, he's probably a member of the British aristocracy. Which would explain the funny clothes, I realise, peering at him uncertainly. He must have been hunting or fishing or something.

"Oh, I'm sorry, I didn't realise," I begin apologising. "I had no idea you lived here. I didn't mean to intrude."

His dark eyes are sweeping across me like searchlights and I'm suddenly aware I'm doing this flicky thing with my hair that I always do when I like someone. Feeling like a dork, I stop doing it immediately and fold my arms self-consciously.

"You are not. I am merely visiting."

"You are?" I feel a rush of relief. "Snap. Me too." I smile, then holding out my hand, add, "I'm Emily."

He seems slightly taken aback by my introduction and for a moment there's an awkward pause. Shit. I'm

**92**

probably being too chatty. I do that sometimes when I'm nervous. And he does seem kind of shy.

"Forgive me," he apologises. "I have not introduced myself properly."

Flicking out his black velvet coat tails, he steps towards me and, ignoring my outstretched hand, bows his head politely. Then he looks up and fixes me with the most intense, velvety brown eyes I've ever seen.

"I am Mr Darcy."

# CHAPTER
# EIGHT

I stare at him in bewilderment.

*What the . . .?*

For a moment I'm too startled to say anything. I don't know how to react.

Then I burst out laughing.

"Oh, ha, ha, very funny! I get it." I grin widely. "This is one of those working museums and you're one of those people who dress up in costume and role-play, aren't you?" Suddenly it's all making perfect sense. The clothes. The formality. The quaintly old-fashioned way of speaking.

"*Role-play?*" he repeats in confusion. "I am afraid I do not understand."

I must say, he's really good at playing Mr Darcy. He's just like I imagine him to be. And just as good-looking. Better even.

"Though it took me a moment to work it out," I confess. "You really had me going there."

"Going where?" he replies innocently.

"You know, with the funny clothes and everything . . ."

Puzzled, he looks down at himself, then back at me. "Forgive me, I was not going to mention it, but I was thinking the same about yourself." He seems to be

**94**

bracing himself for what he's about to say next. "I do not want to be rude, but are those *trousers* you are wearing?"

I look down and immediately regret my choice of clothing. I'm wearing my baggy old pink cords. Stella's been telling me to chuck these away for years, but I've never listened. They're about two sizes too big for me and subsequently really comfy. They're also, for the exact same reason, deeply unflattering.

Insecurity grips. He's right. What on earth *am* I wearing? "Trousers" suggests fashionable and figure-hugging. These are neither. I look terrible. *I look like someone's sofa.*

"Oh, these old things?" I say, trying to brazen it out and pretend I don't care. God, it's always the way, isn't it? Why is it that when you do put on some make-up and blow-dry your hair you don't bump into anyone vaguely attractive, and then when you step out looking like *this*, you bump into *this*. It's like some horrible law of the universe or something. Like having a credit note. Before, you covet everything in that store, but as soon as you get a credit note, guaranteed you'll never find anything you want *ever* again. It's so unfair.

I look at *this* now. Underneath that Victorian costume, he's obviously one of those really trendy types. I can just tell. He looks like one of Stella's friends, with the long sideburns and the dark, floppy hair that falls just so over his forehead. And I know for a fact that hair doesn't do that without a lot of product.

"I got them in a sale. They didn't have my size . . ." I can hear myself gabbling as I always do when I find someone really attractive. It's like my tongue winds itself up like a clockwork toy. ". . . But they were reduced from fifty bucks to only fifteen, so I couldn't say no."

And that's another thing I always do — tell people how much I pay for things — it's as if I have to boast about my bargains and what a savvy shopper I am. Realising I've done it again, I cringe inwardly.

"*Bucks*?"

"Oh, I forgot, we're talking pounds now," I correct myself while doing a quick calculation in my head. "It's probably roughly about ten pounds. Or quid," I add, feeling a twinge of pride that I'm picking up the lingo.

"I think you must be mistaken."

"Am I? Oops, probably. Math has never been my strong subject, I must admit." I quickly redo the figures. "No, I think that's about right." I smile self-consciously as he peers at my cords in disbelief.

"They cost ten pounds?" He looks at me with concern. "I find that very hard to believe. That would be rather a lot of money."

A typical man's response, I note, thinking about the reaction of every boyfriend I've ever had when I've come home from a rare shopping trip and showed them my purchases. Why do men always think clothes should cost the price of a beer?

"Did you have them tailored?"

"No, they're from Gap."

"And where might that be?"

I stare at him, incredulous. "You're telling me you've never heard of Gap?"

His face is serious. "Should I have?"

I'm about to answer when it dawns on me that I'm being completely thick. *Of course* he's heard of Gap, he's just *pretending* not to. This is all part of the act. It's probably really important he stays in the role for his job.

"Silly me, of course not." I smile knowingly.

His face relaxes, and thinking it might be rather fun, I decide to play along.

"But maybe you need to get out more," I tease.

OK, make that flirt.

"I can assure you I do go out," he protests haughtily. "Only last week I went hunting with Mr Bingley."

I stifle a giggle. Honestly, I'm going to have to say something. I won't be able to keep this role-playing thing up. Glancing around to make sure there's no one about but me, I lean towards him in confidence. He smells deliciously of cologne, and my stomach does this funny flip-flopping thing.

"You can drop the Darcy act," I whisper. "I promise I won't tell anyone."

He stares at me in confusion. "I am afraid I do not understand."

"Really?" I persist, raising my eyebrows in a nudge-nudge-wink-wink kind of way.

"Really," he replies, completely stone-faced.

OK, I give up. This guy obviously takes his job very seriously. There's no way I'm going to be able to get him out of character. He's probably like one of those method actors.

"Don't worry, forget it." I smile.

But he doesn't smile back. Instead, he studies my face with his dark, liquid eyes. My chest tightens. There's something very sexy about him, yet I can't work him out. One minute he seems shy and almost gauche, and the next he has an air of arrogance about him. It's a lethal combination.

"Your accent, where is it from?" he's asking now. "I have been trying to place it, but —"

"New York," I blurt, breaking his gaze and looking away. He's making me all jittery.

"New York?" His expression is one of astonishment. "You are from America?"

Just the way he speaks is adorable. He has that lovely deep voice and the sexiest English accent.

Er, hello, now it's your turn to say something, Emily.

"Um . . . yeah. I'm here on a literature tour — you know, a week exploring the English countryside, visiting museums, places of interest, like, for example, Bath and Winchester . . ."

Hearing myself blabbering off my itinerary, I cringe inwardly. Oh, God, what am I doing? I sound like a moron. Normally I can be counted on to come out with a witty one-liner, or at least something vaguely amusing, but today I don't know what's happened to me.

*You like him. That's what happened to you, Emily.*

". . . and it's been really great so far. I've met a lot of interesting people." I break off and see he's watching me with apparent fascination. I wonder if he's got a girlfriend?

98

I smile shyly and this time he smiles back. It's a slight, awkward, unsure smile, almost as if smiling isn't something he does very much, which of course makes it incredibly seductive. Who wants to be smiled at by someone who throws them out willy-nilly? No, this smile feels special. *I feel special.*

"Would that include myself?" he asks quietly.

Flip-flop. There goes my stomach again.

"Um . . . yeah," I manage a wobbly reply. He must have a girlfriend — he's far too gorgeous to be single.

"Well, then allow me to return the compliment."

*Oh, go on then — if you must*, I feel like quipping. Thankfully I don't.

There's a pause and a look passes between us. If he wasn't way out of my league, I'd think he liked me.

"Look, I should be going," I say reluctantly, my voice coming out all high and tinny. I swallow hard and try to compose myself. Honestly, Emily, what's come over you? It's like you've got a crush or something.

"Yes, I too have matters I need to attend to. A letter I promised to write to my sister."

"Well, nice to meet you, *Mr Darcy*," I say pointedly, holding out my hand again to shake his.

He glances at my outstretched hand, then bows his head. "It was a pleasure to meet you, too, Miss Emily," he says, his eyes lingering on me.

OK, so it's official. I have a crush. A full-blown, adolescent crush.

I stand there for a moment, not wanting to leave as I know I'm never going to see him again, but knowing I've got to. After all, I can't stand here all day just *gawping* at him, can I? I have to preserve some modicum of cool. I'm a twenty-nine-year-old New Yorker, the manager of a bookstore, a mature adult with a pension plan and the beginnings of faint pencil lines around her eyes. I can't be going around acting like some giddy, love-struck teenager.

*Even if right now I feel like one.*

Tossing my hair over my shoulder in what I hope is a sophisticated, yet casual move, I turn and walk confidently across the room. Reaching the door, I tug it open, then glance back. He's seated at the little writing table, the fading sunlight from the window casting him almost in silhouette. Huh, he must have moved the plastic barrier as it's not there any more, I muse. Back ramrod straight, he's dipping his quill in the ink, tapping the nib against the glass neck of the bottle. He's obviously found some sheaves of paper from somewhere as, with a steady hand, he begins writing his letter. I have to say I'm impressed. You've got to hand it to the museum: he's pretty goddamn realistic. If you didn't know better, you really would think he's Mr Darcy come to life.

"*There* you are."

Stepping out of the room, I walk into the darkened hallway and crash headfirst into the warm armpit of a corduroy jacket.

"Mumph." I give a muffled yelp and jump backwards.

Of course. It had to be, didn't it? *Spike Hargreaves's* corduroy jacket.

**100**

"Oh . . . hi," I mumble, hurriedly smoothing down my mussed-up hair.

"Jesus, where the hell have you been?"

I feel a snap of irritation at his belligerent mood. "None of your goddamn business," I reply archly.

He throws me a filthy look. "Yeah, well, unfortunately for me, it is. I was sent to look for you." His voice is laden with impatience. "The museum's about to close. Everyone's waiting for you on the coach."

Shit. I feel really guilty. I don't care what Spike thinks, but I do care about everyone else. "I got lost," I say defensively.

"*Lost?*" repeats Spike, his voice dripping with scorn. "Bloody hell. *Women*," he mutters, shaking his head.

As if I'm totally useless, I think, feeling annoyed at both myself and Spike.

"And I got talking to Mr Darcy," I can't resist adding.

Spike looks at me as if I've just gone mad. "Yeah, right. Pull the other one."

"Don't believe me if you don't want to." I shrug. "But the museum has obviously got someone to dress up as him. Maybe you should interview him. For your article," I add, smiling serenely. "Ask him a few questions about what it's like being every woman's fantasy," I say, my eyes flicking to Spike's belly, which is pressing against his crumpled shirt. Automatically he sucks it in. "He's back there, in the parlour."

I can see Spike is interested, but he'd never admit it. I start walking away.

"Are you winding me up?" he calls after me.

I turn and catch him tucking in his shirt tails. He stops immediately.

"Me?" I gasp, pretending to look shocked. "As if I'd do such a thing." Turning back round, I keep walking.

One. Two. Three.

I glance over my shoulder and catch Spike tugging his notebook out of his pocket and retrieving a pen from behind his ear. He doesn't see me, and switching back into confident-journalist mode, he strides into the room.

I tip-toe down the hallway and wait outside the dining parlour, ready to eavesdrop.

Except —

"Ha, ha, very funny," huffs Spike, suddenly reappearing and catching me hiding out in the corridor. I jump back as he fires me a condescending look.

"What do you mean? What's funny?" I snap.

"We obviously don't share the same sense of humour," he continues, not answering my question. "But that's probably because the British actually have one."

"Oh, yes, of course. Your famous sense of irony," I retort. I tell you, I'm really beginning to lose my patience with this guy.

"Well, it's slightly more sophisticated than playing a somewhat childish practical joke," he fires back.

"Who's playing a practical joke?" I gasp, annoyed.

"You," he accuses. "Saying some bloke calling himself Mr Darcy is in there." He stabs a finger towards the parlour.

"But he is," I cry, my temper ignited. And grabbing him by his corduroy elbow, I march him back through the doorway.

Oh.

My indignation caves in as I take in the scene before me. Dammit. He's right. There is no Mr Darcy. How frigging annoying. I can't think of anything worse than being proved wrong by some sanctimonious know-all —

Something makes me stop my internal rant. Wait a moment. It's not just that . . . My eyes flick quickly around the room. Now I'm thinking about it, everything looks different, or should that be the same? The plastic barrier is back by the window, and the fire seems to have gone out in the grate. Puzzled, I glance out of the window and am surprised to see how dark it's become. And it's raining, I notice. Well, I guess that explains why the wallpaper is looking all dingy and faded again . . .

"Like I said. Fucking hilarious," snaps Spike.

His voice pulls me back, and I look at him. "But he was here a minute ago," I protest in confusion.

Spike throws me a filthy glare, shakes his head and pushes past me. "I'll see you back on the coach," he mutters, stalking back down the corridor. "After you've said goodbye to your imaginary friend," he adds sarcastically.

God, he really is a dick. Listening to his footsteps retreating, I flop back against the wall and stare into space. Still, that is weird about the guy disappearing. I glance across at a small doorway in the corner of the room. I wonder if that leads somewhere? Somewhere restricted to the public? I guess he must have left through there. Although *I* only left a moment ago and he was writing a letter over on the other side of the room, I recollect, glancing across at the empty chair.

Hmm, what a shame. He was really nice too.

Wandering over to the writing table, I take a look. Everything is as it was before: the desk with the letter, the feather quill and delicate, square-cut glass bottle of purpley-black ink. Only now there's a letter.

Wow, he wrote that quickly. I take a closer look at it. Addressed to "Dearest sister" and signed "Darcy", the handwriting is typically old-fashioned, all swirls and loops and difficult to read, and yet . . . No, but that can't be right. The paper's gone all yellow and the ink is faded. It looks really old.

I rub my dry eyes and stare at it for a moment. Nope, he can't have written that. It's impossible. It must be one of Jane Austen's original letters that's been moved. It was probably displayed on the dining table or something, and I just didn't notice it. Which isn't surprising, seeing as I was so tired. *Am* so tired, I think, yawning. God, why do I feel so groggy?

I turn to leave and then, suddenly, a thought strikes. Why would Jane Austen write a letter pretending to be from one of her characters?

I think about it for a moment. It doesn't make sense. I know there must be a simple explanation, but I can't figure it out. And right now I don't have time to, I tell myself, zoning back in and throwing my bag over my shoulder. If I don't leave now I'm going to miss the

**104**

coach and then Spike will *never* let me hear the last of it. He'll be even more unbearable than he is already. *If that's possible.*

And you know what? From what I've seen so far of Spike I-think-I'm-so-great Hargreaves, I think it probably is.

# CHAPTER
# NINE

By seven o'clock that evening I'm feeling so much more *with it*.

God, a bath and a fresh change of clothes make all the difference, don't they?

OK, so it's probably got a lot more to do with this Jack Daniels and Coke, I muse, crunching on a mouthful of ice, but still, I feel loads better.

I'm downstairs in the hotel bar getting to know everyone. Stella is right, everyone on the tour is a lot older than me. But whereas I was assuming this would mean lots of cosy chats about knitting patterns and cupcake recipes with a bunch of old dears, I'm fast realising I was mistaken.

". . . so I joined match.com after the divorce and that's how I met Sebastian," announces Hilary, a local magistrate who recently retired from her post as the partner of a top legal firm in London. "We've been together six months and he's like a breath of fresh air." She smiles delightedly and takes a sip of her red wine.

Wow. Internet dating? At her age? I'm impressed.

"Although my sons aren't too happy."

"Oh, is it a protective thing?" I ask politely. "I know girls are like that with their fathers."

"No, I think it's because Sebastian is younger," she says, heaving a sigh. "They have a bit of a problem with it."

"But why? Lots of women date younger guys these days," I cry supportively. "Look at Demi and Ashton."

Hilary throws me a puzzled look as if to say, "Who and who?" and then shakes her head.

"No, I mean younger than *my sons*."

*Close your mouth, Emily.*

"So he's twenty-five years younger than me. So what?" she continues. "Once you get to my age, you don't care what people think any more."

"Absolutely," I manage to croak. "So what!"

By the time I've finished my second Jack and Coke, I've undergone something of a revelation. Older, I've discovered, certainly doesn't mean *old*. In fact, I feel quite embarrassed. What was I thinking? I don't know whether it's the fault of TV, movies and magazines, but for some reason all this time I've been under the impression that it's my age group that are having the fun, interesting lives. Go grey and everything stops. It's like the menopause is some kind of biological Berlin Wall — and who wants to be on the wrong side?

Only now I'm no longer sure which *is* the wrong side.

"I've been practising all my life but only started teaching when the children left home. I'm doing a retreat to Goa, in India, next year," beams Rupinda, a yoga instructor, who, at over twice my age, can get her body into positions that mine can only dream of. "You must come."

A yoga retreat in India? How amazing.

"Umm . . . yes, I'd love to," I reply distractedly.

Except of course I know I'll never be able to take the time off work.

Unlike Enid, a sprightly seventy-year-old with salt-and-pepper hair who's just bought a VW camper van with her husband and is planning to spend six months next year touring Europe. Or Marion, a widow, who makes all this lovely chunky silver jewellery and has her own website.

In fact, if anyone's staying home in their bathrobe and slippers, it's more likely to be me, I realise, taking Marion's business card and feeling secretly disappointed nobody wants to talk about cupcake recipes.

I *love* cupcakes.

By the time dinner is served I've got to know everyone a bit better. Everyone apart from Spike Hargreaves, that is. *Him*, I spend all evening avoiding like the plague. I duck into the washroom when I spy him walking towards me down the hallway; I strike up a conversation about "women's troubles" with Enid and Rupinda when he tries to mingle at the bar. And now I've seated myself as far away as possible at the dinner table and have suddenly turned stone-deaf when he asks me to pass him the braised carrots.

Instead, I pick up the dish and calmly help myself to the last of them.

He shoots me a murderous look.

I respond by smiling innocently, piercing a braised carrot with my fork and casually taking a bite. Nobody puts Baby in the corner, I think defiantly.

*Actually, that's* Dirty Dancing, *Emily.*

Well, whatever. He's still a big bully. And if he thinks he can go around all week insulting me, he's got another thing coming. Two can play at his game. And feeling his eyes boring into me, I finish off the carrots.

I wouldn't mind, but I hate carrots.

After dinner we're all pretty exhausted. It's been a long day, and following several rounds of yummy wafer-thin mints called After Eights and more goodnights than *The Waltons*, everyone turns in.

Except I'm not tired. Not even slightly. After my earlier exhaustion I'm now wide-awake and raring to go. It's the jet lag. Back in New York it's only three thirty in the afternoon, so the last thing I want to do is go to bed. This is my first night in England. I want to go out, explore my surroundings, be a complete tourist. OK, so it's eight thirty at night and I'm in the middle of the countryside, but there must be *something* to do around here.

I glance around the dining room, empty but for a tableful of black After Eight wrappers and a grandfather clock whose rhythmic ticking is the only thing breaking the silence. Then I have a brainwave. Of course. Ye olde village pub.

I feel a buzz of excitement.

It's only, like, a ten-minute walk into the village. I can go get a drink. Meet the locals . . . Out of nowhere that scene from *American Werewolf* flicks into my head. You know the one — where he goes into a pub on the moors and all the locals ignore him.

I feel my confidence wobble.

Oh, rubbish, Emily, you're being silly. If lone women can venture up the Amazon in dug-out canoes, you can venture down to the local pub.

Buoyed up by my idea, I start making my way towards the lobby. It'll be fine. I'm sure everyone will be super friendly and welcoming, I tell myself firmly. Though it would be nice to go with someone.

"It's your auntie here, just ringing to say hello . . ."

Hearing a quiet voice coming from the far corner, I look over and see a figure hunched over the payphone. It's Maeve.

". . . but you must be out again. OK, well, I'll try you again tomorrow. Bye for now." Blowing kisses down the phone, she places the receiver on the cradle. For a moment she remains very still, her hand resting on the phone, her face incredibly sad. She appears deep in thought. Then, seeming to sense something, she looks up and sees me.

"Oh, hello . . ." she says, pulling together the edges of her cardigan and smiling self-consciously. "I didn't see you there."

"I was just going to grab my coat," I explain, gesturing upstairs. "I thought I'd take a walk. Check out the village pub."

"Oh, I see." She nods.

There's a pause, and I wonder if I should invite her. I don't really want to, but it seems only polite. I mean, she seems nice and everything; I just wouldn't really know what to say to her as we don't have anything in common. Well, apart from the fact we're both single, I

**110**

think, noticing her empty ring finger. Earlier, at the meet and greet, I tried to talk to her, but she barely said two words before going to sit by herself on the sofa. Saying that, it's mean-spirited not to ask. And I'm sure she won't want to come, anyway.

"Would you like to join me for a drink?"

There. At least now I've asked.

"Oh, no," she answers hurriedly, recoiling back into her turtleneck sweater. "No, I don't think so . . . But thank you."

See.

"Well, goodnight, then." I nod, and continue on to the staircase.

I'm halfway up when I hear: "It's Emily, isn't it?"

I turn and see Maeve standing at the bottom wringing her hands. "I was just wondering . . ." she says nervously, ". . . about that drink."

For a split second I feel a clunk of regret, but quickly squash it.

"You've changed your mind?" I smile warmly.

Immediately her face relaxes. "Well, a sherry would be nice."

"Cool," I reply.

So this is how I'm going to spend my first night in England. Me and Maeve, grabbing a sherry or two at the local pub. Talk about girls gone wild, I think glumly.

And then, quite unexpectedly, a giggle rises in my throat. If Stella could see me now, she'd pee her pants. There she is living it up in a bikini on a tequila-soaked beach in Mexico, and here's me in my old sweater hanging out with a bunch of senior citizens in the middle of the English countryside.

Covering my mouth, I try to smother another giggle. God, it's just too funny. Even more so because, given the choice, I'd *still* rather be going to the pub with Maeve than doing the conga with a bunch of drunk college boys.

Maeve's looking at me with a puzzled expression, and I throw her a big grin. "I'll just go grab my coat."

Maybe Stella is right. Maybe I am a kook.

Outside, the temperature has dropped dramatically and despite my layers of thick coat, woolly hat and mohair scarf, there's an icy wind blowing that cuts right to the bone. We set off at a brisk pace to try to keep warm. The ground is covered in a layer of white frost and the gravel makes a satisfying crunching noise as we head off down the driveway.

For a while we don't say anything and it's just the noise of our footsteps, first on the gravel, then the asphalt of the sidewalk and finally the cobbles of the street. We walk side by side, clouds of white breath punctuating the darkness of the night. Thankfully, I had the foresight to borrow a flashlight from the front desk as it's dark dark. Not city dark, like in New York, where the night-time skies glow marshmallow pink. Instead, overhead is an inky blackness, dotted only with millions of glittering pinpricks.

"So what's New York like?" asks Maeve, after we've been walking in silence for at least five minutes.

I turn to look at her but it's so black I can't see her face. "Have you never been?"

"No, I've never been to America," she sighs. "I've not been anywhere, really. Apart from a couple of trips to London when I was a lot younger. And I went to Paris once." She gives an embarrassed laugh. "I'm afraid I'm very boring."

"You're doing this book tour," I point out. "That's not boring."

Having reached the edge of the village, we're under the street lamps now and I see her absorb this. "Aye, I guess you're right." She nods and gives a small smile.

"And we're going to the pub, and that's not going to be boring," I continue, trying to buoy her up. Despite my initial reservations, I'm really beginning to like Maeve. There's something about her, something more than you see on first impressions, a silent appreciation for things, a quiet dignity.

"I'm afraid I must warn you, I'm not very good company —" she begins apologising, but I cut her off.

"Rubbish," I admonish. "Where did you get that idea?"

I suddenly feel very protective of Maeve. God knows what happened to wreck her self-esteem, but it must have been something pretty bad. She's just so down on herself the whole time.

Maeve throws me a grateful look. "You'd never guess, but I used to be the life and soul before . . ."

"Before what?" I ask, as she trails off.

She hesitates, as if battling with something inside of her, then says flippantly, "Before I got old," and smiles.

**113**

And that's the other thing about Maeve. She can't tell fibs either.

We continue walking. Ahead of us we can now see the pub. All lit up, it's wrapped in ivy that's turned deepest red, like a great big Christmas present, and high above the door swings a sign that reads, "Ye Olde King's Head." It looks so inviting — a snug refuge from the prickling cold of the night — and as we grow closer I can almost smell its beery warmth.

"It's nothing like this."

"Eh?"

"New York," I explain, turning to Maeve. "You asked me what it was like." I pause, trying to work out how to describe it, then give up. "It's a million different things to a million different people. You should go experience it for yourself."

"Aye, I'd love to," she says dreamily, her eyes bright behind her glasses.

And for a brief moment it's as if I can see a real spark inside Maeve, the spark of a young girl, the spark of someone with big dreams and possibilities.

"Maybe if I was younger, if I had my time again, eh?"

But now it's gone again, and she's got that resigned look back on her face. It's almost as if she's determined to put herself down, not to get her hopes up. I wonder why? What's she so scared of? What could have happened to Maeve to make her give up on everything? To leave her with zero self-esteem. To make her so goddamn sad?

But of course I can't ask her, can I? I've barely known her two minutes. And anyway, it's none of my business, is it? Who do I think I am — *Dr Phil?* And reaching for the handle, I push open the wooden door and we go inside.

# CHAPTER
# TEN

We're greeted with a rush of noise, heat and cigarette smoke. The ceiling is low with thick, gnarly beams running across it, and the uneven walls are painted a dark maroon and hung with horse brasses, faded sepia photographs and sets of antlers. A Christmas tree stands in the far corner, fighting for space among the wooden benches and tables.

It looks like the entire village is crammed in here. Middle-aged couples eating bar food, groups of older men downing pints and a bustling crowd of twenty-somethings in skinny jeans and full Friday-night make-up.

And there was me expecting a few sleepy locals, I realise, feeling slightly taken aback to see such a modern crowd. A couple of ruddy farmers maybe, with muddy boots and flat caps, playing dominoes, like in the James Herriot books.

Which were set in Yorkshire, not Hampshire, during the Second World War, reminds a little voice inside my head.

Embarrassment twinges. Honestly, talk about being the cliché of an American tourist. If I'm not careful I'll soon be wearing a pair of Bermuda shorts and calling everything "quaint."

"What can I get you?"

After finally manoeuvring our way to the bar and squeezing between a couple of elbows, I manage to attract the attention of the bartender — sorry, barman.

"Maeve, what would you like?" I ask, tugging off my hat and gloves and making a start on peeling off the numerous layers of clothes I'm wearing. But before she's had a chance to answer I hear a male voice.

"I'll get these."

I turn sideways. A man in a checked flannel shirt is standing next to me, smoking a pipe. He looks really familiar but for the moment I can't place him.

"Ernie. Your coach driver," he explains, seeing my confusion.

"Oh, yeah, of course." I smile. "Sorry, for a minute there . . ."

"I know. Mine's an easy face to forget," he jokes, his eyes twinkling.

Instantly warming to him, I laugh. "I'm Emily . . . and this is Maeve." I gesture towards Maeve, who blushes at her introduction.

"Maeve? Now that's an interesting name," replies Ernie, giving her his full attention.

Maeve looks as if she wants to disappear through the stone-flagged floor. Avoiding his eye, she looks instead at her feet.

"It's Irish," she says, her voice so quiet it's practically lost in the din of the pub.

Puffing on his pipe, he nods. "It means 'intoxicating'," he adds evenly.

Startled, she looks up and meets his eye. He smiles warmly, and finding herself caught, Maeve has no choice but to smile back.

Watching from the sidelines, I get the feeling that didn't just happen by accident on Ernie's part. Still, I'm impressed. That's the first real smile I've seen from Maeve all night.

"Now, then." Turning his attention back to both of us, Ernie asks brightly, "What can I get you two ladies to drink?"

I'm not usually indecisive — I'm strictly a Corona, Sauvignon Blanc or Jack and Coke girl — depending on whether I'm in the mood for beer, wine or liquor. But on this occasion I'm faced with something different: *cider*. Not that they don't have cider in the bars in New York, but usually it's just a choice between apple or pear. Here they've got all kinds of different varieties, called such bizarre names, like, for example, Old Pig's Squeal, Punch Drunk, Badger's Brew . . .

I summon up my courage and go for one called Legless but Smiling.

"So, how is it?" asks Ernie, raising his bushy eyebrows.

I glance at my half-pint of cloudy amber liquid and take a tentative sip. It's warm and sort of wheaty and makes my teeth feel furry, like they do when I've eaten rhubarb. I swish it around my mouth for a minute, then

**118**

swallow. It's got that kick at the end that you only get when there's serious amounts of alcohol involved.

"Trust me, it's not called Legless but Smiling for nothing," quips the barman, who's leaning on the bar, also waiting for my response.

"Well?" echoes Maeve, who's sipping a sherry.

"I like it," I decide after a moment.

"See, what did I tell you? This New Yorker's got balls," cheers Ernie proudly.

Shaking his head, the barman throws me a look of respect. "There's not many that can stomach that brew, I have to tell you."

"In that case, I'll have a pint."

A voice cuts into our conversation and all four of us turn to see where it came from. I spot a familiar figure further along the bar and my heart sinks. *Great.* It had to be, didn't it? *Spike frigging Hargreaves.* Where did he spring from?

Seeing us all staring at him, he nods amiably. "And whatever these two ladies are having," he continues to the barman, ignoring Ernie.

Because obviously he didn't see him, I assume, but then I notice a look pass between them. What the . . .? And I thought outside was icy.

"Why, thank you, but I'm fine . . . We're fine . . . thank you," replies Maeve, while Ernie looks down and mutters something under his breath that sounds like "troublemaker".

My ears prick up at once. "Are you talking about Spike?" I hiss.

Ernie gives me a look that says I shouldn't have heard that.

"Why do you say that?" I persist, intrigued.

"Journalists. Always sticking their nose into other people's business." He shrugs, but I get the distinct feeling there's something he's not telling me.

"Oh, no, you must have got Mr Hargreaves wrong," protests Maeve, leaping to Spike's defence. "He's not like that. He's always been so charming."

"Not to me he hasn't," I retort. "He's been an asshole."

I look at Ernie, who nods in silent agreement. I'm dying to quiz him more, but Maeve, I notice, is now looking quite disconcerted. Reluctantly I drop the subject, but as Ernie changes the conversation to grandchildren, I can't help watching Spike taking a sip of his pint of cider. Honestly, how pathetic. Ordering a whole pint because I ordered a half. Feeling all riled up again, I watch him a moment longer, and then before I know what's come over me, I hold my breath and swig back the rest of my cider.

"Actually, I'll have the same again," I manage to croak as I gulp down the dregs. Putting the empty glass defiantly on the bar, I throw down the gauntlet. "This time make it a pint."

I can feel glances flying around me, but I ignore them.

"I thought you Americans didn't drink," smirks Spike from across the bar. "Being fitness freaks and into all those faddy diets."

"That's LA. I'm from New York," I reply dryly.

*Like you'd know the difference. Moron.*

"Great," says Spike tightly. "Well, in that case, why not make it a pint this time?"

Boy, is he pissed off about those braised carrots.

"Yeah, why not?" I reply, forcing my brightest of smiles.

As I watch the barman draws two pints of frothy I feel a twinge of concern, but I brush it aside indignantly. *Please.* I spent three years at college drinking Jägermeister. No need to worry about me. I'll be just fine, I tell myself, as my pint is placed in front of me.

"Cheers." Holding his own aloft, Spike looks me directly in the eye.

It feels like a game of chicken.

"Cheers," I reply archly, picking up my pint and steadfastly meeting his gaze.

I mean, c'mon. How much stronger than Jägermeister can this stuff be?

Quite a bit, actually.

Ten minutes later I'm chatting to Ernie and Maeve when my lips start feeling a bit funny. It's the strangest sensation. A bit like when I go to the dentist and he gives me an injection to make my mouth go numb.

". . . and that's Theresa. She's a bonny lass. Nearly nineteen now, I'll be damned, and studying to be a nurse . . ."

And I'm finding it hard to concentrate. Ernie's produced pictures of his grandchildren from his wallet, but I can feel myself zoning out.

". . . and little Thomas, only six and already a rascal. Do you have grandchildren, Maeve?"

"Um . . . no, no, I don't."

Maybe I should try to mingle, meet some people my own age. Yeah, that sounds like fun. I peer woozily around the bar. Hmm, saying that, everyone here seems to know everyone already. It could be kind of tricky. I mean, what am I supposed to do? Go up to a complete stranger and tap them on the shoulder?

Someone taps me on my shoulder.

I twirl round unsteadily and come face to face with a tiny, ebullient blonde wearing a tie-dyed T-shirt and a disarming grin.

"Um . . . hi." She gives a little wave, then stuffs her hands into the pockets of her combat pants. "Your friend told us you're staying up at the Old Priory . . ."

"My *friend*?" I repeat, puzzled.

"Yeah." She nods, gesturing over to Spike, who's now deep in conversation with a tall, shaven-headed guy.

"Oh, well, I wouldn't call him a friend *exactly*," I confide.

She looks triumphant. "I knew it!" Dipping her head to hide her face behind her hair, which I can now see has all these tiny little braids woven in it, she leans closer and hisses, "I said to Lee, there's no way those two are just friends."

Er, what?

"I could just tell. Straight away."

The cider has dulled my reactions so it takes me a moment to realise she's completely misunderstood.

**122**

"I'm like that, you know. I can just read people."

"Oh, no, I didn't mean —"

"I'm Caroline, by the way."

"Oh, hi, I'm Emily." I smile, concentrating hard on appearing sober. I'm fast realising why this cider got its name.

"Friends call me Cat. Like Cat Deeley, you know, on the telly —" She breaks off and tuts loudly. "Bloody hell, I'm such a dummy. You probably won't know who she is, will you? Being from America . . ."

"Actually, she presents some show in the States."

"Does she *really*?" Cat greets this news with such genuine, wide-eyed fascination you'd think Cat Deeley was a personal friend. "That's great. I really like her. And she's so pretty. In fact I wish we shared a bit more than a name." She lets out a snort of laughter and quickly covers up her nose with her hand. I notice she's got a little tattoo of a star between her thumb and fore-finger.

"Yoah, Cat."

We're interrupted by a loud yell from across the pub and I turn to see the shaven-headed guy standing with Spike over by the pool table beckoning her over.

Cat breaks into a huge smile. "That's Lee, my boyfriend," she explains. "We're coming," she yells loudly, then turns back to me sheepishly. "I'm supposed to be inviting you to join us for a game of pool, but once I get talking . . ." She rolls her eyes. "So, are you up for it?"

Her invitation catches me by surprise. *Am I?* On the one hand I don't want to be within a snooker cue of

Spike Hargreaves, but on the other hand Cat seems really lovely and a game of pool does sound like fun . . .

"Yeah, sure. That sounds great." I smile, tipsily. "Um, but there's just one thing. About Spike —"

"Don't worry, I understand," she interrupts, her face suddenly serious. "I won't let on I know. I can be very discreet when I want to be." And before I've got a chance to explain, she links her arm through mine and begins steering me towards the pool table.

Four games later I've eaten my first ever packet of pork scratchings — which I thought were going to be gross, then I tasted one and discovered they *were* gross, but also delicious — learned that Cat loves Lee, the Killers and TopShop (that's the second time I've heard about this place. Like Stella, she referred to it in a hushed, reverential voice) *and* finished my pint of cider.

Which in total means I've polished off one and a half pints and I'm feeling quite drunk. Or, as Cat taught me they say here in England, *pissed*. But it doesn't matter, as I'm actually playing really well. Funny, as for the last three shots I haven't even been able to focus on the ball without getting double vision, but it's not a problem as I've worked out a really easy way to fix that. I just close one eye. Clever, huh?

Screwing up one eye, I watch Cat, who's zipping around the table, potting ball after ball with alarming skill and ease. At the moment we're winning — girls against boys.

"Whoo-hoo, you go girl," I cheer, raising my empty pint glass. "Get 'em by the balls."

124

Oh, my God. That's so funny, isn't it? *Balls. Pool. Men.* I suddenly get the giggles.

"Hey, come on, Cat," whines Lee, pretending to beg as she goes to pot our last ball. "Have mercy on us."

"Oi, speak for yourself," grumbles Spike, looking over at me with this really sour expression as if he's just sucked on a lemon. I don't know why but it makes me giggle even harder. "We don't need any favours."

"I think we do, mate," smiles Lee good-naturedly. "Cat's a pub champion."

"True, but she's got a handicap," says Spike pointedly.

"Oh, is it like golf?" I cry excitedly, though I'm not exactly sure why as I don't play golf, or know anyone who plays golf, or is even remotely interested in golf for that matter. Grinning, I direct my question at Lee, who like Cat, is totally adorable. I mean, really. I just love these guys. They're such a sweet couple. In fact, I think I'm going to invite them to stay with me in New York.

"Um, no," replies Lee awkwardly. He throws Spike a look.

"But then I don't understand . . ."

I trail off. Oh, I get it. *I'm* the handicap.

"Bugger. Missed it," gasps Cat, grabbing everyone's attention before I've got time to come back with a crushing put-down for Spike. Because I'm sure I'd think of one, it's just it's escaping me right now.

We all look at the table, just in time to see our last ball gliding past the pocket in the far corner and gently tapping the side, where it comes to a halt.

"Bad luck, ladies," tuts Spike, who's doing this thing of stretching the cue behind his shoulders. His shirt tails pop out of his trousers and I suddenly catch more than a glimpse of his pot belly, which is all freckly and *covered* in blond fuzz. It runs all the way down past his navel to —

*Oh, yuck.*

"You were so near."

"And yet so far," finishes a grinning Lee. Ducking a playful punch from Cat, he looks at Spike. "So, who's gonna show them how it's done?"

Shrugging, Spike puts down his cue.

*Thank God.*

"Leave it to me, mate." He winks.

We all wait as Spike begins circling the table, working out his next shot. Back and forth he goes, leaning across the table from one side, then from the other, until finally satisfied, he stands upright and begins making a big show of rubbing chalk on to his cue as if he's Tom Cruise in *The Color of Money*.

Oh, please. And this from a man who's so far managed to pot just three balls. *Two of which were ours*.

"For Christsakes, just get on with it," I can't help muttering under my breath.

At least I thought I muttered it, but it must have come out a bit louder as Spike looks up and shoots me daggers.

*Oooh. Grumpy.*

Looking away, I catch Cat's eye, who throws me a "secret smile", as if to say, "Aw, look at you two,

**126**

pretending to argue." I pull a face and try shaking my head to show her she's got completely the wrong idea, but she just grins all hippy-dippily and wraps her arms drunkenly round Lee.

For a wistful moment I watch them, all coupled up and happy, and I get a sense of hope that maybe there are some decent guys out there, then I glance back at the table. About to take his shot, Spike is leaning so close to the table his belly is almost resting on the baize. In fact — uggh — it is.

As Spike flashes me his naked stomach yet again, an image of the stranger I met this afternoon in the museum suddenly pops into my head. I bet his belly wouldn't rest on the table, I muse, imagining the six-pack that was no doubt lurking underneath his shirt.

I watch Spike sliding the cue through his fingers.

He has bitten fingernails. I *hate* bitten fingernails.

That's one thing I really remember about the guy in the museum. He had lovely hands, with long fingers like a piano player. In fact, I know I'm supposed to be off men, but this guy was different. There was something really — how can I put it? — *dignified* about him.

Unlike Spike, who's now making a noise like a pig.

Honestly, the man really is a slob, I think, letting out a burp. Oops, excuse me. This cider is making me a bit gassy.

"Uggghhh." Grunting, Spike hits the white, misses his ball and instead pots the black.

"Oh, shit, mate," gasps Lee, but his voice is drowned out by Cat, who erupts like a shrieking volcano and rushes over to me.

"Yippee, we've won, we've won!"

"Put it there," I hear myself exclaiming, high-fiving Cat.

She laughs delightedly. "Oooh, I love how you Americans do that."

"Yeah, I know," I laugh back, though to be honest I don't really, as I never high-five anyone — in fact, I don't know what just possessed me to high-five Cat.

"I think that deserves a drink," laughs Cat. "Your round, boys."

At that moment a bell sounds twice. How odd. I thought I heard a bell five minutes ago.

"Sorry, that's the end of last orders," grins Lee. "You weren't quick enough." Then seeing my puzzled expression, explains, "That means closing time."

"Awww," groans Cat, her face falling. "Well, we'll have to do this again sometime."

"Definitely." Honestly it's amazing, I've only known Lee and Cat a few hours, but I'm feeling quite emotional. I've even got the hiccups.

I glance over to the bar, where Maeve and Ernie are engrossed in conversation, their heads bent low, their bodies turned towards one another. You'd have to be blind not to read the body language, and as I catch Maeve's eye her face flushes like a teenager on a first date. Aww, would you look at that? They look so cute together.

**128**

Gesturing for her to wait for me, I turn back to Cat and Lee and launch into a round of hugs and goodbyes and the promise of keeping in touch, until we're eventually broken up by the barman, who appears to collect our glasses.

"There you go," I hiccup, passing him my empty one. Stumbling to my feet, I turn unsteadily to leave when I notice that Spike's pint is still half-full.

"Couldn't finish that, huh?" I hear myself slurring. God, I really am a lot more drunk than I thought. Still, I don't think he noticed.

"Nope," he replies, not looking at me as he hands his cider to the barman.

I feel a hot flush of satisfaction. This is so great. First I beat him at pool, then I drink more than him. That'll show him!

"'Fraid I'm a complete wuss when it comes to alcohol. Never could stand the hangovers." He grins smugly.

Huh? What? I hiccup loudly and put my hand up to my head, which is beginning to throb.

"Make sure you drink lots of water," he chortles.

And with that he's walking away across the pub and I'm left behind with a bad case of the hiccups and the woozy feeling that I've just been had.

# CHAPTER
# ELEVEN

"*Beep-beep-beep . . . beep-beep-beep . . .*"

The next morning I sleep through my alarm and wake up with only ten minutes left to make it in time for breakfast. Not that I feel like breakfast. I have the *worst* hangover. My tongue feels like a small furry animal, my mouth tastes like a sewer, and that alarm is like a pneumatic drill boring through my skull.

"Shuddup."

I hit the "snooze" button for the umpteenth time and let my arm flop down on to the bedspread like a leaden lump. It still feels like the middle of the night. Probably because back in New York it still *is* the middle of the night . . . For a joyous, fleeting moment I imagine I'm back home in my apartment and I can sleep for hours, and hours, and hours . . .

But I'm not. And I can't.

I have to get up.

The alarm starts beeping again.

*Like now.*

Dragging myself out of bed, I stagger zombie-like — eyes closed, arms outstretched, groaning loudly — into the bathroom. Once I've taken a really hot shower I'll feel a lot better. There's no better hangover cure than being blasted by strong jets of water for five minutes to wake you up, I tell myself, thinking back to my power shower in my apartment and the countless times it's brought me back to life. God, it's just what I need. Tugging off my pyjamas, I blearily open my eyes. It takes a moment to focus, and then —

No. Surely not. It can't be.

*This* is the shower?

A few minutes later and I'm standing shivering in the small, pink, plastic bathtub, sprinkling myself with a sort of brass hosetype attachment. Having shampooed my hair, I'm now trying to rinse it with the feeble trickle of lukewarm water, but it's not easy. I seem to be doing a better job of rinsing the flowery wallpaper than my scalp. Plus, it's really difficult to get the temperature right. I fiddle with the taps. It's either freezing cold or —

"Argghhhh."

Hot enough to cause third-degree burns.

I drop the attachment. It falls clattering into the bathtub, affecting the water pressure, which suddenly changes from feeble-cum-nothing to Niagara Falls-type gushing and takes on a life of its own, spinning round like a whirling dervish and spraying scalding water everywhere.

"Jesus!"

Trying to get out of the way, I now lose my balance and bash my shin against the tub.

"Frigging hell," I yell, hopping around before promptly slipping on the pink plastic and sort of bellyflopping out of the bathtub and on to the pink shagpile bathmat.

For a moment I lie prostate, cheek wedged up against the bathmat, limbs outstretched, feeling like one of those scene-of-the-crime chalk figures. I close my eyes. I'm tempted to lie here and go back to sleep, but I can't. I'm supposed to be on vacation. A soapsud drips down the side of my nose and I shiver. And I'm not going to let a little thing like a hangover spoil that, now, am I?

A few minutes later I'm finally ready. I've managed to rinse my hair in the sink with a cup, but decided to pass on my fuzzy legs. After all, it's the dead of winter — who's going to see them? And anyway, I need the extra layer to keep me warm. I shiver, walking into the dining room, which is distinctly chilly.

That's another thing I'm learning about English people. They're so hardy! In New York when the temperature dips below zero we're slaves to our central heating, but here they just put on another sweater.

I'm wearing three already.

"Well, good morning," roars Rose through a mouthful of toast.

I've noticed that Rose doesn't really mix with the other ladies on the tour and this morning is no exception. She's sitting alone at an empty table wearing a sparkly black turtle neck and more diamonds than Elizabeth Taylor. By the looks of the screwed-up napkins, toast crumbs and empty teacups, most people have already eaten breakfast.

Yet it's not even nine thirty, I realise, glancing at my watch. Will someone tell me why that is? Why do old people love getting up early? They're retired. They can sleep till noon. Why, when the rest of us would do anything for that extra five minutes in bed, are they getting up at the crack of dawn when they don't have to?

Baffled by one of life's great mysteries, I pull out a chair.

"Sleep well?"

"Yeah, fine," I reply. "Apart from a bit of a hangover —"

"Well, lucky you. I didn't," she interrupts, pouring another cup of tea and adding three heaped teaspoons of sugar. "My room was far too hot, and the mattress was horribly lumpy. I didn't sleep a wink all night."

"Oh, dear," I sympathise, deciding against mentioning that I woke up at 4 a.m. with jet lag and could hear her snoring through the wall. "Poor you."

"Poor me indeed," grumbles Rose, clanking the spoon against the sides of the cup as she stirs. "However, it seems others were enjoying themselves." Leaning closer, she suddenly fixes me with a heavily mascaraed eye. "A little birdie told me you and our journalist friend were embroiled in a little tête-à-tête last night at the local drinking establishment."

My cheeks tinge with colour. "I wouldn't call it that. We just bumped into each other in the local pub," I protest hurriedly, wondering why I feel the need to explain when nothing happened. "We played pool."

Rose raises a painted eyebrow. "Quite," she says, clicking her tongue. Looping her finger through her teacup, she leans back against her chair and sips her tea. It's more than obvious she doesn't believe me, and I'm about to protest further when a teenaged waitress appears in full frilly-aproned garb.

"Would madam care to order breakfast?" she asks, hovering awkwardly at the head of the table, her eyes darting around like a frightened bird.

My stomach is still swilling round like a washing machine set to cycle "nauseous" and I really don't feel like eating anything. But I know I have to. Even if just because I can't take two Nurofen on an empty stomach.

Quickly I scan the menu. Usually breakfast for me consists of snatching a low-bran muffin from the Italian bakery next to the bookstore, but this is all cooked. "Um, what would you recommend?" I ask, feeling a bit fazed.

The waitress stares at me fearfully. "We do a full English breakfast," she suggests meekly.

I have no idea what this involves, but I'm keen to embrace local traditions. "Sounds great." I smile, closing my menu.

The waitress's face flushes with relief and she makes a little scribble on her pad. "And how would you like your eggs, madam?"

"Over easy," I reply automatically. That's how I always have my eggs.

She looks at me with a baffled expression.

"Sunny side up?" I suggest instead, looking at her face for some kind of recognition and, seeing nothing, feeling like a bit of an idiot. God, I must look like a right tourist.

"Um . . . *scrambled?*" I ask uncertainly.

Suddenly she breaks into a smile and I feel a beat of relief.

"And could I have —" I'm about to say egg whites, but decide against it. I don't want to look like one of those fussy Americans who ask for everything to be non-fat and on the side, I think, remembering Spike's comment last night. "Just a non-fat latte," I say instead.

Oh, shit. I just did, didn't I?

"I mean . . . um . . . Tea is just fine," I say, gesturing to the teapot in the middle of the table. "When in Rome . . ." I laugh breezily, but the waitress merely gives me a puzzled look and scuttles away.

"Nothing better than a nice cup of tea," approves Rose, taking a rather loud slurp as if to prove it. "Although of course the tea they serve here is ghastly."

"Oh, really?" I nod, ignoring my hangover, which is screaming out for a coffee. Like I said, I'm keen to try all these English traditions, and this is one of them.

Reaching for the teapot, I squeeze my fingers through the fine bone-china handle. I hold it gingerly, reminded of the time I held my cousin Lisa's newborn baby: at arm's length, away from my chest, terrified I was going to drop and break it. It's surprisingly heavy — the teapot, not the baby — and my wrist wobbles. Saying that, I've also got the shakes from alcohol poisoning, which isn't exactly helping matters.

**135**

"So?"

"Mmm, delicious." I smile, taking a sip of weak, milky tea. "Very refreshing."

*God, I'd kill for a Starbucks.*

Rose purses her lips. "I'm not referring to the tea," she chastises. "I'm referring to your . . ." she hesitates, choosing her words carefully ". . . *encounter*."

Aww, bless, how chaste. Underneath the booming voice and guise of heavy eyeliner, Rose really is still just a sweet little old lady, I think affectionately. "Nothing happened. It was entirely innocent," I say reassuringly.

"I'm sure it was, my dear." She nods. "But let me tell you, men are *never* innocent in their thoughts."

I stifle a smile. No doubt she's now going to warn me about the dangers of men and how I have to protect my honour. How cute.

"I was young once, you know."

I nod kindly and settle back in my chair. What joy. Rose is going to tell me tales of courtship and romance. Of being wooed by handwritten love letters and being recited poetry to under a spreading oak tree . . .

Scenes from novels flash through my mind and I feel a wistful pang. Oh, to be young and single in those days. Things were so very different.

"Long before I became a famous actress in the theatre, I met Larry, my first husband . . ."

I feel a blip of surprise. Her *first* husband? How many husbands has Rose had? I wonder.

". . . He was a US serviceman based here during the war . . ."

**136**

Ah, you see. That explains it. He probably died in action and she was left heartbroken for years. No doubt she only married again later in life for companionship, but she never forgot her first love, their tender moments shared, their slow, sweet courtship.

". . . I was only nineteen years old . . ."

See. I knew it.

". . . and I'd never even seen a penis . . ."

My reverie screeches to an abrupt halt. Hang on a minute. Did she just say *penis*?

". . . I was somewhat of a late bloomer. Tilly, my best friend, had already done it with her young chap . . ."

No. Please. No. There must be some mistake. What happened to handwritten love letters?

". . . several times in fact. Both missionary and from behind . . ."

Arrrggh.

". . . It all came as quite a shock, I can tell you . . ."

For the love of Christ. Make this stop. *I've got a hangover.*

". . . In those days all I was interested in was getting my hands on a pair of nylons, but Larry was interested in getting those great big Ohio hands of his on my —"

"Full English breakfast?" Like a white frilly angel, the waitress suddenly reappears at the table.

I almost cry with relief. Thank God. Another second and I don't think I would have made it.

"Yes, please . . . Oh, thank you." I smile gratefully as the waitress puts a huge plate in front of me.

And I mean *huge*.

My stomach balks. Wow, that's a lot of food for one person. I stare nervously at the glistening mound of eggs, sausages, bacon, beans and some kind of patty. Not to mention the slices of toast. And they say *Americans* eat huge portions.

"Well, don't just sit there looking at it. Tuck in," scolds Rose, who thankfully seems to have been steered off course from telling me all about her sex life. "You need to get some meat on those bones."

Trust me, I have enough meat on these bones to last more than one series of *Survivor*, but I'm not going to argue with Rose. Picking up a fork, I cautiously survey my plate. Hmm, I wonder what this patty thing is?

Shaving off a slither, I tentatively taste it.

I get a very pleasant surprise. "Wow, this is delicious," I enthuse, taken aback. I cut a bigger slice. "What is it?" I ask, savouring the juicy, salty taste. My hangover's starting to feel better already.

"Black pudding," beams Rose. "It's always been a favourite of mine, too."

"Pudding?" I mumble, as I chew hungrily. Those crazy Brits, I think fondly. A savoury dessert for breakfast. What will they think of next? "Mmm, yum, what's it made of?"

"Dried cow's blood," says a male voice next to me, and I turn sideways to see Spike pulling out a chair and sitting down.

My jaws freeze mid-chew. "Excuse me?"

"Black pudding's made of cow's blood," he says matter-of-factly, plonking down his tatty old notebook on to the table and helping himself to a cup of tea.

For a second I'm almost about to heave all over the table. Then I get it. Of course. Spike and his hilarious English sense of humour.

"Very funny," I reply and continue chewing.

"I'm not joking." He shrugs, yawning loudly without covering his mouth. He's even more dishevelled than usual. He's wearing a crumpled sweatshirt with some kind of stain on it, and there are dark rings under his bloodshot eyes. "You can ask Rose if you don't believe me."

"OK, I will." Calling his bluff, I look across the table. "Rose, would you believe it, a certain someone just told me that this . . ." I wave the piece of black pudding that's speared on my fork. ". . . is made of cow's blood!" I give a little sarcastic snort.

Rose purses her scarlet lips. "Nonsense," she tuts, shaking her raven bob dismissively. "It's not made of cow's blood!"

I knew it. I throw Spike a triumphant glance. Cow's blood indeed! As if I was going to fall for that! Defiantly popping the rest in mouth, I make lots of smug chewing noises: "Mmmmm . . . mmmmm . . ."

Then Rose has to go and say something I really don't want to hear.

"It's made of pig's."

Urgggh.

I've cleaned my teeth twice, flossed *and* gargled with mouthwash, and I can still taste that . . . that stuff. OK, so I admit it's delicious, but still. Dried pig's blood?

That has to be the most revolting thing I've heard. It's like eating scabs.

Taking a glug of Diet Coke, I slosh it around my mouth and stare out of the coach window. We're on our way to Winchester to visit the cathedral where Jane Austen is buried, and as we weave through the narrow streets I try to concentrate on the scenery and not my dodgy stomach.

The seat next to me is empty, Maeve is sitting somewhere towards the back, being interviewed by Spike for his article. I bristle at the very thought. No doubt he's still cracking up about breakfast, but I've made a resolution. I'm not going to waste any more time getting annoyed about Spike. He's *so* not worth it. From now on I'm going to Etch-a-Sketch him from my mind and concentrate on my trip.

"We'll be spending the next couple of hours exploring Winchester Cathedral, so if you'd like to gather your things together . . ." our tour guide's shrill voice fizzes over the microphone as we pull into the parking lot and come to a standstill.

Cricking my neck, I stare out of the window and up at the impressive piece of architecture with its intricately carved stonework and elaborate stained-glass windows.

Wow, this looks amazing. As the door swings open I eagerly grab my coat and stand up. I see Maeve making her way down the aisle towards me. For a moment I think she's going to walk right past me. She mustn't have seen me.

**140**

"Hey." I smile as I shuffle into the aisle next to her. "How's it going?"

She doesn't turn round and for a split second I almost think she's going to ignore me, but then she turns and nods. "Oh, Emily, hello." She seems a little flustered, but I ignore it. Maeve often seems flustered.

"So, how did you and Ernie get along last night?" I ask, leaning closer to make sure no one hears. I've been dying to ask her, but I haven't been able to get her on her own. When we got back to the hotel after the pub I left her and Ernie chatting in the foyer and went to bed, and then this morning she's been with Spike the whole journey.

"Oh . . . um . . . all right," she says warily.

"Just all right?" I tease, giving her a little nudge. "I think you two make a lovely couple."

"Yes, well, I'd appreciate it if you kept thoughts like that to yourself," she snaps.

I look at her in disbelief. I don't know who's more shocked that she's snapped, me or her.

"Oh, I'm sorry, Maeve. It was a joke. I didn't mean —" I break off as I notice that her eyes look suspiciously moist behind her glasses. "Hey, are you OK?" I ask quietly.

There's a pause as she swallows hard. We're at the front of the coach now about to disembark, and I see her glance anxiously towards Ernie, who's sitting behind the wheel. For a brief second I think she's going to tell me something, but then she looks quickly away before he sees her.

**141**

"I'm sorry. I'm just a bit under the weather. I think I've got a cold coming," she mumbles, rushing down the steps and into the parking lot to join Rupinda and Rose.

Puzzled, I follow her. I see no evidence of a runny nose or as much as a sneeze. Something's definitely up. But what? Walking home from the pub last night she seemed relaxed and in really good spirits. I was so drunk it was all I could do to put one foot in front of the other, but I remember her laughing at Ernie's jokes and talking glowingly about her nieces and nephews. What could have happened between then and now?

I glance across the parking lot and see a familiar figure pulling out a packet of Malboros from his breast pocket. Suddenly it dawns on me: *Spike* is what happened between then and now.

Hands dug deep in my pockets, I stride across the blustery asphalt. Spike's standing apart from everyone, head bent into his cupped hands, trying to light a cigarette. "Hey, have you said something to Maeve?" I hiss angrily.

So much for my resolution.

"Excuse me?" He looks up, an unlit cigarette dangling from the corner of his mouth.

"Oh, please, don't act all innocent with me," I snap, and I see him flinch a little. "What were you two talking about on the coach?"

"I'm a journalist," he replies, snatching his cigarette from his lips and sticking it behind his ear. Throwing his corduroy shoulders back, he gives me a lofty glare. "I was conducting an interview."

"About Ernie?"

Spike's face is impassive. "About Mr Darcy," he replies evenly. "Perhaps you'd care to answer a few questions yourself. When you've calmed down and got rid of your hangover."

"What hangover?" I say sharply. As if on cue a wave of nausea wafts over me. "I don't know what you're talking about."

And ignoring the lurching feeling in my stomach, I stalk past him. I don't believe him. Not for a second. I definitely think he's said something to Maeve about Ernie. But he is right about one thing: my hangover.

Feeling light-headed, I steady myself on the trunk of a tree. In fact, I think any minute now I'm going to pass out.

# CHAPTER
# TWELVE

Leaving the rest of the party behind, I quickly find a quiet patch of frosty grass behind the cathedral and collapse on to an empty wooden bench. Everything is starting to spin and I close my eyes. God, I'm feeling really dodgy now. Dropping my head between my knees, I start inhaling lungfuls of piercingly cold air.

*In. Out. In. Out. In. Out. In . . .*

I've no idea how long I remain like this, sitting here, taking deep breaths, but the next thing I know I suddenly hear the sound of footsteps crunching. I stop breathing and hold my breath. Who's that? I stiffen and snap my eyes wide open. Probably Spike, come back to hassle me about the interview, I realise, with a horrible sinking feeling.

Remaining perfectly still, I keep my head between my knees and my eyes focused on the ground, childishly wishing that perhaps if I can't see him, he won't see me. Well, it used to work when I was five years old and playing hide and seek with my grandparents, I tell myself hopefully.

The crunching is growing louder, closer, *right by me*. A pair of feet suddenly appear in my field of vision. Just the tips. Then stop.

Double shit.

"Ahem."

He clears his throat and waits for me to look up. So he can gloat, no doubt, I tell myself, feeling tempted to ignore him and pray he gets the message and goes away. But I know there's no chance of that. Spike's a journalist. Persistence is his middle name.

I stare at his shiny boots a moment longer, bracing myself for the onslaught of jokes — seeing as I am one now, I think huffily — then lift my head. Except in the split second it takes to do so, something registers as not quite right. Hang on a minute. Spike's boots are scuffed and always unlaced.

As I look up, I'm hit by a sudden headrush.

*They're not Spike's boots.*

"Are you feeling unwell?"

*It's him again.* The man from the museum. I stare blankly at his impossibly square jaw with the sexy cleft in his chin and take a moment to absorb this. As I do so, two thoughts are whizzing through my head:

1. What a weird coincidence. What on earth is he doing here?
2. What brilliant luck. I never thought I was going to see him again.

"You look a little pale."

"No, I'm fine. I was just feeling a little . . . erm . . . light-headed."

He looks at me with concern, then reaches for his temples and rubs them in consternation. "I am also feeling a little light-headed. Would you mind if I sit down?"

"Oh . . . um . . . sure — of course." I nod, shuffling up a bit to make room for him. I suddenly feel ridiculously nervous, the way I always feel when I'm really attracted to someone. I glance surreptitiously at him. He's still wearing the same funny clothes he was wearing yesterday, but even so, let's not beat about the bush here. Fancy-dress costume or not, he's still drop-dead good-looking.

Flicking out his thick black winter frock coat, he sits down next to me. My heartbeat quickens at his close proximity. So what if he's wearing a frilly shirt, tight breeches and fob watch? I dated a man who wore white cowboy boots, remember?

Er, hello, Emily, you're not dating him.

*Yet*, pipes up a little voice inside me.

Jesus, what's come over me? Since when did I get so *predatory*?

There's a long pause, and for a few moments we both just sit there, side by side. Me, hugging my knees and trying to check him out by peering sideways without being caught. Him, sitting completely erect, rubbing his temples and frowning.

At least that's what he seems to be doing, but have you ever tried to peer sideways at someone? It really hurts your eyes.

"I believe we met yesterday at Chawton Manor," he says, turning sideways and catching me staring right at him.

**146**

I blush hotly. Honestly, could I get *any* less cool? "Er, yeah," I say uncertainly, wondering what's going to come next.

"Miss Emily, the American, is it not?"

As he looks at me I can't help noticing the way the light catches his eyes and how you can see these faint flecks of amber around the edges. "And you're Mr . . ." I trail off awkwardly.

"Darcy," he finishes firmly. "Mr Darcy."

Oh, right, I see, so we're still playing this game. I stare at him for a moment, trying to weigh him up. "Do you . . . um . . . do this for a living?" I ask.

"Do what?" he asks innocently.

*Be all charming and sexy around single American girls.*

"I mean, are you an actor?"

"An actor?" He seems surprised. "Why, no." He smiles, seemingly amused by my question. I smile back, but to be honest, now I'm a bit lost. I mean, I'm not sure what to make of it. If he's not an actor, then who is he?

Still feeling a bit woozy, I try thinking of some logical explanation to what's going on here. Is he playing some joke? Is someone going to jump out from the bench in a moment and shout, "You've been punked!" or whatever they shout here in England.

I glance around, but everything is peaceful and quiet. There's absolutely no one around. Just me and this dark, handsome, English stranger.

Then I get a scary thought: what if he's some weirdo murderer who goes around pretending he's Mr Darcy to lure gullible young women like me to their doom?

In my mind I suddenly see a newspaper spinning towards me, like in one of those old black-and-white movies, and the headline:

## THE TRAGIC DEATH OF A HOPELESS ROMANTIC — MURDERED BY HER LOVE OF LITERATURE

"We begged her to come to Cancún," says close friend Stella, recently engaged to Scott, 29, an advertising executive. "But she wanted to meet Mr Darcy."

Right, that does it. I've got to just come out with it.

"Look, what's going on here?" I blurt, looking him straight in the eye. Hell, I'm American. We like to straight-talk.

He seems shocked by my abruptness. "Pardon me, but I am afraid I do not quite follow."

"You. Turning up again. In that outfit. Saying you're Mr Darcy," I continue, feeling emboldened. "If you're not an actor, then who are you?"

"Mr Darcy," he says simply.

I look at him for a moment, trying to figure him out and failing. I really like this guy, but a joke's a joke. "I'm sorry, but that's impossible."

"How can that be impossible?"

"Because you don't exist," I say simply. "*Unfortunately*," I add with a rueful murmur.

"In that case, could you explain to me how I happen to be sitting here next to you? Are you suggesting that I am in fact a ghost? A figment of your imagination?" he replies archly.

Now he's saying it, it does sound a bit far-fetched.

Er, hello? More far-fetched than him saying he's Mr Darcy?

"If it's any consolation, I too find your presence a little disconcerting," he confesses, seeing my discomfort. Leaning forwards, elbows on knees, he rakes his fingers through his hair. "And I am also confused as to why our paths keep crossing."

I glance sideways at his hunched figure and feel an unexpected warmth of affection. "Not as confused as I am," I reply softly.

"Yesterday, after seeing you in the parlour, I wondered if I had seen you at all."

"Me too," I say, nodding vigorously.

"You seemed to appear from nowhere and then disappear into thin air."

"*Exactly*," I gasp. I feel a wave of relief. So I'm not going loopy. There's obviously a rational explanation for all of this.

But *what*?

For a few moments we remain perfectly still. Neither of us speaks, but the unspoken questions are whirling around us, as if we're two figures in a snowglobe. *How . . .? Why . . .? Who . . .?* I close my eyes. I feel dizzy.

"I wondered if perhaps I'd imagined you."

I hear his voice, low and measured, and I open my eyes to see he's gazing at me as if he can't quite believe it himself.

He leans back against the bench and folds his arms. "I must tell you, Miss Emily, everything about you, from your dress to your speech to your manner is like nothing I have ever experienced before."

"I could say the same about you." I smile shyly.

Moreover, there's definitely something happening *between* us. And I'm definitely not imagining that.

"Is that true?" he demands, never taking his eyes from mine.

"Absolutely." I nod. I feel slightly flustered. Is he flirting with me? My stomach tipple-tails. Jeez, this is crazy. I almost have to pinch myself.

I pinch myself.

Nope, he's still here. On the bench. Sitting next to me. *Flirting.*

Feeling my crush rearing its lovesick head, I meet his gaze and for a beat we just look at each other. Only it's a bit longer than a beat — it's sort of like you've slowed it down and stretched it to make it last just that little bit longer. Long enough to make it feel significant. Long enough to feel a tingling all the way up your back to the nape of your neck . . .

"So, what are you doing here in Winchester?" I ask, partly out of suspicion, partly in an attempt to drag the conversation back to some kind of normality. As much as I'm loving sitting here with a handsome stranger, I need to at least *try* and get a grip.

"I travelled here with my good friends, who are fascinated by the stained glass in the windows. However, I am afraid that I am not, and so instead I chose to come outside. My intention was to read my newspaper . . ."

He waves it at me as if in evidence that he's not really stalking me, and it's then I see something. My breath catches in the back of my throat.

*What the . . .?*

Printed in black and white and staring out at me from the corner of the newspaper is the date. Only instead of saying, "29 December 2006," it reads, "29 December 1813." I look at it, rub my eyes and then look back at him.

"They've printed the date wrong."

"You seem to make a habit of not believing things. First me, then *The Times of London*," he says, his dark eyes flashing.

"But it's wrong . . ." I protest, taking it from him and scanning the headlines. Hang on, it's not just the date, all these articles don't seem right either. They seem to be referring to things that are part of history. As if this paper really is nearly two hundred years old. It just doesn't add up. *Unless . . .*

My head starts spinning, and I look up at the man sitting next to me, taking in his shiny riding boots and tight black breeches, his frock coat and fob watch, his stiff white starched collars, his cravat, the cleft in his chin . . . My mind casts itself back over the last twenty-four hours: his appearance at the museum yesterday, the fire burning in the grate, the wallpaper, his formal introduction, how the plastic barrier seemed to vanish . . .

And now the images are becoming muddled, thrown out of sequence as I try to remember everything. Big things, little things, freaky things, *unexplainable* things. The letter to his sister, his newspaper dated 1813, his sudden disappearance when Spike entered the parlour and his reappearance out of the blue today . . . I look about me. And there's never anyone around when he's here, just me . . .

It could all be an elaborate foil, but — I take a deep breath to steady myself for what's coming next — what if I allow for the possibility that it's not? I pause, knowing I'm about to think the unthinkable. What if he really is who he says he is?

*What if he really is Mr Darcy?*

"You're shivering, would you like my scarf?"

I snap back to see him unknotting the white silk scarf from round his neck. I nod mutely. There has to be a rational explanation, *there just has to*, but I can't think of one. And the part of me that's in love with Mr Darcy and has spent the last year going on one shitty date after another *doesn't want* there to be.

As he wordlessly leans close and tenderly places his scarf round my shoulders, I catch my breath. *None* of this makes sense, but what if sometimes things don't *have* to make sense? That just because you can't explain it doesn't mean it's not real. Like UFOs and ghosts and crop circles . . . and a character from a book come to life.

Emily, stop it. You're being ridiculous. This is crazy. This guy's obviously bananas and it's rubbing off on you! Come on, girl, get a grip.

152

Suddenly I'm struck by an idea, and diving into my bag, I rummage around until I find what I'm looking for — my copy of *Pride and Prejudice*. Tugging it out, I brandish it at him in evidence. "Mr Darcy is a character in a book. *This book*," I say out loud as if to silence my insane thoughts.

He seems genuinely surprised. "I? Am in a book?"

"Yes, by Jane Austen. It's all about you — I mean, Mr Darcy," I correct myself quickly. God, even I'm at it now. "Look," I gasp exasperatedly. I thrust my copy of the book into his hands. Now some rational explanation will have to appear. Well, he can't argue with this evidence, can he?

For a moment he sits very still and erect, the slim volume in his hands, a look of suspicion on his face.

"*This is a book?*"

I nod feverishly.

"How strange. There is no cover," he says, looking genuinely perplexed.

"Haven't you ever seen a paperback before?" I retort impatiently.

And then a thought hits. In Mr Darcy's day books would have been bound in leather, paperbacks didn't even exist, which would explain —

Quickly I brush the thought aside. Like I said, it's impossible.

Slowly he turns the book over, his thumb rubbing the cover, his brow furrowed, then cautiously he opens it and turns to the first page. I watch his eyes scanning the text. Totally absorbed, he flicks over a few more pages. He looks completely bewildered.

"You are indeed right," he says measuredly after a few moments.

"I know," I reply with a sense of satisfaction. But there's something else: a stab of disappointment. He almost had me thinking it must be true, what with the outfit and the newspaper. OK, so it's completely insane and impossible and a complete fantasy, but what girl wouldn't want to meet the real Mr Darcy? I mean, can you imagine? That would have been pretty amazing.

He looks up at me, his face sombre. "I am in a book. As are my dear friends Mr Bingley and his sister . . ." With the book laid open on his knee, he looks down again at the pages, as if deep in thought, and then, almost imperceptibly, I catch a faint smile appear on the corners of his mouth. "I have to admit I am most flattered that someone should write a book about me."

*Er, wait a moment, that wasn't the reaction I was expecting.*

"Thank you for showing me this. I feel honoured. It is quite a compliment, isn't it?" he continues, looking up at me. The pride is audible in his voice, and I have to say, he seems very pleased with himself. "Although it rather disproves your theory that I do not exist," he adds, his eyes twinkling. "Not only am I here in the flesh, but I am also here in black and white."

Completely thrown, I open my mouth to say something, although I'm not quite sure what. I mean, is this guy simply crazy? Admittedly, he seems perfectly normal, apart from his clothes, and he is really attractive . . . God, that would be just my luck, wouldn't it? I finally meet someone I've got real chemistry with and he turns out to be a total fruit-loop.

"But there is one thing I don't understand . . ."

I snap back to see my dark, handsome stranger flicking through the book, his smile having vanished. "Why are the rest of the pages empty?"

"Empty?" I repeat.

Oh, God, I was right. *He is crazy.*

"Look."

With my heart sinking, I watch him hold out the book and fan through the second half.

*Typical, just typi* —

Hang on a minute.

I feel a jolt of astonishment. Instead of the pages being full of printed text, they're all entirely blank.

But how could that be? It's impossible.

All at once I wobble and a tiny flicker of doubt catches alight inside me. Something very weird is going on here. I was just reading that book on the tour bus. That book was normal before, and yet now —

"How did you do that?" I gasp, snatching it from him.

"I didn't do anything," he says simply.

I'm thumbing through the book now, as if somehow expecting the rest of the story to reappear, but the pages remain resolutely blank. There's probably a hundred or so of them. White, empty pieces of paper. I stare at them in disbelief, trying to think of a rational explanation. But there isn't one. How can words from a page simply disappear? Vanish into thin air?

"Is it some kind of trick?" I gasp in confusion. I've seen my dad make playing cards disappear up his sleeve, but actual *text* . . . "Are you a magician or performance artist — you know, like David Blaine?"

He looks troubled. "I'm afraid I am not aware of this Mr Blaine, but I assure you *I* am Mr Fitzwilliam Darcy. Why will you not believe me?"

"But then how . . .?" I trail off. "It just doesn't make sense," I mutter, shaking my head.

"Miss Albright?"

I'm suddenly aware of a shadow falling over me and I twirl round on the bench to see Miss Steane standing right beside us.

"Have you heard a word I've been saying?"

How long has she been there? I've clearly been so transfixed by Mr Darcy that I didn't hear her coming. I turn back to Mr Darcy, ready to explain —

Except the bench is now empty . . .

"I was saying we're due to leave any minute. If you don't hurry inside immediately you will miss out on the opportunity to visit one of our most important literary sites."

*Where's he gone?* I feel a crushing disappointment. With my heart thumping I run my hand over the space next to me on the bench. It's still warm from where he was sitting. I couldn't have imagined him. And yet — I put my hands to my throat — his scarf isn't there any more.

"Miss Albright?"

"Um . . . yeah, coming," I say, feeling all disorientated.

**156**

"Well, come along now. Chop chop," she cheers, vigorously clapping her tiny leather-gloved hands together. "Even though I say it myself, I think you'll find the stained glass fascinating." There's a pause, and then she peers at me suspiciously. "Are you all right?"

"Er . . . yeah . . . I was feeling a bit light-headed, but I'm fine now," I reply, trying to sound casual when I'm anything but. I press my throbbing temples. We didn't even get the chance to maybe arrange to see each other again. I stand up shakily. That's if he was even real in the first place.

"Forgive me if I'm intruding, but I understand you were at the local drinking establishment last night."

Gosh, what is it with everyone? I'm like the talk of the whole tour.

"Um . . . yes, I went with Maeve. The two single girlies," I say jokingly.

If I'm expecting her to disapprove, I'm wrong. "Excellent. Friendship is certainly the finest balm for the pangs of disappointed love," she says wisely, then adds confidingly, "I would, however, advise staying away from the cider."

Oh, my God, who told her?

"Alrighty. Ready?" she barks, advice over.

"Um . . . yes . . . absolutely."

Taking a deep lungful of fresh air, I stick my hands in my pockets, but as I turn to follow Miss Steane she cries, "Oh, look," and points at something half hidden in the grass underneath the bench.

"What's that?" I ask, feeling a thump of excitement.

"He must have dropped his scarf," she remarks, before continuing her brisk pace towards the cathedral.

As she walks away, her footsteps crunching rhythmically on the gravel, I bend down to pick it up. *So I didn't imagine it.* I feel butterflies inside as I press it against my nose. It smells just like him. That same distinctive mix of cologne and shaving cream.

I quickly tuck the scarf in my coat pocket and hurry after my tour guide. Which is when something suddenly registers. Hang on a minute.

"Miss Steane?"

About to walk through the doorway, she turns. "Yes?"

"You just said *he* must have dropped his scarf."

She looks at me, her face impassive, completely unreadable. For a second there I could have sworn I caught a flash of uncertainty, a flicker of something, but now it's gone again and she's ushering me inside.

"Did I? Oh, silly me, a slip of the tongue," she says breezily. "I meant *you*." And without further ado, she thrusts a pamphlet into my hand and launches into her guidebook speech. "Now, if you look straight head you'll see the impressive Gothic nave built in 1858 . . ."

# CHAPTER
# THIRTEEN

I am going crazy.

Actually, scrub that.

I *am* crazy. Totally, utterly, back-in-college-doing-tequila-shots-on-acid crazy.

Back in my hotel room later that night, I'm lying in bed and staring up at the ceiling, thinking about the afternoon's events. It's nearly 11p.m. and I've been trying to fall asleep for the last hour, but it's not happening. My mind is whirling round and round, sloshing all these insane thoughts together in a jumble, like dirty laundry in the washing machine. What was that back there? An out-of-body experience? My overactive imagination? *A fictional character come to life?*

Gasping loudly, I grab my pillow and turn it over, trying to find a cool spot. Honestly, Emily, this is ridiculous. Agitated, I begin tossing and turning, causing the wooden bed frame to start squeaking violently. In the next room Rose bangs on the wall.

"Do you mind!" she complains loudly. "Some of us are trying to sleep."

Great. Now I'm being accused of having sex. I wouldn't mind if I *was* having sex, but I'm so not. I'm lying here, wearing fleecy pyjamas with cherries all over them and a plastic mouthguard to stop me from grinding my teeth, and thinking about meeting Mr Darcy this afternoon . . .

Did I just say *meeting Mr Darcy?*

Right, that's enough. I've got to get up.

Grabbing my copy of *Pride and Prejudice*, I tug on my jeans and an old sweatshirt, and go downstairs. The hotel is quiet. Everyone else seems to be already in bed and fast asleep, I muse, padding into the deserted drawing room.

Lit by various lamps with the kind of tasselled lampshades your granny would have, and decorated with dozens more hunting scenes, the room has a surprisingly cosy feel to it. It's the antithesis to all those hip hotels you get in New York, with their minimalist modern furniture, bare steel and concrete designs. Here, it's chintz, chintz and more chintz, I muse, looking at the couple of lumpy-looking sofas over by the mullioned windows and an old button-back leather chair.

I, however, rather like it.

I walk over to the stone fireplace, where there's a real fire. It's died down, but there's still a few logs glowing in the grate. Next to it I spy a stash of newspapers. Guilt stabs. God, I feel like such a philistine. This is my second day and I haven't *looked* at an English newspaper yet.

Apart from the one today, but that was nearly two hundred years old, interrupts a voice in my head.

**160**

It gives me a little jolt, but I ignore it and, grabbing the *Daily Times*, cosy up on the leather armchair. Whoo-hoo, look at me, I feel like the lady of the manor, I think with amusement. Smiling to myself, I flick open the newspaper and begin scanning the pages for something interesting to read.

"Lover of disgraced MP recalls affair", "Nurses threaten strikes", "£3-million fraud case revealed" . . .

Hmmm, it seems the news isn't any different whichever side of the Atlantic you live on, just a mixture of gloom and gossip. Idly I begin scanning the various articles. Nothing sparks my interest. I flick over the lifestyle pages. I think I'll carry on with my book as I'm just at the part where —

*Spike Hargreaves.*

The name jumps out at me from the newspaper. I blink again and look at it. There, in small print, underneath an article about an Irish actor I've never heard of, are the words "Interview by staff writer, Spike Hargreaves". Wow, so he really is a proper journalist. The *Daily Times*, huh? So it's true. A begrudging sense of respect creeps over me. I hate to admit it, but I'm rather impressed. This isn't some local rag, it's a national newspaper.

Saying that, let's not get *too* excited. After all, it's not the *New York Times*, is it? It's not *that* amazing. I chew my lip and eye the article. Part of me desperately wants to ignore it, to refuse to read it on principle. And yet . . .

C'mon, how can I resist?

Curiously, I begin reading, even though I have no clue who this actor is. Not that it matters. I just want to confirm that it's badly written. As soon as I've established that I'll stop. Which I'm sure will be only a matter of lines . . .

Hmmm. Actually, the introduction isn't bad. But no matter, I'm sure it's going to get worse.

Only it doesn't. It just gets better. By the third paragraph I'm seriously impressed. Spike certainly has a distinctive voice. He's neither effusive about his subject nor over-descriptive in his style; instead, it's just good writing. Insightful, respectful and rather charming.

Damn. How disappointing. I really wanted to rip him to shreds.

Even worse, he's really very funny in parts, I realise, giggling to myself at a comment he makes about men looking better than women in high heels. Who would have thought it? Alert the media. Spike Hargreaves has a good sense of humour.

"Something funny?"

I look up to see the writer himself appear from behind my chair, nursing what looks like a large brandy.

"Umm, no. Not really," I reply stiffly, furious with myself for being caught actually laughing at something he's written.

"Is that the *Daily Times*?"

"I don't know. Is it?" I fib, pretending I hadn't noticed. With a loud crunching of pages, I hurriedly shut the newspaper and stuff it down the side of the

162

leather seat cushion in an attempt to get rid of the evidence.

Spike's eyes glance from me to the newspaper. Then, without saying anything, he walks over to the fireplace, leans against the mantelpiece and, cradling the bowl of the glass, studies his brandy with careful consideration.

God, is he just going to stand there? Annoyed at the intrusion, I'm half tempted to get up and leave. But my pride stops me. I was here first, so why should I? And anyway, like I said, I've turned over a new leaf. I'm not going to let him get to me any more. I'm just going to carry on as if he's not even here. Tra-la-la . . .

Nonchalantly I pick up *Pride and Prejudice*. Right, where am I? I scan the paragraphs. Oh, yes, here, where Darcy is beginning to pay attention to Elizabeth:

Occupied in observing Mr Bingley's attentions to her sister, Elizabeth was far from suspecting that she was herself becoming an object of some interest in the eyes of his friend. Mr Darcy had at first scarcely allowed her to be pretty; he had looked at her without admiration at the ball; and when they next met, he looked at her only to criticise.

Hmm, like some others I could mention. I'm still piqued by Spike's comments about me on the coach yesterday.

But no sooner had he made it clear to himself and his friends that she had hardly a good feature in her face, than he began to find it was rendered uncommonly intelligent by the beautiful expression of her dark eyes. To this discovery succeeded some others equally mortifying. Though he had detected with a critical eye more than one failure of perfect symmetry in her form, he was forced to acknowledge her figure to be light and pleasing; and in spite of his asserting that her manners were not those of the fashionable world, he was caught by their easy playfulness.

Spike clears his throat as if to say something, but I don't look up. If he thinks he's going to engage me in conversation with him, he can think again.

Resolutely, I keep reading.

Of this she was perfectly unaware; to her he was only the man who made himself agreeable nowhere, and who had not thought her handsome enough to dance with.

"You and I have got off on the wrong foot, haven't we?"

For a stubborn moment I think about pretending I haven't heard him, then I remember my new leaf. My mature, composed and *infinitely* cool new leaf.

Casually marking my page by turning over the corner, I close my book and look up.

Resting his chin on the rim of his glass, Spike's fixed me with his pale blue eyes. I fidget under the spotlight of his attention.

"The wrong foot?" I repeat coolly.

"It's a turn of phrase," he explains.

"I know what it is," I say crossly.

**164**

Watching me, he breaks into an amused smile, revealing a surprisingly neat row of white teeth.

For an English man, that is.

"Apparently, it originates from the old days when people believed it was unlucky to put your left foot on the floor when you got out of bed. Incredible, huh? How all these phrases and words we use today have all this history attached."

I look at him blankly. Is he being *nice*? I mean, he *seems* genuine, but I can't be sure.

"How interesting," I say tightly.

*Remember: new leaf, Emily. New leaf.*

"Isn't it?" agrees Spike, seeming not to notice my sarcasm. "I think that's partly why I became a journalist —" He breaks off, and smiles self-consciously. "Sorry, I'm boring you, aren't I? I can see the glazed look in your eyes and you're thinking, What is this bloke going on about? But once I get started I just can't help it. I find the English language fascinating. Don't you?"

Staying mad at him is proving harder than I thought. I'm beginning to realise that Spike and I are much more similar than I would like. Feeling my defences rapidly melting, I fleetingly consider diving into a discussion about literature and authors and writing. Then I remember. "*pretty dull . . . average-looking . . . and she's American.*"

Immediately, my defences go back up again.

"I wouldn't know," I reply tartly. "After all, *I'm an American.*"

If he's got any idea what I'm referring to he doesn't show it. "You don't think we speak the same language?" he asks with interest.

"No, I don't."

"Really? Why?"

OK, now would be a good time to change the subject, advises the little voice inside my head. Except the thing is, I've never really been one to listen to advice, not even my own.

"I don't say mean things about people," I blurt.

Spike flinches and a deep crevice splits his brow. I brace myself for an angry, defensive outburst. Well, he started it, I think to myself, somewhat childishly.

But it never happens. Instead, the storm passes and his offence dissolves into an astonishingly wide smile. The kind of smile I had no idea he had in him. It hugs the corners of his eyes, flares his nostrils and stretches out his mouth to show off those straight white teeth of his.

Aha, but it's as I thought, I note with a sense of satisfaction Now I can see his bottom ones I notice they're all crooked. Not too bad, but definitely orthodontically challenged, I decide, trying to find some small reason not to find him attractive and realising that it's not working. He's annoyingly attractive. Even with those insanely crooked bottom teeth.

"Crikey, you don't mince words, do you?" he's saying, shaking his head and scratching the patch of bristles on his chin.

"Neither do you," I reply.

**166**

He looks at me, not understanding.

"Yesterday. We were on the coach, you were on the phone," I begin, feeling self-righteous. "I was in the bathroom."

He crinkles up his forehead, trying to think back. "I don't know what you're talking about . . ." he begins, then suddenly trails off. All at once his smile crumples and he inhales loudly through his teeth. "*Oh, fuck.*"

He looks so mortified I feel an intense sense of satisfaction. And then — I get a niggle. I thought I'd feel really triumphant, but actually, his discomfort isn't making me feel that great. And as for all the anger I felt towards him, it appears to have disappeared and instead I'm . . . I flail around, trying to grab the tail of my thoughts. To tell the truth, I'm not sure what I am.

"I thought you were referring to the article in the *Daily Times*. I saw you reading it when I came in."

I feel my cheeks tinge as he gestures towards the newspaper I've tried and failed to hide down the side of the armchair.

"Listen, I know you must think I'm a complete bastard —"

"*Now* we're talking the same language," I cut in belligerently.

He ignores my sarcasm. "Look, I can explain. You've got me all wrong. You're taking it all out of context. I didn't mean it like that, I was in a shitty mood, I'd had a huge row with my girlfriend . . ."

"*You?* Have a *girlfriend?*" I mock, pretending to be surprised.

There's a pause and I can tell he's dying to retaliate, but instead he clenches his jaw and continues: "I was talking with a friend, just joking around, taking the piss. It's an affectionate thing. It's what we British do," he adds.

He looks desperate.

"I might be American, but I'm not stupid," I retort. "Just *pretty dull and average-looking.*"

He winces.

"Unlike your *hot French girlfriend,*" I blurt, unable to stop myself.

Oh, shit, where did that just spring from? Why did I just say that? It's not as if she was that hot, anyway. So she wore red lipstick and had that chic turtle neck and scarf thing going on. So what?

For a moment Spike looks shocked, then his face floods with realisation. "Oh, *that's* what all this is about." Squaring his shoulders, he seems to reinflate.

"What?"

"Nothing."

"Whoah . . ." Stretching out my hand, I stop him right there. "You can't pull the 'nothing' trick on me. I'm a woman, remember. Nothing always means something."

"And I wonder why I've never understood women," he mutters, taking a gulp of brandy.

I shoot him one of my scary looks.

"Look, let's drop it, shall we?" he suggests.

I think about it. *For, like, a second.*

"No, I'm not going to drop it," I reply stubbornly. Even though while I'm saying it I know that I should.

**168**

But that's my biggest fault, I'm stubborn to the point of mulish.

He hesitates, as if weighing me up to see if I'm serious enough. "OK, have it your way." He shrugs in surrender. "You're jealous," he says simply.

"*Jealous?*" I gasp, feeling little hot knives of anger pricking me all over. "Of what?"

"Emmanuelle," he says, as if it's obvious.

Simultaneously my brain registers two thoughts: (1) Not only does she look fabulous in bright-red lipstick, which makes my teeth look yellow; *and* look stylish in chic turtle-neck sweaters and knotted Hermès scarves, while I stumble around H&M like a drowning woman clinging to anything sparkly, but her name is really pretty and sexy and so much nicer than boring old Emily. (2) You arrogant fucking asshole.

I go with thought number two.

"You arrogant asshole," I curse.

Spike's head goes back, like a boxer who's just taken a jab.

"I am not remotely jealous of any woman that has to go out with a man who has zero personality, appalling manners and wears corduroy jackets with patches on the elbows."

We both glance down at his jacket.

"You don't like the patches?"

His innocent question disarms me, pricking my anger as if it's a balloon. I want to be angry. I've a right to be angry. But for some reason, I just can't *stay* angry.

**169**

Surveying his jacket, I wrinkle up my nose. "They're a bit Simon and Garfunkel.

He absorbs this comment. "I like Simon and Garfunkel," he says simply.

"I do too," I confess.

He meets my eye and smiles. I smile back, albeit begrudgingly.

There's a pause.

"So, when do I —"

"Well, I guess —"

We both start speaking at the same time and then stop.

"You first," he gestures.

"No, it's OK, go ahead."

He shrugs. "I was just wondering when you were going to tell me about Mr Darcy."

His question completely blindsides me. I try not to let even a flicker cross my face, but it's like someone just dropped a ten-ton weight on my chest.

"Me and Mr Darcy?" I squeak. Oh, shit. What does he know? What did he *see*?

Spike gives me a curious look. "Yeah, I need to interview you, for the paper."

"Oh, yeah, of course." I nod, feeling both relieved and a bit ridiculous.

"Tomorrow?"

I'm all jumpy, but I try to appear casual. "Sure, whenever." I shrug, acting like a pouty teenager instead.

"Now it's your turn."

"Um, excuse me?"

"You were saying . . .?"

That I met Mr Darcy again today and I really like him and I can't stop thinking about him and — oh — *I think I'm going mad.*

"Um . . . nothing. Just that it was getting late."

I try to gather my thoughts. Easier said than done when your thoughts are whirling round all over the place like leaves in a storm. Spike. Emmanuelle. Mr Darcy. Spike. Mr Darcy. Spike. Mr Darcy. Mr Darcy. *Mr Darcy.*

Right at that moment the grandfather clock next door begins softly chiming.

Saved by the bell.

"Wow, midnight. I should go to bed." Quickly releasing my knees, I hoist myself up from the snug of the leather armchair. "Before I turn into a pumpkin," I quip, making a feeble attempt at humour.

"And I turn into Prince Charming." Spike smiles ruefully.

I look at him uncertainly.

"That was a joke," he adds.

"Obviously," I reply.

There's a pause and he regards me for a moment as if he's thinking about something, but I can't read his face.

"Well, night, then."

"Yeah, night."

He sort of salutes me with his brandy and I give an awkward little wave. I came down here to clear my mind, but I've only made it worse.

A yawn overwhelms me and I suddenly realise how tired I am. No wonder I'm all confused. I'm so jet-lagged I can barely remember my own name. And clutching my book to my chest, I turn and head out of the drawing room. Once I've had a good sleep I'll feel loads better.

# CHAPTER
# FOURTEEN

I wake up the next morning feeling like a different person. Invigorated, energised and completely clear-headed. Yesterday all seems like a dream. I've heard of jet lag doing funny things to you: I once read about an English woman who'd ripped off all her clothes on the Heathrow Express and straddled a businessman demanding sex because, according to her defence lawyer, she'd been travelling fifteen hours without any sleep on a flight from Singapore — and I thought that was *outrageous*. But meeting Mr Darcy? Honestly.

We check out of the hotel after breakfast (after yesterday's disaster I go for the safe option and order Continental) and set off on the journey to Bath. It's a gorgeous day. Still, with a crisp frost, brilliant blue skies and bright sunshine. It's the kind of day that almost makes you want to start humming about brown paper packages tied up with string. Well, *almost*.

Leaning my face up against the window of the coach, I watch the matchstick trees whizzing by, the blur of hedgerows and the villages that seem to finish before they begin with funny names like Upper Dumpling — or something like that. I still can't get over how different England is from America, with its vast sprawl, straight roads and huge horizons. Here, everything's in miniature, with skinny winding roads, blind corners (I'm still trying to get used to driving on the left without my stomach leaping into my mouth), the patchwork of fields and church spires. It's all so pretty.

*Pretty*. That's such a lame word. Only I honestly can't think of a better way to describe it. After the chaos and concrete that is New York, everything here is so neat and tidy and, well, *pretty*. I mean, look at all those cute little sheep dotted about in that field. And that little bird over there with a red breast. In fact, *is that a robin?* I squint at it as we trundle past. Jesus. I've never *seen* a robin in real life, only on Christmas cards.

Gosh, listen to me. You'd think I've never seen nature before, when in fact I've been to Hawaii, and Mexico, and camping in Montana. (OK, so it wasn't *strictly* camping as I was in my friend's log cabin, but there was no shower and I was in a sleeping bag.) But this is different. I'm only five thousand miles away from New York, but I feel about a million miles away from my life there. And with every mile the coach travels it's as if I'm moving further and further away from it, as if I'm entering a whole new world.

Gazing out of the window, a smile plasters itself dreamily across my face. Boy, did I need this vacation.

Arriving in Bath some time later, I discover a scene that could have been torn straight from the pages of Dickens's *A Christmas Carol*. The blue skies have turned white and it's started to snow faintly. In the large cobbled squares vendors are roasting chestnuts and selling hot mulled wine, garlands of tiny lights are strung between the old-fashioned lamp posts and rows of shops have decorated their bow-fronted windows with glittering strands of silver and gold tinsel.

I swear, any minute now Tiny Tim's going to hobble past on his crutches.

Our coach is too wide for the narrow side streets, so we disembark and wheel our suitcases the last few hundred cobbly yards to our hotel, a Georgian townhouse with fake snow sprayed jauntily in the corners of each windowpane.

"Ooh, isn't this lovely," chorus Rupinda, Maeve and Hilary as we walk into the lobby, where we're greeted by a Christmas tree so weighed down with baubles and tinsel it looks like it might collapse at any moment.

"If you like that kind of thing," says Rose querulously.

Rose, I'm fast learning, is a bit of a snob and never seems to have a good word to say about anything. OK, so I agree, that tree is not going to win any style awards, but she is being a bit bah-humbug. What happened to getting into the festive spirit?

Instead, with a disapproving expression on her face, she turns her attention to the far wall, which is strewn with signed photographs of stars who have stayed here. Suddenly she perks up. "Oh, look, there's my dear friend Dame Judi," she says loudly, pointing to a headshot of Judi Dench.

But no one's listening. They're still busy cooing over the Christmas tree, with Hilary enlightening everyone on how to stop the pine needles dropping with the clever use of hairspray.

"Just give it a couple of liberal squirts when you first buy it — not the firm hold, but the flexible. Make sure you get the flexible."

"She was my understudy, you know," tries Rose again, only this time louder.

Plopping myself down on the small flowery sofa by the front desk, I look across at her. Standing apart from the rest of the other ladies in her full-length fur, which looks like something befitting an Eskimo, and too much rouge, she cuts a rather sad figure. I feel a bit sorry for her.

"Wow, really? That's pretty cool, Miss Bierman," says Spike, coming to her rescue.

It's like someone just flicked the spotlight on her. Rose transforms with his attention, smiling vibrantly and pretending to look surprised that someone's heard her.

"Not that I'm boasting of course," she adds coyly.

"Of course," nods Spike evenly. Walking over to her, he sticks his hands in his pockets, scrunches up his forehead and surveys the wall. "They need to get a photo of you up there," he says after a moment.

A look of delight floods Rose's powdered face, but she quickly tries to hide it. "Oh, you're a darling." She laughs girlishly and throws her diamond-encrusted hand against her chest. "But it's been a while since I trod the boards . . ."

Watching Spike chatting to Rose, I feel myself soften towards him. That was kind of him. He didn't have to do that.

"Rubbish," he's saying now dismissively. "I reckon they'd love to have you up there."

Maybe I've judged him too harshly. First impressions and all that. Maybe he's not as bad as I thought. Though, saying that, he really shouldn't tease Rose about hanging her photo on the wall.

"Oh . . . *mais non . . . mais non . . .* " Rose is protesting. Dipping her head in an affectation of modesty, she hides behind her curtain of hair — for, like, a second — then looks back up again. "Do you really think so?" Her eyes are flashing with excitement.

"Oh, yeah. Definitely."

"Well, I do think I might have a black-and-white headshot *somewhere*," she acquiesces, trying to sound casual, while at the same time unzipping her Louis Vuitton hand luggage and, without any rummaging necessary, pulling out a crocodile-skin folder.

She feigns astonishment. "Well, I never. I just so happen to have some here with me!"

"Wow, what a coincidence," says Spike humouring her. He glances across at me and catches me watching. Despite myself I have to smile.

"Though they're really just snapshots," she's saying self-deprecatingly as she tugs out several large, glossy, black-and-white prints. "They're not very flatter-ing . . ."

"Oh, I doubt you can take a bad picture, Miss Bierman," says Spike.

Rose blushes.

"Now, come on, let's have a look."

"Well, if you insist," she sighs, handing them over without any insistence necessary.

"Everyone, if I could have your attention, please . . ."

Engrossed in watching Spike and Rose, I'd almost forgotten about everyone else, but now I turn to see Miss Steane, our tour guide. Circling the lobby energetically, she's trying to round everyone up like a sheepdog.

"Leave your luggage here, it will be taken care of," she's instructing. "And now if you'd all like to follow me, we shall begin our short walk to 4 Sydney Place, Jane Austen's former home."

Dragging myself off the sofa, I glance over at Spike. But he's not there any more. Just Rose, regaling her Judi Dench story to no one in particular.

". . . and so I said to her, 'Judi, darling, don't you worry about fluffing your lines. It happens to even the best of us,' and, oh, my goodness, she was so very grateful, because of course, as you know, I was a very famous theatre actress in those days . . . in fact, the hotel is going to hang a signed photograph of myself on the wall . . ."

Damn. This is what I was afraid of. Now Rose has gone and got her hopes up.

Spike is nowhere to be seen. Obviously he got bored of humouring her and now he's disappeared to do his interviews. I feel a snap of anger. Everything's always a joke to him, and always at someone else's expense.

Poor Rose is going to be *so* disappointed, I think, turning back to her and throwing her an enthusiastic smile. "What an amazing story! Tell me some more."

And linking arms with her, I listen as she launches into another anecdote — this one being about Tallulah Bankhead and the time they got drunk together — as we make our way across the lobby and step outside on to the street.

A couple of hours later and I'm all tourist-ed out.

Bath is just oozing with incredible history and architecture and there's tons to see. First off is Jane Austen's home and a lecture by its owner, then it's the famous Pump Rooms, the Regency tea rooms and finally the Jane Austen Centre. Which is all very interesting and fascinating at first, but then I get a bit, well — *overwhelmed* would be one way of putting it.

*Bored* would be another.

"And here we have a rare collection of original cross-stitch samplers, as made at the end of the 1700s . . ."

Don't get me wrong. I like architecture and history to a point, but there's only so much a girl can take before lunchtime. Plus, I'm dying to see if I can find an old traditional English bookshop, as well as exploring some of the really cool-looking boutiquey-type shops I spied earlier. Tucked away down tiny cobbled streets, they appeared to sell all kinds of stuff like vintage furniture, handmade stationery and cards, and these amazing lights shaped like teapots that you can hang in your garden.

Not that I have a garden, and they're probably crazily overpriced like designer-type shops always are. But still, they are really cute . . .

That's the thing about me. I might not shop for clothes, but I sure well make up for it by shopping for other things.

Wandering aimlessly around the gift shop, I feel an itch to spend some money. This is my third day on vacation and I still haven't bought anything and my credit card is burning a hole in my pocket. I flick through a couple of guidebooks and cast my eye wide across the various shelves and compartments. Needlepoint cushions, cross-stitch sampler sets, ostrich-feather quills, *Mr Darcy soaps* (can you believe it?), cameo brooches . . . I toy vaguely with the idea of buying a cameo brooch for Stella as I'm sure I read somewhere that Victoriana is the new boho. Or was that boho is the new Victoriana? Oh, God, I can't remember.

I spot a carousel of postcards. Ah, that's a much safer option. I start turning it slowly around, looking at all the different cards. Oh, look, there's a good one. I think about sending it to my parents, then catch myself. They won't be there, will they? I feel a twinge of something that feels like disappointment, but I quickly dismiss it. Mom's never been the kind of mom to stick postcards on the fridge, anyway, or even our drawings when we were kids. No doubt it would just get lost under the pile of mail they'll have to open when they get back from their trip. Anyway, it doesn't matter, I'll send it to Mr McKenzie instead — I'm sure he'll appreciate it. And I'll get one for Auntie Jean, too, I muse, turning the rack of postcards.

It turns right back.

What?

I turn it again. It stays like that for a few seconds, but then revolves slowly to the right. Huh. There must be someone on the other side. Gently, but firmly, I move it back to where it was and continue looking at the postcards. Hmm, this one is quite nice . . . It twirls round again.

This time I feel a pinch of annoyance. I push it back, only harder this time. Right, that should do it, I think, feeling triumphant. Immediately it swings back. I glare at it, infuriated. Honestly, sometimes people are so rude. I grab hold of it, but now it won't move. There's sort of a tussle. "Excuse me . . ." I gasp, giving it a sharp tug ". . . but I happened to be looking at these first . . . *Yeowwwikes.*"

Suddenly it's released and it twirls round furiously, nearly rattling off its pedestal.

I jump back as a face appears. It's Spike.

"Oh, it's you." I scowl.

He's wearing a woolly beanie hat and chewing on a red liquorice twirl. He looks at me for a moment, then holds up a postcard and waves it like a little white flag. "This is a good one."

I glance at it. It's a picture of Matthew Macfadyen playing Mr Darcy. He's gorgeous, but even so, he's not a patch on *my* Mr Darcy.

"You know, I have to say, I just don't see what all the fuss is about," tuts Spike, wrinkling up his brow and peering at the postcard.

I smile. Is that a twinge of jealousy I can detect in his voice? "Well, you wouldn't, would you. You're a guy." I shrug.

"What? You mean you *agree* with all those women in the poll? He's your ideal date too?"

"Uh-huh." I nod. I feel as if I'm bursting with this great big secret that I can't tell anyone. "I've had a crush on him since I can remember."

"A tough act to follow, huh?"

"Meaning?"

"For us regular blokes," he says, sucking on his liquorice. "We're never going to be able to live up to him, are we? It's like everything. The reality is always more disappointing than the fantasy."

I look at Spike's shambolic figure. In his case it's most definitely true.

"I'm the same. My first love was Betty Blue. I adored her. Passionate, sexy, *French*. Normal girls didn't match up. But in reality, do I really want to go out with a nutcase who stabs her own eye out?"

I smile, despite myself.

"Trust me," he continues, "a passionate affair with a sexy French woman might look great in the movies, but in reality there's *nothing* sexy about constant rows and broken crockery."

"You sound as if you're speaking from experience," I say, getting a flashback of him arguing with his girlfriend in the parking lot.

"Emmanuelle has broken every plate in my flat. Now I have to eat off paper ones." He smiles ruefully, but I get the feeling he's not joking. She did have a pretty mean temper on her. "No, what I *really* want is someone I can have a proper conversation with, who's going to help me get the clues in the *Daily Times* crossword that I can't, who'll laugh at my shitty jokes and share my passion for spaghetti Westerns."

"So why don't you go out with a girl like that?"

"Now there's a thought," he says, cocking his head on one side as if he's only just considering the idea. "I dunno. Maybe because a girl like that is real. And that would mean being in a *real relationship*," he says, emphasising the words and rolling his eyes in mock horror. "I'm not sure if I'm ready for that. To be honest, I think it scares me." He smiles sheepishly.

"What? More than having plates thrown at you?"

"Yeah." He nods. "I can always try to duck the plates. Emmanuelle's a pretty crap aim."

He smiles and looks at me in a way that makes me feel I should say something, but his honesty about his relationship has thrown me. I wasn't expecting it.

A pause opens up, and feeling awkward, I turn back to the rack of postcards and resume choosing. Out of the corner of my eye I can see Spike studying me thoughtfully.

"Can I ask you a question?" he asks after a moment.

I glance up at him warily. "Is this for your article?"

"No, I'm just curious." Having difficulty biting off a piece of twirl, he clamps it between his back molars and tugs hard.

"About what?"

"About why a girl like you is spending New Year by herself on a book tour." He begins gnashing the red liquorice between his teeth.

"Who's a girl like me?"

OK, so I'm being defensive, but do you blame me? So far I've already had "pretty dull" and "average-looking".

"No, I didn't mean . . . I meant . . ." He gives up and sighs. "Don't tell me. You're a reporter and you're writing an article too."

I eye him warily, then decide to let him off the hook. "I manage a bookstore in New York," I say, trying to keep the pride out of my voice.

"Crikey, that's great," says Spike in admiration.

I feel a beat of pleasure, but don't let him see. "And I saw an ad and . . ." I trail off. Actually, now I come to think of it, I don't really want to admit how this trip came about. How I'd sworn off men after my last disastrous date and booked this tour on an impulsive whim to avoid being coerced on to an 18 — 30 holiday where I'd no doubt have to meet lots of men *and* enter a wet T-shirt competition. "I thought it sounded interesting," I say simply.

He gives me the same look that Stella gave me.

"Blame my parents. They're total bookworms. Hence my name: Emily Brontë Hemingway Albright."

"Blimey," he says aghast.

"I know. It's a bit of a mouthful, isn't it?"

"Well, it's not as bad as mine."

I look at him curiously.

"Napoleon Caesar Nelson Hargreaves," he rattles off, his face serious. "My father was in the navy. He's obsessed by military leaders." He rips off another chunk of liquorice.

**184**

"Naturally." I nod, trying to stop my mouth from twisting into a smile. "He'd have to be, with a name like that."

"Uh-huh," chews Spike.

"So tell me. How did you get the nickname Spike?" I ask, busting him.

"Actually, it's funny you should ask that," he replies unfazed.

"Isn't it?" I stifle a giggle.

"It's, um . . . the name of a battle," he replies, keeping a completely straight face. "The Battle of Spike."

"Oh, you mean the *famous* Battle of Spike." I nod, playing along.

"You've heard of it?" he asks, his eyes twinkling.

"Oh, yeah, it's very well known in America." I nod gravely. There's a pause and then, "Tell me, what were they fighting over again?"

"Um . . ." He scrunches up one eye as if thinking hard. "I think it was postcards."

"Ah, yes, of course, I'd forgotten." I tut. "*Postcards.*"

Our eyes meet briefly and despite our straight faces amusement flashes between us.

"Talking of which. You're right."

"I am?" He looks surprised.

"Yep, that is a good one." And plucking the postcard out of his fingers, I turn and head towards the cash register. Battle of Spike, indeed. With my back to him I break into a smile. That's the annoying thing about Spike. He can be kind of cute when he wants to be.

# CHAPTER
# FIFTEEN

*Dear Mr McKenzie,*
   *Well, here I am in Bath, England, home to one of our bestselling authors! Having a great time. Wish you were . . .*

Shit. I can't put "wish you were here" to my boss, can I? I don't wish he was here. Even if he is a sweet little old man with natty taste in bowties and not really like a boss at all. I cross it out and replace it with:

*You would love it here. Hope things are all OK in the store.*

As I think about the store I feel a seed of worry. That shop's like my baby. Before I left I wrote masses of Post-It Notes and stuck them everywhere, together with a list of my contact numbers in case of an emergency, but even so . . .
   Emily, quit panicking. It's a bookstore. What kind of emergency is there going to be, for Godsakes? You run out of copies of *He's Just Not That Into You*?
   Actually, that did happen once, and I had to deal with a store full of irate females, but since then I've

always made sure I've got tons in stock. Anyway, I'm sure everything will be fine.

Chewing the end of my biro, I look back at the postcard. There's still quite a bit of blank space left. I agonise. God, I never know what to put on these things. I always want to sound witty and interesting, and I always end up writing something really obvious. Like "Here I am in Bath, England" when it's pretty obvious I'm here in Bath, England, as that's what it says on the front of the postcard. Oh, I give up.

BACK VERY SOON. [I write it in big letters and underline that bit twice.]
Love, Emily x

"There you go, dearie."

It's lunchtime and I'm sitting upstairs in a cosy, traditional-looking café, tucked away in a flock-wallpapered corner. I look up at the waitress, who is holding out a plate piled high with thick, chunky-cut chips, a golden hunk of battered cod and something described fascinatingly on the menu as "mushy peas".

"Fish and chips?"

My stomach gives a loud gurgle of approval. "Mmm, yes, please."

I hastily clear away my postcards to make room for her, and she puts the plate down in front of me, together with a big plastic ketchup tomato and a bottle of something called Sarson's Vinegar, and bustles off, her opaque tights rustling against her nylon underskirt.

I inhale deeply. Just the smell makes my mouth water and I suddenly realise how hungry I am.

Yum, England's famous fish and chips. Unrolling my knife and fork from the pink paper napkin, I eye my plate hungrily. Well, it would be rude not to try the national dish, wouldn't it?

I squirt a dollop of ketchup on to my plate. That's the amazing thing about going on vacation: it's a get-out-of-jail-free card when it comes to calories. Like money in airports. It's not real money, just like they're not real calories.

Offering up a silent thank-you that I'm not Stella right now and don't have to be squeezing into a string bikini, I forgo my fork and pick up a chip with my fingers. Well, that's the only way to eat chips, isn't it? It's hot and burns my mouth, but I persevere. They're real chips, big and chunky, not like the skinny fries we get at home.

"You look like you're enjoying that."

I turn sideways and suddenly notice Ernie sitting across from me at the next table. He's wearing a tartan shirt, rolled up to reveal his tattooed forearm, and is reading a newspaper.

"Mmmm . . . ummm." I can only manage to half grunt, as my mouth is full of red-hot potato.

Ernie laughs. "I'll take that as 'yes', then."

I finish chewing and swallow. "Sorry, they were just too delicious to wait."

"I bet." He nods. "'Fraid the doctor won't let me within a mile of fish and chips," he grumbles and pats his tartan paunch with a certain pride. "I'm having the baked potato. Tuna and sweet-corn. No butter."

I throw him a look of sympathy.

"Blimey, those chips do smell bloody good."

"Want one?"

He hesitates for a moment. "Go on, then," he whispers. "One isn't going to kill me, now, is it?"

At that moment his baked potato and tuna makes an entrance. Even with the jaunty attempt at a salad garnish, it still looks really boring. I watch Ernie peer at it, see his ruddy face collapse and a weary resignation appear in his eyes.

"Hey, why don't you join me?" I suggest brightly. "You can steal a few chips. There's far too many for me anyway, and that way it doesn't count."

"How do you reckon that?" he asks, raising a bushy eyebrow.

"Oh, it's an old female trick," I confide, scooting over to make room for him and grabbing some cutlery off his table. "You have the salad but you get your boyfriend to order the fries. Then you spend the whole meal stealing them off his plate until they're all gone. But that's OK, you don't have to feel guilty. *You* only ordered the salad."

Ernie smiles. "I'll have to remember that."

"Oh, yeah, it's great. It works with other things too. Dessert at restaurants . . . popcorn at the movies . . . hot dogs at the game . . ." Pushing away his baked potato, I move my fish and chips into the middle of the table so we can share. "It's pretty incredible."

Ernie laughs. "So is that what you do with your boyfriend back in America, then?"

"Oh, no." I shake my head. "I don't have a boyfriend. I'm single."

I try a scoop of mushy peas. They taste like Mexican refried beans. Only they're green.

To be honest, I don't really like them.

Ernie, however, appears to love them. "Get away!"

I laugh. "I know. It's unbelievable, isn't it?" I say ironically.

Shovelling a spoonful of peas into his mouth, he smacks his lips. "I bet you're fighting them off."

I get a flashback to me a few weeks ago, standing on the sidewalk in New York while John, the architect, tried to shove his tongue down my throat. "Kind of." I take a bite of fish and offer a piece to Ernie. It's delicious. We fall silent for a few moments as we eat.

"No one you've got your eye on?"

My stomach flutters as I think of the handsome stranger at Winchester Cathedral. My Mr Darcy.

"Actually, yeah," I say, trying not to blush and blushing anyway.

"What? Back home?"

"No, I met him here, on the tour."

Ernie's face suddenly pales and his smile fades.

"Yeah, well, you be careful," he warns.

"Of what?" I laugh, and then suddenly realise he's being deadly serious. "Ernie?"

He looks away, and won't catch my eye. "Oh, nothing," he mumbles.

"Tell me, *what*?" I persist.

He hesitates for a moment, then sighs. "It's not what, it's who."

I look at him, puzzled.

"Look, I shouldn't really be saying anything, but I'd hate you to get hurt."

I relax. Oh, it's that old chestnut again about broken hearts and being older and learning from experience.

"Physically hurt, I mean . . ."

I drop my fork from my mouth. Did he just say *physically hurt*? Fuck. Don't say there's a murderer in our midst or something. My thoughts suddenly leap to Mr Darcy. No, surely not.

"Who are you talking about?" I say in a low voice, leaning towards him over the table.

"Why, Spike Hargreaves of course," says Ernie, frowning.

I don't know whether to feel relieved or horrified.

"Spike Hargreaves?" I repeat in disbelief. For a split second I almost take it seriously, then I burst out laughing at the sheer ridiculousness of it. "No, you've got it wrong. I know he can be a bit of an asshole, but —"

"He punched me once."

"*He punched you!*" I gasp.

"Broke my nose."

"*He broke your nose!*"

Not only am I in total shock at what I'm hearing, but the power of speech seems to have deserted me and all I can do is repeat after Ernie in a strangulated, high-pitched squeak.

191

"It was five years ago now, but I still have trouble breathing . . ."

Oh. My. God. I'm staring at Ernie across the table as he proceeds to put a thumb against each nostril to demonstrate how his septum has been irreversibly damaged, despite two operations, but his voice has become a sort of blurry noise, as if I'm underwater, and all I can hear is the hammering of my heart against my chest.

*Spike punched Ernie.*

Nice, jovial, pensionable Ernie who eats bacon sandwiches despite doctor's orders, drives about twenty miles an hour and showed me pictures of his grandchildren. My mind is whirling.

"But why?" I finally manage to stammer.

In the middle of giving a graphic description of his rhino-plasty, Ernie looks at me, astonished.

"Didn't he tell you?"

"No, he didn't."

"I courted his mother."

Surprises are being fired at me thick and fast. I'm reeling over my cod and chips.

"*His mother?*" I repeat.

Shit. I'm back to that again.

"I used to work as one of the drivers at the *Daily Times*, that's how I met Iris. She came a few times to visit her son, and we got chatting and, well . . ." His voice trails off. "We were very much in love." He sees me looking at him in astonishment and obviously misinterpreting my dropped jaw and wide eyes, adds, "People my age can still fall in love, you know."

**192**

"Oh, of course," I say hurriedly.

"Just because you get to my age, doesn't stop you being a romantic," he says sadly.

"I know, I'm a romantic too," I gasp in solidarity. "My friend Stella even calls me a hopeless romantic."

Ernie smiles weakly. I don't know what's happened, but he seems to have suddenly shrunk in his tartan shirt and his eyes look suspiciously moist.

"And then her son decided I wasn't good enough."

Suddenly I get really angry. "Jesus. How dare he!" I cry, slamming down my knife and fork. I'd suspected Spike was a snob, but this? This is so much worse than I'd thought. Suddenly I understand Maeve's sudden change of heart after talking to him. No wonder she'd seemed strange. God only knows what lies Spike told her about Ernie. "I had no idea. What a bastard," I hiss, my voice low.

Ernie chews thoughtfully on his mouthful of baked potato and tuna.

"Told me I had to stay away from her, or else."

"He threatened you?" I'm aghast. This is getting worse and worse.

"But I couldn't. I loved her. That's when he hit me."

"What? Without provocation?"

"Well, I guess I did provoke him by being in love with Iris."

I can't believe it. This is terrible. Beating someone up because he's in love? I've got a good mind to punch Spike I'm-a-bully Hargreaves myself. And trust me, I am not a violent person. I can't even kill the spider that's been living in my bathroom for the past year and a half, terrorising me every time I get in the shower.

"Provoke him? Of course not!" I cry. "I bet he was jealous of the attention his mom gave you."

"I suppose it's just a son being protective of his mother," Ernie says kindly.

Suddenly I like him even more than before.

"There's being protective and then there's being a great big bully," I admonish. "You must be twice his age."

"Well, not quite —"

"And he's a pretty big guy . . . to use violence."

Ernie is nodding silently.

"It's disgusting."

Spitting expletives, I sit back in my chair, watching Ernie eating his baked potato, trying to get my head round this new information. And to think I've been so civil to him. All the ladies on the tour think he's so nice, but imagine what they'd think if they knew this!

"Did Iris ever find out?"

"No." Ernie shakes his head. "I didn't tell her. I didn't want her to think badly of her son, to be ashamed of him. I loved her too much for that."

God, Ernie is such a nice man. This is heartbreaking.

"I just made up some excuse that I was moving away, that I had a new job as a coach driver. Well, I couldn't stay there, could I?" Wiping clean his plate with a slice of bread, he looks up at me and sighs. "In fact, I haven't told anyone this story until now — I didn't want anyone to ever find out, in case it got back to Iris. But then, when I saw Spike again, well . . ." he breaks off and shakes his head, I thought I should warn you, in case you were thinking of getting involved . . ."

"Oh, no. God, no," I protest, shuddering.

"If you don't mind, could you keep all this to yourself? I'd hate for it to get back to Iris — she'd be devastated. And I don't want any trouble from her son . . ." he finishes, looking worried.

"Of course I won't say anything," I promise. Reaching across the table, I squeeze his sandpapery hand. "I'm sorry, Ernie."

"I know."

I look at the little old man sitting opposite me. I'm shocked. Utterly shocked. I've never heard such a horrible story. I don't know what to say. I'm dumbfounded.

"Are you not eating that, dearie?" All of a sudden the waitress makes a reappearance, her rosy-cheeked face looking at me inquisitively.

I glance at my lunch. The plate of cod and chips lies cold and practically untouched on the table. The mushy peas congealed. With everything that's just happened I'd forgotten all about it.

"Um, no . . . thank you," I manage to stammer. "I seem to have lost my appetite."

Abruptly the café seems very stuffy and claustrophobic and I feel the urgent need to leave. My mind's reeling. I don't know what to think.

Mumbling my excuses to Ernie, I leave some money on the table and stumble outside. It's bitterly cold and I take some deep breaths, trying to clear my head. But

**195**

all I can think about is Spike. About how much I hate him. And how, at this moment, I honestly don't think I've ever hated a person more.

# CHAPTER
# SIXTEEN

After dinner our tour guide had planned an "evening of themed conversations on Jane Austen", but I skipped it and went straight to bed. Partly due to the fact that I couldn't keep my eyes open long enough to make the dessert, and partly because I am beginning to discover that whereas I might be a fan of Jane Austen — there are fans *and then there are fans*.

Propped up against my pillows, I'm reading instead. Or rather, I'm supposed to be reading, but in truth I'm staring at the pages of my book, my mind churning over what transpired this afternoon. I can't stop thinking about it. Ernie's revelation knocked me for six and I'm still trying to get to grips with it.

Spike, *beating up* Ernie?

I mean, I know he can be an asshole, but to hit a sweet little old man who can't defend himself?

And yet, the more I think about it, the more it seems to make sense. The way Spike reacted to Ernie when he first saw him on the bus, Maeve's odd behaviour after she'd spoken to Spike . . . and I know Spike's got a temper because I saw him shouting at his girlfriend that first day in the parking lot. But to actually punch someone and break their nose? And just because they were in love with his mother?

God, it's so dastardly. He's like the villain in some book. It's like some great big Shakespearean tragedy. Just think, Iris will believe Ernie deserted her, and all along he left because he loved her and was protecting her from the truth about her son.

My eyes prickle. Honestly, it's just the saddest thing I've ever heard. It makes me want to burst into tears.

After I've punched Spike's frigging lights out.

Hit by a hot burst of anger, I take a few deep breaths. Calm down, Emily, just calm down. So far I've managed to control my temper. I promised Ernie I wouldn't tell Spike I knew. So all the way through dinner I was polite and cordial, smiling at his jokes, passing the gravy boat. But, God, it was hard. Trust me. I was *this close* to tipping the scalding-hot gravy all down his T-shirt. I resisted. But for how long?

Fighting back the temptation to jump out of bed, march down the corridor, bust into Spike's room and pin him against the wall in a good cop, bad villian-type scenario, I turn back to my copy of *Pride and Prejudice* in an attempt to calm down. Which reminds me, I really must e-mail Mr McKenzie tomorrow and tell him that we've got a faulty batch. After I got back from Winchester Cathedral I double-checked to make sure I hadn't imagined the blank pages, but nope, they still remain blank. Obviously it's some kind of printing error. Good job I discovered it, though.

Well, technically it was Mr Darcy, or rather the mystery man *calling* himself Mr Darcy — *boom*. There he is again. A snapshot of him in my head. Tall, dark and utterly gorgeous. Automatically my mind flicks back to yesterday afternoon, sitting on that bench outside the cathedral. I can hear his voice, smell his cologne, feel the warmth of his body right up close to me. And yet looking back now with a clear head and no racing hormones, the whole thing feels surreal, even if at the same time I can't remember anything feeling *more* real.

But still, let's be honest, it's all a bit *Kate and Leopold*, isn't it? Apart from the fact I look nothing like Meg Ryan and my guy looks way sexier in a tailcoat than Hugh Jackman ever did. However, while I might have a rational explanation for all the blank pages, I haven't yet got one for my Mr Darcy . . .

Snuggling down underneath the blankets, I turn back to my book. I'm still on volume one, at the part where Elizabeth has met Wickham, the cute blond guy in the military. The one whom everyone, her included, fancies the pants off. (God, isn't *"fancies"* just the coolest word? Cat taught me it and it's heaps better than "got the hots for".) Anyway, this is the conversation where Wickham is telling Elizabeth about what a bastard Darcy has been to him by cheating him out of his inheritance:

"His behaviour to myself has been scandalous; but I verily believe I could forgive him any thing and every thing, rather than his disappointing the hopes and disgracing the memory of his father."

**199**

God, he's such a great actor, isn't he? I read on quickly to get Elizabeth's reaction.

> "This is quite shocking! He deserves to be publicly disgraced."
> "Some time or other he *will* be — but it shall not be by *me*. Till I can forget his father, I can never defy or expose *him*."
> Elizabeth honoured him for such feelings, and thought him handsomer than ever as he expressed them.

Shit, I love Elizabeth, but she's a freakin' idiot sometimes. She thinks she's such a great judge of character and so right all the time and yet she gets it so wrong here. Wickham is a real cad, and yet she gets totally sucked in. Honestly, she's so blind! How can she be taken in by him?

> "I had not thought Mr Darcy so bad as this — though I have never liked him, I had not thought so very ill of him — I had supposed him to be despising his fellow-creatures in general, but did not suspect him of descending to such malicious revenge, such injustice, such inhumanity as this!"

Indignation stabs. I always get so riled up at this part. Talk about misjudging Darcy. He's so honourable. As if he'd ever stoop so low as to do something like that!

A wave of tiredness washes over me and I glance at my alarm clock. Jeez, it's past 2a.m. I need to get some sleep, but I just know I'm going to wake up with jet lag at some weird hour like I have done the last couple of nights. Another yawn rips through me. Right, that's it . . .

Digging around in my bedside cabinet, I pull out a small bottle. I brought some sleeping pills with me that I had from when I had my wisdom teeth removed. I don't really like taking them, but one's not going to do any harm and it will definitely zonk me out. Climbing out of bed, I pad into the bathroom to fetch a glass of water, and on the way back I notice I haven't drawn my curtains. Tugging them closed, I climb into bed and take my pill. I wash it down with a few mouthfuls of water, then snuggle under the covers.

Mmmmm. Night, night. Sweet dreams . . .


I must have fallen asleep straight away, because the next thing I know I'm being woken by the sound of hailstones rattling against the windowpane.

*Rat-a-tat-tat-tat-tat-tat-tat.*

Wow. It's so loud, you'd think it's going to break the glass, I muse, snuggling gratefully back down under the heavy blankets. Thank God I'm not outside.

Except now suddenly it's all gone quiet again. Huh, how strange. I guess it must be one of those freak storms and now it's passed over, I decide, curling up into the foetal position and hugging my lumpy feather pillow.

Still, at least now I can go back to sleep.

*Rat-a-tat-tat-tat-tat-tat.*

I sit bolt upright. Shit. There it goes again. Only now it seems even louder.

Curious, I peel off the blankets and clamber out of bed. It's freezing in my room, even in my fleecy pyjamas, and I pad, shivering, over to the window. Pressing my nose against the glass, I peer out into the darkness. It's like one minute there's hail and then the next minute —

*There's Mr Darcy.*

My stomach lurches as I spot his figure in the bushes beneath my window. I catch a flash of his white shirt, then he disappears again into the shadows. I rub my eyes to make sure I'm not seeing things, then I open them again — just in time to see him grabbing a handful of gravel from the path and preparing to chuck it up at my window. Suddenly he sees me and freezes.

"Hang on," I gesture, tugging at the catch on the sash window. Only it's jammed with thick layers of paint and won't budge. Shit. My heart thumping, I signal to him that I'm coming down, then dash from the window, tug on my jeans and sweater — the pink glittery one that always looks nice against my complexion — and hurry downstairs. He's here, Mr Darcy's here, I can't believe it.

OK, that's a fib. Ever since yesterday at the cathedral I didn't know how, or where, or when, but I knew I'd see him again. I just knew.

As I slip out of the front door he emerges from the shadows. He's taller than I remember, but just as cute. My chest tightens and I feel a thrill of excitement.

202

"We've got to stop bumping into each other like this," I quip, trying to be all nonchalant.

Mr Darcy looks at me blankly.

"It's a saying," I explain, smiling tentatively. Standing opposite him on the gravel drive, I suddenly feel shy.

"Ah, I see." He nods, obviously not seeing at all.

There's a pause and we both stand facing each other, neither of us speaking.

"How did you know where to find me?" Curiosity gets the better of any attempt to be cool.

Taking off his top hat, he rakes his fingers through his shock of black hair. "I'm not entirely sure," he admits. "I was taking a walk by your hotel and I happened to see you in the window. I wanted to catch your attention . . ." He pauses and bows his head. "Please forgive the impropriety."

He's so courteous I feel myself melting. "You're forgiven," I reply, with mock formality.

Looking down at me, his brooding eyes meet mine. "Perhaps you would care to join me?"

Gosh, could he get any more adorable? "That sounds great." I smile.

As I slip my arm through his I feel a delicious tingle all the way down to my groin. I don't know if it's chemistry, pheromones or good old-fashioned lust, but, *God*, he is hot.

"So, where are we going?"

"Down to the lake," he says assuredly.

The lake? I get a buzz of anticipation. I've got a feeling that this is going to be *so* much better than any of the other first dates I've ever been on.

We set off at a leisurely walk. Everything is so peaceful. It's like the whole world is asleep but me and Mr Darcy. It's a full moon tonight and the glow is shedding a milky whiteness on everything. It almost has a dreamlike quality to it, I think, casting a sideways glance at him from underneath my eyelashes just to check he's still there and hasn't disappeared in a puff of smoke, or turned into a pumpkin or something.

Oh, he's still there all right.

I slide my eyes across his firm-set jaw, his Roman nose, his dark eyes staring directly ahead, the gleam of his white shirt in the moonlight. I feel the warmth of his body against my arm. It still doesn't make sense. Mr Darcy isn't supposed to be real. And yet . . .

Without even glancing down at me, he seems to sense me looking at him and wordlessly places his free hand reassuringly across mine. And yet, the funny thing is, Mr Darcy feels more real to me than any of the men I've been on first dates with.

I'm not sure how long it takes for us to reach the lake. Time seems to blur, until I'm no longer aware of it passing and I see the lake, stretching out before us like a pale, silvery ink blot. Picking up a stone, Mr Darcy skims it across the water and I watch it bounce, one, two, three, four, five times, the moonlit ripples spreading ever outwards.

"Here, let's see how many you can get," he says, handing me a stone.

I laugh and protest that I'm useless. "Look, not even one," I groan, as my stone plops into the water and disappears.

"Try again." Handing me another stone, he stands behind me and curls his fingers round mine. "Like this."

I get a sudden shortness of breath. "Oh, I see," I murmur, feeling the warmth of his breath of my neck and the solidity of his body behind me. Gosh, I hadn't realised skimming stones could be so much fun.

We stay like this for a while before Mr Darcy finds an old row boat hidden under a weeping willow and rows me out into the middle of the lake. I can't quite believe what's happening. I feel as if I'm in one of those romantic movie sequences — you know the ones, a montage of cheesy moments over which plays a Coldplay song — only in my case the soundtrack is just the lapping of the water against the boat and the gentle sound of the oars.

And then Mr Darcy stops rowing and, tilting his head, declares, "Look, there's Orion."

Gazing upwards into the velvet darkness, I trace the glittering pinpricks of light. Like millions of tiny diamonds. In the past I've never been able to make out any star formations, but sure enough, there it is, clearly visible, the hunter and his belt. I feel a burst of joy and suddenly it hits me: I don't know exactly what's happening, and I can't explain it, but honestly, right now this feels so wonderful, I don't care.

"You know, I've dreamed of a moment like this," I whisper. "Of meeting you."

There's no reply, and as I turn my gaze away from the sky I look across at Mr Darcy. He's staring at me intently, and even when I catch his eye, he still doesn't feel the need to say anything. Wow. I feel a shiver all the way up my spine. Mr Darcy is so completely different from all the other guys I've been out with — I'm so used to the crappy jokes and easy small talk that are usual in these kind of scenarios, but he's just so *intense*.

In fact, if I were to have one *teensy-weensy* criticism about Mr Darcy, it would be that he can be a little *too* intense, I decide, feeling a little self-conscious and looking away again. I mean, all this brooding is lovely in *theory* and he looks very handsome with his brow all crinkled up like that, but in reality it's all a bit — well — *heavy*.

Not that I don't like heavy. I'm not saying that. Heavy is good. Especially after some of the idiots I've been out with who laugh at their own farts and can't be serious for a minute. Only sometimes it's nice to have a *little* light relief. A *bit* of chit-chat about the usual stuff: you know, current events, the latest celebrity gossip, what's on TV. Maybe even have a bitch about the contestants on *American Idol*.

But of course I'm being ridiculous. This is Mr Darcy. He doesn't do chit-chat; he broods and smoulders and strides around setting pulses racing. And that's why I love him, right?

Afterwards he rows back to the side, chivalrously helps me out of the boat, and we walk back into town. And then, before I know it, I'm back outside my hotel again, and Mr Darcy is saying, "Well, I shouldn't keep you out all night."

No, keep me out, keep me out, pipes up a little voice in my head, but instead I just nod and smile. To tell the truth, this evening has left me in something of a trance.

"Goodnight, Emily." He bows politely.

Of course. No goodnight kiss. I feel a stab of disappointment. Oh, well. What can I expect? He's a gentleman, remember?

"Goodnight, *Mr Darcy*," I add with emphasis.

He waits dutifully as I climb the step and dig my night key out of my pocket. Sliding it into the lock, I turn the key and open the door. Then falter. I can't just walk into the hotel and close the door behind me, allow him to disappear into the dead of night without knowing what happens now. I just can't.

"When am I going to see you again?" I ask, twirling round.

My voice is urgent and high. I am *so* not cool. But I have to ask.

Having begun to walk away, he stops under a street lamp and turns, and with his trademark composure, replies enigmatically, "Soon."

# CHAPTER
# SEVENTEEN

I wake up early the next morning.

*Soon.*

What exactly does that mean?

Trying to figure it out, I lie in bed, staring up at the ceiling. It's such a frustrating word. So vague. So ambiguous. So open to misinterpretation. It could mean ten minutes, as in "I'll be ready soon." Or anything from a few weeks to a few days, as in "See you soon." In fact, I told my Auntie Jean I'd see her soon, and that was last Christmas.

*Great.*

Plunged into gloom, I roll over on to my stomach and bury my face in my pillow.

Honestly, couldn't he have been a bit more specific? I mean, what's wrong with *tonight*, for Godsakes?

The way I see it, words like "soon" shouldn't be allowed when it comes to love and romance and affairs of the heart. They should be outlawed. Otherwise you're just hanging around waiting for "soon" to happen.

Or lying face down on your bed obsessing about it.

Damn.

Feeing suddenly annoyed with myself that I'm doing everything I promised myself I'd never do again over a man — any man, not *even* Mr Darcy — I take a few deep breaths like we do in yoga (which is about the only thing I can *do* in yoga) and pull myself together.

Right, that's it, I decide firmly. I'm going to put it right to the very back of my mind. It's no big deal. I'll see him again whenever. I take another deep inhalation. See, I'm totally chilled out already.

I hear the faint burbling of my phone.

Oh, my God, that could be him!

I flick up my head sharply, making all these little black dots suddenly appear in front of my eyes, and throw myself over the side of my bed. Furiously groping for my bag, which seems to be submerged under a pile of clothes, I drag it out, stick my hand inside and frantically scrabble around, my fingers grasping at everything but my phone. *Shit, it's going to ring off, it's going to ring off, it's going to —*

Got it!

"Um . . . good morning," I say, lowering my voice a couple of octaves and trying to sound all cool and seductive into the mouthpiece.

Instead I sound like my brother.

"Emily, is that you?"

"Oh, Stella, hi," I say over-brightly, flopping back on my pillows.

God, I am an idiot. What am I thinking? Of course it's not going to be him.

"How's it going?" I ask, hiding my disappointment.

**209**

"Can I just say something?

Suddenly I get a heavy, weary feeling. I know what this means.

"Men suck!"

Stella has called up to vent. Not because she wants to have a conversation. Or find out how I am and how my trip is going. Or even to ask my advice.

No, Stella's just annoyed about something. (In this case it's men, though in the past we've had subjects ranging from her neighbours' "frigging yapping chihuahua that kept me awake all night" to "Why does it cost three dollars for a cup of tea at a café when a tea bag only costs ten cents?")

"I was supposed to see Scott tonight and he totally blew me out . . ."

I don't actually have to *say* anything. I just have to listen, quietly and without interruption, apart from the occasional "Uh-huh" or "Seriously?" interjected at relevant points.

Like, for example, now.

"*Seriously?*"

"Yeah. Can you believe it? We arranged to go out for dinner tonight — he was taking me to this fancy restaurant over in Playa del Carmen — but he never called . . ."

Sitting upright, I swing my legs out from underneath the blankets and sit there for a moment trying to come round. I've never been one of those people who can just leap out of bed on a morning all bright-eyed and bushy-tailed.

". . . and I thought, There's no way I'm going to stay in, mooning over some guy . . ."

"Uh-huh."

Silencing a yawn, I glance at my watch. Yet again I've managed to wake up with just ten minutes to spare before breakfast finishes. I need to get ready.

Stumbling into the bathroom and resting my fleecy elbows on the basin, I peer at my reflection in the mirror. Ugh. It's not pretty. I'd like to blame it on the unflattering overhead lighting (which makes me think every electrician in the world must be a man, as no woman would *ever* install overhead lighting), but I have a sneaky feeling I really do look this rough. Though it's not surprising: I hardly slept.

Well, you shouldn't have been such a dirty stop-out, should you? Gallivanting around Bath in the early hours with Mr Darcy.

At the memory I feel a buzz of something warm and gloopy inside.

". . . so I went clubbing with Beatrice to Amigos . . ."

I zone back in with a "*Seriously?*"

"You're damned right I did!" she exclaims.

Careful only to turn on the cold tap a trickle, I dampen my facecloth. One of the rules when listening to Stella's rants is that I am required to give her my full concentration. No matter that she might have called me up in the middle of something crucial — I have to drop everything. I am not allowed to be caught — heaven forbid — *multi-tasking*.

". . . and I wore my new hotpants, the ones with the silver stripe down the side, and tied one of those sarongs I bought from Chinatown round my boobs. It made this adorable little tube top . . ."

Finishing washing my face, I grab my toothbrush. Hmm, now this could be tricky.

I squeeze on a squiggle of toothpaste and attempt to brush my teeth with my mouth closed. It's surprisingly effective. Although toothpaste does froth up pretty quickly.

"Uh-huh . . . uh-huh . . ." I mumble, my mouth full.

"Anyway, so Bea and I were in the club sharing a pitcher of margarita . . ."

Spitting it silently in the basin, I forgo rinsing in the name of friendship and wipe my mouth on a towel. So far so good. And at this rate I'll make breakfast.

". . . and guess who I saw?"

But first I need to pee.

"Scott!" she shrieks down the handset.

"Um . . . seriously?" Honestly, why is it that I always need to go at the most inconvenient of moments? I think, having a flashback to that day on the coach and Spike. Maybe I should start drinking cranberry juice or pomegranate or whatever it is that's good for your bladder.

Quietly I lift up the toilet lid. I might have pelvic-floor muscles of steel, but there's no way I can hold this. I've gone from wanting to go to desperate to go in under five seconds. I have the Ferrari of bladders.

"And he was there with a whole bunch of girls. Right there! In the middle of the dance floor!"

"Seriously?" I begin quietly unravelling the toilet roll, careful that the holder doesn't rattle and give me away.

"*Seriously!*" she cries. "They were all over him and he was all over them. I nearly didn't see him because of all that foam."

I dip the sheets of toilet paper into the bowl, crisscrossing them backwards and forwards across the U-bend to form — how shall I put it? — *a soft landing*.

As you can probably tell, this is not the first time I've peed while on the phone.

"So I marched right up to him and threw my margarita in his face. And I know what you're going to say, Em . . ."

Really? 'Cos I don't, I muse, sitting down on the "loo", a word I've picked up from Maeve.

"'What a waste of good tequila' — but I was so goddamn angry . . ."

I chime in with a sympathetic "Uh-huh."

"The slimeball!"

This time I go for an enthusiastic "Uh-huh."

"Bastard!"

Followed by a wearily resigned "Uh-huh."

"Fuck-face!"

Building to a you-go-girl "Uhuh!"

God, it's amazing what you can convey through intonation, isn't it?

"Loser!" she gasps, then corrects herself. "Well, actually he's not a loser, is he?" she says dryly. "He's rich, handsome and successful and probably having an orgy right now."

I finish peeing and go to flush the toilet. Then remember . . .

"God, I feel like such a fool," she adds quietly and, if I'm not mistaken, I'm sure I can hear a tremble in her voice. "I was totally taken in. I thought he really liked me."

There's a pause, and then I hear it: a sniff.

It's my cue to speak.

"But did you really like him?" I ask gently.

"Yeah." She sniffs, only louder this time and I can imagine her sitting on her bed in her hotel room, dabbing her eyes with her Chinese sarong. "Well, he could be a bit arrogant . . ." she trails off doubtfully.

It's her first admission that Scott might not be the god she thought he was, and I seize the opportunity: "Just a bit?" I coax. I feel like Harvey Keitel in that film with Kate Winslet — you know, the one where she's in a cult and he has to de-indoctrinate her.

"Mmmm," she murmurs, still sniffing into her sarong, but I can tell she's starting to think about it. There's a slight hesitation and then, "He did go on about his bonus a lot and how this year he'd made his company a fortune so he was expecting a really huge one . . ."

"Really?" I ask, trying to sound surprised.

"Yeah, all the time," she replies, as if she's surprised too. "Plus, he was always flashing his platinum Amex about . . ."

"Tacky," I chime in. All she needs now is a bit of encouragement and she'll be on a roll. "And what about his clothes?" I prompt, fingers crossed.

"Oh, my God, didn't I tell you about his jeans?" she cries.

214

*Bingo*! That's it. She's criticising his fashion sense. The spell's definitely broken.

"They were *hemmed*!"

I don't know quite what's wrong with wearing hemmed jeans, but it's obviously worse than being a serial killer in Stella's eyes.

"And he wore a belt with a big silver buckle," she's now shrieking. "Oh, Em, it was hideous. It was like something David Hasselhoff would wear." She bursts into a fit of howls. "Jesus, what was I thinking? I was so impressed by everything —" she breaks off, and sighs. "He was such good fun, though," she confesses.

"So are roller coasters, but after a while they make you nauseous."

Stella laughs. "Thanks, Em."

"What for?"

"For listening to me."

"Hey, any time." I stifle a yawn.

"Shit, I have no idea what time it is over there. Did I wake you up?"

"Um, yeah . . . sort of . . . I was out late." Scooping my glittery pink mohair sweater off the floor from where I dropped it when I got in last night, I drag it over my head. It still smells of night-time, and chimney smoke, and him.

"Let me guess. Playing dominoes," she teases.

"No, actually. I was with a man."

*So there.*

There's a stunned silence. It turns out to be a delayed reaction.

"Holy shit!" she shrieks, then repeats *ohmyGodIcan'tbelieveit* over and over (I take this opportunity to flush the toilet and wash my hands), until finally drawing breath, she gasps, "You were on a date?"

I think about it for a moment. I hadn't thought of it like that until now, but —

"Yeah . . . I guess so."

"I don't believe it!" she says again.

Neither do I, I think, brushing out my hair and staring at my reflection. Memories of last night come wafting back to me: walking arm in arm, skimming stones, rowing on the lake, looking at the stars . . . At the time it was amazing, but I guess it does all seem a bit cheesy now I'm thinking about it.

"I can't believe you've waited until now to tell me!"

I wouldn't call being pinned to the earpiece listening to her ranting "waiting", but I'm not going to split hairs.

"Tell me all about him," Stella's demanding.

Oh, hell, of course. She's going to want details. I hadn't thought of that. Suddenly I'm fast regretting telling her.

"Well, um, it's a bit complicated —"

"Don't tell me. He's married," she cuts in.

"No, of course not," I snap crossly.

"Oh, silly me, it's *me* that's married," she laughs self-deprecatingly. "So what's the problem?"

Shit. Where do I start? He's a fictional character and yet he's also real. We've met a couple of times, but he has this habit of vanishing into thin air and I never

**216**

know when or *if* he's going to show up again. Oh, and he's also incredibly famous and every woman wants to date him. And let's not forget, whereas I live in New York, he lives in England — but probably about two hundred years ago.

Confused?

So am I.

"Well, it's kind of a long-distance relationship," I say, choosing my words carefully.

"A *relationship*? Wow, that sounds serious," says Stella, impressed. "How long have you known this guy?"

"He was my first love."

Well, if I'm being honest.

"Whoah, you're kidding me!" she exclaims, then laughs. "Wait a minute. Not Arnold Bateman. The guy you used to tell me about who would pull your pigtails?"

"No, not him!" I gasp, then hesitate. Shall I tell her? Part of me wants to, but the other part of me is remembering our conversation back in New York. The bit where she insisted Mr Darcy didn't exist. But maybe if I explain, about the quill, the mysterious blank pages in the book, the newspaper, Mr Darcy himself . . .

Oh, come on, Emily. Listen to yourself. She's never going to believe you. And do you blame her? *You* still can't quite believe it and you've seen it all with your own eyes.

"So, who is it?" Stella is persisting, somewhat suspiciously. "What's his name?"

But if I don't tell her the truth, what do I say? My mind draws a blank. I don't want to lie to her, but —

"Um . . ." Walking back into the bedroom, I notice the postcard Spike chose for me resting on top of my dresser. I haven't written that one yet. Absently I pick it up and turn it over. On the back is written "Matthew Macfadyen as Fitzwilliam Darcy."

"Fitzwilliam," I blurt.

"No, what's his *first* name?" she asks.

"That *is* his first name."

"Wow, what a crazy name," she replies. "But cool, I like it," she adds decisively.

I feel oddly relieved. He's been given the Stella seal of approval.

"Well, look, hon, I'm dying to hear more, but I should go to bed. It's nearly 3 a.m. here and I need to get some beauty sleep. Plus, T-mobile is gonna bankrupt me. Do you know what they charge per minute international?"

"A lot," I say, feeling a wave of relief. Thank God, no more awkward questions.

"I swear, this is costing me the equivalent of a pair of Prada shoes."

Perching myself on the edge of my bed, I tug on my socks and boots. "OK, go. I'll call you next time. It's my turn."

"OK. Night. Big kiss."

"Actually, it's morning here." I stand up.

"Whatever." She laughs sleepily. But then just as I think I've got away with it scot-free she asks, "Hang on a minute. How can it be long distance if you were with him last night? I don't understand. It doesn't make sense."

I allow myself a small smile. "Like I said. It's complicated."

# CHAPTER
# EIGHTEEN

And things only get more complicated as the day goes on. Fast-forward to later that afternoon and after having spent most of the day on a sightseeing tour, which included a quill-writing workshop (mockery aside, it actually turned out to be pretty good, but inky, fun), I'm walking back to the hotel with Maeve and nibbling on hot, roasted chestnuts that I've just bought from a fingerless-gloved teenager on the corner.

It's grown even colder. The tip of my nose is almost frozen and I can barely feel my toes, despite two layers of woolly socks. The air is so glacial it almost hurts to breathe, and it smells of winter and woodsmoke and pubs. We pass one now, its door flung open as a group of office workers spill on to the sidewalk, intoxicated by laughter and high spirits.

And about half a dozen pints no doubt, I think, watching them stumble round, arms round shoulders, tinsel draped round their necks like silver and gold ties.

"Don't you just love this time of year?" whispers Maeve. "New Year's Eve always feels so magical, don't you think?"

I feel a jolt as I remember. "New Year's Eve," I murmur. "Wow, I totally forgot."

"You forgot," repeats Maeve in disbelief. She looks at me aghast. "But it's the big ball tonight."

"God, yeah, of course," I gasp, suddenly thinking about it. "I lost track of time, what with the time difference and travelling . . ."

And meeting Mr Darcy, I think, my mind flashing back to last night. Just a few hours ago I was walking with him across this very square, which had been deserted but for the two of us. It had been magical. Thinking about it now, my stomach flutters with excitement and I bury my nose in his white silk scarf, which I've taken to wearing, and inhale its delicious scent.

"I understand," nods Maeve, not understanding at all. "It can be a difficult time when families are apart. Sometimes you just want to forget about it." Patting my arm reassuringly, she peers at me intently, her face reminiscent of an owl's in her huge wide-framed spectacles.

I'm about to tell her she's mistaken and I'm absolutely fine being apart from my family, when I get the sense that she's actually talking about herself.

"Are your family back in Ireland?" I ask cautiously. I don't want her to think I'm being nosy. Since the other day when she snapped at me on the bus I've been careful to keep our conversations very surface, which is one of the reasons why I decided not to tell her what Ernie told me. Part of me wants to set the record straight, but the other part is afraid to get involved. Shoot the messenger and all that. Plus, he did make me promise to keep it a secret. Still, it's such a shame. I think Ernie and Maeve would have been great together.

"Oh, there's only my brother, Paddy, and he's spending Christmas and New Year's Eve at his daughter's villa in Spain . . ."

She's smiling brightly as she talks, but her eyes betray a certain sadness. I've always presumed Maeve was single, but now it strikes me that perhaps she's a widow. That would explain the sad look she always has, as if she's in mourning for someone, I think, glancing at Maeve's ring finger. I'm sure I didn't notice her wearing a ring before, but maybe —

"I never married," she says, catching me looking.

"Oh, I . . . didn't mean . . ."

Seeing my embarrassment, Maeve quickly reassures me. "It's all right, dearie, people often wonder."

"So you never wanted to?" I ask curiously.

She hesitates for a moment, as if thinking about something, then says matter-of-factly, "It just never happened for me, that's all." Stuffing her hands in the pockets of her rather drab woollen coat, she gestures across to a group of children building a snowman in the square. "My goodness, will you look at them. Isn't that wonderful?"

And with that our conversation ends and we pause for a few moments to watch them, all bundled up in stripy scarves and woollen mittens, their faces bursting with innocent excitement as they make eyes out of buttons and a nose from a carrot. And no doubt the topic would have switched to something else entirely and I would have forgotten all about it if I hadn't

222

happened to glance across at Maeve and see a look in her eyes that belies the smile on her face. It's that haunted look again. And right there and then I know for sure there's a lot more than Maeve's telling me. I just don't know what it is.

But this time I'm determined to find out.

"What is it, Maeve?" I begin uncertainly.

She doesn't answer and continues staring resolutely ahead, but I can see the muscles in her jaw clench tightly. Regret stabs. Oh, shit. What did I do that for? I shouldn't have said anything. What's it got to do with me?

"Look, I'm sorry," I'm now saying quickly. "It's none of my business . . ."

"I had a daughter."

I'm silenced.

"When I was eighteen. She was the most beautiful thing I had ever seen. I named her Orla," she continues, speaking in the past tense. "They only let me hold her for a few minutes and then they took her away."

I feel a rush of sadness. Oh, God. So *that's* what it is. That's why she always looks so terribly sad. Maeve had a baby girl and she must have died. How awful.

"I think about her every day."

I look at Maeve. Her eyes are watering behind her thick glasses and I want to say something to comfort her, but I don't know what. The tried-and-tested words seem so trite. There's a whole canyon of grief that she's kept bottled up inside. How can I even begin to imagine what she's been through?

"I wonder where she is, what she's doing, if she has her own children now," continues Maeve, who's talking quietly to herself.

I feel a jolt of confusion.

"She's grown up?"

Maeve nods. "She turned thirty-seven this year."

"But I thought, I mean, the way you were speaking —" I break off.

"That she died?" finishes Maeve, and smiles sadly. "No." She shakes her head. "I gave her up for adoption. I was the one who died that day." She looks at my face, and seeing I don't understand, adds quietly, "I died the moment I gave her away."

Suddenly it all makes perfect sense. That sadness that Maeve always seems to be carrying around with her. Maeve is in mourning. She lost not just a daughter, but herself.

"*Gave.* It sounds so easy, doesn't it," Maeve is now saying. Swallowing hard, she looks straight at me, her eyes shining brightly. "It was the hardest thing I've ever had to do. It broke my heart."

I place my hand on her arm and squeeze it supportively. There's so many questions that I want to ask, but I get the feeling that Maeve has kept this secret hidden for a long, long time, and now she just wants to let it all out. So I just listen as she talks.

"His name was Seamus. I met him at the fair. He had long, dark hair. Blue eyes. Cheekbones to cut you with. And the most beautiful hands — long, delicate fingers, smooth, pale skin — I'd never seen hands like that before. Men's hands were always rough and

224

calloused and ingrained with dirt from working on the land."

Without prompting she starts telling the story, staring off into the middle distance as she talks.

"But he was a painter. Landscapes were his thing. Big, dark canvases that filled the tiny flat he was renting . . ." Her voice trails off and I can see she's back there again, with him in his flat, experiencing all those feelings she had for him all over again. "I'd never known anyone like him. I'd lived on a farm my whole life, I didn't know what a hippy was. I didn't know anything. I was so naïve."

She shakes her head in disbelief at her younger self.

"He told me he loved me and I believed him. Everyone warned me against him, but I wouldn't listen. What did they know? I was young and headstrong and invincible. And I was in love."

Knowing Maeve now, it's hard to imagine her being a strong, vibrant, confident person.

"But then I got pregnant. And suddenly he didn't love me any more," she says simply.

I'm silent for a moment, then I have to ask: "What happened to him?"

"I don't know." She shrugs. "He left town. Ran away. And there was I. Eighteen, unmarried and pregnant. Suddenly I wasn't so invincible any more."

She smiles ruefully.

"The priest told me I'd brought shame on my family. My brother threw me out. I had nowhere to live. No job. I couldn't support a baby."

I try putting myself in her shoes, but I can't. My parents would never disown me over something like that. Times have changed. Being unmarried and pregnant is no big deal. It's practically the norm these days. How sad to think that something that would barely raise an eyebrow today had such a devastating effect upon her. Poor Maeve. God, she must have been so scared and alone. No wonder her self-esteem has been wrecked.

"I had no choice," she says now, wiping away a lone tear that's slowly trickling down her cheek. I squeeze her arm tighter in support. "Except that's a lie, isn't it?" She sniffs, suddenly angry at herself. "I had a choice. I could have said no. I could have run away with her. Found a place to live. A job. I was a coward."

"No, you weren't," I cry indignantly. "Things were different back then. You mustn't blame yourself."

"Why not?"

"Because you can't keep punishing yourself. You did the best you could."

"But did I? Did I really?" she demands, and I suddenly get just a glimpse of the guilt she's been carrying around with her for years. "All she had was me. Her father deserted her, and then I did too." Her lip trembles and she bites it. "I'm so ashamed of what I did. I don't deserve to be happy ever again. I did a terrible thing, Emily. I deserve to be punished. She probably hates me and I don't blame her."

"You don't know that," I disagree.

Maeve sniffs loudly, her eyes still focused on the kids building the snowman.

226

"Have you ever thought of looking for her?" I ask gently.

There's a pause. "Once," she says quietly. "When she would have turned eighteen, but —" She breaks off and shakes her head, as if finding it difficult to speak. "I dream about her, you know. I picture her in my head, and try to imagine what she's like. What it would be like to have a daughter, to be someone's mother." Turning to face me, her pale blue eyes search mine. "You and your mother are very lucky. To have each other."

I think about Mom. We've never had the traditional relationship between a mother and daughter, and now, listening to Maeve, I feel cheated. I mean, look at Maeve. She'd do anything to speak to her daughter, and yet my mom rarely ever makes the effort to come and see me, or even pick up the phone.

And yet, you're not exactly blameless, are you, Emily? When was the last time you asked her how she was and really wanted to know? Instead of being satisfied with the obligatory "fine".

"You know, me and my mom aren't really close," I confide to Maeve. "We don't talk much."

"You don't?" asks Maeve. "But why?"

I think about her question. It's one I've asked myself hundreds of times over the years, and yet I still don't have an answer. "I don't know, really." I shrug. "When I was a lot younger I remember hanging out with her more, having fun, but then as I got older . . ." I trail off. "She's always been so busy with her career, charity work, travelling, Dad, my brother — I didn't want to bother her with stupid things that happened at school or boyfriend troubles. Instead, I shared that personal stuff with my friends. I still do."

"But surely she would have wanted you to share those with her. She wouldn't have thought they were stupid. If they were important to you, they would have been important to her."

I smile. "You don't know my mom."

"Are you sure *you* do, Emily?"

I falter.

"Have you ever asked? Have you ever tried to talk to her? Share those kinds of things with her? Confide in her?" Maeve continues. "You may be surprised, Emily. Perhaps she's hurting as much as you are."

"I'm not hurting," I protest quickly.

"Aren't you?" asks Maeve quietly. "I've learned people don't always say what they feel and because of that, others make a lot of assumptions, without knowing the real truth. Sometimes people even do such a good job of covering up their feelings and acting as if they are just fine that they almost convince themselves . . ."

Listening to Maeve, I don't know whether she's talking about me, my mom or herself. Maybe, in fact, she's talking about all three of us, I realise. And she would be right. Until now I've always maintained that I'm fine with the relationship I have with my parents, my mom especially, but that's because I *wanted* to be fine with it. If I'm honest with myself, I want to be able to talk to her like I can talk to Maeve. To have this kind of close relationship. In fact, if anything, this conversation has made me realise how I barely really know my mom. How she barely knows me. Our phone calls and e-mails involve book recommendations and reminders for dad's birthday. We never talk about the stuff that matters, we never talk about us.

"You know, your mother is very lucky to have you as a daughter, Emily," reassures Maeve, and I zone back to see her looking at me, her face filled with genuine concern.

"And your daughter would be very proud if she knew you," I say quietly.

"You really think so?" she asks as if too afraid to hope.

"Absolutely," I say without a moment's hesitation.

She squeezes my hand tightly and I smile.

"It's getting late. We should head back."

"Aye." She nods, pulling her coat tightly round her. She pauses to take one last look at the children playing with the snowman, and for the first time I see a real smile break across her face. Then linking her arm through mine, we set off across the cobbles.

# CHAPTER
# NINETEEN

Letting myself into my room, I flop down on to my bed and dig out my crumpled itinerary. I'm still reeling from my conversation with Maeve and the news of her secret adoption, but with only a few hours to go until the ball, I force my mind to turn to the evening ahead.

Included in the tour are tickets for a charity ball. Entitled "A New Year's Eve Extravaganza", it's being held tonight at the town's ballroom, famous for housing the actual balls that Jane Austen attended as a young woman, and which were subsequently the inspiration for those described in her novels.

> . . . so put on your finest and enjoy a Regency ball, just as if you're a character in one of Jane Austen's novels.

I feel a flutter of anticipation as I think about Mr Darcy. I wonder if he's going to show up again tonight at the ball? The way he appeared outside my window. It was like something from *Romeo and Juliet*. Feeling all warm and gooey inside, I wonder where he is, what he's doing, when I'm going to see him again. If only he'd call me.

But of course he won't. And I can't call him either. Neither can I text him, e-mail him or instant-message him, I realise, thinking about all the staples of modern-day dating I've taken for granted. The flirty text messages, funny e-mails, hours spent lying in bed at night giggling on the phone . . .

Gosh, I'd forgotten how much fun that can be, I think, feeling a teensy bit disappointed that there won't be any of that.

But never mind, there's always letters and they're a lot more personal and romantic, aren't they? I tell myself encouragingly. Although saying that, I can't remember the last time I wrote a letter, apart from to my bank manager, and trust me, there was nothing romantic about that. But still, I adore the idea of writing a proper letter. There's all that gorgeous textured writing paper you can buy, and I can use real ink and a fountain pen, and maybe even a little wax seal with a stamp with my initial on it. And I could tie up the replies in a bundle with a faded pink ribbon and keep them in the attic, where I'll find them when I'm an old lady in years to come and reread them and —

Er, hello? Before you get completely carried away, Emily, where exactly are you going to send these love letters? Seriously. What are you going to do? Address them to Mr Darcy, c/o Pride and Prejudice, England?

Suddenly the whole thing strikes me as even more ridiculous and impossible than it was before — if that's possible — and even more complicated. It's like trying to figure out a really difficult math problem: the more you think about it, the more confusing it becomes.

So I'm not going to, I tell myself firmly.

But there is one thing for sure: this time I'm going to make certain I make more of an effort than I did last night. Just in case . . .

Glancing up from the itinerary, I hoist myself off the quilted eiderdown and tug open the pine closet that's stuffed under the eaves. Alrighty, so where's my dress? I peer inside the closet for my black nylon garment-holder. It must just be at the back somewhere. I rattle through the coat-hangers. Huh, that's weird, it's not there. I could have sworn I hung it up in the closet, but now I come to think of it . . .

Screwing up my forehead, I glance around the room. Maybe it's behind the door under the coat. Or chucked on the floor along with my suitcase. Or for some strange reason in the bathroom.

But it's not in any of those places, and padding around my hotel room, picking up T-shirts as if a large, black nylon carryon might suddenly appear from underneath, I'm beginning to feel a tinge of alarm. Where the hell is it?

I try retracing my steps. When did I last see it? Well, that's easy, that would be . . . I draw a blank. Actually, for the life of me I can't remember when I last saw it. Here in Bath? Umm . . . actually, no. At the last hotel? Um . . . no again. Panic is beginning to rise. On the coach? When I first arrived at Heathrow? At check-in at JFK?

No. No. No.

In the cab to the airport?

N —

Hang on a minute. My memory focuses in like a long lens.

Oh, shit.

Suddenly I can see it, lying next to me on the back seat. I hadn't wanted to put it in the trunk as I didn't want to crush it. I'd insisted on placing it on the other side of the armrest, folding it carefully in half. Black nylon on black leather. Easy not to see if you're in a hurry. To forget about if you don't have change and have to ask passing strangers if they can split a hundred. To leave on the back seat because your driver has a bad back and you're left to struggle with your ridiculously heavy suitcase.

My heart plummets.

Somewhere in Manhattan my sparkly black dress is hanging around in a nylon garment-holder, missing out on the party. And I'm here in England, with a New Year's Eve ball to go to. With absolutely nothing to wear.

I didn't think my heart could plummet further. But it can. And it does.

What a bummer. I spent ages choosing that dress. And despite what Stella thought, it was a really nice dress, I tell myself, imagining myself in it now, dancing around a ballroom. Disappointment clunks. God, I'm such an idiot.

What am I going to do now? For a split second I entertain the thought of rushing out and buying something else, but it's late, all the shops are closed. In desperation I dive on my suitcase. I haven't unpacked properly yet. There must be something I can wear in here instead.

I flip it open and survey the jumbled contents. Abruptly any hope I might have had stalls. Oh, dear. Perhaps Stella was right. Perhaps I was a *little* heavy-handed with my reading material. Peering gloomily at the suitcase full of books, I wish I'd listened to her. I mean, I can't exactly wear *Sense and Sensibility*, now, can I?

Quickly I begin unpacking the paperbacks and stacking them up in wobbly piles on the eiderdown. I've always thought that you can never be truly alone if you've got a book to keep you company. You can be stranded at an airport, alone in a strange country or stuck in a motel room on a business trip, but if you've got a good book with you, you'll be OK.

Saying that, this is *slightly* ridiculous.

I tug out a large volume of *North and South* in the vain hope that there might be something vaguely appropriate to wear underneath. And find that, no — it's only Emily Brontë lurking in the corner. Damn. I feel a certain inevitability.

Didn't I bring *anything* to wear as a back-up?

A scene flashes through my mind of a chandelier-lit ballroom, guests milling around in their finest, quaffing champagne, engaging in polite conversation, *staring open-mouthed at the American girl doing the two-step in pink velour pyjamas . . .*

No! Stop!

With a screech the scene grinds to a halt and I try shaking the image free from my mind. Come on, Emily, you must have packed something suitable for Plan B. My heart racing, I push up the sleeves of my grey sweatshirt and dive back in. Please let there be something in here. For the love of God, *please*.

Hang on, what's that?

Feeling a tentative whoosh of relief, I pounce on something black. I knew it! I knew I would have packed a little black dress. I mean, who goes anywhere at Christmas without a LBD?

*I do.*

I glare accusingly at the item in my hands. Because it's not a dress — no siree — it's the dreaded DKNY cashmere sweater, goddamn it. Dismay resonates so heavy inside it's almost audible. Frigging hell. I'm supposed to be dressing up in my finest, not looking like my auntie Jean. Flinging it on to the cream carpet, I sit on the bed, fold my arms and survey the mess around me. Shit, shit, *shit*.

Outside in the corridor I can hear a flurry of excitement and the sound of doors opening and closing as the ladies flit into each other's rooms to show off their outfits. I glance at my watch. I have fifteen minutes. And no dress.

At once my panic crumples into a weary resignation. I'm totally useless. I didn't pack anything suitable to wear. I feel a wetness on my cheek. There's no way I can go to the ball now.

So this is it. Me. On my own. In my hotel room. On New Year's Eve.

A knock on the door interrupts my disappointment.

"Who is it?" I call out, wiping my cheeks with the cuff of my sweatshirt.

There's no answer and I half think I've imagined it. I wait a moment, but hearing not a sound restlessly pick up a copy of *Emma*, open it at random and start reading about the Christmas Eve party that the characters all go to. Only instead of feeling OK, my theory is shot to pieces as now I'm feeling glummer than ever.

I eye the door. You know, it did *sound* like a knock.

Hauling myself off the bed, and sending my little pile of books toppling, I pick my way through the debris on the carpet. Most likely it's Maeve or Rose wanting to see my outfit, I think miserably, tugging open the door.

Huh, that's strange. There's no one there.

Standing in my doorway, I glance up and down the pastelpink hallway. Nope. It's empty. No doubt all the ladies have already got dressed and gone downstairs by now, I realise, glancing at my watch. It's seven thirty. The coach will be leaving shortly. Sniffing back any rogue tears, I turn to go back inside and happen to glance down. There's a package. Curiously, I bend down. It has a tag on which is written, "Emily Albright."

I feel a stab of delight.

*For me?*

I dart back inside my room and start ripping it open. I've never been one to carefully unwrap gifts.

Top layer of wrapping off, I discover a second layer underneath. This time it's in shiny gold festive paper with little Christmas trees dotted all over. My curiosity is bubbling over. Someone must have sent me a belated Christmas present. But who? I don't recognise the handwriting on the label — besides, who would have my address here? Squeezing the contents, it feels sort of soft and squidgy, some type of clothing maybe, like a scarf or a pair of gloves . . .

Or a gorgeous slinky dress made from chocolate-brown satin and embroidered with tiny crystals.

I gasp as it spills out on to the eiderdown. Oh, my God. Looping my fingers through the delicate spaghetti straps, I hold it up and gaze at it in stunned amazement. Who would send me a dress? And not just *any* old dress, but a dazzling, exquisitely made, figure-hugging dress. Jumping up from the bed, I rush over to the full-length-mirror and, pressing it up against my body, angle the mirror's brass stand to see my reflection.

I catch my breath as I snap into view.

Holy shit. I can't quite believe it. It's the kind of dress I'd look at in shop windows but would never have the balls to wear.

*Or a ball to wear it to.*

Excitement thumps.

*Stella.* It has to be. I remember now, her sitting on the sofa bed in my New York apartment, watching me pack. She was reading the itinerary and kept asking me what clothes I was taking. She must have sent me this as a surprise, a sort of secret Santa. God knows how she got the address, but she has been a little detective of late, just look how she got Mr McKenzie to come in and cover for us over the vacation . . .

A thought thuds.

Oh, hell. I only got her a scented candle.

Snatching up my cell phone, I speed-dial her number. I glance at my watch. I've got just over five minutes. If I quickly wash my face, squirt on a bit of deodorant, pin up my hair and do my make-up on the coach . . . My mind racing, I start dashing around the room, my phone wedged in the crick of my neck as I dig out my one pair of stilettos. Stella insisted I bring them, just in case. Now I know why.

"Hey, you've reached Stella. I can't come to the phone right now, but if you'd like to leave a message . . ."

"Hi, it's me, Em," I gasp, turning on the taps in the bathroom and splashing my face with icy-cold water. "I just got your present and I wanted to say thank you. It's beautiful, Stella, really beautiful." My voice is muffled as I roughly dry my face on a towel. "And I'm sorry I only got you a scented candle, but it's wild fig and made of soy wax and the woman in the store told me it was supposed to bring you serenity and joy, or something. Look, I gotta go, but I'll call you later. And thanks again, honey. I love it!"

Hanging up, I unzip my jeans, hop back into the bedroom and, chucking my phone on to the cluttered eiderdown, begin stripping off my clothes. I pull off my sweatshirt, unhook my bra and wriggle out of my comfy undies. I'm breathless with excitement. Oh, my God, I've never been brave enough to even *try* on a dress like this. I mean, look at it, it's just so *va-va-va-voom*.

238

For a moment my excitement stalls. Do I really dare wear this? I mean, can I pull this off? Don't you have to have a figure like a supermodel to wear this?

Yeah, probably, I decide, my eyes gliding longingly over the folds of chocolate satin fabric. But I don't have one. So I have two choices: (1) Stay in with a good book. (2) Put on a sexy dress and breathe in.

Scooping up the dress, I slip it over my head, and as it cascades to the floor I suck in my stomach for all I'm worth. Forget staying in with a good book. *This* Cinderella is going to the ball.

# CHAPTER
# TWENTY

*In a minicab.*

Sitting on the back seat of an old silver Mercedes, I drum my fingers against the velour armrest and peer impatiently out of the window.

Despite getting ready in record-breaking time, I rushed downstairs only to discover the coach had left without me. Which meant I had to catch a cab. Easier said than done. Bath is not Manhattan. Not even close. There's no stepping outside and hailing one off the bustling streets.

Trust me, all you'll catch on these streets will be a cold, Emily, I'd told myself, as I shivered on the sidewalk and peered into the silent emptiness.

In the end I went back inside and found the number of a local firm, but it was well over an hour before the creaky old Mercedes pulled up outside the hotel, its body sunk so low on the suspension it nearly scraped the cobblestones. Plenty of time to panic, reapply my make-up too many times, try out a new hairstyle and drink two Smirnoff miniatures from the minibar in my room.

"So, you're not from round these parts, are you?"

Above the noise of Band Aid's "Do They Know It's Christmas?" playing loudly on the radio, I hear a gruff voice. Turning away from the window, I see my driver peering enquiringly at me in his rear-view mirror. He's looking at me in the way people from town look at people from out of town. As a stranger, a foreign tourist, an object of curiosity. Quite amusing, really, considering he's wearing a fake red Santa hat wrapped in tinsel and, with his almost-white beard and matching cotton-candy eyebrows, looks like a real-life Santa Claus.

Albeit in thick prescription glasses and a navy-blue parka.

"No, I'm from New York," I yell to make myself heard over the rousing chorus.

"So good they named it twice, huh?" My driver laughs and I smile politely. "Me and the wife went to Florida once. Ever been to Florida?"

"No, never," I reply.

Only I don't think he can hear for Boy George singing the descant, as he begins telling me all about his trip to Fort Lauderdale to see his brother who has angina. After a few minutes I feel myself zoning out.

Out of the corner of my eye I notice a tiny, fake Christmas tree glued to his dashboard. Illuminated, it's flashing on and off in different sequences and my gaze is drawn to it. I haven't eaten yet and the alcohol is giving me a warm, slightly woozy feeling — the type of feeling that makes a miniature plastic Christmas tree fascinating to watch as it blinks on and off, on and off, on and off —

I'm broken from my hypnotic trance by the shrill warbling of my phone. I quickly dig it out of my bag.

"Hello?"

"So, how's England treating you?" asks a faint and crackly voice on the other end of the line.

I don't immediately recognise who it is as it's difficult to hear — not helped by my driver, who's in the middle of his monologue: ". . . and we went to Disneyland. Ever been to Disneyland? You don't know what you're missing. They've got some cracking rides, you know . . ."

Then it registers: "Freddy!" I cry, partly for the benefit of the cab driver, but mostly because I'm so pleased to hear from him. "How are you?"

"Good, good," he replies brightly. *Too* brightly.

"Great," I enthuse, playing along. Freddy and I are friends, but we're not the kind of friends to call each other for cosy chats. There's obviously something up. And I've got a pretty good idea what — or who — that is.

"Actually, to be honest I'm pretty terrible. I miss Stella," he confesses dolefully.

"Oh, Freddy," I sigh quietly.

"I know, I know," he acknowledges. "I'm a lost cause."

"You're not a lost cause, you're a great guy," I protest, trying to lift his spirits. He sounds really down. New Year's Eve sucks for unrequited lovers. "Stella's just an idiot," I tut.

Forget the loyalty. I love my friend, but sometimes I want to shake her.

242

"Do you think I should just give up and move on?" asks Freddy resignedly.

"God, I'm hardly qualified to give relationship advice, am I?" "Me. The girl who's spent the last year going on one disastrous date after another . . ."

"Sometimes you've gotta kiss a lot of frogs —"

"What? Before I meet Prince Charming?" I finish, smiling ruefully. "I didn't know you were such an old romantic, Freddy."

"For my sins," he quips.

"Hey, me too," I console.

"Maybe you and I should have got together, Em," he suggests teasingly.

"Maybe." I smile, playing along. "But you're forgetting one thing . . ."

"Oh, yeah?"

"You're in love with Stella, Freddy."

It's the first time it's ever been said out loud and as soon as I say it I wonder if I've overstepped the mark. For a moment there's silence on the other end of the line.

"I know," he says finally, his easy demeanour gone.

Regret bites. "Oh, Freddy, I'm sorry, I didn't mean to —"

"Hey, Em, don't be sorry, you're right," he cuts in wearily. "But you wanna know something?"

"Sure," I say quietly.

"This being-in-love business frigging sucks."

I so much want to talk more to Freddy, but I become aware of the Mercedes slowing down and, as we shudder to a standstill, am forced to cut our conversation short. Apologising, I promise to call him the moment I get back to New York, and we quickly say our goodbyes. I really feel for him. He sounds so down, but what can I do?

Troubled, I turn to look out of the window and suddenly everything else slips from my mind as my attention is grabbed by a stunning row of Regency houses. Shaped into a crescent and artistically lit by a row of wrought-iron lamp posts, they look too perfect to be real, as if we've happened upon a movie set and any minute I'm going to hear "Action" and see Keira Knightley appear in a corset.

The driver yanks on the handbrake. "Here we are," he announces cheerily.

"Thanks." Opening the car door, I step out into the glacial evening.

"So what brings you to Bath at New Year? A fella?"

Passing the driver ten pounds for the fare, I smile. "No, quite the opposite," I reply, feeling rather proud of myself for being all cultural. "My love of Jane Austen."

"Oh, right." He nods.

His head disappears back into the cab to get change, but I motion for him to keep the rest as a tip. In New York we're big tippers — twenty per cent is the norm — but I've heard stories about how the British simply don't tip.

But see what a difference it makes, I note, as he looks at me as if he can't quite believe it, then beams at me so broadly I feel like Angelina Jolie. Obviously giving a tip isn't quite the same as being a UN ambassador, but it's still a good deed. Infused with a virtuous glow, I smile generously and pass him an extra pound coin.

"I saw a programme about your type on telly recently . . ." He grins, sticking the cab into gear.

"You did?" See, it's all about showing appreciation and respect. I appreciate him as a cab driver, and he respects me as the passenger. Delighted to have done my bit for American tourists everywhere, I smile graciously as he pulls away from the kerb.

"Aye, and I tell you what, I'd never have put you down as one of them lipstick lesbians." He sighs, shaking his head in disbelief. "That Jane Austen is a very lucky woman."

In disbelief I watch him waving at me as he drives off down the hill. Then, gathering the satin hem of my dress as I hurry up the stone-flagged steps, I start to giggle. I wouldn't mind, but I'm not *nearly* trendy enough to be a lipstick lesbian. If Stella's gay friends from art college had heard him, they'd have laughed their Prada pants off.

"Good evening, madam, shall I take your coat?"

Magically the door opens and I'm greeted by a doorman in a penguin suit and white gloves.

Quickly stifling my laughter, I put on a serious face. "Why, thank you," I reply, slipping off my thick woollen coat and passing it to him. He whisks it away and I'm left standing in the marble entrance hall, feeling, I have to say, a teensy bit nervous.

The sounds of a string quartet and the popping of champagne corks waft towards me.

Actually, you know what, make that *very* nervous.

I head towards the noise. It's coming from the other end of the hallway, and as I round the corner I suddenly catch sight of the magnificent ballroom, its doors flung open wide. I hang back, overwhelmed. I've never seen anything quite like it. I've been to some lavish parties in New York, even a fancy black-tie do at the Ritz Carlton, but this is something else.

Six dazzling chandeliers spill down from the ornate ceiling, although it seems like more than a hundred as they're reflected over and over in the vista of mirrors. Running all the way round the walls, they create a sea of glittering diamonds, and for a few moments I just stand there, staring upwards, drinking it all in like I used to when I was a child and I'd gaze at our Christmas tree for hours. There's something magical about all these tiny lights, I realise, feeling that same flutter of anticipation. I feel as if anything can happen.

Dragging my gaze away, I blink away the brightness, and as my eyes adjust, I take in the red silk bows, shiny green holly wreaths and impressive Christmas tree positioned directly behind the string quartet. The ball is already well under way and the room is thronging with people.

Nervously I scan the crowd for Mr Darcy — just on the off-chance — but there are so many people it's hard to see. As women flit past I see flashes of silk and taffeta dresses, like chocolate wrappers, in amongst the monochrome dinner suits. There's an elderly lady in electric-blue velvet, a tall, skinny brunette in scarlet ruffles, a glamorous blonde in a purple off-the-shoulder . . .

I pull at various bits of my dress. Before I got in the cab I was feeling quite confident, but now I feel all lumps and bumps. I suck in my stomach even harder, shove back my shoulders as far as they'll go and try elongating my body to look taller. God, I've never worn anything like this before. Do I look ridiculous? It's so revealing and clingy and, well, *vampish*. Plus, with all this flesh on show, I'm suddenly feeling a lot broader than usual.

Then my stomach lurches. There's a woman wearing the same dress, standing right in front of me! *And* she looks so much better in it! Crestfallen, I sigh and slump forwards. At the same time I notice she does too. Then I fiddle with my hair. Huh, how funny. So does —

*Hang on a minute.*

I do a little twirl, from side to side, and my face breaks into the biggest smile.

That's me! That's my reflection!

I pause in disbelief. Wow, I can't believe it. I'm entranced by my own reflection. Even though I say it myself, I look great. Totally transformed. As if I'm going to the Academy Awards or something. I do another little twirl, revelling in how the fabric seems to swish out around me. Gosh, if wearing a dress like this can make me feel like a princess, I wonder what else I've been missing out on? Stella's so right. What have I been doing all this time in Gap combats and T-shirts? Pulling a straight face, I do a little shimmy up and down.

*Swish. Swish. Swish —*

"Champagne, madam?"

A waiter swoops down on me bearing a silver tray filled with champagne flutes.

"Oh . . . um, great," I say, abruptly stopping mid-swish and blushing hotly. I take one gratefully. I'm determined not to drink too much tonight, not after my night at the pub with Cat, but I guess one tiny little glass isn't going to hurt, is it? It will just help to take the edge off my nerves. The doors to the ballroom are wide open, and pausing at the entrance, I take a large, fizzy gulp.

After that I'll stick to water. Promise.

# CHAPTER
# TWENTY-ONE

Except the trouble with promises is they tend to get broken.

No sooner have I finished off the first glass than another magically appears in my hand, only it barely registers, as I'm too busy chatting to Maeve, who I found tucked away in the corner with Rupinda and Hilary. She's wearing a plain blue shift dress, and although every now and then she's still in the habit of hugging her pale, freckled elbows to her body, as if trying to hide behind them, she seems more relaxed, unburdened somehow. As if sharing her secret has gone some way to setting her free.

"What a pretty dress. The colour suits you."

I look up to see Miss Steane bearing down upon us. She's wearing what looks like a copy of a Regency dress and is smiling approvingly.

"It brings out the colour of your eyes."

"Oh, wow, thanks." I smile appreciatively. "A friend bought it for me as a Christmas present."

"How very fortunate," she says, her eyes twinkling as she looks me up and down. "I'm sure you will be a huge hit with the gentlemen tonight."

"Oh, I'm not looking to meet anybody," I say quickly.

She looks indignant. "Nonsense," she replies firmly. "To quote Jane Austen: 'To you I shall say, as I have often said before, "Do not be in a hurry, the right man will come at last."'"

How prophetic. Mr Darcy pops up in my head. I get butterflies just thinking about it.

"But how will I know he's the right man?" I quip, smiling.

Fixing me with her hazel eyes, she takes my hands between hers. "Because you will meet somebody more exceptional than anyone you have yet known. Who will love you as warmly as possible. And who will so completely attract you that you will feel you never really loved before."

Wow. *Heavy*. I feel myself blush.

"But first you must be open to the possibility that the right man might not be as you expected," she says wisely, and for a moment I feel as if she's almost talking directly about Mr Darcy. As if she knows about him. But of course that's impossible. "Remember, don't let pride or prejudice stand in the way of love," she finishes, and smiles wryly.

"Poppycock!" interrupts a booming voice. "If you ask me, love is completely overrated."

Turning sideways, I see Rose bustling towards us in a peacock-green satin dress, with matching full-length gloves. "And I should know, I've been married more times than I care to remember."

**250**

"Hello, Rose," chorus Rupinda and Hilary, shooting each other glances and suddenly deciding it's time to take a bathroom break and disappearing.

"Gosh, what an amazing dress," gushes Maeve, her eyes nearly popping out on stalks at Rose's impressive cleavage, which is dripping with diamonds.

"Yeah, you look great," I agree distractedly, taking another mouthful of champagne. My mind is lingering over Miss Steane's words.

"Rubbish! I'm invisible," sniffs Rose. "Nobody sees me any more. Waiters, taxi drivers, shop assistants . . ."

For the first time I notice she's holding a cigarette-holder, and taking a lipsticked puff, she blows a perfect smoke-ring that can only come with years of practice.

"Nobody pays any attention to an old woman like me."

Trust me, there'd be more chance of paying less attention to a tap-dancing monkey than Rose.

"No way," I protest. "You're always the centre of attention."

"Always," echoes Maeve and I catch a flash of wistfulness. Not for the first time do I wish I could share what Ernie confided in me. I have no idea what lies Spike told her, but she'd feel so much better if I could tell her the truth, if I could explain why she shouldn't believe him. But I can't. I promised Ernie.

"Men are fascinated by you," she's now saying.

"*Were*," corrects Rose, waving a gloved hand dismissively. It comes to rest on my shoulder. "I'll let you into a secret, my dear," she continues, leaning closer. "When I was a child I used to wish that I could be invisible. That I could go wherever I wanted, do whatever I wanted, and nobody would pay any attention to me. Oh, the freedom I believed it would bring —" She breaks off to laugh bitterly and take a glug of champagne, leaving behind a thick magenta smudge of lipstick on the rim of her glass. "Well, mark my words, I got my wish, Emily, dear. It came true. That it certainly did." Waving her glass, she gestures around the room, across the vista of people milling around, engaged in a flurry of introductions, conversations, flirtations. "When you get older nobody notices you any more." She turns to me, her heavily powdered face close to mine. "You simply disappear," she whispers, clicking her fingers. "*Poof.*"

I open my mouth to argue, but she silences me with a painted eyebrow.

"When I was your age I would walk into a room and everyone would notice me. Every single person would turn their head to look at me. Every man was captivated. Every woman fascinated." Taking a puff from her cigarette-holder, she turns from me to gaze back at the room. "I was quite something in those days." She drains her glass and waggles it in the air, wanting a refill. Being ignored, she sighs heavily. "Now I'm lucky if I can get the attention of a waiter."

"Ladies . . ."

We're both distracted by the sound of a voice. Being held aloft above the crowd are a pair of hands, two full champagne glasses in each, and as they approach I see their owner, Spike. At least I think it's Spike. He looks so different. Unlike the rest of the men, who are either in tuxedos or full Regency costume, he's wearing a black moleskin suit, black shirt and black tie, which make his hair look even blonder and his eyes even bluer. Reaching us, he begins passing around the drinks to appreciative noises. He reaches me last.

I haven't spoken to him since Ernie's shock revelations yesterday. He wasn't on the sightseeing tour earlier, and to be honest, I'd been relieved as I've got nothing to say to him. I'm still angry at how he treated Ernie, how he's upset Maeve, but I can't break Ernie's confidence. And so I've got to just pretend everything is normal and be civil. *Cold but civil, cold but civil, cold but* —

"Would you like some champagne?"

He offers me a glass, but I shake my head.

"No thanks, I'm not really drinking tonight," I reply stiffly.

"Fair enough." He nods, then adds appreciatively, "Nice dress."

"Nice suit." I nod back, my voice tight. Although his shirt is slightly creased and his jacket bears evidence of a hairy pet, he looks much more groomed than usual, though he still hasn't shaved and what was once stubble is now definitely a beard.

There's a pause and I'm painfully aware of Maeve, Rose and Miss Steane, all standing around with their drinks, watching with interest. Honestly, they'll be breaking out the popcorn next.

I fidget uncomfortably. Talk about a stilted conversation.

It limps along painfully.

"You did something to your hair," I remark. Usually it's an unruly mess with bits sticking out all over the place, but tonight he's gelled it into submission. In fact, it actually looks quite stylish. Well, apart from the tufty bit he's missed at the back, I notice.

"So did you," he replies, and gestures to the tiny little butterfly clips I used to clip up my hair.

I touch it self-consciously. "Um . . . yeah."

I got the idea from Stella. I've seen her wear her hair like this and it always looks really pretty and casual, with all these little tendrils hanging loosely down at the sides. Only have you *any* idea how hard it is to make tendrils look tendrily? And not as if you've been dragged through a hedge backwards and you have clumps of hair sticking out all over the place?

But of course I don't want Spike knowing I've made a really big effort, so I reply nonchalantly, "Yeah, I couldn't be bothered washing it."

And then immediately regret it. Shit. Why did I just say that? I now look like trailer trash. I cringe. Great. Britney in a balldress.

For a brief moment Spike seems taken aback, and then his mouth twitches with amusement. "Is that so?"

Annoyance rankles. I'm trying to be cold but civil, not make him laugh. "It's the shower," I snap. "The attachment thing on the tub doesn't work properly. I can't get the shampoo out. It goes hot, then cold, then scalding hot again . . ."

I can hear myself prattling like an idiot and I'm furious with myself. Just shut up, Emily. *Shut up.*

254

"You need to turn on the hot first, *then* add the cold," suggests Maeve helpfully from the sidelines.

I shoot her a look. "Thanks," I mutter, feeling my face flushing bright red. "I'll remember that."

"So, Spike, young man," begins Rose, puffing on her cigarette-holder, "I see Emily here doesn't have a partner. Do you dance?"

Now it's Rose's turn to be shot a look. Honestly, these women.

"Not if I can help it," he replies.

I feel a sting of rejection.

Huh! As if I want to dance with you. *Old-man-basher.*

"Me neither," I reply quickly. "Not in these shoes." And picking up my hem, I wave a three-inch stiletto at him for further evidence. Except I'm not used to wearing heels, and wobbling dangerously, I grip the nearest thing to balance.

The nearest thing being Spike's chest.

It all happens so quickly I don't have time to think about it. One minute there we all are, having a polite conversation of sorts. The next, my right hand is grasping at the thin cotton of his shirt and I'm squeezing his left pec as if it's a ripe melon.

"Oops, sorry," I stammer, taken aback even further by the realisation that instead of it being soft and squidgy, it's surprisingly firm. Mortified, I snatch my hand away and regain my balance. How embarrassing. "It's these heels," I fluster, trying to explain.

"You want to be careful with those, they look dangerous," he warns, throwing me a wicked look.

"I will," I say coldly, furious at myself.

There's a pause, and just to make things even more awkward, the quartet strikes up and people begin moving to the sides to make way for the couples lining up on the dance floor. Women on one side, men on the other.

"Oh, splendid," remarks Miss Steane, who this whole time has been a silent observer. Clapping her hands together in girlish excitement, she smiles broadly. "This is an original Regency dance, popular in Jane Austen's day. The perfect opportunity for ladies and gentlemen to get to know one another." She looks at Spike and me pointedly.

"How fun," murmurs Maeve, hugging her elbows even tighter and looking longingly at the dance floor.

"Not for us wallflowers," remarks Rose, taking a drag on her cigarette-holder.

Maeve's face drops and she buries it in her champagne flute.

Indignation stabs. Right now she could be dancing with Ernie if Spike hadn't deliberately put her off him by saying God knows what. I shoot him an icy look. *Love-wrecker.*

"Did Mr Darcy dance?" asks Spike, switching into journalist mode.

I feel my stomach flip. At the mention of his name, I try covertly glancing around the room. I wonder if he's going to turn up? Damn, it's hard to see in here, it's so frigging busy.

"Reluctantly," Miss Steane answers authoritatively. "He didn't like to, but he was a good dancer. One of the finest."

"Not like me, eh?" laughs Spike.

My attention snaps back. "No, he's not like you at all," I reply quickly.

*Too* quickly, it seems, as I'm thrown a few curious looks.

"You sound like you know him," says Spike amiably.

"In the book, I mean," I qualify, nervously. "Not in real life. Obviously."

Shit. Me and my big mouth.

There's a pause and I'm aware of glances flying around me. I can see Miss Steane studying me with a strange expression on her face, but just as the conversation is about to turn even more awkward, a short man wearing a kilt interrupts.

"Ahem, excuse me . . ."

We all turn to face him.

"Would you care to dance?" he asks, directing his question at me. He's sweating slightly and is all pink in the face. He blots his forehead with a tissue and smiles eagerly. He has bad teeth.

"Like I said. *Invisible*," mutters Rose into her champagne flute.

I hesitate. I'm caught between a rock and a hard place. The hard place being staying here, answering Spike's awkward questions about Mr Darcy. The rock being the guy in the skirt. I glance at Spike. He's still got that investigative journalist look on his face.

I go for the rock.

"That would be great." I smile, turning back to him. "Lead the way."

# CHAPTER
# TWENTY-TWO

Barry, my dancing partner, turns out to be a marketing manager for a large pharmaceutical firm in Aberdeen, and for the next twenty minutes he leads me around the dance floor while telling me all about a new breakthrough drug for indigestion. I ask him all the pertinent questions, smile at all the right junctures, and I say "wow" a lot. Men, I've learned from my many dates, like to hear the word "wow" a lot when they're talking about their career.

But what I really want to do is ask him what the new break-throughs are for boredom, as I'm about to die of it quite shortly.

". . . but the most exciting thing about this drug is how it works on your acid reflux. It neutralises the bile in a whole new way," he's saying brightly.

"Wow." I force a smile, but I'm not really listening. Instead, my mind is tied up with thoughts of Mr Darcy. As Barry launches into a monologue about an exciting new development in fungal creams, I glance wistfully around the ballroom for a dark, handsome figure, wondering when he's going to turn up.

That's "*when*", not "*if*". Because I'm confident I *am* going to see him again. After all, this isn't some flaky guy I've met in a bar; this is Mr Darcy.

"May I interrupt?"

My heart jumps into my mouth. Is that . . .? I twirl round excitedly.

And get a thud of disappointment.

*Spike.*

"Well, actually, me and this bonnie lassie were in the middle of a conversation —" begins Barry.

And usually I would have agreed. After all, the last thing I want to do is dance with Spike. Except that's not strictly true. I might hate Spike, but I hate the idea of spending any more time with Barry and his fungal remedies more. So, like a drowning man spotting a lifeboat and seeing his chance of being rescued about to pass him by, I cut in, "But now we've finished," and quickly untangle myself from Barry's grip.

"Thought so," smiles Spike.

I throw him a frosty look. So what if he's rescuing me? I still don't have to like him.

Meanwhile Barry hovers blinking in the middle of the dance floor, not quite sure what just happened. Guilt twinges. I feel mean abandoning him.

"I actually have some free samples in the car," he says hopefully.

On second thoughts I don't feel *that* mean.

"Wow. Maybe I could look at them later?" I smile and, without further hesitation, move quickly away and clamp my hand on Spike's shoulder. Sometimes in life you just *have* to put yourself first.

We start dancing — well, it's not really dancing, it's more holding your partner and shuffling around the room. The awkward, clumsy type that needs conversation and jokes and witty observations about the party, otherwise you end up feeling like a self-conscious idiot and all you can think about is the fact you've got your boobs pressed up against a man's chest, and the only thing between you is a flimsy bit of satin and a cotton shirt.

"I thought you didn't like dancing," I blurt, saying the first thing that comes into my head.

"I don't," he agrees, and, as if to prove it, promptly steps on my foot.

"Ouch," I yelp.

"Bloody hell, sorry," he apologises. "Are you OK?"

Crouching down to rub my sore toes, I glare up at him suspiciously. "Did you do that on purpose?"

"On purpose?" he repeats in astonishment. "Why would I stomp on your foot on purpose?"

"Because you think it's funny," I accuse, making a big fuss of rubbing my toes all the more, even though, to be honest, they're not *that* bruised.

"Trust me, there's nothing funny about having two left feet," he replies, reaching out his hand.

Ignoring it, I pull myself upright and wordlessly he slips his arm round my waist. We resume dancing. This time I make sure to keep my feet firmly away from his. Neither of us speaks. Deliberately refusing to catch his eye, I glance around the ballroom. All the other couples are laughing and chatting, emphasising the silence between us. Even so, I'm determined not to be the one to break it. Why should I? I don't want to talk to him anyway.

"Picture this. I'm eighteen. In a nightclub. And it's two a.m . . ."

Spike, however, appears to have no such problem breaking it. Seemingly oblivious to my stony expression, he starts telling his story. "You know what that means, don't you? *The last slow dance.*" With a woeful expression he shakes his head. "Nobody ever wanted to slow-dance with me."

I try picturing him as his eighteen-year-old self, with teenage acne and a floppy blond fringe, and find it surprisingly easy.

"I'm the worst dancer," he continues. "I have no rhythm, zero moves and was once compared to a pregnant duck."

He smiles sheepishly, but I refuse to smile back. I keep getting the image of Ernie, sitting across from me at the table, his eyes brimming with tears as he talked about Iris. If Spike thinks he can charm me with a few funny comments, he's got another thing coming.

"I bet even your dad is a better dancer than I am."

"Now *that* I find hard to believe," I reply sarcastically, prompted to say something about the image that has popped into my head of my father jigging around at a cousin's wedding. "My father thinks hip hop is a Dr Seuss children's book."

"Isn't it?" he asks innocently.

I'm amused, but quickly hide it.

"No, that's *Hop on Pop*," I snap, instead.

Spike's straight face crinkles into a mischievous grin and I realise this is his famous English sense of humour and he's joking with me. Again. I feel a wave of irritation.

*Followed by an idea.*

"In that case, how about I give you your first dance lesson?" I suggest over-brightly.

Well, if he wants to joke around, it would be churlish of me not to play along, wouldn't it?

Spike's smile fades and he looks at me doubtfully. "What? Here? Now? Are you being serious?"

"Totally." I nod. "I'm a good teacher. I studied dance until I was in freshman. Modern, classical, tap, ballet."

"Wow, I'm impressed," he says in admiration.

Me too, I tell myself. My entire dance knowledge comes from watching *Fame* as a kid and wearing leg warmers, but that's not going to stop me having some fun. Spike has been having a laugh at my expense for too long. It's about time he got a taste of his own medicine.

"You see, first you need to loosen up your hips . . ."

"Um . . ." Uncertainly, he begins bending one knee and then the other.

"No, you need to shake them more," I instruct.

God, I can be evil when I want to be.

"Like this?" Brow furrowed in concentration, Spike begins earnestly wiggling his hips.

"Exactly." I nod solemnly. "But you need to take your hands out of your pockets."

"Oh . . . right . . ." Obediently pulling out his hands, he holds them out to the sides as if they're a pair of ornaments he doesn't know where to put and continues jiggling his hips even faster.

Ha, ha, ha, he looks like such an idiot, I think, feeling a sense of satisfaction.

I stand back as if I'm a teacher observing their student. Like in *Fame*, I think to myself, wishing I was like Miss Grant and had a little cane so I could hit the floor and cry, "Fame costs, and here's where you start paying for it." God, I loved that show.

"Hey, I think I'm getting the hang of this," Spike is enthusing. Grabbing a strand of shiny pink tinsel from a nearby holly wreath, he tosses it flamboyantly round his shoulders like a feather boa. "Well, might as well get into the festive spirit, hey?" He grins.

I watch, dumbfounded. I thought he'd fall for the joke, but I never thought he'd fall for it *quite* so hard. Not only is Spike gyrating his pelvis like Elvis on acid, but he's concentrating so hard he's doing the white man's underbite. Sweating profusely he's causing such a commotion people are starting to stare. I stifle a laugh. He looks so ridiculous. That'll teach him to always make fun of other people.

Only the thing is, he doesn't even realise the joke's on him, I think, feeling a tad disappointed. Instead, he just seems to be obliviously enjoying himself, which wasn't the idea.

"It's actually really quite easy when you know," he's panting.

Just at that moment a waiter passes behind me with a tray of champagne and Spike pauses to reach out and take two glasses.

"All that dancing's thirsty work." He grins, passing me one. He begins mopping his brow with a napkin. "So tell me, when do I get to interview you?"

"Aren't you going to misquote me, anyway?" I say archly.

"Only if you want me to," he laughs, taking a swig of champagne.

"Well, I know how you like to play with the truth," I reply, thinking about Ernie.

But if he knows what I'm talking about I don't get a reaction.

"Journalists call it artistic licence," he corrects, smiling.

"How convenient," I remark. I can feel myself getting more and more annoyed. I know I'm not supposed to say anything, I know I promised, but it's proving impossible. He's just so *smug*.

"I'll have to take you to lunch and do it."

"Talking of lunch, I had lunch with Ernie yesterday."

I'm sorry, but I *tried* biting my tongue.

The effect of mentioning his name is immediate. Spike stiffens and his face suddenly whitens.

"He's such a sweet old man," I continue pointedly.

"Well, you know what they say about first impressions," he mutters gruffly.

I can't contain it any longer.

"Well, mine were right about you," I snap back, my anger bubbling up to the surface.

Spike looks shocked. "Meaning?" he demands.

But before I have a chance to answer, a phone suddenly starts ringing, its tone loud and warbling.

"Shit, that's me," he curses. "Hold this —" Shoving his glass of champagne at me before I can refuse, he begins frantically checking all his pockets, until finally he finds it.

Well, at least now he's going to turn the darned thing off.

He glances at the screen.

Doubt twinges. Surely he's not going to answer it. We're in the middle of an argument.

He answers it.

"Yeah, hi, it's Spike . . . yeah . . . Spike . . . Can you hear me?" He frowns into the earpiece, shaking head. "Christ, the reception in here's terrible."

Right, that's it. I've had enough. I turn to leave.

"Hold on. Don't move," he hisses, pressing his BlackBerry to his chest and flinging out his hand in a sort of "Stop" sign. "This is only going to take a moment."

I hesitate. I suppose this *could* be some kind of emergency. Something to do with work. A breaking story or something. I hold on.

He turns back to his BlackBerry. "Oh, c'mon, don't be angry at me, Sugarplum."

"*Sugarplum?*" I gasp.

He shoots me an apologetic look. "I know, I know . . ." he continues pacifying, then quickly covering the mouthpiece hisses, "It's Emmanuelle."

For a split second my chest tightens, but I quickly put it down to anger. I mean, honestly. I don't frigging believe it. Does he think I'm just going to stand here like a lemon, holding his drink, while he whispers sweet nothing to his girlfriend?

Actually, yes, Emily, seeing as you *are* standing here like a lemon, holding his drink, while he whispers sweet nothings to his girlfriend.

Argghhh.

Furious with myself and Spike, I shoot him one of my scariest looks, then turn on my stiletto heel and, still holding a glass of champagne in each hand, march off the dance floor. Anger is swishing around inside of me like hot lava and I'm in serious danger of erupting all over some poor, unsuspecting person.

At the far end of the dance floor French windows lead on to a large balcony, but no one is allowed out there. I make a beeline for them. They're not locked. And nobody's looking. I slip through and step outside.

# CHAPTER
# TWENTY-THREE

OK, now just chill out, Emily. Chill.

The balcony is empty, and apart from the muted strains of the string quarter playing softly inside, it's also still and quiet. It's a welcome relief after the noise and chatter of the ballroom. Pacing over to the edge, I place both champagne flutes on the balustrade, spread my arms far apart and, gripping the cold stone beneath my fingertips, stare out into the darkness.

I take a deep breath.

I'm fuming about Spike. I was right the first moment I ever laid eyes on him. He really is an asshole of the first degree. The way he behaved towards Ernie is despicable. As is telling lies about him to Maeve.

And as for shoving his drink in my face and answering his phone like that and then just *ignoring* me!

I exhale, watching my breath escaping in large white clouds. It's freezing out here and I'm shivering like crazy in my flimsy dress, but I'm too angry to go back inside. It's times like this I wish I smoked. That's what people always do in movies when they're pissed about something, isn't it? They drag heavily on cigarettes and somehow it seems to make them feel better.

A peal of laughter disturbs my thoughts and I look over to see a group of twenty-somethings who have snuck outside too. They're huddled together at the far end of the balcony, laughing at some joke or other. But what interests me most is one of them appears to be smoking.

Emboldened by my shitty mood and the numerous glasses of champagne I've consumed during the course of the evening, I walk over to them.

"Erm, excuse me . . ."

They turn towards me. Up close I see they're all really young, probably in their late teens and early twenties: three lanky guys in novelty ties, and two girls wearing matching feather boas who Stella would describe as "sturdy". They're drinking straight from a bottle of Moët, its gold tinfoil neck glinting mischievously in the moonlight as it's passed around them. I watch each of them taking a swig. They remind me of when I was in college.

"Hi." I greet them with a sort of little wave. "I was wondering if I could steal a cigarette." Then I add the classic non-smoker's line: "I'm supposed to have given up, but, hey . . ."

"Are you American?" slurs one of the guys who, with a floppy brown fringe and goofy smile, would be indistinguishable from the others, had it not been for his tie: black-and-white zebra print.

"Um, yeah." I nod, and then as if to prove it I flash them the smile that cost my parents twenty thousand dollars in orthodontist's fees.

"And you wanna bum a fag?" grins one of the other guys whose tie appears to be made from a Union Jack flag.

Now obviously here in the UK this must mean something *very* different than it does back in the States. "Um . . ." I falter, but I'm saved from answering as all the boys burst into hysterical laughter, slapping their knees and giggling hilariously.

I'm a bit taken aback. Wow, talk about high-spirited.

"Shut up, Henry," scolds one of the girls, punching him on the shoulder. She looks at me and smiles. "Ignore him, he's an idiot," she confides, taking a long drag of her roll-up cigarette. I get a pungent whiff of something and it's not tobacco.

And that's not a roll-up, I suddenly realise. It's a joint.

Oh, God, I'm such a dope, I think, no pun intended. Cringing inwardly, I kick myself. No wonder they're all giggling their asses off out here. They're all completely stoned.

"Yeah, sorry, no offence meant," chimes in Henry, throwing me a sheepish grin and taking a generous swig from the champagne bottle.

"Want some?" The girl holds out the joint to me.

Now considering the last time I smoked pot was at college and I threw up all over the back seat of Johnny Rosenbaum's new VW Rabbit (embarrassing enough in itself, but made worse by the fact both Johnny and I were lying spreadeagled on it having sex), I should probably say no.

Saying that, it would be kind of fun to get high, wouldn't it?

"Thanks, don't mind if I do." I smile, reaching out and taking it from her.

Plus, like I said, I need to chill out.

Have you ever noticed how beautiful the stars are? They're all twinkly and glittery, like millions of little diamonds on a big, big, big, *big* cushion of black velvet . . . a million celestial engagement rings stretching away into infinity . . . for ever and ever and ever . . . Wow, it's so romantic . . .

The group have gone back inside and I'm resting my elbows on the balustrade staring up at the sky. I can't remember how long I've been here — ten minutes, half an hour maybe, who cares? It's as if everything has stopped, and I'm in this big, warm, fuzzy bubble that's sort of floating. I'm not even cold any more. All I can think about is the sky, this big, beautiful black sky. I swear I don't remember it ever being so amazing. I'm totally mesmerised . . .

I'm also, of course, as high as a frigging kite.

Smiling contentedly at nothing in particular, I take a sip of champagne. That joint really hit the spot. I don't feel sick or anything, just totally chilled — or *stoned*, depending how you want to look at it — in which case, maybe now's the time to go back inside and rejoin the party. If I bump into Spike, who cares? It's not as if I have to talk to him. I'll just be totally cool and ignore him, like he did to me. Not that I'm being *petty* or anything. Like I said, I'm totally chilled now. And draining the rest of the glass, I pick up the second glass and turn to walk back inside.

And bump slap bang into Mr Darcy.

"Shit." Still clutching the two glasses, I bounce off him, spilling champagne.

Startled, he looks at me. "Emily?"

"Jeez, sorry, I had my hands full and I didn't see you there and . . ." I'm babbling. Meanwhile Mr Darcy is here. On the balcony. *Right in front of me.*

Holy shit.

I go from chilled to Code Red in less than a second.

". . . um . . . *hi*," I manage to croak, trying to regain my composure while my stomach thinks it's in the Cirque du Soleil and starts doing all *kinds* of acrobatics.

"Good evening," he replies, bowing his head politely.

He looks up, and as we both take each other in I can feel the whole world around me melting away into the cold evening air.

"Am I intruding?"

I snap back to see him frowning at the two champagne flutes in my hands.

"Er, no . . . no, not at all," I mumble, looking for somewhere to put them. Spotting a small table over by a pillar, I hurry over and plonk both glasses down. "I was just a bit, er, thirsty," I say lightly, turning round to face him.

Only I turn round a bit too quickly and everything starts spinning. Oh, dear. I get a flashback of me projectile-vomiting on the back of that VW Rabbit and feel a stabbing terror. No. Please, God. No. Anything

271

but that. I grab on to the balustrade to steady myself and look up to see Mr Darcy striding towards me.

Everything freezes.

Men these days don't stride. They shuffle and trail like Spike, hands slung low in their pockets, shoulders hunched, feet dragging. But not Mr Darcy. I'm staring at him now and it's like watching one of those slow-motion movie sequences. With his chest out, chin up, jaw set determinedly. If you had to look up "dashing" in the dictionary, I swear you'd see a picture of Mr Darcy.

Involuntarily my body gives a little shudder of pleasure. And while you've got that dictionary out, look up "smitten" and you'll see a picture of me.

He pauses a few feet away and looks at me intently. Unlike many of my dates who have no concept of personal space, Mr Darcy keeps a respectful distance.

"I've been looking for you," he replies, his face serious.

"You have?" I squeak.

OK, so I'm excited to see him again, but sounding like I just inhaled a helium balloon is neither cool *nor* sexy. And I'm aiming for both.

I clear my throat. "You have?" I say it again, forcing my voice deeper.

"I wanted to tell you I very much enjoyed your company last night."

"Me too." I nod, and feel myself blushing.

God, talk about the understatement of the year.

I wait for him to say something else, but he doesn't, and what began as a pause is now being drawn out like

272

a long breath and I'm thinking I should say something, but my mind has just gone completely blank, like a floppy disk wiped clean, and I'm just staring at him and wondering how long before we do it.

*Emily Albright! What did you just say?*

I feel a slap of recrimination. Oh, God, I'd forgotten, but *now* I remember why I came to end up in the back of the VW Rabbit. I always get unbelievably horny when I'm stoned.

"So, how is the ball?"

Finally he speaks.

"Oh . . . you know," I say vaguely, trying to drag my mind away from my raging libido.

"Have you danced?" he continues.

I think about Barry and Spike. "I don't know if you'd actually call it *dancing*." I smile ruefully.

But Mr Darcy doesn't smile; instead, his expression remains serious. "I was afraid that because I had arrived so late I was going to have to steal you away from another."

I have a flashback of Spike on his BlackBerry. *Steal me away?* Spike wouldn't have noticed if I'd been tied up and kidnapped right under his nose. "Don't worry. I'm all yours," I joke.

Mr Darcy looks slightly taken aback. "You are?" he replies, and I realise he's taken me literally.

"Oh, no, it's a saying," I say quickly. "Sort of like a joke," I try explaining.

"I see," nods Mr Darcy, although I'm not sure he does really, but I'm no longer thinking about it, as his eyes are sweeping over me like searchlights and my heartbeat is quickening. Wow. I've gone from being ignored to being the focus of someone's full attention. It's as if he can't take his eyes off me. Which is incredibly flattering. I'm just not used to it.

*But you can get used to it, Emily.*

We both fall silent again. With no drink to sip, I fiddle with the tendrils of my hair. "Well, this is nice," I say after a moment.

*Nice?* Did I just say, *nice?*

"Indeed," nods Mr Darcy and stares at me gravely.

The conversation stalls again, and not knowing what to say, I peer down into the inky darkness. It's New Year's Eve and in the distance I can see fairylights glittering, someone's Christmas tree in a faraway bay window, a party taking place in a house across the communal gardens. I drum my fingers against the balcony. Gosh, it's so quiet. I can actually hear myself breathing.

I rummage around in my mind for something to say that doesn't involve some quip. I know I won't be able to joke around with Mr Darcy like I did with Spike, which might bother some people, but I'm totally fine with that. In fact, the more I think about it, the more I think a good sense of humour is totally overrated. I want a real man, not some idiot, I decide, picturing Spike doing the funky chicken on the dance floor.

I stifle a smile at the memory. OK, so I admit it was very funny, but if I wanted to date someone funny I'd go out with a comedian, I tell myself firmly.

"I love this time of year, don't you?" I blurt finally, breaking the silence.

Wow, I never thought I'd be so pleased to hear the sound of my own voice. In books it always sounds so profound and romantic when the characters spend hours staring into each other's eyes without speaking. In reality, however, you'd have to be a Benedictine monk.

"It's bearable," he replies shortly. "If you like silliness and fripperies."

"Oh," I say, feeling shot down. "Yes, I suppose it is a bit silly," I agree, that same image of Spike twirling round with his tinsel feather boa springing to mind. "But being silly can be kind of fun sometimes."

Mr Darcy frowns as if he's never heard of the concept. "And are you having fun now?"

"Of course," I reply over-brightly.

Well, I wouldn't call it fun *exactly*, but that's hardly surprising. I'm too nervous. And anyway, like I said, I'm not here to have fun, I think, sneaking a peak at Mr Darcy and feeling a swell of lust and pheromones at all that repressed passion I know is bubbling under moody arrogance. In fact, I could have sworn I just caught him glancing at my cleavage.

I send up a silent thank you to Stella, thanking her for sending me this gorgeous dress. For once I feel sexy, instead of frumpy.

"Would you like my coat?" he offers.

See. As well as being sex-on-legs he's even Mr Chivalrous. Not like abandon-you-on-the-dance-floor Spike.

"Oh, no, thanks. I'm not cold." I smile, gesturing flirtily to my un-goosepimply shoulders on to which I've rubbed this glittery bronze body cream.

"I insist," he says, draping it round my shoulders.

"No, honestly —" I protest, but it's too late, I'm already being swamped in a black frock coat. I feel a twinge of disappointment. It covers up every inch of shimmery shoulder and completely hides my sexy sequinned spaghetti straps.

"It's to protect your modesty," he explains. "Your dress is very revealing."

"It is?" I say with surprise, "Oh, OK, thanks."

Of course! I hadn't thought of that. I'm so used to living in a world of J-Lo and Madonna and dresses slashed to the navel that my dress doesn't seem revealing at all. But I guess it's very different for Mr Darcy: he's used to women being covered up. If we were to go out with each other I'd probably have to be much more demure. Which is a bit of a shame, as I do have some nice little tops I wear in the summer.

"So how are you liking your stay in Bath?" he asks, moving closer.

My chest tightens. "Oh, it's so beautiful here. All the buildings and the architecture and the river," I gabble nervously.

On second thoughts, I'm not *that* fussed about those summer tops. I like turtle necks. And things that button up to the chin. Yep. I *lurve* things that button up to the chin. In fact, I'll just do up this collar right now.

"Ah, yes, the River Avon." He nods, and I feel his warm breath against my cheek.

Mid-buttoning, my fingers seem to get all tangled up.

And did my knees just wobble?

"I have a surprise for you."

276

"You do?" My heart gives a little hiccup. I *love* surprises. What can it be?

"Allow me." He holds out his arm for me to take.

I remember John, the architect, letting the door swing in my face a few weeks ago. How I walked home alone in the snow, freezing my ass off and dreaming of meeting a man like Mr Darcy.

And now look at me, I marvel, glancing up at the real thing and hitting "delete" on the memory button of bad dates and erasing every last one of them. *Delete, delete, delete.*

"Why, thank you, sir," I say, my mouth twisting into a smile.

I link my arm through his and for a moment he studies my face, his dark eyes drinking me in. Then abruptly his mouth breaks into a smile. "Shall we?"

God, he's just so *masterful*.

And, yes, I know it's shockingly unfeminist of me to find that incredibly sexy.

A cage of butterflies releases in my stomach and I nod happily.

So go ahead: shoot me.

# CHAPTER
# TWENTY-FOUR

We walk arm in arm. Mr Darcy leads me to the far side of the balcony, down a flight of steps and on to a small path that winds its way through the gardens. Everything is so still and quiet. Just the sound of footsteps tapping rhythmically against the paving stones.

After a few minutes we turn a corner. Ahead of me is a huddle of outbuildings and as we near them Mr Darcy makes a beeline for the one on the far left. My mind goes into overdrive. Is this the surprise? Is there something in there? Is he going to give me a present? The door swings open and I get a whiff of hay.

My mind comes to a screeching halt. Holy shit. It's a hay barn. And *everyone* knows what happens in hay barns, don't they? I feel an almighty tremor in my chest. So this is the surprise.

*He's going to seduce me.*

Suddenly every bodice-ripper I've read comes flashing back to me in all their breathless urgency. He's brought me here so he can roll around in the hay with me. To have his wicked way. To make mad, passionate love with the stars twinkling through the gaps of the old timbered roof and his warm, muscular body pressed up against mine . . .

I want to feel offended that he thinks I'm going to put out on the first date, but I can't. I'm *way* too excited.

Well, I'm hardly an innocent virgin, now, am I? Despite what my mother likes to think. In fact, I can't think of anything I'd like to do more right now than roll around in the hay with Mr Darcy.

And it has been a while, I think, eyeing him lustfully.

He leads me inside. Only it's not a barn. It's a stable. I feel a twinge of uncertainty. Followed by a strong whiff of something that smells suspiciously like —

*Horse shit.*

I feel a crash of disappointment. Of course. This is Mr Darcy. He's a gentleman. He would never try and have his wicked way.

Damn. Damn. *Damn.*

"Meet Thunder," announces Mr Darcy, opening the stall to reveal the back end of a big black horse, who, right at that moment, decides to lift up his tale and dump a huge dollop all over the floor.

Watching it pile up, my sexual fantasies of rolling around in the hay suddenly disappear. Funny that.

"Um . . . hello," I say lamely, quickly stepping backwards before my gold stilettos get sprayed in excrement and getting my spiked heel caught. "Whoah," I cry, quickly steadying myself. Maybe I overdid it a bit with the champagne-and-marijuana combo.

"Don't worry, there's no need to be afraid, Emily," continues Mr Darcy, misinterpreting my stoned lurch with a cry of fear. "This isn't your horse."

He's obviously unaware of my inebriation, I realise thankfully. Well, why would he be? I don't remember any of the ladies getting stoned in *Pride and Prejudice*. And they were always going to parties.

Hang on a minute. Rewind that again.

*Your* horse?

I turn to say something, but Mr Darcy is already striding over to a neighbouring stall, flicking open the dead bolt and opening the door to reveal the most beautiful thoroughbred I've ever seen.

Pure white, her powerful, muscular flanks seem to be almost glistening in the light. I'm used to the kind of horses you get in Central Park: old piebald faithfuls who dutifully pull the carriages of tourists and pose for photographs. But this is a different breed of animal. Her whole body is quivering with pent-up energy, like a racehorse just before the starting gun, and her ears flick back as she hears us.

Suddenly she smashes her hoof against the ground, the metal horseshoe making a loud noise against the stone flags. I jump slightly. Jesus, talk about frisky. You'd have to be a brave person to ride her, I decide, noticing she's tacked up with shiny stirrups and a polished leather saddle.

"You're riding Lightning," says Mr Darcy, as if reading my thoughts.

Me. Riding. Lightning.

The words string out in front of me in little cartoon bubbles, but as yet I seem to be having difficulty in joining them up. He obviously can't be suggesting what I think he's suggesting. I'm wearing a balldress and three-inch heels. I look from Mr Darcy to the horse and back again.

Oh, I get it. He's fooling around. Ha, ha, very funny.

"Right, yeah, absolutely." I grin, playing along with the joke. But his face is serious and then it hits me. *Mr Darcy doesn't joke, remember?*

As he takes Lightning's reins and walks her calmly out of the stall, her ribcage rising and falling, her thick white tail swishing, I can't help but feel a snap of annoyance. I can't believe he hasn't even *asked* me if I want to go horseriding! I mean, don't *I* get a say in this? I'll freeze to death in this outfit.

"Never having been to America, I do not know your customs and traditions on such occasions as these," he's saying gravely. "However, I have taken the liberty of arranging a moonlight ride for us both."

Saying that, as Mr Darcy comes to a halt in front of me, in his white shirt and tight breeches and holding the reins of a beautiful thoroughbred horse, I'm suddenly overcome by the vision before me. It's so absurdly romantic I feel dizzy.

Usually it's tickets to the movies and a carton of popcorn if I'm lucky, but *this*. It's the stuff of fantasies. Of the novels that line the shelves of McKenzie's bookstore. This kind of stuff doesn't happen to me: Emily Albright from upstate New York.

The only thing I ever get to ride these days is the subway into work.

"I trust it meets with your approval."

"Um . . . yes . . . of course," I stammer, brushing any annoyance I may have felt quickly aside. Well, come on, Emily — you can hardly stay mad at him, can you?

"Good," replies Mr Darcy with satisfaction, and it strikes me that he never really doubted that his suggestion would be met with approval. In fact, I've never seen Mr Darcy be anything but confident, I realise, watching him take Thunder by the reins and assuredly lead both horses out of the stable.

But that's what makes him so darn attractive, I tell myself firmly. A sensitive, modern-day man who's into making joint decisions over the new kitchen blinds and asking your opinion over whose turn it is to load the dishwasher might make the better boyfriend. But it's hardly the stuff of sexual fantasies, now, is it?

Anticipation buzzes and I follow him out of the stables. "How did you manage to arrange all this?" I ask, wrapping myself tightly up in his coat.

"A gentleman never gives away his secrets." He smiles enigmatically.

And to think I've been making do with going Dutch at pizza restaurants, watching bad foreign art movies and fighting off drunken advances on first dates my whole life.

"I thought we could ride up to Sham Castle."

My stomach flips. Oh, wow, I read about Sham Castle this morning in one of the guidebooks.

282

"Awesome," I enthuse, trying to keep my excitement under wraps and completely failing. Well, do you blame me? A horse-back ride. With Mr Darcy. To a castle. *Please*.

Buzzing, I watch Mr Darcy loosely tying Thunder to a gatepost. Then, still holding Lightning's reins, he turns to me. "I presume you've ridden before."

"Oh, yeah, loads," I enthuse.

"Splendid. In that case, what are we waiting for?"

# CHAPTER
# TWENTY-FIVE

OK, perhaps *loads* is a slight fib.

I used to have lessons when I was younger, but I gave them up when my affections suddenly switched from Prancer the pony to Bruce in seventh grade. Which means I was . . . Wow, was I only fourteen?

Doubt prickles, but I quickly dismiss it. That isn't *that* long ago. OK, so it's fifteen years, and I know that's technically more than half my life, but time speeds up when you get older so you can't count it like that. And anyway, I'm sure it's just like riding a bicycle. It will all come flooding back to me just as soon as I get back in the saddle.

"Would you like me to help you mount?" Mr Darcy politely holds out his hand.

"Thanks, but I'm fine. I can manage," I reply, smiling confidently.

Obviously he's not used to modern-day women doing things for themselves, I think, feeling all capable and independent as I turn to Lightning. Only up close, she seems much bigger than before. And for some strange reason those stirrups seem much shorter than I remember. My eyes travel upwards. Wow, you really need to be flexible to get your leg up there, don't you? I feel a wobble of doubt, but I quickly brush it away.

I do yoga. No problem.

Throwing back my shoulders, I take a deep breath, hitch up my dress and with one seamless move hoist my stiletto into the stirrup.

"Urrrgggghhhh."

Grunting loudly, I pull myself up on to the saddle and swing my other leg across. Except I hadn't realised just how that joint has affected my balance. With one leg in the air, the other foot suddenly twirls round in the stirrup, twisting my ankle. A sharp pain shoots up my leg and for a moment it's touch and go as I clutch on to Lightning's mane, legs akimbo, butt in the air. Fortunately, however, I think I do a really good job of regaining it and before you know it I've slid my other foot over and am sitting upright.

There. Easy peasy.

Smiling triumphantly, I glance over at Mr Darcy. He looks stunned. I feel a beat of pride. It's as I thought. He's obviously really impressed. In fact, he's almost speechless.

"Do . . . um . . . women not ride side-saddle in America?" he enquires, stumbling over his words.

"Oh, no, we ride Western-style like the men," I say. Smiling modestly, I try getting comfy in my saddle which I suddenly realise isn't like the ones back home. That's funny, I can feel a draught.

I glance down and notice my dress has ridden up and is now sort of concertinaed round the tops of my legs in bunches of chocolate satin. At the same time I realise Mr Darcy is staring agog at my naked thighs.

Oops. Tipsily I tug down the hem. "Ready," I trill happily, looping my fingers round the reins, just like I remembered. See, I knew it. It's all coming back to me.

"Um . . . splendid," he stammers. Gosh, what's wrong with him? He seems a bit dazed. I wonder if he had a few drinks too beforehand?

But if he did, it hasn't affected his balance, I notice, as he unties Thunder and mounts him with the slick ease of a professional rider.

"This way," he's saying now and, clicking his tongue, he jabs his boots into his horse's flanks and trots ahead.

I do exactly the same and feel a tingle of excitement as Lightning dutifully follows. It's been a while since I've ridden, but like I said, it's just like riding a bike. Only much more romantic.

After a few minutes we go through a gate (note to Mr Hair Plugs: Mr Darcy dismounts to open it for me) and out into open countryside. Wow, isn't this great? Smiling happily to myself, I sneak a sideways peek at Mr Darcy, who's riding alongside me. Erect in his saddle, his strong shoulders thrown back, his jaw clenched, his eyes looking directly ahead, he might as well have "I am the sexiest man you have ever seen" written on his forehead. I feel an ache in my groin.

And no, it's got *nothing* to do with the hard leather saddle.

"The castle is over on that hill," he announces, gesturing ahead of us. "You won't be able to see it yet, as it's hidden by the woods."

286

Woods? A castle? God, it's like something out of a fairytale.

"Oh, great," I reply, trying to keep my voice level, as if this kind of thing happens to me every day in New York.

We pause for a moment and then Mr Darcy breaks into a brisk trot. Lightning follows suit without me having to do a thing. I feel a glow of satisfaction. Jigging up and down, I grip harder on to the reins. This really is amazing. I'd forgotten just what a buzz you get from riding.

Mr Darcy picks up the pace. His white shirt billows out behind him, and I wipe my eyes to see better. They're beginning to water a bit now because of the wind, but luckily I've used waterproof mascara. I take a deep lungful of cold night air, enjoying the sensation of it rushing through my nasal passages. Wow, this really clears your head, doesn't it? Before, I was feeling a bit woolly, but now I feel so clear and focused and —

A dew drop from my nose falls on my sleeve.

Oh. Euggh.

I sniff hard and refocus. It's so great being in the great outdoors. Maybe I should think about quitting the city and moving to the country. It can't be good for your health, all that pollution and stress and —

Gosh, I'm really quite sniffly. I sniff harder, but it's no good. I need a tissue to blow it. I wonder if Mr Darcy has one . . . I feel in his pockets. But nothing. Hmmm. The wind is blowing harder now and my nose is . . . well, running would be one way of describing it, *streaming* would be another. Shit. And I've got nothing to wipe it on. Unless . . . a thought stirs. I've got Mr Darcy's silk scarf in my little sequinned purse.

Immediately I catch myself.

Honestly, what am I thinking? I can't go and blow my snotty nose on that, can I? It's got that lovely sexy cologne smell of his. It's a keepsake.

And yet my nose seems to have suddenly turned into what my grandmother used to call the "candle factory". And I'm on this big full-on romantic date. I can't very well get to the castle with two big snotty candles hanging from my nostrils, now, can I?

I tug out the slip of white silk and blow hard. My nose makes a noise like a trumpet, but fortunately the wind's blowing the other way so Mr Darcy doesn't hear.

"Isn't this incredible?" hollers Mr Darcy from ahead.

"Amazing," I yell back, quickly scrunching up the snotty scarf and shoving it back in my purse. Never mind. I'll just have to wash it later.

We're cantering across the fields now, up towards the woods, and as the ground rushes beneath me I experience a whoosh of freedom. We pick up even more speed and suddenly, before I know it, Lightning has broken effortlessly into a gallop. Rushing through the darkness, hooves thundering, I feel as if I'm flying.

I feel alive. Euphoric. Exhilarated.

*In agony.*

Ouch! I wince in pain as I jig up and down in the saddle. Whose bright idea was it to go bra-less? My boobs are bouncing around like a couple of eager puppies here! Holding the reins with one hand, I try cradling them in the crook of my arm. Trust me, I'm not a big girl by any means, but every woman needs more support than sequinned spaghetti straps.

Squashing them into my arm, I grimace at every thudding hoof. I don't remember it being like this for Julia Roberts in *Runaway Bride*. Galloping across fields with the wind in your hair and a floaty dress always looks so fab in movies — it's one of those big, romantic fantasies — and yet here I am, getting chafed nipples, I think despairingly.

Thankfully, after a few moments we reach the woods and Mr Darcy slows down as we begin weaving our way through the trees. Relieved, I do the same. Well, skin only has so much elasticity. Any more of that and my pert little B cups will end up looking like something out of *National Geographic*, I tell myself, letting go of my breasts and quickly smoothing down my tangled hair, which has come undone in the wind.

"There it is."

I pause from unbuttoning Darcy's coat in an attempt to appear a bit sexier and look up. Before me is the castle. It's so amazing I'm rendered speechless.

"It was commissioned by Ralph Allen to improve the view of his townhouse, and from a distance it appears to be the genuine article. However, it is in fact merely an impressive façade," he continues, as we come to a standstill.

"It's like a prop from a movie," I gasp, before I realise what I'm saying.

"A what?"

"Oh, nothing," I say, quickly brushing it aside. I don't want to spoil the mood by getting bogged down in explanation, and instead we remain quietly side by side on our horses, both gazing up at the "impressive façade."

Well, actually, I tell a lie. I'm peeking at him.

"Still rather magnificent, though, don't you think?" he says after a moment, his eyes never leaving the castle. Not that he should be looking at me, I'm just saying.

"Yeah," I manage quietly. "Yeah, it is."

But I'd still much rather be gazing at you, I think, getting that jittery feeling again as it registers that we're here, alone, just the two of us . . . and what with the moonlight, it's all very seductive. My eyes trace the sharp silhouette of his cheekbone, the proud arch of his nose, his strong, confident mouth —

He turns to look at me. His dark eyes lock with mine and I feel another spasm in my groin.

Oh, God, *this is it*. This is the part where he kisses me.

My heart is hammering so loudly in my chest I'm surprised he can't hear it, and as he leans towards me I close my eyes in delicious anticipation. I can feel his warm breath close against my neck. Smell his cologne. Feel his lips . . .

"O, Rose, thou art sick!"

I jolt slightly, startled by Mr Darcy's voice in my ear.

"The invisible worm . . ."

*Invisible worm?* I feel a jerk of confusion. *What on earth's he going on about?*

290

"... That flies in the night, In the howling storm ..."

Oh, *now* I get it, I realise, recognising the words from the time I reorganised the poetry section at McKenzie's: it's a poem by William Blake.

Furtively I open one eye, just a tiny little bit, and sneak a peek at Mr Darcy. He's right there, only inches away, staring at me intensely.

Drawing a deep breath, he continues: "... Has found out thy bed, Of crimson joy ..."

He's *reciting poetry* to me.

Oh my God, he's so passionate I don't know where to look! Heroes are always doing this in novels, but I've never heard of it happening in real life before. It's incredible.

Except . . .

I don't want to sound ungrateful. What woman wouldn't want Mr Darcy reciting poetry to them, in that gorgeous cut-glass accent of his, beside a moonlit castle, on New Year's Eve?

"... And his dark secret love ..."

But to be honest, I'd rather have that kiss.

An icy chill whips off the turrets and I shiver. Now we've stopped riding, I'm fast realising just how cold it is. I try wiggling my toes, but they're so numb I can't feel them any more. Unlike the rest of me. My whole body is aching. My butt, my boobs, my ankle. As if on cue, it twinges. No doubt by tomorrow that's going to be black and blue and the size of a cantaloupe.

"... Does thy life destroy," finishes Mr Darcy with a dramatic flourish.

God, it's all a bit heavy isn't it?

Irritation bites. I've come all the way out here, on a horse, in the freezing cold, and I don't even get one little kiss? So what am I supposed to do now? Applaud? Swoon? Or —

My thoughts are silenced as Mr Darcy suddenly pulls me close.

Oh, OK. I take it back. So *that's* what happens now.

All my life I've dreamed about being kissed by Mr Darcy, and now it's actually coming true . . . Closing my eyes, I lift my face to his expectantly. Everything seems to slow down. I angle my body against his, but the satin of my dress is slippery in the saddle, and as his lips brush against mine I have to dig my heels against Lightning's ribcage to keep my balance.

Oh, my God. So this is it. The kiss. *Finally.*

"*Arggghhhhh!*" I shriek.

Suddenly, without warning, Lightning lets out a loud whinny and rears up on her back legs.

"*Arggghhhh.*"

Instead of a passionate embrace, I'm now being thrown backwards into the air. Clutching at the reins, I hang on for dear life as Mr Darcy's coat slips from my shoulders.

Holy shit!

That moment in the air feels like for ever until — *thwack* — all four hooves hit the floor and I'm propelled forwards again. Relief floods my body. *Oh, thank God, thank God, thank —*

It lasts all of about two seconds.

Then she bolts.

292

"Hold on!" shouts Mr Darcy.

"*Argghhhh . . .*"

That's all I can do. Shriek at the top of my lungs in sheer terror.

"Whoah, easy girl." Masterfully he swings his horse round and tries to grab the reins, but Lightning rears up again, knocking him off his horse with sheer brute force.

"My Darcy," I scream with horror as he crashes on to the muddy ground.

"Emily," he gasps, winded by the fall.

I glance back. I can hear him shouting something else, but as Lightning charges off his voice is whipped away by the wind and disappears into the night.

"Help," I scream at the top of my lungs as we plunge deep into the woods and I'm thrown around in the saddle. "Help," I yell again. But it's hopeless. There's no Mr Darcy to rescue me.

And now we're galloping out of the woods and across pitch-black fields. The moon seems to have disappeared behind a cloud and I can't see a thing, just dark shapes in the distance. Dark, scary shapes that loom out at me like monsters. My stomach jumps into my chest. Jesus! What's that over there? Brushing underneath branches of trees, I crouch down low, but it's too late.

*Whack*.

I feel a sharp blow to my forehead. Then it all goes black.

# CHAPTER
# TWENTY-SIX

Where am I?

I wake up lying face down. Slowly I roll my head to the side. It thuds dully. Ugghh. Next I curl my fingertips into the palms of my hands, feeling crisp, starched cotton beneath them. I'm in a bed. I peel open my eyes a crack. My bed.

I experience a lurch of relief, swiftly followed by confusion. How did I get here? I don't remember going to bed. In fact, I don't remember anything since — I feel a slight panic — *I can't remember*.

I try focusing, but my head doesn't seem to want to work properly. Not the memory bit, anyway. Befuddled, I peer blearily through my eyelashes. My room is still in darkness but for a lamp casting a glow in the far corner.

For a few seconds I don't move. I just lie here, doing nothing but breathing in and breathing out, cocooned in a snug of blankets and praying for this fog of sleep and amnesia to lift. And now, slowly, my eyes are starting to adjust. Fuzzy shapes are appearing out of the Anaglypta shadows and coming into focus: in the corner, the nylon jaws of my suitcase lie wide open, and there are items of clothing strewn everywhere —

294

T-shirts, jeans, sweaters — a swathe of chocolate satin slung across the full-length mirror.

Of course. The dress. The New Year's Eve ball. It's all coming back to me now. Dancing with Spike, smoking that joint, bumping into Mr Darcy —

*Mr Darcy.*

Tentatively I roll my head across the pillow to the other side. My eyes follow like those in a haunted-house painting. My hangover starts thumping like a bongo drum. Slowly, slowly, *slow-lee* . . .

The pillow next to me is empty.

I stare distrustfully at it for a moment, almost expecting Mr Darcy's dark head to materialise on the paisley cotton, then indignantly shove the thought aside. Of course I didn't sleep with him! I'm not that kind of girl, and he's not that kind of guy.

*More's the pity*, whispers the lustful little voice inside me.

Ignoring it, I try recollecting the evening's events. We were talking on the balcony, I remember that, and how sexy he looked, yup, I *definitely* remember that bit and — Ouch — my butt gives a painful twinge — of course, we went horseriding and my horse bolted and then . . .

Blank.

"You're awake."

A voice startles me and I take a sharp breath as I see a figure looming over me.

A face coming into close-up.

*Spike.*

Make that two Spikes.

Woozily I look up at him and try focusing. For a horrible moment there's not just one selfish lying pig of a journalist, there's another selfish lying pig of a journalist until, squinting hard, both blurry images merge into one.

"What time is it?" I mumble groggily.

He glances at his watch. "Nearly four a.m."

I try to sit up, but he stops me with a wet flannel.

"No, you need to lie still."

"Huh?" I groan, then realising my head is killing me, I flop back down on to the pillow.

"You've got a bit of a nasty bump on your head, but don't worry, you're going to be OK," he soothes, pressing the cold flannel to my forehead.

Tentatively I touch my forehead. "Ouch," I whimper, flinching as my fingertips brush against a lump the size of an egg. "What happened?"

"I don't know exactly. I went looking for you — after the phone call," he adds, looking sheepish. "When I found you, you'd completely passed out."

"Where did you find me?" I murmur, still desperately trying to piece everything together.

"Near the stables."

"Oh . . ."

My mind starts whirring. I must have hit my head on something and blacked out, and yet somehow managed to stay in the saddle until Lightning found her way back to the stables . . . Or maybe I rode back to the stables but I just can't remember because I fell off as I was dismounting and hit my head on the floor and it's made me lose my memory . . . Or maybe —

"I bumped into some kids when I was looking for you." Spike interrupts my confused cerebral ramblings. "They said they'd last seen you smoking a joint with them."

"Oh . . . right, yeah."

Now *that* might explain my amnesia.

"And drinking two glasses of champagne."

*That* as well.

"One of them was yours," I point out weakly.

Spike sighs and scratches self-consciously at his burgeoning beard. I notice he's taken off his jacket and tie, undone his collar and rolled up his sleeves to reveal two thick, hairy forearms, one of which is now disappearing into the neck of his shirt. He starts awkwardly scratching his collarbone. He's obviously feeling guilty about the whole thing. Either that or he's got fleas.

"Look, I'm sorry," he begins self-consciously. "I feel somehow responsible — that's why I offered to watch you — make sure you were OK. Someone had to stay. You were pretty out of it."

"Thanks," I say stiffly. Jesus, how embarrassing. Why did it have to be Spike who found me? Talk about bad luck. He must be crowing right now. "But I'm fine now, so you can go," I add, and pull up the bedcovers in a "closed for business" kind of metaphor. Which is when I suddenly realise that I'm not wearing my pyjamas. In fact, I am not wearing anything.

I am totally butt naked.

Mortified, I sharply tug the eiderdown even tighter to my chest. I don't even want to *think* about who took off my clothes. "If you could close the door behind you," I prompt.

Spike looks at me as if he's going to say something, but then picks up his jacket and tie and snatches at the door.

He opens it, hisses, "Fuck," then slams it shut again. I jump.

He turns to me, his face flushed, his jaw set hard. "Look, it's no good, there's something else I've been wanting to say to you, but there's never been the right time and — well — I'm just going to come out and say it . . ." He steps towards me.

Bracing myself for an angry outburst, I mentally start frantically stacking up ammunition to retaliate.

"I'm crazy about you."

I stop stacking and look at him in total astonishment — and confusion. His hands are held stiffly down by his sides and his body is rigid.

"Is this supposed to be one of your jokes?" I manage to stammer.

"No, not at all," he replies quickly. "I'm totally serious." He pulls up a chair and sits down, straddling it with his legs and hugging the back. He looks at me, waiting for my reaction.

Now, when I say I'm totally speechless, I mean it. I stare at him incredulously. He's got to be joking, right? We hate each other's guts.

Only he's not smiling or winking or doing any of the stuff he usually does, which means —

Oh, shit. *He's really serious.*

"I can't stop thinking about you, Emily," he's now saying, his words coming out even faster than normal, falling over themselves in their haste, "and I know this is all probably coming as a bit of a surprise, but I just wanted to tell you that I think you're amazing . . ."

Someone please tell me I'm still out cold and this is some bizarre nightmare. This cannot be happening. It just can't.

". . . Really amazing."

But it is.

Oh, God.

Oh, God. Oh, God. Oh, God.

All this time I thought Spike hated me, and yet all along he was really *into* me.

I almost feel myself blushing. Despite the fact that I hate Spike I can't help feeling just the *teensiest* bit delighted. Flattered even. I mean, who doesn't like being showered with compliments? Even if they are from a liar/love-wrecker/old-man-basher.

"Even though you know that when I first saw you I didn't fancy you in the slightest . . ."

Hang on, what was that?

". . . far from it. Blondes are usually my type. In fact, I'm a total sucker when it comes to the whole glamorous red-lipstick thing." He smiles with embarrassment. "And you didn't have any of that going on . . ."

*Excuse me?* My delight is suddenly taking a U-turn.

". . . and if I'm honest, I thought you were a bit dull . . ." He laughs ruefully.

Stunned. There's no other word for it. STUNNED.

". . . but these past few days I've really got to know you as a person, and even though I tried to dislike you, and trust me I've tried, I can't. I mean, I'm mad about you, Emily. I've even managed to overlook the fact you're an American . . ." Having obviously warmed up now, he emits another chuckle at what he obviously thinks is a joke.

But I'm not laughing. I'm angry.

". . . I always swore I could never go out with an American — you know I always had this thing about French girls . . ."

Very angry.

". . . but you're different . . ."

Fucking furious. Damn right I'm different, you fucking asshole, I want to scream.

". . . and so, well, I just wanted to tell you how I feel and I was wondering . . . well, hoping, really, that you might feel the same way. About me, that is. And that maybe you'd have dinner with me tonight, if you're not doing anything."

He stops talking — finally — and, evidently pleased with his monologue, looks at me expectantly. I survey him with every drop of restraint holding my anger tight inside me.

He *says* "hoping", but there's no doubting he's pretty confident he's going to get a positive reaction. That I'm going to suddenly swoon into his arms with grateful relief. Now, more than ever, I want to slap him.

Instead, I fold my arms and look at him coldly. "And what about Emmanuelle?"

Not only is he a liar, love-wrecker and an old-man-basher. It would now appear he's also a potential cheat. God, how can I resist?

"Oh, didn't I mention it? We broke up last night," he says as if to reassure me.

I feel a twinge of something that could be mistaken as pleasure, but I quickly reject it.

"It was never right between us. We fought like cat and dog. You were right the other day when you said I needed to go out with a normal girl."

"And I'm normal, am I?"

"Yeah," he enthuses, pulling his chair closer. "Absolutely."

I feel stung. No girl ever wants to be called "normal", do they? You want to be called "special" and "amazing" and "sexy" and "passionate" and a million other words that mean you're unique. "Normal" is just another word for "boring".

"Jeez, I'm flattered," I say sarcastically. "Thanks."

He looks at me uncertainly. It's the first flicker that things might not be going the way he'd planned.

"I can't think what I've done to inspire such love and affection," I continue calmly. "Truly, I'm very flattered. Privileged, even." With the anger building inside, I discard the flannel and gather myself up as best I can in a sheet. Sticking out my chin, I say determinedly, "But if you even *think* I might feel the same way about you, you're very much mistaken."

Spike seems to take a moment to register what I've just said. And then his smile seems to freeze and he goes a funny colour. For once he's lost for words. This is obviously not the reaction he was expecting.

"And even if you were the last man on earth, I wouldn't go out to dinner with you," I declare ferociously.

A whole range of emotions flit over his features. Shock, anger, disbelief, incredulity, hurt. In fact, he looks really hurt, but then he quickly buries it and, composing himself, says stiffly, "You know, I find it really hard to talk about emotional stuff, and it took me a lot of balls to tell you how I feel about you."

For a second regret stabs. Determinedly I push it aside.

"So you don't feel the same way. Clearly," he adds, grim-faced. "But you didn't have to be such a bitch about it. I do have feelings, you know."

He stands up, the injured party, and turns to leave.

Which is when I lose it.

"You have feelings?" I exclaim, my face flushing. Jumping out of bed, my sheet wrapped round me, I grab my bathrobe and — while trying to cover myself fully — tug it on. "What about my feelings?" I demand. "You stand there and tell me that you thought I was this, that and the other when you met me, but that you've decided to like me against all your better judgement, and that it's *so* out of character for you, but you've struggled against it!" I break off, panting, my chest heaving up and down. "And then you expect me to be *nice* to you?"

"Oh, come on, I didn't mean it like that," he retorts. If he thinks he's going to start talking he's got another thing coming. It's my turn now.

**302**

"Yes, you did," I cry, cutting him dead. "And who do you think you are? Criticising me! Insulting me! You're not so perfect, you know. Far from it."

"OK, so I thought those things then, but I'm just being honest, isn't that what you're supposed to be with each other? Totally honest?"

"Oh, you want us both to be brutally honest, do you?" I'm shouting now, my voice high and hoarse, but I don't care. "Well, in that case, let *me* be honest with *you* about a thing or two . . ."

As I step towards him I see Spike flinch.

"Let's imagine, for one ridiculous moment, that I *did* happen to like you. That I *did* feel the same way about you. Do you even *think* —" I spit out the word "think" as if it's got a nasty taste "— I would ever consider going out with a guy who thinks it's perfectly OK to go around punching a defenceless old man and threatening him to stay away from his mother or else?"

It's as if Spike's been slapped. The muscle in his jaw starts clenching furiously. He looks demonic, but he's not saying anything.

"Well, are you going to deny it?" I yell.

"I don't want to talk about it," he says coldly, refusing to be drawn.

"You can't, can you? You can't deny it!" I'm demanding.

Spike's face turns red with anger. "No, if we're talking about Ernie Devlin, I'm not going to deny it," he snaps.

I look at him, shocked that he's actually admitting to it. He's not even trying to make up some excuse.

"I did everything in my power to keep that bastard away from my mother, and if I had to do it all over again, I would."

"But you hit him!" I gasp.

"Yes, I did." He nods. "And trust me, I've never hit anyone in my life before."

He seems so genuine I falter slightly, but pull back.

"Trust you? After everything that's happened?" I snort sarcastically. "I'm sorry, but I don't believe you."

"Jesus, you've really got a great opinion of me, haven't you?"

"You lied to Maeve. I know you did. You wanted to prevent any kind of relationship between her and Ernie."

"You're damn right I wanted to keep him away from Maeve."

I can't believe it! He's not even making an attempt at arguing.

"God, you're pathetic," I gasp. "You couldn't stand your mom loving Ernie, could you? You were so jealous you broke up their relationship. You beat him up and broke his nose, causing him to be so terrified of you he had to quit his job and disappear. You broke your mom's heart."

Spike looks so angry that I might feel afraid if I wasn't so angry myself.

"But then to destroy any other relationship that Ernie might enter into is just vindictive. How could you? Maeve's just the sweetest person and she's been sad for such a long time. But you wouldn't have any idea about that, would you? You wouldn't know that she had to have her baby girl adopted when she was just eighteen, that she's been wracked with guilt ever since, that on this trip, maybe for the first time in years, Ernie made her smile. Made her laugh. Made her feel worth something again. You wouldn't care about all that, would you?" I break off, realising I've said too much. I didn't mean to tell him about Maeve, but I couldn't help it. I'm just so angry. I pause, my heart thudding. I'm out of breath. "And you went and ruined it for her," I add quietly.

"That's what you think of me, is it?" asks Spike, finally speaking. "That I'm a thug and a liar and a vindictive bastard? That I'd ruin something for Maeve because of my own feelings towards — God, I can't even bear to say his bloody name." He breaks off and gasps, shaking his head. "You think that this is all about me?"

"You said it," I reply bitterly.

We face each other, me with my arms folded, Spike with his hands shoved firmly into his pockets. Animosity wafts between us like the chill from a freezer cabinet.

"You talk about your first impressions of me, well, let me tell you mine. From the moment I met you you've been rude, selfish and arrogant. You're so self-obsessed you think the whole world is about you."

"I think you've said enough, don't you?" he says, his voice trembling.

"I haven't even started."

"Well, I'm not going to stand here and listen to any more of this crap," he says determinedly. "You've made

**305**

your feelings pretty clear. I'm sorry I bothered you. I'm sorry I've taken up so much of your time." He pauses, as if to say something else, then adds simply, "I hope you feel better tomorrow." And with that, he turns, pulls open the door and slams it so hard behind him it nearly comes off its hinges. I flinch.

"And a Happy New Year to you, too. Asshole," I yell loudly. And then, to my utter astonishment, I burst into tears.

# CHAPTER
# TWENTY-SEVEN

I wake up the next morning with "crying eyes".

You know the ones: the horrible swollen peepers that you get when you combine crying + sleeping. Bloodshot slits with big puffy bags that refuse to respond to any of those age-old beauty tips involving tea bags, cold teaspoons and Preparation H, and leave you with no option but to hide them.

Which explains why I'm going down to breakfast wearing my sunglasses. In *January*.

Leaving my hotel room, I let the door fall closed behind me and hobble slowly along the patterned pink carpet. My ankle hurts and I'm still feeling a bit shaky. Last night I must have been suffering from shock. I didn't realise it at the time, but that's obviously why I burst into tears. It had nothing to do with anything Spike said — even though it might *appear* like that — no, it was definitely the shock of the fall.

Plus, of course, the concussion I got from hitting my head. I rub my forehead. The lump's still there, but it's shrunk quite a bit. I'll probably end up with a nasty bruise as a souvenir from my trip.

I feel a twinge of self-pity. When I booked this trip I'd had visions of myself wafting around the English countryside in various colour coordinated outfits, my H&M spangly scarf thrown nonchalantly over my shoulder, a copy of *Pride and Prejudice* in my hand. I was going to be sexy, yet bookish. An American girl abroad, turning her back on the shallowness and disappointments of modern-day life and embracing a world steeped in history and literature. A world filled with quaint country pubs and roaring fires — in front of which I'd be curled with my book, sampling a local custom or two and making jovial banter with the villagers, most of whom would be wearing tweed.

I wasn't supposed to be going around getting drunk *and* stoned, into huge arguments and knocked off horses and *nearly* killed.

As if to remind me, my head begins to throb naggingly.

I'm distracted by the faint burble of my phone, and digging it out of my bag, I look at the display. Stella. I feel a wave of relief. Boy, do I need a friend right now.

"Hey, Happy New Year. Got the message," she says cheerily as I answer. "I wanted to find out how the ball was."

"Oh, it was great," I reply with forced cheeriness in an attempt to match hers. Reaching the staircase, I pause and sort of hover near the grandfather clock.

"So tell me all about it."

"Well, it was in this amazing house, and there was a string quartet and dancing and champagne and . . ." My eyes start watering again. "Oh, God, Stella, I had the most awful row," I blurt.

"No way."

"Yeah, I did. And it was a really huge one . . ." My voice goes all wobbly and high-pitched, and I start furiously blinking back tears.

"Aww, Em, what did you go and do that for?" she reprimands me teasingly, trying to make me laugh. "My fling went and flung himself at about twenty other women, so I need to live vicariously through yours."

I don't laugh, and hearing nothing but a faint sniffling on the other end of the line, she gets serious. "Come on, tell Auntie Stella, what did you and this Fitzwilliam guy argue about?"

Suddenly I realise she thinks I'm talking about Mr Darcy.

"Oh, it wasn't with him."

"It wasn't? Well, who was it with?" she asks, surprised.

"Spike."

"Sorry, you've lost me, Em. Who on earth's Spike?"

"The asshole." I sniff.

"Ahhhh, the *cute* asshole," says Stella. And there's something in the way she says it that makes me feel defensive.

"I never said he was cute," I protest.

"You didn't have to," she replies knowingly.

"What are you, some kind of psychic?" I snap, annoyed.

"Oh, so he *is* cute."

"OK, OK, so he's cute," I admit under pressure. "Now will you stop going on about it?" I'm starting to feel very frustrated that this phone conversation is not going the way I wanted. You know, lots of female support, the "Yes, he is a dickhead; no, of course none of it's your fault" kind of thing.

Instead, I'm being badgered and insinuated at.

There's a triumphant silence on the other end of the line.

See what I mean?

"So what did you guys argue about?"

"It's a long story," I sigh wearily.

"Well, I'm not going anywhere," offers Stella kindly.

I hesitate, then before I can stop it, the floodgates open and it all comes pouring out.

"Well, first I discovered he'd told lies about our driver, Ernie, to Maeve, this sweet Irish lady who I think really liked him, and then yesterday Ernie told me himself that Spike had punched him for going out with his mom . . ."

"Jesus."

". . . and then last night at the ball we were dancing and his girlfriend called him, and he just ignored me so I ended up smoking a joint . . ."

"You smoked a joint?"

". . . and went horseriding . . ."

"In a balldress?"

". . . but then I must have hit my head and blacked out because the next thing I know I'm waking up naked in bed and Spike's there . . ."

"No way!"

". . . and he tells me he's crazy about me . . ."

"Holy shit."

". . . and then we have this huge argument and he storms off."

310

There's a stunned silence on the other end of the line.

"Stella?"

"Fucking hell, Em, I'm supposed to be the one on the 18 — 30 holiday. Jeez, if I'd known a book tour could be that wild I'd have come with you!"

I smile. "I guess it does all sound a bit crazy."

"Crazy? It sounds fantastic!" gushes Stella, enviously. "Trust me, Mexico is totally dull in comparison. All that's happened here is a couple of pathetic wet T-shirt competitions and a few all-night margarita parties. I never thought I'd say it, but believe me, I don't want to see another margarita again. In fact, to tell the truth, I'm really looking forward to going home . . . Talking of which, have you heard from Freddy? He hasn't returned any of my texts."

I think about my conversation with Freddy last night. Him telling me how much being in love sucked. All at once I feel very emotional again.

"Hey, are you OK?" asks Stella, suddenly aware of my silence.

"Not really," I reply feebly.

"Sorry, there's me prattling away. So. How do you feel about him?"

"Who? Spike?"

"Well, you've barely mentioned the other guy," says Stella pointedly.

I bristle. "I still think he's an asshole. Even more so now," I say defiantly. "In fact, now I also think he's a liar and a bully."

"So what are you gonna do?"

"I don't know. What did you do about Scott?" I ask, remembering our last conversation.

"You mean after I threw a pitcher over him?" laughs Stella. "Simple. I ignored him. If you do that he'll soon get the message."

"Well, that's what I'm going to do," I decide firmly, pulling myself together. It's the lack of sleep that's making me emotional. Nothing more.

"What? You're going to take my advice?" she gasps in disbelief. "Wow, that's a first. What's come over you?"

Leaning back against the wall, I think about this last week, about everything that's happened. I'm still struggling to get my head round it all. "I'm not sure exactly," I say finally. "I'm really not sure."

We say our goodbyes, and of course as soon as we hang up I remember the dress. Damn, I meant to mention it again. Though I wonder why she didn't. I guess it must have slipped her mind, I decide, descending the staircase; after all, Stella's not exactly *renowned* for having the best memory.

Entering the dining room, I try to appear as if it's the most normal thing in the world to be wearing ten-dollar fake Gucci sunglasses at 9 a.m., on New Year's Day. Hopefully no one will pay any attention and I can just slip in and out.

"So you're alive!"

On second thoughts, perhaps not.

I glance over to see Rose, Maeve, Hilary and Rupinda. Sitting round a table, they've all stopped what they're doing to stare at me. Now I know how it must feel to be famous.

And not in a good way.

"Well, good morning, Emily," Rose is barking. "And a Happy New Year."

Her voice slices right through me and I smile weakly.

"Got a little bit of a hangover, have we?" she chortles loudly, waving a thickly buttered English muffin at me.

"A little bit." I nod, sitting down at the empty chair they've pulled up for me. Smiling gratefully, I reach for the coffeepot. My hand trembles. This morning I think I'm allowed to dispense with the English traditions and forgo the Earl Grey.

"We were all very worried about you," whispers Maeve, leaning close and placing her hand reassuringly upon mine.

"What happened exactly?" demands Hilary, reaching for a slice of toast.

Oh, God, questions, questions. I feel a flurry of panic. This is what I was dreading.

"I'm not sure . . ." I reply, feeling my cheeks flushing with embarrassment. "I hit my head."

"You were gabbling all kinds of nonsense," chimes in Rose.

"I was?" I feel a beat of alarm. Hurriedly I take a sip of coffee. I need the caffeine urgently.

"Romantic horserides, moonlit castles, poetry . . ."

"Mr Darcy," adds Hilary, raising an eyebrow.

I freeze, my mouth filled with coffee. It's lukewarm and slightly bitter. Hilary looks at me suspiciously. Or maybe that's just me being paranoid. I try thinking of an excuse.

"Well . . . er . . . you see . . ." I start my sentence not having a clue where it's going.

Fortunately, I'm rescued by Rupinda. "No need to explain, we all have our fantasies about Mr Darcy." She winks, taking a sip of her usual hot water and lemon. "Though I must say, yours are a lot more inventive than mine."

"Oh, I've always had an overactive imagination," I joke. "Ever since I was a little girl." I smile gratefully at Rupinda, relieved to have escaped what was no doubt going to be a very awkward conversation.

"Thank goodness Spike found you, hey?" says Hilary.

Only to find myself slap bang in the middle of another.

"Um . . . yeah . . ." I murmur vaguely. I really don't want to talk about Spike.

The ladies, however, obviously have other ideas.

"Ah, yes, the wonderful Mr Hargreaves," smiles Rupinda dreamily.

"Well, I have to say, I think it's very romantic," comments Hilary, who has changed her mind about the toast and is now chewing a mouthful of All Bran.

"Romantic?" I repeat dismissively, before I can help it. "Hardly."

"But he came to your rescue," whispers Maeve, her eyes shining behind her glasses. "He saved you."

The ladies have been hell-bent on setting up us "two young ones" since the beginning of this tour, and now they're obviously using this turn of events to back up their theory. God, if only they knew what really

**314**

happened in the early hours of this morning. It was anything *but* romantic.

"Oh, I don't know about that —" I begin, but I'm cut off by Miss Steane, who suddenly swoops upon the table with a clipboard.

"Yes, indeed, Miss Albright. You were very fortunate to be found by Mr Hargreaves. If it wasn't for him, you could have caught your death of cold out there —"

"We wanted to take you to the hospital, but with it being New Year's Eve accident and emergency would have been packed —"

"But luckily Spike had done a first-aid course so he checked you over —"

"And he even offered to stay with you in your room, just to make sure —"

"Concussion can be a funny thing, you know."

As all the women speak at once, chiming in over one another, my feelings towards Spike wobble. Gosh, I had no idea he did all that. I never even said thank you. In fact, I said all those mean, horrible things instead — *rude, selfish, self-obsessed, arrogant, liar* — I wince as I remember a few. God, I really went for it, didn't I? That's not like me at all, I sound like such a nasty bitch.

Probably because you were such a nasty bitch, Emily.

Guilt punches me in the stomach with a mean left hook and winds me, but I'm not going to take it lying down. Yes, but what about Ernie? I hear myself cry in justification. What about the abominable way he behaved towards him? Spike deserves everything he

**315**

gets. Why should you have been nice to him? He wasn't nice to Ernie, was he? I think indignantly.

"Speaking of which, where is our wonderful Mr Hargreaves?" booms Rose. "I haven't seem him at breakfast this morning."

My stomach lurches with dread. Oh, Jeez. Justified or not, I can't face him now. I just can't. Bracing myself for him to walk in at any moment, I bury my face in my coffee cup. Talk about awkward.

"He's gone back to London," says Miss Steane matter-of-factly.

What? My head flicks up. "Gone back?" I gasp in astonishment, and then, even more astonishing, feel a stab of disappointment.

"Yes, he had to leave early. Urgent business to attend to."

There's murmuring at the table — they are evidently as surprised as I am.

"But what about the article?" Hilary is asking, folding her arms in readiness to cross-examine Miss Steane. It's not hard to imagine her as a partner in a top legal firm and a local magistrate.

"It's as good as finished. He's done all his interviews," she replies simply.

"But he never interviewed me," I suddenly hear myself protest.

My outburst catches me by surprise, and I see Miss Steane glance over at me.

"Perhaps you gave him the impression that you didn't want to be interviewed," she opines.

"Yeah, perhaps." I nod, although I know there's no perhaps about it.

"In my experience, Emily, when anything concerns a man, you have to make things very clear. Women love figuring a man out, and we're very good at it. But men have no interest in figuring us out, isn't that right, ladies?" Miss Steane looks around the table for approval and is met with chuckles of concurrence. "And this is never more true than when it applies to affairs of the heart. As Charlotte Lucas said in *Pride and Prejudice*, 'It is sometimes a disadvantage to be so very guarded. In nine cases out of ten, a woman had better show more affection than she feels.' "

As Miss Steane finishes speaking I catch her looking right at me and I get the same feeling I had last night at the ball. As our tour guide I know she's simply quoting Jane Austen, but you'd almost think the words of advice are her own, as if she knows a lot more than she's letting on.

"Well, that's a shame," booms Rose. "Nice chap. I would have liked to say goodbye."

There are nods of agreement, and as everyone begins murmuring their regret at not having wished him a Happy New Year, invited him to drop in anytime he was passing, or attempted to fix him up with their "single but adorable" niece, I make my excuses and leave the table.

So that's it, then. Spike's gone back to London. And I catch a late flight to New York the day after tomorrow. Which means we'll never have to see each other again.

No more arguments. No more anything. It's over. The end. Boy, what a relief.

But even as I'm telling myself that, I can't shake the feeling that I'm trying to convince myself. That somewhere, deep inside of me, is a nagging doubt that I might have made a really big mistake. And that this isn't relief I'm feeling, it's regret.

# CHAPTER
# TWENTY-EIGHT

Being New Year's Day, we're given a break from our busy itinerary. Instead, a whole day of screen adaptations of Jane Austen books are going to be shown in the drawing room, followed by a series of discussions. First up on the list, and scheduled for right after breakfast, is the movie adaptation of *Pride and Prejudice*, starring Keira Knightley and Matthew Macfadyen. I decide to pass. It's a great movie, and Matthew Macfadyen is a babe, but I've seen it on DVD twice already. And anyway, I don't feel in the mood for watching a movie.

To be honest, I don't think I'd be able to concentrate on anything for thinking about last night. But not the parts I *want* to think about. Like, for example, my moonlight ride with Darcy, how he recited poetry to me, that delicious moment when everything sort of stopped and he was about to kiss me, *Spike calling me a bitch* —

See! It's done it again. That's exactly what I'm talking about. As soon as I try to think about my evening with Mr Darcy my mind veers off course and snaps back to what happened with Spike.

*Stop it*, a loud voice barks inside my head. I don't care, OK? I don't care about Spike, or what he had to say. Like I said, It's over. I'm never going to see him again, so what does it matter?

Walking into the lobby, I'm about to just go back to my room and catch up on some more sleep, when I spy a computer tucked away in the corner. Actually, maybe I should check my e-mails while I'm here. Not that I'll have many, what with it being over the holidays and everyone being away. Plus, all my friends and family have my cell-phone number, so if there was anything important they'd call or text. But you never know. And anyhow, it will only take a few minutes.

Clicking on to Internet Explorer, I access my web server and type in my address and password. I watch the little egg-timer as the page waits to download. The hotel is big on its miniature soaps and showercaps, but modern technologies such as high-speed Internet or wireless are still light years away and instead it's good old-fashioned dial-up.

Finally it connects, and I move the mouse on to my inbox. It opens up, showing me I've received twenty-four junk e-mails offering me Viagra and thirty per cent off books at some book club. That's my mom for you. I told her the last thing I needed was to buy books online, but she signed me up anyway, and now I get all these e-mails cluttering up my inbox.

Highlighting them all, I delete them and continue down. The first one I see is from Freddy — he e-mails me occasionally, usually around Stella's birthday, though sometimes it's just to see how I am. He's sweet like that. I open it. Sure enough, he's saying it was nice to talk to me yesterday, apologising for not enquiring after my trip and hoping I'm having a lovely time, and then there's something else:

As Stella's best friend, I want your advice on something. I know you've always been aware of my true feelings for her — and yesterday you made me face up to those feelings. I love Stella, I always have, but I guess I've just been burying my head in the sand as I know she's not in love with me. But while she's been away I've been doing a lot of thinking. (Don't panic, I'd already made this decision before our conversation, so don't feel responsible!)

Anyway, I decided that, you know what, perhaps she's right. We *can* only ever be friends. So with that in mind I've been on a couple of dates this past week. Nothing serious, but I'm not sure how to tell Stella, which is why I haven't returned her calls. I don't think she's gonna be upset — knowing Stella, she'll probably be really pleased for me — but it still feels a bit weird. That was partly the reason I called you yesterday, I wanted your take on it, but we didn't have time to talk properly. Anyway, I thought I'd send you an e-mail instead. She texted me just this morning asking me if I was OK, so I feel I have to say something. Any suggestions how to break the news?

Wow. So Freddy's finally got fed up with waiting for Stella. I knew it was going to happen eventually, but I can't help feeling disappointed. I really wanted those guys to get it together. Saying that, I've got a feeling that Freddy's got it wrong about Stella being pleased for him. Despite all her protestations to the contrary, I've got a sneaky feeling that when she discovers he's dating again, Stella might just realise her feelings are not as platonic as she thought.

A thought strikes. Immediately I dismiss it. No, I can't. That would be wrong. Freddy told me in confidence. Then again . . . maybe he was secretly hoping I would . . .

Would what, Emily? *Hit "forward" and type in Stella's e-mail address?*

As I press "send" and I watch the e-mail disappear from my screen into cyberspace, I feel a touch guilty. Who do I think I am? A modern-day Cupid? Firing e-mails instead of arrows?

But I get over that pretty quickly. Maybe this will finally make Stella see sense. Maybe it won't. Maybe they're both going to kill me. But I think it's still worth a shot. Just because I've made a total mess of my love life, it doesn't mean everyone should.

I turn back to my inbox. OK. Now, what else?

Hmm, there's a Hallmark card from a friend in Chicago, a couple from my bank . . . Oh, there's one from Mr McKenzie. Automatically I feel a stab of worry. I hope there's no problem with the figures for the stock orders, I think, clicking on it anxiously. Oh, hang on, maybe we've had some complaints from customers about those copies of *Pride and Prejudice* we just got in, the ones with all those blank pages. I meant to e-mail Mr McKenzie about that, but it slipped my mind. Kicking myself, I start reading:

Dearest Emily,

This is Audrey McKenzie here, and I'm writing on behalf of my husband, William.

Only this e-mail isn't about incorrect stock orders or complaints about misprints. I only wish it was.

Two days ago he suffered a slight stroke and had to be admitted to hospital. It was all a bit of a worry, but fortunately we were very lucky. William is a tough old boot and he's going to be absolutely fine. I'm not sure I will be, though! He's currently recuperating at home and is already complaining he's bored and badgering the doctors to let him go back to work!

However, in the meantime I've got him under lock and key. We've currently closed the store until your return, at which point we'll need to arrange a meeting to discuss the store's future, and obviously your position.

But I would like to use this opportunity to thank you from the bottom of our hearts for all the hard work and dedication you've shown for McKenzie's over these past five years. And to apologize for bringing you such news over the holiday season, but William and I felt it was better that you were kept informed about everything, at all times.

Safe trip back and let's speak on your return.

Best wishes,

Audrey and William McKenzie

*   *   *

Of course my initial reaction is to thank God he's OK. Mr McKenzie is more than just a boss to me. If anything happened to him I'd be so upset.

But I'd be lying if I didn't admit my thoughts then immediately turn to myself. This doesn't bode well for the store. Ever since Mr McKenzie stopped working in the store, his wife has been pushing him to officially retire and sell the business, but he's always managed to persuade her to keep it on. But now? I feel a pang of dread. Who knows what will happen.

I send a cheerful reply, wishing him a full recovery and telling them both not to worry, that I will be back soon and can't wait to take over things again. I try to make myself sound as positive and capable as ever, but the worry is there. I know I can always get another job in a bookstore, but to work anywhere else would be like going from driving around in an Aston Martin to getting on the bus. And what about Stella? What would happen to her?

I try to calm myself. No need to panic just yet. Nothing is going to happen right away. I've got a few weeks to think of something. Maybe I could borrow the money to buy him out?

Yeah, right. And maybe you'll win the lottery, Emily.

I feel a wave of tiredness as I look at the flickering glare of the computer screen. So much has happened in the last twenty-four hours, right now all I want to do is curl up under my bedcovers and catch up on my sleep. I go to log off but a new e-mail pops into my inbox. I don't recognise the address and the subject line is

324

"Please read". I peer at it suspiciously. It's probably junk. I move my mouse over it to delete, then pause: Sbh@thedailytimes.com. The *Daily Times*? Isn't that Spike's newspaper?

Then I realise. Of course. Sbh. I don't remember one of his middle names beginning with B, but these must be Spike's initials.

My heart thuds. Immediately two thoughts hit me: (1) How's he got my e-mail address? (2) What's he going to say?

I click on it with slight trepidation. I'm not sure what I'm expecting — a few sharp lines, an apology, a bitchy PS — but as I watch the e-mail opening up I'm taken aback to see it's a letter. I move my mouse downwards. One that runs into six, seven, *eight* whole pages.

I stare at them for a moment. Each page is filled with text, but at the bottom are pasted what appear to be extracts from newspapers.

"Excuse me, have you nearly finished?"

Someone is talking to me and I look up sharply to see a few people hovering in the lobby, obviously waiting to use the computer.

"Oh, sure . . . Just give me a minute." Turning back to the computer, I press "print". There's no hurry. So he wrote me a letter? So what? I'll read it later, when it's convenient.

Who am I kidding?

Less than two minutes later I'm sitting on the edge of the bed in my hotel bedroom, the pages of Spike's e-mail clutched in my hand. Catching my breath, I start to read.

Dear Emily,

The chances are you'll delete this e-mail before you ever read it. But, on the off-chance your curiosity is greater than your hate for me, right now you're probably thinking I'm about to reiterate those sentiments that last night were so disgusting to you.

In which case, let me put your mind at rest and tell you that you don't have to worry. You made your feelings pretty clear — in fact, I don't think they could have been ANY clearer, so I think the faster we both forget about that, the better.

OK, that out of the way, I'll cut straight to the chase. Last night you accused me of some pretty serious stuff and for personal reasons I was not prepared to explain or defend myself as I didn't know what I could and should reveal. And anyhow, you'd made up your mind, so what was the point?

However, since then I've had time to think about it, and although it's unlikely we're ever going to see or speak to each other again, I still want you to know my side of the story. I would hate to think that you never knew the truth.

Now, obviously you don't have to read this e-mail. You can delete it, banish it to cyber hell for ever with just a click of your mouse — it's up to you. But there's some stuff you don't know. There's some stuff you SHOULD know. Afterwards if you still think I'm guilty, still believe I'm a liar and a vindictive bastard, then so be it. But to judge me without knowing all the facts isn't fair — to you or me.

Last night you laid two serious offences at my door:

1. Lying to Maeve about Ernie and therefore basically ruining her first chance at happiness in years, maybe even her entire life.

2. Behaving despicably towards Ernie, a poor, defenceless old man who did nothing wrong but fall in love with my mother, causing me to fly into a jealous rage, make repeated threats to him, and culminating in me beating him up and breaking his nose without any provocation. And then — it gets worse — forcing him to quit his job at the *Daily Times*, which he did, as he was so terrified of me.

OK, so now we've established what you believe to be the truth, let me tell you my version of events:

I first met Ernie Devlin when he came to work at the *Daily Times* five years ago as one of the drivers of our courtesy cars. We would say hello and goodbye, exchange small talk, discuss football scores, that kind of thing. And he seemed like a nice enough bloke.

Then one night my mum came to meet me after work. That's how she met Ernie. I was on a deadline, couldn't get away from my desk, and so she had to wait half an hour in the lobby. The two of them got chatting — Mum loves to talk — and, well, the upshot was Ernie asked my mum if he could take her out and she said yes.

Now, I know you're not going to believe this, but when she told me she'd been invited on a date I couldn't have been more pleased for her.

My dad died when I was sixteen and since then it's just been the two of us, but that doesn't mean I don't want her to have another man in her life. On the contrary. I loved my dad, but he's gone now, and I don't want her to be alone for the rest of her life. I want her to meet someone and live happily ever after. Who it is and what they do is irrelevant. I'm not a snob. He doesn't have to be rich or successful. He just has to be a good bloke. And he has to love my mum.

So my mum and Ernie go on their date and then they go on another and another, until pretty soon they're "courting", as my mother likes to call it. I was delighted for her. She was the happiest I'd seen her since before my dad died. It was as if she was young again. And Ernie? He called when he said he would call. He was always punctual. Every time he turned up he'd have flowers or a small gift. He seemed like the perfect gent.

In hindsight, I think I should have been suspicious. He was too perfect.

But I think seeing Mum so happy again blinded me. I didn't have my investigative reporter head on. When he talked about his past and how his wife had died tragically in a car accident, I didn't try to corroborate his story, dig deep into his past or check the facts. After Dad died there were months, years even, when I never thought I'd see my mum smile again, and yet here she was smiling and laughing — it was as if she'd come back to life.

I actually felt *grateful* to him.

And seeing as I'm being totally honest, I'll admit to you something that I have difficulty even admitting to myself. I was also relieved. I had a girlfriend. I had a life. A job that took up long hours. Now I didn't have to worry about my mum. Didn't have to feel guilty that she was alone at Christmas when I went snowboarding.

God, that's so fucking selfish of me, isn't it? My mum, who'd given me everything in life, and there was I, thinking about myself. I still beat myself up about that now. I regret to this day that I didn't ask more questions, pay more attention, spend more time getting to know Ernie Devlin. Maybe then I could have uncovered some clue, something that would have made me suspect. But I didn't, and I can't turn the clock back now, can I?

Ernie proposed to my mum just three months after they'd met. Got down on one knee and gave her an antique diamond ring that he said was his mother's. She was over the moon. She cried when she told me the news. They were going to have a small wedding in the summer, with a reception at the local golf club and a honeymoon on Lake Garda.

But they weren't the only plans they'd made. They'd also decided to sell both of their houses and buy a place together, make a fresh start. In fact, they'd made an offer on a bungalow in a nearby village.

To be honest, it did all seem a bit soon, but like Mum said, they loved one another and at their age why wait? Put like that, who was I to spoil things? So I was sentimental about selling my childhood home, so what? I'd moved out, moved on with my life, why shouldn't she?

They booked the registry office for June, which was only two months away, and preparations began in earnest. Flowers, invitations, menus, cars. One day I discovered Mum's credit-card statement and saw that everything for the wedding had been paid for by her. That's when I got my first inkling that Ernie might not be everything he seemed. When I asked her about it, she breezily explained that Ernie didn't use credit cards, he only had a cheque book, and so it was easier this way. "And anyway, like Ernie says, once we're married, what's mine is his and vice versa," she'd reasoned.

I got a bad vibe, but I tried to brush it off. I was just being over-protective; it made sense to pay by credit card rather than cheque; he hadn't actually done anything wrong.

By this stage they were also getting ready to move into their new bungalow. Both Mum and Ernie had found buyers for their respective houses, and their solicitors were getting all the paperwork ready. All that was needed now was their ten per cent cash deposit so they could exchange contracts.

Ten per cent.

That's thirty thousand pounds. Which, in today's current exchange market, is nearly sixty thousand dollars. That's a lot of money. And some people will do anything for that kind of money.

They'll even break someone's heart for it.

Unbeknown to me, the week previously, Ernie had gone over to Mum's and told her that his buyer had pulled out at the last minute, that it might take weeks to find a new one, and what was he going to do? Apparently he was distraught they were going to lose their new bungalow and so Mum told him not to worry and wrote out a cheque for the entire deposit. Only she couldn't remember the name of the solicitor, so Ernie told her to just leave that bit blank — he would fill it in later as he had all the paperwork back at his house.

The first we knew something was wrong was when the solicitor called Mum a week later, the day before her wedding was meant to be, asking where his money was, and several urgent phone calls to Ernie went unanswered. My mum was beside herself. She thought he must have had some terrible accident. That he was lying hurt somewhere. "Something awful must have happened," she kept saying, over and over, and I knew she was thinking of my dad, of the day she'd found him in the study, how he'd suffered a massive stroke, how it had been too late.

That's when we got the police involved and it didn't take long for them to discover Ernie had made the cheque payable to himself, deposited it in his bank account, calmly waited for it to clear, then left the country.

When Mum found out the truth she was actually relieved. That's my mum for you. Jilted a day before her wedding, by a man she thought loved her and wanted to spend the rest of his life with her, who'd stolen her life savings — and yet she's still thankful he's not hurt. She's such a bloody good person, my mother.

Me?

I wanted him dead. I wanted to kill him with my bare hands. Not only had he destroyed her hopes and shattered her dreams. Not only had he humiliated her in front of her friends and family. Made her a laughing stock among her neighbours. Betrayed her trust, robbed her of thirty thousand pounds, run up huge debts on her credit card and left her with a huge mess of a wedding to cancel and committed to a house she no longer wanted to buy.

He'd also broken her heart.

And you want to know the worst thing? He'd done it intentionally.

You don't know my mum, Emily, but everyone who's ever met her will tell you she's the kindest, most loving person you'll ever meet. She trusted Ernie Devlin, and she was willing to give him the whole world, yet he cold-heartedly set out to destroy her with his greed and selfishness. As if she meant nothing. And to him, she didn't. She was just a means to an end.

I wish I could say that was the end of it, but there were more shocks to come.

Six weeks later Ernie was arrested when he tried to return to the UK. Turns out that Mum wasn't the only woman he'd duped. Dozens of women had come forward. They all told the same story — he was a widower, they were supposed to get married, they were buying a house together but he didn't have his share of the deposit . . . Well, you can see where this is going, can't you?

Mum didn't attend his trial, but I did. But if I thought I was going to see some remorse, I couldn't have been more wrong. He didn't apologise to his victims, ask for forgiveness, or show any shame for what he'd done. As he left the court on the first day he even had the audacity to smile for the photographers.

That's when I hit him.

I couldn't help it. Something just snapped inside of me. After everything he'd put my mum through, to see him smiling was just too much. I jumped in front of the reporters and wiped the smile of his face. I was promptly arrested, but because of the circumstances, the police let me off with just a caution. I've never been in trouble with the law my whole life, apart from a few parking tickets, but I still don't regret it. I'm not defending my actions, but as far as I'm concerned, after what Ernie Devlin did, he got off lightly.

On 24 May 2003 he was found guilty and got six years for deception and theft. He was ordered to pay

Mum back all that money, plus legal costs, and also had to repay the money he'd stolen from the other women. He declared himself bankrupt. Eighteen months later he was let out for good behaviour.

They say time heals, but I don't think my mum will ever get over what Ernie did to her. And I know I'll certainly never forgive him. When I saw him again on the tour after all this time, I admit I wanted to kill him. Or at least beat the living daylights out of him. But we know how the legal system works. I already had a caution. If I laid a finger on him I'd be the one going to jail. Personally I wouldn't have cared, it would be worth it to wipe the smile off his face, but Mum's had enough upset in her life. She didn't need to see me in court, to have it all dragged up again.

So I decided to just ignore him. To avoid him. To pretend he didn't exist.

But then, that night, I saw him with Maeve. The way he was, all laughing and jokey, showing her pictures of his grandchildren, I realised he hadn't learned his lesson. That's exactly how he was with Mum. (By the way, just for the record, they're not his grandchildren. He doesn't have any. Neither did he ever have a wife who was tragically killed in a car accident. And that engagement ring that was his mother's? Stolen from one of his "ex-fiancées".) I couldn't bear to see him doing it again. Taking advantage of someone like Maeve.

So that morning on the coach on the way to Winchester Cathedral, I decided to tell her in confidence about my mum. She was shocked. Who wouldn't be? She was probably disappointed and upset too, and for that I'm sorry. But the way I see it, I saved her from getting a whole lot more hurt in the long run. This way, Maeve will never have to go through what my mum and all those other women had to go through.

To this day, my mum's never seen a penny of that thirty thousand pounds. She's due to retire soon and it was meant to be her nest egg, but to be honest, it was never about the money. Money is just money, but you can't put a price on a broken heart, can you?

I know what you're thinking right now. It's my word against his, right? And he's the kind old man and I'm the asshole. Which is why I've included some press clippings from the time. I don't expect you to believe me, Emily, but it's there in black and white — so you decide for yourself.

But before you read them, I'll say bye. For what it's worth it was good meeting you. And if you've made it this far, thanks for listening.

Spike

# CHAPTER
# TWENTY-NINE

I don't know how to describe my feelings reading Spike's e-mail. I think I went through every emotion possible. Indignation, disbelief, anger, annoyance, horror, guilt, remorse. I do know that I sat down on my bed with every intention of not believing him. As far as I was concerned, I'd already made up my mind. He was guilty of every accusation I'd thrown at him.

And yet, the more I read, the more my prejudices began to crumble. With every page I turned, the evidence became more and more overwhelming. Until there was no doubt in my mind: I'd judged him and I'd got it wrong. Horribly, *horribly* wrong. I didn't even need to see the newspaper articles to know that.

I read them anyway. The headlines screamed out at me. "LOVE RAT", "THE RUNAWAY GROOM", "HE STOLE HER HEART AND HER SAVINGS".

Accompanying them were pictures of a man with dyed brown hair and moustache, but there was no mistaking it was Ernie. Sweet, defenceless Ernie. The innocent victim. Survivor of a jealous attack by Spike, a man half his age.

Shit. How did I get it so wrong?

I sit on the edge of the bed, breathing, trying to stay in control. My mind is reeling. I have no idea what to do. My first instinct is to run downstairs and send Spike an e-mail apologising, but after everything I said, all my accusations, the way I behaved towards him, it seems pretty lame. An e-mail, after what I've said and done? To be honest, I wouldn't blame him if he told me to go to hell.

Maybe instead I should just leave it. After all, I've done enough damage already. Just try to forget all about it. Pretend it never happened.

But it did.

Remorse stabs. I think about Ernie, about how I was utterly taken in by him, how I was so quick to believe his stories about Spike. Why? Because I *wanted* to believe them. Because they supported my opinion of him, confirmed my first impressions. I wanted to be right.

And yet you couldn't have been more wrong, could you, Emily?

Guilt and shame wash over me — and fear. It's a scary thought when you realise you can't trust your own judgement. That your pride and prejudices can completely blind you to the truth. It makes me wonder how many times I've got it wrong before — I just never found out.

The room suddenly feels stuffy and claustrophobic. I need to go out and get some fresh air. Try and clear my head. So much has happened I can't think straight. What with these revelations from Spike about Ernie and the e-mail from Mr McKenzie's wife, my head's all over the place.

Tugging on my boots and thick winter coat, I go downstairs. You can rent bikes from the front desk and I choose a black one with a straw basket. It's more Miss Marple than Lance Armstrong, but trying to look cool is the least of my concerns right now, and climbing on to the saddle I set off up away from the town.

It feels good to be on a bike. I fill my lungs with cold air and push down on the pedals. Soon the roads turn into lanes and the houses give way to open fields. I keep cycling. I don't notice my sore buttocks, or the twinge of my ankle, just the regular motion of the pedals, the feeling of the cold wind ruffling through my hair. With every revolution of the wheels, I feel myself growing calmer, more steady, as I leave the city behind and climb higher and higher. None of it makes sense, but this does. Cycling is so straightforward. You pedal, you move forwards. Why can't life be as simple?

After a while the burning in my thighs becomes too much, and I dismount and lean my bicycle against an old metal gate adjoining a stone wall. Up ahead, there's some woods and through the clearing in the trees I can see a castle. Oh, wow, that must be the same castle I rode to last night with Mr Darcy. What was it called? Ah, yes, I remember now: Sham Castle — because it's not actually real.

I start heading towards it. The hill's pretty steep and by the time I enter Bathwick Woods I'm out of puff. I slow down. The going is a lot tougher here. It's hard to make out the path and there's plenty of exposed rock

**338**

and tree roots to catch you out — God knows how I negotiated it last night on horseback — but after about five minutes I come out on the other side. The castle is to the right of me, and yet it looks completely different in the daylight. Not at all how I remember. Made of creamy-coloured Bath stone, it had looked totally genuine last night, but now up close I can clearly see it's all a sham.

In summer this place is probably teaming with tourists, but now it's deserted, and sitting down on the grass, I rest my head against the stonework and take in the view. Surrounded by seven hills, the city of Bath lies beneath me, its Georgian architecture, which had seemed so grand and impressive at street level, now looks like a miniature model from a town-planner's office.

I rub my puffy eyes and tilt my head to look at the grey sky above me. It looks like it might rain. A typical New Year's Day. Except it's not, is it? There's nothing typical today. That heavy feeling I had inside returns and I heave a sigh. I can't think about it any more. I'm too tired. I didn't sleep well last night. And what with the after-effects of the ball, the concussion, the revelations, I just want to close my eyes for a moment and block everything out.

After a few moments I feel a warmth on my face and open my eyes to discover the sun emerging from behind a cloud. Shafts of bright sunlight pierce through the gaps of blue and I have to shade my eyes with my hand to see anything. In the far distance I notice someone approaching. I squint, trying to make them out. It's a man, I realise, as he fast approaches. And he's on horseback.

*Mr Darcy.*

Overjoyed, I watch as he gallops up to me, his cheeks flushed with the January wind, his dark, heavy brows almost obscuring his eyes.

"I was hoping I might find you here," he says, dismounting and striding towards me.

I smile and jump up to greet him. After everything that's happened I have a sudden desire for a hug, for someone to hold me tightly and tell me everything's going to be OK.

Impulsively I throw my arms round him and bury my face in his broad shoulder. "Boy, am I glad to see you," I gasp, closing my eyes and breathing in his familiar cologne.

Happiness mixes with relief. Gosh, he really does have the best shoulders to cry on, I think, feeling all the tension in my body release with his embrace.

Although, hang on, he's not *actually* embracing me, I notice, suddenly realising how stiff he is. In fact, *I'm* the one hugging him. He's just standing here with his back ramrod straight and his hands held firmly down by his sides.

I pull away self-consciously.

"Um . . . Happy New Year," I say lamely.

"Yes. Indeed." Mr Darcy coughs awkwardly and stares at the ground. For the first time I get a glimpse of what it would be like to go out with someone who's brooding and dark and has all these repressed

**340**

emotions. I mean, it all sounds very attractive and sexy in the book, but in real life I want someone who can give me a bear hug.

"I have been looking for you," he begins, clasping his hands behind his back in a gesture that doesn't need a body-language expert to tell me he's obviously extremely uncomfortable with my public outburst of affection.

But then it's not his fault, is it? I tell myself, feeling a bit sorry for him. I suppose the ladies of his day didn't go around flinging their arms round men and expecting bear hugs. They just made a sampler or something.

Swallowing hard, he looks up at me and meets my eyes. "I was very worried about you, Emily. I went back to the stables last night in the hope that you would have made it back safely. When I found Lightning but no sign of you, I rode to your hotel. However, there was no light at your window, and by then it was very late and . . ." He takes a breath and composes himself. "It gives me great relief to find that you are not hurt."

Oh, God. With everything that's been happening, I'd completely forgotten that the last time I saw him he had been knocked off his horse. But now, listening to him speaking, I suddenly realise I haven't even asked him if he's OK. Even worse, I hadn't even *thought* about it until this very moment.

"Thanks." I smile gratefully. "But what about you? I saw you fall —"

"Thrown," he bristles.

"Oh, right, *thrown*," I repeat, feeling a little piqued by the way he just corrected me.

"Fortunately, I am a skilled equestrian and therefore I escaped injury."

"Phew, that's lucky."

"Oh, it had nothing to do with luck," he says arrogantly.

That told you, Emily.

A line from *Pride and Prejudice* about Mr Darcy suddenly springs to mind: "One cannot wonder that so very fine a young man with family, fortune, everything in his favour, should think highly of himself. If I may so express it, he has a *right* to be proud."

Yeah, well, I don't, I think irritably.

"So, have you eaten lunch?" he asks.

His tone is once more polite, but I'm half inclined to fib and say yes, as I'm still feeling a bit rankled. My pet peeve is arrogance. Saying that, I haven't eaten anything at all today, just the coffee at breakfast. As if on cue my stomach gives a faint gurgle of complaint.

"No, not yet," I mumble.

"Excellent. I brought us a little something." He nods, and strides over to his horse.

Trepidation stabs. Oh, no, not that again. I don't think my buttocks can take another horseride. This time I'm just going to come out and say no.

"No need to look so worried," he adds, catching my expression. "It is not like the last surprise."

Unfastening something from behind his saddle, he lifts down a small wicker picnic hamper and a thick woollen blanket from one of the side panniers. He unfolds it and lays it down on the ground, meticulously making sure it's straight. Then, unfastening the leather

342

straps of the hamper, he begins pulling out various things.

"We have some bread, grapes, cheeses, goose-liver pâté, a bottle of vintage Bordeaux to wash it all down with . . ."

"Oh, wow," I gasp, somewhat taken aback.

". . . and here are the cutlery and plates . . ." he continues.

Forget the paper and plastic variety. He's brought real silver knives and forks, and white china plates.

". . . and I brought you a little something to keep you warm," he adds, unrolling a large fur.

"That's so sweet of you." I smile. I feel a wave of affection. So he can be a bit arrogant. So what? He's also really thoughtful, I tell myself, as he sits down next to me on the blanket and places the fur over my legs.

Next, he carefully arranges the plates, takes out a delicate silver knife with a mother-of-pearl handle and proceeds to cut thin silvers of cheese and slices of bread with a surgeon's precision. Then he twists opens the glass jar of pâté, flicks open a starched white napkin and fastidiously wipes the rim, removing every last invisible smear of pâté. Finally, the grapes: he examines each one, before plucking off exactly three and arranging them as a piece of artful decoration.

I watch him in fascination. Gosh, everything is so proper and careful, I note, as he hands me a plate.

"Why, thank you." I smile, popping a grape in my mouth. Mmm, yummy. Hungrily biting into the cheese and bread, I glance across at Mr Darcy. With a knife and fork, he divides a grape into halves, cuts a small square of cheese from the slice and then, layering the two on the prongs of his fork, puts them neatly in his mouth.

His manners are impeccable. Embarrassed, I immediately stuff the rest of the cheese and bread in my mouth before he notices, dropping crumbs all over my coat in the process. Oh, God, I'm such a pig. Brushing them off, I look up to see him peering at me quizzically.

"Messy eater," I laugh sheepishly.

I wait for him to laugh with me, but he just says, "I see," and continues eating.

A vague feeling of unease descends on me, but I ignore it and reach for my knife and fork. Copying him, I spear a grape with my fork. But as the prongs puncture the skin, there's a sudden squirt of juice and pips. It lands on Mr Darcy's white shirt. Well, it would, wouldn't it?

"Oops, shit," I gasp, horrified.

He frowns, puts down his knife and begins dabbing the starched white cotton with his napkin.

"God, sorry," I continue apologising.

"It is perfectly fine, no need to worry," he says, still dabbing.

"I'm sure it will come out," I reassure him.

"Indeed." He nods, pouring water on his napkin and returning to the stain.

Which you can't even see any more, I think, watching him fussing. I feel a twinge of irritation. He's being a touch overdramatic, isn't he? I mean, it's just a bit of grape juice.

"When you get home, just put a sprinkle of salt on it and soak it in the sink."

"Thank you. I will suggest it to one of the servants."

"*Servants?*" I squeak. God, I'd forgotten how posh he is. I mean, who on earth has servants apart from the Queen?

"Why, yes, of course," he replies. "Surely you have servants back home in America?"

His assumption is so comical I have to stifle a laugh. I try imagining a butler and a maid bowing and curtseying in my little studio apartment. I can't. There wouldn't be enough room for a start.

"Not really. You can't get the staff these days," I joke, grinning.

Not even a flicker. But then he's busy pouring me a glass of wine, so he probably didn't hear me, I decide, noticing how deftly he turns the bottle to prevent spilling a drop, just like they do in restaurants.

I try chasing another grape around my plate with my fork for a few moments, then give up and abandon my silverware with impatience. Well, it *is* a picnic, I tell myself. There's no need to be so *formal*. I mean, it's not as if we're in some fancy-schmancy restaurant, is it? I tear off a bit of bread and use it to scoop out the pâté. "Yum, this stuff is delicious," I enthuse. "Did you make it yourself?"

"No, it was my cook."

Ah, yes, of course. The servants again. I'd forgotten about them.

"I'll have to get the recipe." I make an attempt at lightening things up. "Take it back to America with me."

"When do you leave?"

"Just a couple more days. Tomorrow we're driving north to Lyme Park Hall and then on Wednesday night I leave for New York."

"Can you not extend your stay?"

"I'd love to . . ." The e-mail from Mr McKenzie's wife pops back into my mind.

"But, no, I can't. Having blocked it out this whole time, I suddenly feel the familiar ache of worry. Taking a gulp of wine, I stare into my wine glass.

"What is it, Emily? You seem troubled."

Mr Darcy's tone is kindly, but I don't answer. Gazing at the burgundy liquid, I'm wondering where on earth to start. Now I've opened the door to my worries, they all come barging in again. Spike, Ernie, Mr McKenzie . . .

"It looks like I might lose my job at the bookstore," I hear myself blurting after a pause. "My boss, Mr McKenzie, might be selling the store. He's not been well. I understand, but . . ." I sigh despondently. "I don't know what I'm going to do."

It feels good to just say it out loud.

"You are employed?"

I look up to see Mr Darcy gazing at me in total astonishment. In fact, he's looking more astonished at this suggestion than anything that's happened these past few days.

"Yup. In one of the best bookstores in New York. McKenzie's," I say, with more than a little pride in my voice. I can't help it. It happens every time.

"You work in a bookshop?" he repeats in disbelief.

346

I'm not sure what I was expecting, but it was more along the lines of sympathy and understanding.

"Well, for the moment."

"But surely you have a private income from your family? A trust fund, perhaps?"

"'Fraid not." I grin, thinking about Mom and Dad. A *trust fund?* I don't even get a postcard. "But anyway, even if I did, I'd still want to work. I love my job."

My Darcy rakes his fingers through his hair and studies my face. He seems to be having difficulty computing what I've just said.

"I must confess I am shocked, Emily," he says after a moment.

His voice is thick with disapproval and I feel my smile slide.

"An educated woman such as yourself should not be working."

I feel myself stiffen. "But what about your servants? Aren't they women?" I counter, trying to keep my cool.

"Well, yes, of course. But domestic employment is both acceptable and a necessity for the lower classes."

Now it's my turn to look at him in astonishment. "Servants" was bad enough, but did he just say the *lower classes?* I look at him incredulously. I honestly can't believe what I'm hearing. I knew he was posh, but I had no idea he was such a *snob.*

"A woman's place is in the home. As a wife and mother."

Yes. He really did say that.

"But that's so sexist," I cry.

He looks bewildered, as if he's never heard of the word.

Probably because he hasn't, I realise. In fact, he's probably not even aware of the concept. In which case I shouldn't really be angry at him, should I? I mean, it's not his fault he's totally ignorant. I can't accuse him of something if he doesn't even know what it is.

"Surely you are not suggesting women should seek out a living the same as men?" he's asking pompously.

I take it back. Yes, I can.

"Of course!" I gasp, infuriated. "Why shouldn't women work the same as men? My career is very important to me."

"Obviously your customs are not the same in America," he says gravely. "But here we do things differently. And, I have to say, properly."

"Bullshit!"

His face pales and he struggles to repress his emotions. Watching him, I have a flashback to Spike losing his temper and part of me can't help wishing Mr Darcy would do the same. But of course he won't, he's always so goddamn composed the whole time. I used to think it was sexy, but now I just find it frustrating.

His eyes flash moodily and as I look into his dark irises with the tiny flecks of grey, I think about all the months and years I've fantasised about dating Mr Darcy. Wanting every man to be him.

And now here we are. Together. *Arguing*.

"Look, I didn't mean to snap," I begin. First Spike, now Mr Darcy, what's wrong with me? "It's just —" I break off.

**348**

Just what, Emily? It's that voice again. Only this time it's more persistent. That he's acting like a selfish, sexist pig? A stuck-up snob? A crashing bore?

"I should be getting back," I finish quietly, trying to block out the voice.

"I understand." He nods solemnly. "I also have matters to attend to." His chest heaves, as if there's a lot going on underneath the surface, and he turns away from me to look out towards the valley. "I forget how beautiful it is here, with the view of the town," he says quietly, after a brief pause.

I follow his eyes. He's right. It is stunning. "Yeah, it's awesome," I murmur in agreement.

For a moment we stay like that, gazing out at the majestic scenery that sweeps beneath us, the rolling hills set against the backdrop of the vast expanse of sky. It's quiet. There's no one around. Just the two of us.

Out of the corner of my eye, I see Mr Darcy turn to me, his brow furrowed. "Perhaps we can just sit a while longer?"

I don't answer immediately. Instead, I continue staring resolutely out towards the skyline. It's so big it puts everything into perspective. Does it really matter if I don't share the same views as Mr Darcy? I mean, of course he's going to have a different opinion from me on certain things, it's totally understandable. We're from two completely different worlds. Right?

"I think I can manage a few minutes," I say finally, meeting his gaze.

"Excellent."

He reaches for my hand, but as he interlaces his fingers through mine, I can't help feeling disturbed by our row. Our opinions are so different. Too different. I don't know if I can ever reconcile myself to those of Mr Darcy. And more importantly, would I want to?

Troubled, I rest my head on his shoulder and silence those nagging doubts.

For now, anyway.

# CHAPTER
# THIRTY

I must have fallen asleep because the next thing I know I'm being woken by the cold. Opening my eyes, I discover the sun's disappeared, and with it, Mr Darcy.

Shivering, I stretch out my stiffened limbs and glance around me. Nope, he's definitely gone. And with him all the picnic stuff. He's even taken the fur, I notice, looking down at my lap with surprise. Huh, that's not very chivalrous of him, is it? I think, feeling miffed.

In its place is a single snowdrop. Mr Darcy must have had to go attend to those matters he was talking about and obviously didn't want to wake me. Instead, he left me this as a parting gift. I pick it up and twirl it between finger and thumb, looking at the delicate white petals.

Quite frankly, I'd rather he'd left me the fur. I'm frigging freezing.

As I'm hoisting myself up from the ground I hear the faint burbling of my cell phone. With frozen fingers I pluck it out of my pocket and see it's Stella. That's odd, I only spoke to her this morning. I wonder why she's calling. I pick up.

"Em?"

"Hey," I croak, pulling my coat tight and stamping my feet on the ground to get the circulation going. "It's good to hear your voice again."

"Is it?" she snaps grumpily.

For a moment I'm puzzled, then I realise. Oh, shit. So she got the e-mail, then.

"Freddy's dating," she continues.

"I know, I forwarded his e-mail, remember?" I reply. Though now I'm really not sure I did the right thing, I think, feeling my earlier resolve wobbling.

"Well, I can't believe it," she cries.

"Why not?"

"Because it's *Freddy*," she gasps, as if that makes it obvious.

I suddenly feel very defensive of Freddy. Stella might be my best friend but she's still out of order.

"So? The last time he looked he had a penis, didn't he?" I retort.

"Em," breathes Stella, shocked, "I can't believe you just said that — you *never* say things like that."

"Well, I'm sorry, Stella, but someone's got to be harsh with you," I continue firmly. "What did you expect? That Freddy was going to turn into a monk because you didn't want him?"

"Oh, c'mon, Em, I didn't say it like that," whines Stella, audibly shaken.

"True," I acquiesce. "You didn't say it *exactly* like that. No, it was more along the lines of 'We're complete opposites. We'd drive each other crazy if we were really a couple. Freddy's the sweetest person in the whole

352

world, and he'll make someone a wonderful boyfriend, but not mine' . . ." As I trail off there's silence on the other end of the line.

"But we *are* married," she quips weakly, after a moment.

"Only for a green card. Aren't you the one who's always pointing that out?" I remind her.

Again there's silence, only this time it's not broken by a quip. Instead, there's a heavy sigh.

"Oh, God, I've been such an idiot, haven't I?" she whispers finally, her voice thick with remorse.

"You mean you've only just realised?" I say, but there's affection in my voice. Stella's not a bad person, she just didn't see what was right under her nose.

There's the sound of a tut and I can imagine her smiling, despite herself.

"I don't want Freddy dating other girls," she says quietly, almost to herself.

"Why? Because even though you don't want him, you don't want anyone else to have him?" I propose a little unkindly. I don't think that's true, but I have to ask.

"No, that's not the reason," she fires back, full of indignation. "That's not the reason at all."

"So what it is?" I prompt.

There's a pause.

"I love him."

Her voice is quiet but steady and as I hear those three words I feel like punching the air and yelling, "Yes!" But I'll leave that to Freddy. And so, containing my excitement, I reply, "I think you need to be telling someone else that."

After making her promise that she would call Freddy and keep me posted, I say goodbye to a somewhat dazed Stella. My hands are almost frozen solid with holding the phone. God, it's cold.

Rubbing my hands together to try to warm them up, I think about Stella and Freddy, trying to imagine what their conversation might be, what's going to happen. I hope they can work it out. Stella's been an idiot, but it seems to me that sometimes you have to lose something before you realise its true value.

*Like Spike?*

My stomach churns and then — *boom* — there's Spike's e-mail again, the newspaper articles about Ernie, Mrs McKenzie's e-mail . . . Problems, worries, revelations . . . they all come rushing back. With Mr Darcy gone, I'm faced with reality again and with it, a feeling of dread. I know I can't escape from this any more. I've got to deal with it. I've got to — Oh, I don't know what I've got to do, but I've got to do *something*. Stuffing my hands in my pockets, I take one last look at the view. Hiding away up here isn't going to help. I need to go back to the hotel and face up to things. Try to figure things out. My eyes search the skyline, as if looking for some clue, some answer, some solution, but of course it's never as easy as that, is it? And turning away, I set off back down the hill.

354

Half an hour later I'm freewheeling down a road that leads into the city. Gradually it's starting to level out and so, not wanting to lose speed, I start pedalling. I turn a corner. The road narrows and winds to the left, then turns into a one-way street. The asphalt gives way to cobbles. So pretty to look at, but brutal when you're on a bicycle, especially one that doesn't have a particularly springy saddle. In fact, I'm just thinking about the havoc it's wreacking on my butt when I nearly collide with a pedestrian.

"Hey, watch out," I yell, braking suddenly and nearly going over the handlebars.

"Oh, dear. I didn't see —"

"*Maeve?*"

In the middle of a breathless apology she stops and pushes her glasses further up her nose to peer at me. "Emily! I didn't see it was you!"

"You didn't see it was anyone," I gasp, coming to a standstill.

But if she hears my remonstrations, she doesn't acknowledge them. "Where have you been? I've been looking everywhere for you," she's exclaiming instead. Her voice is breathy and high and she looks agitated.

Immediately I feel a thud of dread. "Why? What's wrong?" I ask.

Maeve seems unable to speak.

"What? Tell me!" God, now I'm really worried.

Wringing her gloved hands, she bites her lip and looks at me. Oh, hell, I'm right. She's bracing herself to tell me bad news.

"Right, c'mon," I say, taking charge. "We need to get you a drink."

"OK, tell me what's going on."

We're ensconced in the only place we could find open in Bath on New Year's Day: the Gate of India, an empty, flock-wall-papered restaurant with bad lighting and delicious poppadoms, which Maeve is absently crumbling as her words tumble over themselves.

"This morning I received a phone call."

"A phone call from whom?"

"From my brother, Paddy."

"You mean the brother in Spain?"

"Aye, I've only got the one." She nods furiously, making a start on demolishing a new poppadom. "He was in Spain with his daughter for Christmas, I think I mentioned it . . ."

"Oh, yeah." I remember now. I nod. And you also mentioned he was the brother who threw you out when you were pregnant, I think coldly, remembering her story from yesterday — though it feels like days ago — and how I'd resolved to hate him ever since.

"Well, he's back in Ireland now, and he rang me this morning, after breakfast. At first I was worried — I thought something bad must have happened."

"Why?"

"Well, Paddy never rings me, especially not on my mobile. Says it costs far too much money."

What? Not even to wish you a Happy New Year? I want to protest, but we're interrupted by a waiter who comes to take our order. I ask for a couple of brandies, then change it to peppermint teas at Maeve's request. The waiter looks grumpy and tries to push some garlic naan on us before finally giving up with a weary resignation and leaving us to continue our conversation.

"So?" I encourage.

"So, anyway, I knew something was up. At first I thought it was the children." Maeve pauses and takes a deep breath. "But thank goodness, no, they're fine." She smiles as she thinks of them. Then, remembering herself, continues: "It's to tell me I've had a phone call from a woman by the name of Shannon."

I gesture her to go on.

"She was looking for a Maeve Tumpane."

"How did she get your number?"

Maeve shrugs. "Mine's a rare surname — there aren't many in the directory. I suppose it was just a case of ringing them all up." Pushing her glasses up her nose, she peers at me uncertainly.

"And what did your brother say?" I prompt. Despite Maeve's initial eagerness to tell her news, she seems somewhat dazed by it.

"He asked what her business was." Maeve smiles, almost apologetically. "Paddy can be very brusque on the phone."

"I don't doubt it," I murmur, before I can help myself.

"He's not a bad man, you know, Emily. He did what he thought was best."

I look at Maeve's pleading expression and realise that I'm doing it again. Letting my prejudice get in the way.

Maeve's right. He probably did do what was best at the time, and who am I to judge him for it now? Nearly forty years later. A girl from the noughties who lives in New York City, where men can walk down Fifth Avenue in drag and no one bats an eyelid.

"Of course he did." I smile, and reaching across the plastic tablecloth I squeeze her hand. There can be no doubt that Maeve has forgiven her brother for what happened all those years ago. It's just a shame that it took her so long to forgive herself.

"So what did she say? This Shannon?" I ask, bracing myself for bad news.

"That the Maeve she was looking for would be in her late fifties now, and if there was such a person fitting that description living there, to pass on the message that Shannon O'Toole wanted to get in touch."

A look passes between us.

"And there was something else," says Maeve quietly.

My chest tightens. I daren't ask.

"She said it was very important to tell me that her middle name was Orla, as it was the name first given to her when she was born."

For a moment neither of us speaks. Oh my God, this isn't what I was expecting at all. I look at Maeve's face across from me at the table. Her pale blue eyes wide behind the lenses of her glasses. Her small, delicate features now worn with age. I can't begin to imagine the enormity of this news for her.

"It's my daughter, Emily. It's my daughter come to find me," she whispers eventually.

"But are you sure?" I say gently, feeling both a sense of fear and joy. "I mean, I don't want you to get your hopes up — there could be some kind of mistake . . ."

"I've spoken to her."

Wham. Out of the blue. Just like that.

"*You have?*"

"She left a number. I called her."

I can feel my eyes saucer-wide. It's not so much that Maeve has spoken to her that's so astonishing, it's the way Maeve seems so pro-active. So determined. So fearless. The old Maeve would never have picked up that phone. She was too guilty, too heavy with remorse, too scared.

"And?" is all I can manage to say.

"She sounded lovely, Emily," says Maeve quietly, but I detect the sound of relief and pride in her voice. "She's a social worker and lives in Birmingham with her husband, Richard. She told me that she'd always wondered about me. That she'd wanted to find me for a long time, but while her adoptive mother was alive she never felt it was right to ask her about me, out of respect for her feelings.

"But then when she passed away she got in touch with an agency that helps you trace birth parents. They found me straight away, but then she started to have doubts. What if I rejected her? What if I had a new life now, with more children of my own? What if I was ashamed of her and wanted to keep her a secret?" Maeve looks at me incredulously, as if she can't believe that anyone could ever think such a thing.

"She kept my details in a drawer for over a year, then apparently she heard from the agency that they'd had an enquiry about a Maeve Tumpane's daughter . . . Actually, that was the bit that I didn't understand . . ." She breaks off and shakes her head. "Or maybe I got that bit wrong. I don't know, I can't remember now. I was so overwhelmed by it all, Emily, I could barely take it in."

"Oh, Maeve, I'm so pleased for you," I whisper.

Having been listening to everything she's been telling me, my fears have been slowly falling away until now I'm just left with a cautious excitement.

"But I know it's not going to be easy," Maeve continues. "I'm not expecting us to be suddenly like mother and daughter. I mean, she had a mother for thirty-five years — I don't want to replace that, but I hope we can get to know each other, become friends."

The way she says that is so humble, so hopeful, that she almost breaks my heart.

"I'm sure you will," I say encouragingly.

"And do you want to know the best bit? When I confessed to her about how all this time I've been punishing myself for giving her up, she said it was *her* that should be thanking *me*. For giving birth to her and making the ultimate sacrifice by allowing her to be adopted by a wonderful couple who couldn't have children of their own. And who gave her two brothers — who are also adopted — the best childhood anyone could have ever had."

I smile, the bitter-sweetness of the story conjuring up all kinds of emotions within me. I look at Maeve, who's wiping a tear from underneath the lens of her glasses, and I squeeze her hand even tighter.

"And you know what else she said to me?" Sniffing back her tears, Maeve suddenly breaks into a smile. "She said, 'You're going to be a grandmother.' "

My mouth drops open, and I shriek, "Maeve! Oh, my God, Maeve!"

Jumping up from my chair, I rush round to the side of the table and wrap my arms tightly round her. "Maeve, that's fantastic! Though of course you don't look old enough," I add. Breaking into the widest smile, I squeeze her so hard I nearly squeeze the air right out of her, and in an almost comedy moment, the waiter finally reappears with our teas, only for us to send them back with orders for banana splits with extra cream, to celebrate.

Later that evening, after Maeve and I have got back from the Gate of India and I've watched four episodes back to back of the BBC dramatisation of *Pride and Prejudice* starring Colin Firth, I'm in my hotel room, about to go to bed. Except there's one thing I need to do first.

Tugging out my phone, I scroll down my list of contacts. I'm not expecting anyone to be there, but I can still leave a message. Finding the number, I press dial and listen to it ringing. As expected, it clicks on to voice-mail. "Hi, Mom and Dad, it's me. I'm just calling to say I love you both —"

"Emily?" My mom's voice. "Is that you?"

I'm startled. "Oh, yeah, it's me. I didn't think you'd be back from your trip already."

"We got back today. Are you still in England?"

"Um ... yeah." God, this is silly, I should have waited until I got back to New York.

"Are you OK, honey? What's wrong?"

I think about saying, "Nothing, I was just ringing to wish you a Happy New Year." But then if I do that, I know it might be another twenty-nine years until I make this phone call again. And then it might be too late.

I hesitate, and then, before I know it, I just come right out with it. "Next year, can we spend Christmas all together. At home. As a family?"

There's a pause. I can tell my mom's caught by surprise. Then she says with genuine pleasure, "That's a lovely idea, Emily. I think your father and I can hang up our backpacks for one year."

Five minutes later, after we've said our goodbyes, I hang up the phone and flop back against my pillow. See. It was so easy. I was expecting a row, imagining I'd have to persuade them, but I was so wrong. Turning off the light, I close my eyes. It was as simple as just picking up the phone and asking.

# CHAPTER
# THIRTY-ONE

Today we're leaving Bath on the last leg of our tour and travelling north to Cheshire to visit Lyme Park, used by the BBC as the setting for Pemberley for their *Pride and Prejudice* adaptation and the famous lake scene with Colin Firth.

It's an early start. We're due to leave after a 6a.m. breakfast, and after packing my things quickly — "pack" being a rather euphemistic word for screwing up clothes and stuffing them into my suitcase as if I'm trying to mop up a leaking washing machine (having recently mopped up my own leaking washing machine, I know this to be true) — I dash downstairs to the lobby to send an e-mail.

Since last night I've made three big decisions:

1. I can't do anything about Spike. It's too late. That horse has bolted, as my grandmother would say, which is rather apt considering my New Year's Eve experience. So I'm just going to have to try and forget all about it.

2. But I can do something about the e-mail I received from Mrs McKenzie. Instead of waiting until I get back to New York, I'm going

to bite the bullet and write another reply asking them outright if they are planning to sell the business. I'd prefer to know now, rather than prolong the agony and spending the next forty-eight hours worrying about it. It's like ripping off a plaster: painful but over quickly.
3. I'm going to stop using all these ridiculous sayings.

Ten minutes later and I still haven't sent my e-mail to Mr McKenzie.

Having opened up the mail from Mrs McKenzie and pressed reply, my resolve has failed me and now I'm sitting here, fingers poised on the keyboard, staring at a blank e-mail and a blinking cursor. I don't know what to write. I've already sent them that e-mail hoping Mr McKenzie gets better soon. What I really want to write is, "Do I still have a job to come back to?"

Immediately my stomach starts churning and I feel a heavy foreboding descending upon me. On second thoughts, maybe I should give biting bullets a miss for the moment.

I press "delete".

"So that's where you've been hiding!"

With my finger still on the key, I twirl round in my chair to see Rose bearing down upon me in a pungent cloud of perfume that I don't know the name of. But then I never cease to be amazed by those girls who the moment they meet you gasp, "Oooh, is that Dolce & Gabbana you're wearing?" As someone who's been wearing White Musk since the age of fifteen, I wouldn't be able to recognise a Chanel No. 5 from a Glade air freshener if you paid me.

"What on earth are you doing tucked away like a little mouse in that corner?" she's declaring loudly.

I force myself to sound casual. "Oh, I was just sending an e-mail," I shrug.

"To whom?" she demands, raising her eyebrows. "Privacy" is not a word in Rose's dictionary.

"My boss. To see if I've still got a job."

Well, what's the use of fibbing? Everyone's going to know soon enough, I think glumly.

Rose looks perplexed. "Well, why shouldn't you, my dear? I'm sure you're very good at your job. A hard worker." She says that with a nod of approval and her diamond earrings rattle agreeably.

I smile gratefully. Rose is being very sweet, but she's also being very naïve. Gone are the days when being a "hard worker" guaranteed success. Now it's more about having a famous rock star for a parent.

"Thanks, but I'm afraid Mr McKenzie, that's my boss, the owner of the bookstore, hasn't been very well. He's been talking about officially retiring for ever, but now I think he's really going to do it. And that means selling the business."

"Oh, I wouldn't worry," she pooh-poohs. "A bookshop will always need a manager. Who else is going to do all that tedious paperwork and what-not . . .?"

God love her. Only Rose would think insulting my job description like that will cheer me up. And yet, ironically, it does a bit.

My face creases into a smile. "I know, but it won't be the same. It won't be McKenzie's any more. Some big company will buy it and it'll get all refurbished and modernised and totally lose its charm. I can see it now. Espresso machines, wi-fi, loud music . . ." I heave a sigh, and sink down in the plastic chair. "Everybody wants new these days. No one seems to put any value on age and history."

"I know, I know . . ."

I glance up at Rose, who's nodding pensively, deep in thought.

"Actresses, bookshops, it's no different," she's murmuring to herself, and I remember what Rose was saying at the ball, about being invisible.

"Oh, sorry, I didn't mean —" I begin quickly. Shit. I don't want her to think I'm insulting her. But Rose silences me with the palm of her hand.

"Emily, dear, you have *nothing* to be sorry about. It is *society* that should be sorry." And closing her eyes, she rests the back of her hand on her brow and takes a huge, shuddering sigh.

I'm almost tempted to applaud. For the first time I see Rose not as the diamond-clad senior citizen on a Jane Austen book tour, but as the youthful twenty-something who wowed theatre audiences as leading lady. And I can see why. She's actually pretty good.

"Excuse me, Miss Bierman?" The manager of the hotel pops his head round the wall. Small, with lopsided features like a Picasso painting, he smiles nervously. Stuck to his chin is a piece of pink tissue where he's cut himself shaving.

"Yes?" Rose snaps her eyes open and transforms herself from tragic victim to demanding diva as she rounds on him. "Yes?" she barks even louder.

The manager swallows, his Adam's apple bobbing up and down furiously. "I wondered if you'd care to take a look now. I think you'll find it's to your *exacting* standards."

His brave stab at sarcasm is punished by an icy look.

"Well, thank you, Mr Geoffries. Let's hope it is, shall we?"

"What is?" I hiss at Rose, as she turns away to follow the manager, who's disappeared back round the corner. No doubt with relief that his head is still attached to his shoulders.

Smoothing down her bob, Rose flashes me a bright smile. "Come and see."

The woman smiling down at me in the black-and-white photograph on the wall of the lobby has cheekbones like coat-hangers, delicate almond-shaped eyes and lips so full they'd send Angelina Jolie running for the collagen.

"Wow, she's beautiful," I murmur. She looks about the same age as me, but it's hard to tell from a photograph. I glance across at Rose, about to ask her, when I notice she's just standing there, staring up at the framed photograph, her face filled with pride.

Of course. How could I not notice the resemblance? OK, the lips are not nearly as full, and the eyes are now heavily crinkled in the corners, but there's no denying it's Rose. I peer at the signature in the corner. Yup, there it is: Rose Raphael. Her stage name.

And then I remember her conversation with Spike. His suggestion she put a signed photograph of herself up in the lobby, along with all the others, next to Judi Dench, and how I thought he shouldn't be teasing her like that.

I feel a beat of regret.

Well, that's another thing I got wrong, isn't it?

"Don't you think it should be a little higher?"

Rose is looking at me, eyebrows raised.

"No, I think it looks great there." I smile brightly.

The manager, who's standing behind us, holding a hammer and a box of nails, braced for action, shoots me a grateful look. I get the feeling there's been more than one nail hammered in the wall this morning, trying to get this hung right.

"But are you sure I'm not clashing with Judi?" persists Rose.

"No, I think you've both got plenty of room to breathe," soothes the manager.

I shoot back a look of admiration. He's obviously a professional at this. Judging by the number of photographs on the wall, he's obviously had to deal with his fair share of demanding luvvies.

"Hmm, do you think so?" Rose is saying, but she's allowing a smile to creep across her face. "I mean, I wouldn't want to overshadow her or anything."

I have to stifle a smile. Only Rose could worry about overshadowing an Academy Award-winning actress.

"And she does look rather old next to me, don't you think?"

Considering that your photograph was taken probably fifty years ago that's hardly surprising, I want to say, but of course I don't. This is Rose's moment, and she's thoroughly enjoying herself. In fact, this is the happiest I've seen her all tour. The last thing I want to do is spoil it by giving a reality check.

"Yes, I think she does," I reply, and turning to Rose, I wink.

She breaks into the broadest smile. "Perfect. Then let's leave it there, shall we?" she announces, turning to the manager.

A look of relief floods his lopsided face.

"And as for you, Mr Geoffries . . ."

*Oh, God, what now?* scuds across his features.

Grabbing him by the shoulders, she plants a large kiss on his astonished cheek. "*You* are an absolute star!"

Rose's picture draws quite a crowd. Until now, I think most of the women had secretly thought Rose boastful and her tales of her "renowned beauty" and "theatrical prowess" somewhat exaggerated. But now, with their memories jogged and the evidence indisputable, they're full of admiration and questions:

"Ooh, did you act with Sir John Gielgud?"

"I *thought* I recognised you! I saw you on stage at the Old Vic in 1955."

"Rose Raphael? You're *the* Rose Raphael?"

"Tell me, what is Judi like?"

Rose, of course, is utterly delighted. Fielding questions like a seasoned politician, she seems to really come alive, recounting anecdotes from her theatre days to an eager audience. In fact, it takes all of Miss Steane's skills as a tour guide to break up the crowd and chivvy everyone out of the lobby to board the waiting coach.

I hang back. The thought of seeing Ernie after everything that's happened isn't something I've been much looking forward to. After that whole made-up story he told me, all those lies about Spike, what on earth am I going to say? Anything? Nothing? Should I just ignore him? Confront him? *What?*

Walking across the parking lot, I go backwards and forwards, different scenarios playing in my head: Ernie's reaction when confronted with the evidence of the newspaper cuttings. He's angry, furious — Shit, what if he turns violent? I flinch at the thought. He might be an old man but he could still pack a punch with those forearms. Then there's the scenario of us both pretending nothing's happened, politely greeting each other, yet a silent look passing between us that acknowledges he knows that I know.

But whatever happens I can't put it off any longer. I'm the last to board, and as I climb up the steps I brace myself for our confrontation. Stay calm, Emily, keep your cool, don't go making a scene in front of everyone. I reach the top step. Hilary is in front of me, but I can see a peaked cap. OK, I've made a decision. I'm just going to tell him I need to speak to him privately, that there's something we need to discuss, that —

Hang on a minute —

"You're not Ernie," I blurt in bewilderment.

The boyish figure in the peaked cap turns to me. "Well, I wasn't the last time I looked," he quips, and cocks a smile.

I stare at him blankly. He has a goatee and pimples and looks about twenty-one. Nope, he's definitely not Ernie.

I laugh awkwardly. "It's just that we . . . um . . . had a different driver before," I explain, trying to regain my composure, but I'm bursting with unanswered questions. Where's Ernie gone? Was he fired? Did he leave of his own accord? What happened exactly?

"Oh, right, yeah, so I heard," nods the new driver. "I was called in to cover. Something about him having to leave at short notice, some problem . . ."

"What problem?" I demand, dying to know what happened.

"I dunno." He shrugs. "No one tells me anything round here."

"Now if you'd all like to take your seats, please," instructs Miss Steane, charging up the aisle towards me, clipboard in hand. "That includes you, Miss Albright, if you would be so kind." She glances between me and the driver, and I can tell from her expression she knows exactly what's happened, but she isn't letting on. But then I often get the impression that Miss Steane knows more than she's saying.

I sit down and look out of the window. And for the first time it dawns on me that for someone who sure knows a lot about everyone else, I don't know the first thing about our enigmatic tour guide. Not one little thing.

# CHAPTER
# THIRTY-TWO

Of course it soon gets round about Ernie's disappearance and it doesn't take long before rumours begin circulating. According to Hilary, who has it on good authority, Ernie was spotted on New Year's Eve with a woman from the ball.

Apparently they appeared "deep in conversation", is how Hilary puts it, which reminds me of those murder mysteries you get on TV, where the victims are always last seen "deep in conversation" with a stranger before their untimely death. Not that I'm implying Ernie has now turned from a con man into a murderer, I'm just saying.

Credence is further added to this story by Rupinda, who, with much jangling of the dozens of thin, gold bracelets she wears on her arms, relates her visit to a newsagent's yesterday where she'd encountered Ernie and the aforementioned mystery woman (now a blonde, with bad posture that could be dramatically improved by yoga, according to Rupinda). Ernie, however, did not see Rupinda, and he and the blonde were overheard talking about their last-minute vacation to Jamaica.

Or at least that's what she *thought* she heard, admits Rupinda, when quizzed by Rose, but then perhaps it wasn't that at all. In fact, now she's thinking about it, she can't be one hundred per cent sure it was Ernie after all, as she was too busy flicking through *Spiritual Health Monthly*. There's universal groan of disappointment from those on the coach who've been listening to all this with bated breath, and Rupinda is crossly accused of having an overactive imagination by Miss Steane, who then tells everyone to stop making idle assumptions and to look to the left as we're passing a famous viaduct built by the Romans.

Me? I don't know who or what to believe. Maybe Hilary and Rupinda are right, maybe Miss Steane is, or maybe none are and it's something completely different. Either way, he's gone.

I glance sideways at Maeve. Her face tilted to the window, she's gazing at the scenery and smiling absently to herself, and I know that even if we never find out what happened to Ernie, one thing is certain: she's had a lucky escape. And for that, we have Spike to thank. Because if it wasn't for him, this story might have had a very different ending altogether.

It's a long drive to Cheshire and an hour into our journey we've left the countryside far behind and are on the grey concrete monotony of an English motorway.

I think about Bath. About leaving it behind. Part of me is sad, the way you're always sad when you've looked forward to visiting somewhere or doing something for so long, and now it's over, but to be honest, I'm also rather relieved. It's got a lot of wonderful memories, most of them revolving around Mr Darcy — our amazing first date on the lake, riding up to the moonlit Sham Castle on New Year's Eve, the butterflies in my stomach when he turned to kiss me — but it has some pretty painful ones too.

My mind leapfrogs back to my furious row with Spike, then leapfrogs off again.

But like I said, there's nothing I can do about that now. I've just got to try to forget about it.

Half an hour of fidgeting later, my sweater screwed up underneath my chin in a makeshift pillow, I give up trying to snooze like everyone else is doing. It's impossible. There's too much going on in my head. Sitting upright, I dig around in my bag, pull out my copy of *Pride and Prejudice* and turn to my bookmarked page.

With everything that's been going on, I haven't got very far in — I'm still only near the beginning. Saying that, this is one of my favourite scenes in the book. It's where Elizabeth and Mr Darcy are at Netherfield Ball, and Mr Darcy has just asked her for the next dance. Taken by surprise she says yes, but when he walks away, she wonders what on earth she was thinking. Her friend Charlotte tries to console her:

"I dare say you will find him agreeable."
"Heaven forbid! *That* would be the greatest misfortune of all!

To find a man agreeable whom one is determined to hate! Do not wish me such an evil."

God, I totally know how she feels, I muse, thinking about Spike, then quickly trying not to. Remember your decision, Emily? I tell myself firmly. Turning over the page, I continue reading about what happens when they actually get on the dance floor: I always feel a bit sorry for Elizabeth here. She's so earnest in her defence of Wickham and yet she totally gets it wrong.

"I remember hearing you once say, Mr Darcy, that you hardly ever forgave, that your resentment once created was unappeasable. You are very cautious, I suppose, as to its *being created*."

"I am," said he, with a firm voice.

"And never allow yourself to be blinded by prejudice?"

"I hope not."

"It is particularly incumbent on those who never change their opinion, to be secure of judging properly at first."

Saying that, she's such a hypocrite. If anyone's blinded by prejudice, it's Elizabeth! I think, my mind flicking back over the earlier scenes. She's been totally against Mr Darcy from the very beginning, ever since he hurt her pride by calling her "pretty dull" and "average-looking".

I catch myself.

*What?* No, I've got that wrong — it was *Spike* who called *me* that. Mr Darcy called Elizabeth "tolerable" and "not pretty enough". I shake my head. How weird. Where did that just come from? Brushing it aside, I turn back to the page.

"May I ask to what these questions tend?"

"Merely to the illustration of *your* character," said she, endeavouring to shake off her gravity. "I am trying to make it out."

But she's not *really*, is she? I tell myself. It's pretty obvious Elizabeth has already made her mind up about Mr Darcy, and she's using this to have a dig. I mean, let's face it, the only reason Elizabeth was so quick to believe Wickham's story, and without even a scrap of evidence to support it, was because it backed up her opinion of Mr Darcy as a total bastard. It made her feel right. It justified her dislike of him.

And the only reason I know this for certain, is because I felt exactly the same that day in the café when Ernie told me *his* story, I think regretfully. Honestly, talk about a coincidence.

Except —

Suddenly the parallels are too many to ignore and it's like a light goes on in my head. Hang on a minute. This could be written about me and Spike, just replace the names and it's us.

No sooner has the thought struck than I can't believe I haven't noticed this before. I start flicking through the pages in the book. In fact, the more I'm thinking about it, the more similarities are jumping out at me, I realise, my memory simultaneously flicking through a rollerdeck of past conversations, arguments, glances, emotions . . .

There was the time we met and he insulted me, our awkward dance at the ball, believing Ernie when he told me all those terrible things about Spike, his letter in the form of an e-mail showing me I'd completely misjudged him, his declaration of love, my awful reaction —

Oh, God. I feel slightly sick.

Because now I'm thinking about it, I realise that, just like Lizzy Bennet, I've got it all wrong. And not just about Spike, but about Mr Darcy too . . .

There. I've admitted it. And as I do it's as if a lid bursts open on a box I've kept tucked away inside myself and all those nagging doubts I've had for the last few days are released and come rushing to the surface. The long, awkward silences, his views about women working, his zero sense of humour and inability to laugh at himself . . .

What was it Spike said that day in Bath? "*The reality is always more disappointing than the fantasy.*" He was talking about Betty Blue, but he could just as well have been talking about Mr Darcy. In *Pride and Prejudice* Jane Austen describes Mr Darcy as "brooding", which *sounds* so attractive, but in truth it turns out it just means he's sulky; "proud", I've fast come to realise, means sexist, and as for him appearing "arrogant", in reality, what it really means is he's actually quite snobbish.

**378**

And finally it hits me. I'm not in love with Mr Darcy. Not even remotely. And you know what? I never was. I was in love with the idea of him and what he represented, but not the reality. Of course that doesn't mean I'm not attracted to him, who wouldn't be? As Stella said back in the bookstore, the man's a female wet dream. But how can anything live up to the airbrushed vision I've created in my head all these years? He can't. And he shouldn't be made to. Because that's the thing about Mr Darcy — he's a female fantasy. But that's all he is, a fantasy. And that's what he should remain.

"Emily?"

A voice right next to my ear snaps me back and I look to see Maeve peering at me.

"My, my, you were away with the fairies, weren't you?" she's chuckling, pushing her glasses up her nose to peer at me even closer. "Haven't you noticed? Look! We've arrived."

She gestures out of the window, and as I turn sideways I see everyone milling about in the parking lot full of excited chatter and anticipation, and I realise the coach is empty.

"Sorry. I was engrossed in my book," I say, making my excuses, and getting up. "You go ahead, I'll follow you."

"Okey-dokey," nods Maeve, and then throws me a smile. "Gosh, isn't this exciting? Home of the famous lake scene. Perhaps we'll see our very own Mr Darcy," she says, and raises her eyebrows.

"I hope so," I reply, watching as she turns and begins making her way down the tour bus.

And I really do hope I see him, I think, as I start quickly gathering together my things. Because I've also realised something else. Mr Darcy and I can never make this work. And ironically it's got *nothing* to do with the weirdness, absurdity and implausibility of it all, and *everything* to do with something a lot more mundane: irreconcilable differences. Or, to put it in layman's terms, we're just too different.

We have views which are, quite literally, worlds apart. And I need to tell him this. But since I don't have a number I can call him on, a mobile I can text or an e-mail address I can write to, I'm going to have to do it the hard way and tell him face to face.

I feel my resolve falter.

The only problem is, how on earth do you break up with Mr Darcy?

# CHAPTER
# THIRTY-THREE

"As most of you probably already know, Lyme Park was turned into one of television's iconic backdrops when it was used by the BBC in their adaptation of *Pride and Prejudice* as the setting for Pemberley, the home of our beloved Mr Darcy. It wasn't entirely loyal to the original novel. Indeed, it's actually Chatsworth House in Derbyshire that is believed to have been Jane Austen's inspiration for Pemberley. However, for all you Colin Firth fans, it is *here* that the famous scene with Mr Firth emerging dripping from the lake was filmed . . ."

There are a few phwoars and whoops of approval from the ladies who have gathered inside the grand entrance of the house to listen to Miss Steane's introductory speech.

". . . and today we are very lucky indeed to be allowed this opportunity. Usually the hall is closed to the general public at this time, but for us Jane Austen fans, the powers that be have made an exception and opened it up to us for a private tour. Bravo!"

Finishing with a flourish, she brings her hands together and sets off a little round of applause. I join in though I wasn't really listening. I'm too busy thinking about Mr Darcy. About how I have to tell him it's over, that I can't see him any more. And how on earth do I find him to tell him?

Wondering where I was going to bump into him again has always seemed so romantic and exciting, but suddenly it isn't fun any more. I feel a flash of frustration. I don't want a man who's mysterious and enigmatic — I want a man I can text. Me, who hates all this constant texting, who's always complaining it's so unromantic and takes away the mystery. Now I'd do anything to be able to text **'Where R U?!'** and press "send".

"Though Chatsworth House, which Jane Austen visited in 1811, may have been the real background for Pemberley, I think you will probably all agree, ladies, that Lyme Hall would probably be of a more manageable size for Elizabeth when she becomes lady of the house . . ."

A couple of hours later and Miss Steane's coming to the end of her guided tour. As she leads the way into the last and final room, I glance quickly around, as I've done with every room in the house, hoping to catch sight of Mr Darcy. Hoping that he'll just turn up unexpectedly as he always does. That any minute now I'm going to step into a room or walk through a doorway or turn to the side and he'll be there. That tall, dark, instantly recognisable figure, the familiar brooding expression, the unmistakable voice with its gravity and perfect vowels.

Yet I've looked around every marble bust, behind every stick of furniture and out of every window and I haven't seen him. Now, with our visit soon to be over, I'm fast losing hope that he's going to show up. And beginning to think that I might, in fact, never see him again.

At the thought, I feel a strange mixture of sadness and relief. I guess it solves the problem of having to break up with him, and yet somehow it doesn't feel right — after everything that's happened, I feel I need to say goodbye properly. I need, to use a dreadful Americanism, to have closure.

After the tour has finished, everyone makes their way to the café and souvenir shop, but instead I go outside and take a look at the view. It really is beautiful here. I hadn't noticed just how stunning this place is. I was too busy with my head in my book when we first arrived to even notice the impressive drive through the deer park, the hall itself which resembles a sumptuous Italianate palace, surrounded by gardens and fronted by the most incredible reflection in the lake. But now, as I stand here drinking it all in, it fairly takes your breath away.

The hall itself is magnificent, if a little overwhelming and stuffed with clocks, tapestries and woodcarvings, while the seventeen acres of Victorian garden, including an Edwardian rose garden, deer park and woodland, stretch out for ever. But it's not just the aesthetics, it's the feel of the place. Lyme Park has got that magical quality to it. I can tell why the BBC chose it. It has a serenity. It's timeless. You could imagine that nothing has changed in a hundred years — it's like time has stood still.

I draw in a long breath and stuff my gloved hands further into my pockets. Alone in the clear, fresh January air, I remain here, gazing out at the lake, absently watching the birds in the distance, squawking and swooping across the water and over the branches of the bare trees.

"Beautiful, isn't it?"

Broken from my reverie, I turn to see Miss Steane walking across the path to join me. I feel a beat of regret. I don't feel much up to talking. I want to be alone.

"Oh, yeah, very." I nod. "We don't get views like this in New York," I add, for something to say. My knack for small talk seems to have deserted me.

"I don't doubt it," she enthuses. Joining me, she stares straight ahead out at the view.

I glance at her out of the corner of my eye, at her delicate features, the curls of hair escaping from her fur hat, which matches her muffler. You know, she really does remind me of someone. I've been wracking my brains all week, but I just can't think who.

"So have you enjoyed your literature lover's trip, Miss Albright?" She suddenly turns and catches me looking at her.

"Oh, yeah." I nod, quickly looking away again. "It's been . . ." I search for the word. Well, what word sums up this roller coaster of a week? I can't think of one. Does one even exist? ". . . Interesting," I manage.

Miss Steane looks satisfied by my reply.

"Which has been your favourite part?"

I hesitate. Before, I would have definitely said Mr Darcy. Well, I wouldn't have *said* it, but I would have thought it. But now? Now, I'm not so sure. Everything is so jumbled up and messy and confused. I don't really know what to think.

"Um . . . all of it," I say finally. "It's all been great."

"And did you read Mr Hargreaves's e-mail?"

"Yeah," I reply, before it registers what she's just asked me. I look at her sharply. Miss Steane is looking at me, her hazel eyes bright in the winter sunshine. "How did you . . .?"

"Know he'd written to you?" she finishes, and smiles. "I gave him your e-mail address." There's a beat. "I hope you don't mind."

I pause for a moment, allowing this to register. "No, of course not." I shake my head. And then, looking back at her, ask quickly, "Did he tell you what happened? What he was going to put in the e-mail?"

"No. I didn't ask and he didn't tell me." She stares at me for a few moments, as if deep in thought, before finally speaking. "Prejudice can be a terrible thing, Emily. As can pride," she says quietly, and looks at me soberly. "You know, Jane Austen always made her heroines feisty. They stuck by their principles, went after what they wanted, were not afraid to admit when they were wrong." She looks at me, her eyes flashing. "Not doing anything can be worse than doing the wrong thing."

I absorb her words. They resonate within me. I turn them over in my mind and am about to say something when I'm distracted by what looks to be someone swimming in the lake. Surely not — it's *January*. I crinkle up my forehead and squint to see better. The swimmer is pulling himself out of the water. Christ, he's still in his clothes. He must be *freezing*. You can see his nipples from here, right through his white shirt that's wet through and clinging to his chest . . .

Holy shit. It's the famous lake scene. Except it's not Colin Firth . . .

"It's Mr Darcy," I gasp, before I can help myself.

As soon as I've said it I clamp my mitten over my mouth, wishing I could stuff the words right back in again. Fuck. Me and my big mouth. Why did I have to go and say that? My tour guide's going to think I'm totally nuts.

I glance at Miss Steane, but she hasn't flinched. Instead she's still standing there, perfectly poised. She turns to me, a faint smile of amusement playing on her lips. "I hate to say it, but he's not a patch on Colin Firth, is he?"

"No, he's not," I laugh — and then freeze.

What the . . .?

Did she just . . .?

I open my mouth but no words come out. Which is weird as there are a million of the things whirling round in my head right now, forming a million different questions.

But I don't have time to ask any of them. I need to talk to Mr Darcy before he disappears again. I look sharply back down at the lake. Shit, he's already striding away across manicured lawns.

"I gotta go," is all I can manage to stammer. And without even a backwards glance, I begin hurtling down the hill after him.

By the time I get to the bottom, he's gone.

I scan left and right, hoping to catch sight of him, but seeing nothing I slow down and come to a standstill by a large hedge. I bend double and drop my hands to my knees to catch my breath. My heart is thumping like a piston, so hard it feels as if it might burst right out of my chest. Jesus, I had no idea I was so unfit.

I stay like that for a few moments, waiting until my breathing returns to normal, staring at my grassy, mud-splattered boots and wondering what I'm going to do next. Heaving a sigh, I push my hair out of my eyes and focus. I might not be an Olympic athlete, but it didn't take me long to run down that hill. He's got to be around here somewhere. But where?

I take a gamble and head towards the gardens. Now, I don't know the first thing about gardens. Living in New York, the most green-fingered I've ever got is growing some chili peppers on my windowsill. I used to have the most beautiful shocking-pink orchid Stella bought me, but when all the flowers fell off I thought I'd killed it and threw it away. Only to learn that, apparently, that's what's supposed to happen, and new flowers grow. Suffice to say, Stella *killed* me.

However, you don't have to be an expert to see that these gardens are something else. Even in winter there are all these amazing-looking shrubs and plants, hedges displaying some incredible — and *very* steady-handed

— topiary, manicured borders, ornate trellises, formal nurseries and a maze of pathways winding round. On any other occasion I would love to take my time and wander along them, like when I was little and I used to go to nurseries with my dad and wander around the green-houses, looking at all the different plants, inhaling the humid scent of soil and flowers. But right now there's something I need to do, a conversation I need to have: I owe it to Mr Darcy.

And sticking my childhood memories firmly in my pocket, I hurry off down one of the paths.

After a while of zigzagging backwards and forwards and weaving left and right, on the lookout for a flash of his tailcoat, a whiff of his cologne or the sound of gravel crunching under his footsteps, I'm beginning to lose hope. It's getting late, we'll be leaving soon and there's *still* no sight of him. I'm totally at a loss.

I'm also, I abruptly realise, totally lost.

Shit.

Slowing down my pace, I glance around me, trying to find my bearings. OK, no problem, I just have to find the sun as that will tell me — Actually, I'm not exactly sure what that will tell me — but anyhow I can't find the sun as the sky is now heavy with a dark wadding of clouds and it looks like it's going to rain any minute. Double shit.

I try looking for other clues. Only I've been looking ahead for Mr Darcy the whole time and haven't been paying attention to anything else. I can't remember any clues. In fact, I can't even remember if I just turned left by that fountain or right. Or did I go straight?

I gaze doubtfully at the myriad of paths. It's like a maze with all these tall hedges on either side. Gut instinct is telling me that I came from that direction, but then gut instinct once told me that gate 20 at JFK Airport was "that way" and I ended up going completely the wrong way, nearly missing my flight and being whooshed through the airport on an electric cart with a flashing light and a siren blaring in order to make it. The word "embarrassing" doesn't even come close.

Spotting an old stone bench, I abandon my attempts at orientation and wander over to it. It's tucked away under an even older-looking tree and covered in lichen and moss, but I sit down anyway. Instantly I can feel the cold seeping through the denim of my jeans. I try tugging my coat underneath myself, but it's not long enough and won't stretch. Defeat stabs.

Ever get that feeling that nothing's going right? That you've totally messed up? That whatever you do, you're not going to be able to make it right again? That it's too late?

Pressure thumps against my temples and I feel a flash of weariness. I'm tired. I've had enough. I can't go chasing around the countryside for a man who's not supposed to exist. Just so I can break up with him. Just so I can say goodbye.

Unexpectedly, I feel a wetness on my cheek and a big fat tear rolls down my face. Furiously I brush it away with the sleeve of my coat. But another one appears, and another, and another, until my sleeve is all wet and the tears are coming thick and fast.

I give up. I totally and utterly give up on everything. I give up trying to find Mr Darcy, I give up hoping Spike will forgive me, and I give up believing that somehow I'm going to fix things and there's going to be a happy ending.

And hugging my knees to my chest, I bury my face in my scarf and sob my foolish heart out.

# CHAPTER
# THIRTY-FOUR

I don't know how long I stay like that. Curled up tight into a ball, my shoulders shaking. Or how long I would have stayed like that if I hadn't felt a hand on my arm.

Even before I look up, I know who it is.

"Emily, dear, whatever is the matter?"

Mr Darcy is peering down at me, his sharp features etched with surprise. I sniff frantically, rubbing away the strands of damp hair that are sticking to my clammy face. I want to feel relieved that he's here, I *should* feel relieved, but I don't. Everything's such a mess. I'm such a mess, I think miserably, sniffing again, as my nose won't stop running. God, I must look terrible.

Without saying anything Mr Darcy offers me a white handkerchief. I take it gratefully and wipe my puffy eyes, streaking the cotton with big black smudges of eyeliner and mascara, and then blow my snotty nose. Oh, what the hell. Forget the feminine mystique, I don't care any more. Screwing the handkerchief into a ball in my fist, I finally raise my swollen eyes to look at him.

As usual, he's standing there, immaculately groomed and completely stoic. Stoic to the point of impassive.

"Emily, please. Why are you crying?"

There's a faint air of impatience in his voice and I notice his hand is still resting on my arm. Now more than ever do I want someone to just put their arms round me and give me a hug, instead of being all repressed and brooding.

"I was looking for you, I saw you swimming, but I couldn't find you . . ." I sniff, my voice coming out a bit trembly.

"Oh, Emily, do not distress yourself further. I was never far — I simply put on some fresh clothes and took a walk."

". . . and I needed to see you, to tell you something . . ." I swallow hard, twisting the handkerchief in the palms of my hands as I try to think of the right words.

But before I get a chance to speak, Mr Darcy says, "I feel exactly the same way. I too have something I need to tell you, something very important, something that I cannot hide from you another minute longer . . ."

I stop sniffling and look up with slight apprehension. He's staring at me with that dark intensity, but whereas at first I found it sexy, now it's making me really uncomfortable.

". . . something that will change our lives for ever . . ."

With a thud, what he's saying registers. Oh, sweet Jesus, please don't tell me he's going to do what I think he's going to do.

He drops to his knee in his front of me.

"Holy shit," I gasp, thrown into a panic.

He looks at me, startled. "What is wrong?"

**392**

I falter. This is where you explain, Emily. This is where you tell him everything. About how you don't want to see him any more, about how you're too different, about how you want to say goodbye. About how you're in love with Spike —

*What?* Where the hell did that just come from?

"Um . . . it's all muddy," I manage to stammer. "Your breeches, they'll get filthy."

He looks at me and then gets up again. "That is what I love so much about you, Emily, you are always so sweet and thoughtful and amusing."

I watch as he sits back down next to me on that little stone bench, flicking out his tailcoat, pulling at his breeches. Before, it had seemed so attractive, but now it seems stiff and fussy.

"As I was saying, I have something I must tell you —" begins Mr Darcy.

"Look, I don't think —" I try cutting him off.

"I love you, Emily," he declares, before I can stop him. He waits expectantly for my response.

Oh, God. I pause, then take a deep breath. "No, you don't," I reply firmly.

He looks surprised and, I have to say, more than a little miffed.

"Excuse me?"

"Love me," I reply simply. And then, more determinedly, I repeat it again: "No, you don't love me."

Mr Darcy is taken aback, but he quickly recovers. "Emily! What would make you say such a thing!" he declares, his features darkening.

I pause. And for a brief, magical moment I wonder what might happen if I were to change my mind. If I were to tell him I love him. If I were to choose the fantasy over reality. It's so close I can almost touch it with my fingertips.

"Because you love someone else," I blurt.

"Who? I demand you tell me who?"

"Elizabeth Bennet," I say firmly, and as the words come out of my mouth I know there's no going back.

"You know her?" he asks, struggling to keep his composure.

"Well, not exactly," I admit.

"Well, then, let me assure you, Emily, I do not know what rumours you may have heard, but I met Miss Elizabeth Bennet for only a short time some months ago — November, I think it was — and I have not seen her since. It is you who has stolen my affections —"

"No," I interrupt, shaking my head. "This is all wrong, you've got it all wrong."

"I thought so too," agrees Mr Darcy, his voice low and powerful. "But meeting you has caused a revelation within me, Emily. I do not want a woman like Miss Bingley, I desire someone feisty and opinionated, someone who can match me at my own game."

"Like Elizabeth Bennet," I persevere, partly because I feel a responsibility to the novel, and partly because I'm hoping this way he'll get the message and I'll be able to avoid our "talk".

Mr Darcy throws me an impatient look. "Why do you keep talking about Miss Bennet? I barely know her," he protests indignantly.

**394**

"But you *should* get to know her. I think you'd be perfect for each other," I continue. "I heard she's . . . um . . . really got the hots for you," I say, trying to appeal to his ego.

"*Hots?*"

"It's an American saying," I quickly explain. "It means she really admires you, thinks you're attractive and honourable and . . . um . . . a great equestrian," I finish, crossing my fingers behind my back. God, if Jane Austen could hear me she'd kill me. I'm completely destroying one of her finest heroines.

Mr Darcy looks briefly impressed, and his chest seems to rise an inch or two, but he's still not satisfied. Mr Darcy, it would seem, like most men, cannot take rejection.

"Am I not making my advances clear?" he insists, glaring at me.

For a brief instant I'm struck by my bizarre situation. Here is Mr Darcy, the most dashing hero of all time, telling me he's in love with me. And here *I* am having a panic attack.

"You're not my type," I bleat weakly.

"Type?" he repeats in bewilderment, obviously never having heard of such a notion.

I make another stab. "It's not you, it's me," I say, resorting to the old cliché.

His face changes colour and the muscle in his clenched jaw twitches violently. "But you told me you had dreamed of this moment, that being with me was like a fantasy," he cries. Jumping up from the bench, he begins pacing backwards and forwards, raking his fingers through his hair.

Did I? I can't remember. I was so busy being swept off my feet, I was being swept away from myself.

"It was. I did . . ." I begin, and then falter. God, I've never been any good at breaking up with *regular* guys, but Mr Darcy? What am I supposed to say? That you weren't how I hoped you were going to be? That you didn't — *and couldn't* — live up to the fantasy. But that it's not your fault, because no man could. I'd set the bar so high no one could ever reach it. And maybe I'd done that for a reason.

Because Stella was right. I am a hopeless romantic. A silly, ridiculous, foolish romantic. I live in a fantasy land. I need to get real. And now, for the first time, I'm realising that I *want* to get real. I want a real relationship with a real man in a real world — with all the real problems, faults and whatever comes with it.

I glance up at Mr Darcy. Clasping his forehead, he's leaning his elbow against a tree trying to compose himself, and I know now, more than ever, that I don't want a romantic fictional hero declaring his undying love. Moonlit horserides in ballgowns might sound romantic, but they kill your ass — trust me, I have the bruises to prove it — and instead of someone reciting poetry, I want someone who can crack a funny joke or discuss the merits of the UK version of the *Office* versus the US *Office*.

I want to go out with a man who's nice to my friends . . .

**396**

(I have a flashback of Spike encouraging Rose with her headshot.)

. . . who's sensitive and funny . . .

(Who can forget Spike doing the funky chicken on the dance floor?)

. . . a man who can express his emotions and not smoulder the whole time . . .

(Cut to my huge argument with Spike after the ball and him saying, "*You didn't have to be such a bitch about it. I do have feelings, you know.*")

. . . who doesn't mind me eating with my fingers or wearing sexy dresses . . .

(Remember when Spike looked me over in the ballroom and said, "*Nice dress,*" with a nod of appreciation?)

. . . and is impressed, not horrified, by my job . . .

("*Crikey, that's great,*" said Spike in admiration when I told him about my work.)

. . . who won't expect me to be able to play the bloody piano or sew samplers, but will hang out and watch *Changing Rooms* and —

"Is there someone else?" Mr Darcy is asking me stiffly.

Snapping back, I look at him and hesitate.

Oh, for Godsakes, Emily, just come out and admit it. To yourself and Mr Darcy. You don't want to go out with just any man, you want to go out with Spike. He ticks every goddamn box.

"Yes," I say quietly.

"Are you in love with him?"

The breath catches in the back of my throat. Because as hard as I've tried to hate Spike, I can't. In fact, I've gone and done exactly the opposite.

"Yes," I say, and this time I don't hesitate. "I think I might be," I admit, and I can't help smiling.

Mr Darcy pales. I suspect he's not used to being refused by ladies. But then he'll have to get used to it, I think ruefully, thinking of the famous scene between him and Elizabeth Bennet when he asks her to marry him. And he will ask her. I'm sure of that now.

Quickly recovering, he stands before me now, hands clasped behind his back.

"May I enquire one more thing?" he says, and he says it with such formality that I feel a bitter-sweetness. Despite everything that's happened, I'm going to miss Mr Darcy.

"Of course." I smile, and then with slight trepidation add, "Ask me anything."

There's a pause as he composes himself and then: "What does he have that I don't?"

"He's real."

And as our eyes meet a large drop of rain splashes on to my lap. I glance upwards. As dozens more start to fall, big meaty drops that are splattering all over my face and running down my collar. The grey skies have turned black and threatening, and at that moment a splinter of lightning is followed immediately by a loud crack of thunder.

"Quick, the storm must be directly above us," I cry. "We've gotta find shelter."

Jumping up from the bench, I put my head down and dash for cover, but the rain has turned into a torrential downpour and the paths are all slippery and I can barely see as the rain is lashing my face so hard. And I'm running and running, and all the trees are bare, and there's nowhere to shelter, and I'm getting completely drenched, and I'm never going to find my way out —

I stop dead. There, before me, is Lyme Hall. Large and grand, it's just sitting there as if to say, "What took you so long?" A huge smile breaks across my face and I feel a whoosh of relief. I've found my way out. I'm not lost at all.

I whirl round to tell Mr Darcy, but he's not there. In fact, he's nowhere to be seen, I realise, scanning my surroundings. Shit, where did he go? Maybe I left him behind, maybe he took a different path, maybe he's gone back to wherever he came from.

No sooner has the thought struck than I notice the rain has stopped, just as quickly as it started. The birds are tweetering again, noises return, there's a sweet, fresh smell from the grass. I feel a sudden, unexpected rush of euphoria.

"Oh, look, there she is . . ."

Hearing voices, I turn round and see Rose and Hilary striding towards the grass with two colossal striped golfing umbrellas. I can't help smiling. As someone who insists on wearing heels at all times, Rose is not one for taking country walks, and is picking her way precariously across the wet turf. Obviously the gift shop has proved a disappointment.

"Hi." I wave, pushing my wet hair out of my eyes. "What brings you out here?"

Reaching me, Hilary throws me her "lawyer" smile. "You, my dear," she says firmly.

I look at Rose for an explanation. Winded by the walk, she takes a moment to catch her breath, and then, in an uncharacteristic show of affection, reaches for my hand and gives it a squeeze.

"Can we have a word?"

# CHAPTER
# THIRTY-FIVE

"Cheers." I grin.

Making sure to keep my "little finger out" (as instructed by Rose), I loop my finger through the handle of my goldrimmed teacup and raise it aloft.

"Cheers," beam Rose and Hilary, doing the same.

There's a delicate chink of finest bone china as the three teacups come together, and I feel a burst of happiness.

God, I love England! What a civilised way to do business.

It's the next day and I'm in London, at the Savoy, having afternoon tea with Rose and Hilary. It's our last day of the tour. We arrived here this lunchtime and a lot of people have left already in a flurry of address-swapping and cheek-kissing (Rupinda wouldn't go before making everyone sign up for her yoga retreat in Goa next year) and gone to catch various flights and trains home.

Maeve and I said our goodbyes first thing this morning. She was catching a flight from Manchester back to Ireland, and promised to call me next week after her first meeting with Shannon. She was nervous but excited, and there was a quiet confidence about her that was never there before. Ever since that phone call from her brother, the transformation has been incredible. The person who left today was so different from the anxious mouse I met only a week ago, and as I hugged her goodbye I got quite choked up. When I came on this trip I would never have thought I'd make such wonderful friends, especially not ones old enough to draw their pension. But then I've had a lot of unexpected things happen to me this week.

One of them being the reason I'm sitting here right now in this fancy hotel, on this plush velvet sofa, sipping Earl Grey and nibbling the tiniest triangle of crust-less cucumber sandwich that you've ever seen. I gobble it up in one mouthful. I've got that giddy, nervous exhilaration that makes me want to eat, even though I'm not hungry. I reach for another cucumber triangle. Saying that, these are rather delicious.

Things have been happening so fast I'm still trying to take it all in. When Hilary and Rose asked to speak to me yesterday I had no idea what it was about.

But Rose, being Rose, came straight to the point: "Have you thought of buying your bookshop?" she asked, without even an introduction.

Coming from a woman wearing ten years of my salary in diamonds, I couldn't help but smile. "I don't think I've got enough in my savings account," I quipped ruefully.

To which Rose and Hilary laughed heartily, and Hilary cried, "Oh, I do love the New Yorkers' sense of humour," while Rose added, "No, you silly girl. Don't you know the first thing about business? You don't pay for anything *yourself*. You get someone else to pay for it." I must have looked confused because she went on to explain, "Investors, darling! What you need are investors!"

Which is like telling someone who's run out of gas, that they need to put petrol in the car.

"Great, but where exactly do I find some of these investors?" I asked.

And — now this is the *best* bit — Rose replied, as if it was obvious, "Why, you're looking right at her!"

"Would you care for a fresh pot of tea?"

I hear a voice in my ear and look up to see our young Italian waiter hovering over us with the kind of attentiveness that makes women of a certain age giggle and swoon.

Hilary wafts him away with a flick of her ballpoint pen. "No, thank you," she instructs. Having attempted to flirt with him earlier and discovered he was engaged, she promptly branded him a tease. "Just the bill, please."

Hilary is here in her capacity as a lawyer. She might have retired from partnership at a top London law firm, but she's still got her licence to practise law, and she's going to draw up the legal papers.

Oh, didn't I mention it? Silly me, I'm so excited about everything I can barely think straight. So, OK, I'm going to do a Rose and just come out and say it . . .

I. Emily Albright. Am the new owner of McKenzie's.

Yup. Really! Can you believe it?

No, neither can I, but it's for real. After talking to Rose and Hilary and discovering that, no, this wasn't a practical joke, and, yes, Rose was totally serious, I called up Mr McKenzie late last night and, with trembling hands and a voice that was such a high-pitched squeak I sounded like I was mainlining helium, we talked about me buying the bookstore and agreed on a price for the lease and all the stock. He was delighted. "Now I know it will be in good hands," was how he put it, and I was so over the moon I can't remember what I said apart from a few hundred breathless thank-yous and a lot about it being a dream come true.

Rose, obviously, is my investor. We're going into business together. Day to day, nothing much will change. I'll continue running the store, with a few extra responsibilities, of course, and Rose will be my silent partner.

"Isn't this just marvellous!"

Rattling her diamonds as if they're castanets, Rose leans back in her chair and claps her hands with joy. "I'm so thrilled to be getting my teeth into something new. Makes a change from men, hey?"

OK, I admit, perhaps not so silent.

We say our goodbyes on the pavement (not sidewalk — see, just as I'm about to fly back to New York I'm finally getting into the lingo) outside the Savoy.

"I'll be drawing up the papers first thing and I'll have them FedExed to you next week," Hilary is saying, giving me a firm handshake.

"Great, thanks." I smile, pumping vigorously. "Thanks for everything."

"My pleasure." She nods.

"Well, no need for us to be saying goodbye, is there?" chimes in Rose, bustling up to me in full-length fur and a matching muff.

I turn to her. I'm feeling a bit light-headed and I can feel my eyes prickling.

"No, I guess not," I sniff, "*partner*," I add, attempting a Texan accent.

Rose cackles delightedly and plants two lipstick kisses on my cheeks. "So when's your flight back to the Big Apple? *Ce soir?*"

I smile. "Yeah, I thought I'd do some sightseeing."

"Oh, to be an American girl in London for the first time . . ." Rose closes her eyes as if to swoon. "I remember my first trip to Paris in my youth. Strange cities are always ripe for adventures." She opens one eye and raises an eyebrow.

"Um . . . well, I think I've had plenty of those." I laugh nervously.

Rose gives me a look that says she doesn't believe a word of it. "Well, cheerio, darling," she says briskly. "I'll be in touch."

"I don't know how I can ever thank you enough."

"Nonsense. I should be the one thanking you, Emily."

"*Me?*" I look at her in confusion.

"For showing me the importance of true friendship," she says soberly. "For making me realise that I don't need a chap to make me feel important, to give me self-esteem." Lowering her head, she squeezes my hand tightly. "For the first time, in a long, long time, I don't feel invisible any more, Emily."

"You were never invisible," I reply, and smiling I squeeze her hand back.

Our eyes meet and for a moment we remain like that until we're interrupted by Hilary, asking, "Do you want to share a cab? I'm heading up to Euston Station . . ."

"A cab?" repeats Rose in astonishment, turning to face her. "Why, don't be such a silly goose, you can ride with me in the Bentley."

As she's speaking the biggest, sleekest black car glides up against the pavement and a uniformed driver gets out and opens the door. He's wearing white gloves and a peaked hat.

"Larry, can we give my dear friend a lift to Euston?"

"Of course, ma'am."

*Ma'am?*

Hilary and I exchange incredulous glances, before she disappears behind Rose into a luxurious cocoon of leather upholstery and Larry dutifully closes the door behind them. The engine starts up with a purr and, as they glide away from the kerb, Rose's diamond-encrusted hand appears from a window and gives a regal wave.

I stifle a giggle. God love Rose. You gotta hand it to her.

Finding myself left behind on the busy street, I glance at my watch. I've still got hours to kill before my flight back to New York. I booked a really late one, thinking I'd want time to do lots of sightseeing on my last day:

Big Ben, the Houses of Parliament, Buckingham Palace, the London Eye, the Tate and all those other art galleries they have here . . . Except, now I'm here, the funny thing is, I don't much feel like sightseeing.

Wheeling my suitcase behind me, I start walking. I decided to donate quite a few of my books to the hotel in Bath before we left. Normally I never part with a book, it's like a part of me, but they had the most pathetic selection on their "reading shelves" that I felt duty-bound. I mean, honestly. Dog-eared copies of Danielle Steele? A book on stamp-collecting? *Geri Halliwell's autobiography*? Now they've got rather a nice collection of literary works, and I've got myself an almost empty — and much lighter — suitcase.

The pavements are thronging with tourists and January-sales shoppers, and I weave in among them, my eyes drifting absently over store windows. I soak up all the sights and sounds and smells of this new city. There's a certain feeling you always get when you're alone in a strange city for the first time. The excitement of being totally anonymous, of not knowing what you're going to find when you turn down a street, of having the freedom to do, for just a few hours, anything that you goddamn please (credit card permitting of course).

With this in mind I cut through a couple of side streets and take a left for no reason other than I just feel like it. I have no clue where I'm heading, and for once, I don't care. Considering my appalling sense of direction, I've decided not to even pretend to look at the little tourist map Miss Steane gave me before she left. She was in a hurry as always. Apparently the coach does a quick turnaround at the cleaner's, before heading straight back to Heathrow to pick up a whole new set of passengers, so I barely got a chance to say bye and thanks as she stuffed it in my hands and disappeared off with her clipboard.

TOPSHOP.

The black-and-white sign grabs my attention and stops me dead in my tracks. I look at it, slowly registering. Oh, wow, this is it. *This* is the famous Topshop that Cat was going on about? Stella's own personal Mecca? A place from which, according to both Cat and Stella, I will emerge a transformed person?

Well, c'mon, I gotta see this.

Wheeling my suitcase behind me, I step on to the escalator. As I ride downwards the thumping music gets louder, my adrenalin starts mounting, and the excitement starts building. Although you're going down, you feel like you're coming up.

Well, I haven't always been a mature bookshop owner, you know.

Reaching the basement, I'm greeted by a vista of clothes racks. On and on they go into a sort of fashion infinity. My nerve falters. I can't do this alone. I need help.

*I need Stella.*

Digging out my cell phone, I quickly dial. Even though it's only been a couple of days, it feels like ages since we last spoke. The phone connects and I listen to it ringing. She was due back from Mexico yesterday, so she should pick up . . .

"Hello?"

**408**

"Stella, it's me, Emily."

"Em! Hey, when are you back? I got a phone call from Mr McKenzie saying not to come into work today. What's going on? Is everything OK?"

"Yeah, everything's cool," I say, quickly reassuring her. I'll tell her all about it when I get back. Right now there are more important things to tell her. Like I said, Top Shop is Stella's Mecca.

"So did you hear from Spike?"

"Sort of," I say, and then quickly change the subject. "What about you? Have you spoken to Freddy?"

"Sort of," she replies, equally vaguely. "But I'll fill you in when you get back. Hey, what's all that music I can hear? Where are you? In a nightclub?"

I laugh inwardly at the very thought. Me? In a nightclub? You'd have more chance of seeing the Pope in a nightclub.

I don't begin to explain that actually it's only the middle of the afternoon here, and instead cut straight to the chase and say those little magic words: "I'm. At. Topshop."

There's a loud screech on the end of the line and I have to hold the phone away from my ear.

"Em, that is *so* fucking exciting. I am *so* fucking jealous!" she's now gasping. "Tell me, *what's it like? What's it like?*"

She's almost hyperventilating.

"Well . . . um . . . it's big . . . and full of clothes . . ." I begin uselessly. Overwhelmed by the sheer volume of stuff, I cautiously venture further into the store, my free hand sort of trailing in wonder across racks. ". . . and

**409**

they have these things that look like . . ." I hesitate as I finger a woollen fabric that looks like a coat but is in fact "a cape," I finish.

"A cape?" shrieks Stella. "Oh, my God, they have those capes? I *adore* those capes. I've been coveting them online for weeks now —" she breaks off to draw breath — "I would *kill* for a cape."

"Well, actually, that's one of the reasons I called. I want to buy you a gift to say thanks for my dress —"

After the word "gift" the rest of my sentence is drowned out by another scream.

"A gift? For me? From *Topshop*?" she says the words with the kind of breathless awe usually reserved for religion. But then for Stella, fashion *is* her religion. And she *is* always telling me Marc Jacobs is a god.

"Oh, Em, I don't know what to say . . ."

"Hey, look, you don't have to say anything. I know you were my secret Santa."

There's a pause and then, "Your what?"

"I know it was you who sent me that beautiful dress for the ball," I continue, absently looking through the rack of capes.

"But I didn't send you a dress," protests Stella, sounding puzzled.

Doubt flickers, but I brush it aside. "Oh, c'mon, Stella, I know it's supposed to be secret, but you can admit it."

"Look, I really wish I had, but seriously, Em, it wasn't me. In fact, I feel really bad as I didn't get you anything and you got me that lovely scented candle."

**410**

I stop flicking through the capes. I've had enough years of Stella's fake phone-in-sick-to-work calls when she's got a hang-over to know when she's not telling the truth. But this time she is.

"But I left you a message thanking you."

"Oh, is that what that message was about?" she says breezily. "I remember you mentioning something about a dress, but I could hardly hear what you were saying, so I just deleted it."

My mind is rapidly going through my list of possible secret Santas. So far I've drawn a blank.

"But if it wasn't you, who was it?" I demand. "I mean, who else is going to send me an amazing dress?"

"I dunno," replies Stella impatiently, and I can imagine her now, sitting on her bed, phone wedged underneath her ear, desperately wanting to get back to her cape conversation. "Your fairy godmother?"

I'm about to do a ha-ha-very-funny-type laugh when I remember something Miss Steane said to me at the ball: "*What a pretty dress. The colour suits you. It brings out the colour of your eyes.*"

At the time I didn't think much about the attention Miss Steane was paying me, but now, on reflection, she *had* shown a lot of interest in my dress. And then there was that funny way she looked at me . . .

No, this is ridiculous. Why on earth would my tour guide be going around buying me a ball dress, for Godsakes? I mean, Jesus, I'm not Cinderella. Why would she want me to go to the ball? I flash back to our conversation.

"*A friend bought it for me as a Christmas present.*"

"How very fortunate. I'm sure you will be a huge hit with the gentlemen tonight."

"Oh, I'm not looking to meet anybody."

"Nonsense. To quote Jane Austen: 'To you I shall say, as I have often said before, "Do not be in a hurry, the right man will come at last." ' "

At the time I felt as if she was referring to Mr Darcy, but I suppose she could have been referring to Spike . . .

Shit. I've done it again. Thinking about Spike when I promised myself I wouldn't. Right, that's it. No more of this dress nonsense. I'll have to get to the bottom of that mystery later. Firmly I turn my attention back to Stella, who's still hanging on the line with bated breath. "OK, so what size are you in a cape?" I ask her.

Theres a squeak, and then she launches into, "Well, actually, I'm a size zero, but that's in the US. In the UK they have an entirely different sizing chart . . ."

I end up buying Stella the cape and three pairs of Union Jack G-strings. I also buy myself a few things. But I don't even *try* trusting my own judgement. Even without Stella's reminder that I am a fashion flunky, I know better. Instead, I get myself one of the store's personal shoppers. A personal shopper! I didn't even know there was such a thing!

And now look at me! I think, staring happily at my reflection as I ride back up the escalator. I have a neck. A waist too. And all these wonderful clothes that mix and match. I'm wearing one of the outfits my personal shopper picked out for me, a pair of skinny jeans (yes, me, in skinny jeans!), a pewter-coloured *jumper* (see, I'm practically British now. I'm not going to use the word "sweater" ever again), a pair of cute black ankle boots with these little cuffs that sort of turn over and the most adorable bright canary-yellow pea-jacket. I would never in a million years have chosen it, but it looks really cool and I've already had a few admiring glances. I think about Stella and smile to myself as I imagine her reaction. She is going to *freak out*. She's going to think I've had a brain transplant, not a vacation.

I emerge into Oxford Street a new — albeit poorer — woman. OK, so now what? I hesitate. I could grab something to eat, except I ate all those cucumber sandwiches and I'm not really hungry. Or maybe I could go to an art gallery, but then, like I said, I'm not really in the mood to look at paintings.

*Or you could go see Spike.*

My stomach doubles over and I feel a sort of tugging in my chest. I've been trying not to think about him all day, but the voice pops into my head loud and clear. I ignore it. Alternatively there's always having a mooch around some bookstores. Maybe Charing Cross is near here somewhere and I've always wanted to go, ever since I saw that movie with Anthony Hopkins and Anne Bancroft.

*He works in London. The offices of the* Daily Times *can't be far. You could jump in a cab.*

Stop it. I am *not* going to see Spike. There's no point. Like I said, I'm just going to forget about him.

**413**

Except my memory has other ideas. Pressing play on the tape recorder in my head, I hear Miss Steane's voice: "*Prejudice can be a terrible thing, Emily. As can pride. You know, Jane Austen always made her heroines feisty. They stuck by their principles, went after what they wanted, were not afraid to admit when they were wrong. Not doing anything can be worse than doing the wrong thing.*"

Up ahead I can see a black cab heading towards me, its yellow light on. I watch as it gets closer and closer. Any minute now and it's going to whizz right past me.

I stick out my arm. At the very last moment the cab swerves deftly to the kerb, and quickly tugging open the door, I scramble inside.

"Where to, love?"

The driver looks at me in his rear-view mirror.

My heart is thumping. I feel almost sick with nerves.

"The *Daily Times*, please."

414

# CHAPTER
# THIRTY-SIX

It's one of those modern metal signs that doesn't have the words written *on* it but instead has them inconspicuously engraved *into* it: THE DAILY TIMES. If it wasn't for the cabbie I would never have noticed it, but the newspaper has probably been here for years and it's their way of saying, "We're so famous we don't need a *proper* sign as you'd have to be moron not to know this is the *Daily Times* building."

Which takes me from nervous to borderline panic.

Checking my reflection (again), I take a deep breath and push open the steel and glass doors. Inside, the foyer is all black marble and the heels of my new boots make a loud clip-clopping as I walk across to the front desk.

"Hello, can I help you?"

The overly made-up desk clerk smiles at me politely.

"Um . . . yeah. Could you tell Spike Hargreaves that Emily Albright is here to see him?"

My heart is beating so hard in my chest right now I feel as if it's going to burst open.

"And what should I say it's regarding?"

I swallow hard and force a smile.

"Just tell him I'm here for my interview."

Ten minutes later I'm still waiting. Well, OK, looking at my watch, it's not exactly ten minutes, it's more like six and a bit, but it feels like he's keeping me waiting. It's probably his way of punishing me, I decide, nervously tapping the heels of my new boots against the marble floor. This is probably a really bad idea. Like, a really, *really* bad idea. Like I should just pick up my bags and wheel myself and my suitcase out of the *Daily Times* and never come back again.

In fact, you know what —

"Miss Albright?"

I snap back to see the desk clerk looking over at me.

"Mr Hargreaves is ready for you now. If you'd like to take the lift to the third floor, someone will meet you."

For a brief moment I consider not going through with my plan, gabbling some excuse about having to be somewhere and dashing out of that black marble foyer as quickly as my new Top Shop boots can take me. But something stops me. I'd like to think it was Miss Steane's voice in my head about not being afraid to admit I was wrong, or my innate desire to do the right thing and apologise for my appallingly shitty behaviour.

But I'd be lying. You want to know the real reason why I don't leave? Because I think — I *hope* — that I've actually met someone I give a stuff about and who gives a stuff about me, and if I go now I'm always going to wonder what could have happened.

"Sure . . . Thanks." I smile back at the desk clerk, and picking up my bags I walk across to the elevator and press the button.

Plus, let's face it, to use another phrase I learned from Cat, I fancy the bloody pants off him.

"Emily!"

As the elevator doors slide open Spike is waiting there in all his crumply, dishevelled Spikeness. My stomach lurches. I expected to feel something when I saw him again, I was *hoping* I was going to feel something. That's the reason I came all this way: that "something". But I hadn't expected it to be *quite* so intense. Forget butterflies, I've got frigging rhinos stampeding around in my stomach.

And now it's that awkward bit where we don't know how to greet each other. Having spent the last three floors running through this very moment, I abandon all thoughts of grand gestures and decide to go with pretending it's perfectly normal to be showing up at the office of someone who only a couple of days ago I was calling a lying bastard, and revert to my default greeting of "Hi" and a smile.

Spike, meanwhile, who I thought for a brief, hopeful moment looked pleased to see me, has now firmly pulled down the shutters on any show of emotion and is nodding "Hello" and stuffing his hands resolutely in the pockets of his old cords.

I feel a crush of disappointment. Well, what did you expect, Emily? For him to greet you with open arms? Quite honestly, you should be grateful he's even talking to you.

I step out of the elevator. My legs wobble. I try telling myself it's the new heels.

"I have to say, you're the last person I expected to see here," Spike is saying now as he leads me across the bustling news floor, filled with dozens of journalists all busily bashing away at their keyboards, and into a small office tucked away in the corner. Closing the door behind him, he gestures to a chair.

"No, I bet," I laugh nervously, as I plonk myself down and glance around the office. It's small, and it's one hell of a mess, but it's cosy, with all these interesting pictures on the walls and shelves crammed with books. *Lots and lots of books.* Not only are they lined up in rows, but they're piled on top too, to fill every available inch of shelf, spines jostling against spines, big hardback books, small paperbacks, dog-eared old favourites with their covers missing . . .

I swear I feel like reaching across his desk, grabbing hold of him and demanding we get married right now.

"So, how's things? How was the rest of the tour?"

Leaning back in his chair, he plonks his feet on his desk, his frayed laces plopping into his coffee mug. I notice he has blackened chewing gum on one of his soles. I also notice that whereas before I would have thought, Pig, now I think, Adorable.

Shit, I have got it bad.

"Oh, great, great." I nod, wondering when I can launch into my speech, which I've been rehearsing all the way up in the elevator. "Lyme Park was awesome. Apparently they've got one of the finest collections of clocks and they have some really interesting paint-ings . . ."

**418**

I can hear myself prattling on like a tour guide and I cringe. "Oh, and Rose got her photo up on the wall," I add, remembering.

"She did? That's great." Spikes grins broadly, and I feel a rush of pleasure.

Maybe there is a chance. Maybe he does still like me. Just a little bit.

He opens his mouth to say something, then pauses uncertainly, and just as I think he's going to refer to our last "conversation", he asks, "And how's Maeve?"

My disappointment is tempered by my excitement at telling him the good news.

"Amazing," I enthuse. "She got a phone call from her daughter out of the blue —"

"So she spoke to Shannon?"

"Yeah, apparently she's a nurse and she's married and — oh, guess what? — Maeve is going to be a *grandma*!" I gasp, and then break off as it suddenly registers. "You said Shannon," I say quietly, my mind turning. "How did you know she was called Shannon?"

For the first time ever I see Spike having difficulty articulating what he wants to say. Rubbing his beard with the flat of his hand, he stares down at his keyboard for a few moments, deep in thought, then, looking up, says, "That morning, after the ball, when we spoke about Ernie . . ."

I feel my cheeks redden with shame.

". . . you told me about Maeve having to give up her baby for adoption, and how she'd always felt terrible about it, and I remembered we'd done a story about that a few months ago. About reuniting adopted

**419**

children with their birth parents. There's these great agencies that can help you trace a person, so when I came back to the office I dug around a little, put in a few phone calls . . ."

Suddenly I have a vague memory of Maeve saying something about how someone had made an enquiry about her to the same agency Shannon had.

"It was you who got in touch with the agency?" I ask, starting to fit it all together.

"Hey, I wasn't trying to interfere," protests Spike quickly.

"No, I didn't mean —" I break off. "Maeve is like a different person," I say quietly.

"That's great, really great." He nods, and I can tell he's genuinely pleased.

"Thank you." I smile.

"Hey, don't thank me. I just made a couple of enquiries." He shrugs. "It's what I do. I'm a journalist, remember?"

Our eyes seek each other out across the desk and I can't help thinking how I didn't see this humble side of him before. How could I have been so blinded? More than ever I want to say all the things I came here to say, but my nerve fails me.

"So, the receptionist said you were here for your interview?" says Spike, breaking the silence.

"Er, yeah . . . yeah, that's right."

"Blimey, I didn't know you were so keen to give one — you never seemed that interested before."

He throws me a look as if to say, "You never seemed that interested in me before," and I feel a thudding regret. But maybe I'm just reading too much into it.

**420**

"Well, no, I wasn't . . ." I flounder around for words. "But, well, you see, I've thought about it and I think it's very important that you get both the old and young perspective on Mr Darcy."

Shit. Emily. *Old and young perspective?* What on earth are you going on about?

"Right, I see." Spike raises his eyebrows as if he's impressed. Then again, it's also a look that could be interpreted as him thinking, What kind of nutcase have I got here?

There's another one of those pauses. I fiddle with my hair. He starts tapping a plastic ruler backwards and forwards against his keyboard.

"Is it me or is it really hot in here?" I blurt.

"It would probably help if you took your coat off." He gestures towards it.

"Oh, yeah, right, *duh!*"

Arggh. Fucking hell. If wearing my coat in a central-heated office and then complaining I'm hot doesn't make me look like a complete moron, sounding like something from *South Park* certainly does. *Duh?* I've never said "duh" in my life! Ever. And now, *here*, is where I decide to use it for the first time?

Self-consciously tugging off my coat, I fold it over on my lap. And then, not knowing what to do next, I sort of stroke the yellow bundle as if it's a pet. "I just bought it," I hear myself saying brightly. "From Topshop."

Oh, my God. What's got into me? I am *digging* a grave. And I want to throw myself in it, I think desperately.

Spike's mouth twitches and I'm sure I see a glimmer of a smile.

"Is that so?"

And now he's laughing at me. I feel the familiar stirrings of irritation.

"Yes. I had a personal shopper," I inform him stiffly. Huh, that'll show him.

"Wow." He leans back in his chair and surveys me with amusement. "And what exactly does this personal shopper do?"

I bristle. "Oh, you know," I say breezily, trying to sound as if I'm used to having personal shoppers all the time. "Inform you about new trends, show you how to put together different looks, pick out clothes . . ." My eyes wander across Spike's outfit. He's wearing ancient-looking cords, an unidentifiable pair of sneakers and an old Smiths' T-shirt, which still has what looks like the remnants of this morning's toothpaste down the front.

"You know, maybe you should try one, one day," I can't help adding. Well, I'm sorry, I know I'm supposed to be here declaring my undying love among other things, but still.

"You don't like the Smiths?" he pleads, tugging at Morrissey's face.

Instantly I feel myself melt. God, how does he do that? How does he manage to look so adorable with Oral B all down his front?

"I love the Smiths," I admit, twisting my mouth up into a smile.

"Good girl." He nods with satisfaction.

Disarmed again, I look tentatively at Spike, searching for the right way to start saying what I came here to say. But there's no easy segue into "Sorry, I fucked up", is there?

"So, what was it you wanted to tell me about Mr Darcy?" Spike asks.

Since yesterday my mind's been full of so many things that I haven't thought about Mr Darcy, but now, just the mention of him makes my chest tighten.

"Aren't you going to ask me questions?" I reply.

Damn. I didn't come here to talk about Mr Darcy.

"Well, no, not really," frowns Spike, shaking his head. "It's more of a freeform chat."

Just the way he says "freeform chat" sends a shiver down my spine. How come I never noticed how wonderful his accent is before? I could listen to it all day.

"Just tell me anything you want to share with my readers," he continues, "about why he would be so many women's ideal date."

"Well, he wouldn't," I retort.

Spike's eyebrows shoot up. "Oh? And why do you say that?"

"Well, he's very self-absorbed, and he can be really intense," I confide, leaning towards him.

Spike stares at me, and I suddenly realise what I've just said.

"I mean, I can *imagine* he could be quite intense," I correct myself quickly.

"But I thought that's what you wanted," he says, leaning towards me and making those rhinos start charging around in my stomach again. "Didn't you once say that to me when we were choosing postcards?" he reminds me.

I feel my cheeks prickle. "Um . . . possibly," I nod. "But I've changed my mind."

"You have?"

"Uh-uh." I nod again. "I was wrong."

Spike looks astounded. "*You?* Are admitting you're *wrong?*"

God, I didn't think I was *that* bad.

"Yep," I say firmly. "I've been wrong about a lot of things, actually."

Spike's face is serious. "Such as?"

I take a deep breath. It's now or never.

"You."

He looks at me and makes a sort of "mmm" sound as if to say, "Go ahead, I'm listening."

"Ernie."

"Mmm . . ."

I screw up my courage and lay my heart wide open. "*Us.*"

There. I've said it.

For a moment Spike doesn't move. Instead, he just stares at me across the desk, his face expressionless, his eyes unblinking. Every millisecond feels like an hour. Just say something, I think urgently. *Anything.*

"I see," he says finally, and steeples his fingers.

My heart constricts. Oh, God. This is dreadful. When I said "anything", I didn't mean *anything*. It suddenly dawns on me that the big romantic moment that I'd hoped for, the one where Spike was going to grasp me

424

in some big corny embrace and kiss the living daylights out of me, is not going to happen. I feel like a complete idiot.

"You know, I should be going, perhaps we can do this interview on e-mail," I gabble hastily, standing up, the humiliation pouring all over me. Clutching my coat to my chest as a sort of shield, I head for the door.

Spike stands up and follows me. "When's your flight?"

"Oh, erm . . ." I glance at my watch gratefully. Anything not to have to look at him. "Not for a few hours, but you know, the traffic might be bad . . ." I'm desperate to get out of the door, but now Spike's standing in the way and blocking it with his huge frame.

"Really?" he's saying. "You know, you can do a lot in a few hours . . ."

Something in his tone makes me look up. His eyes are flashing with amusement. Suddenly the penny drops. Of course. The British sense of humour. He was winding me up. How could he do that to me! I feel a white-hot flash of annoyance, followed by total and utter relief.

"And my flat's just round the corner," he's saying.

Well, I guess I did deserve it, I muse, then ask, "What are you suggesting?" pretending to be shocked, while feeling a thumping beat of excitement. I'd be fibbing if the thought hadn't already crossed my mind. I didn't come here hoping *just* to apologise. Well, I *am* human, and his chest did feel very firm that night at the ball when I squeezed his pec.

"Oh, I dunno, we could watch a spaghetti Western, do a crossword . . ." He moves closer.

"You know, I'm pretty darned good at the cryptic ones. I get all the clues," I tease, leaning my body towards him.

"You are?"

"Uh-uh."

"Great," he whispers, and I can feel his breath on my cheek. "But before we go any further, I think I should tell you something."

I look at him. A flutter of nerves.

"Don't look so worried." He smiles. "I'm not going to tell you I'm crazy about you, I've told you that already."

And wrapping his arms round me, he pulls me to his chest and gives me a great big bear hug. I feel a whoosh of happiness. There's nothing quite like being hugged by a big strong guy you're crazy about.

"No, there's something else," he murmurs, his lips brushing against my hair.

"What?" I gasp, a quiver running all the way down to my toes.

"My name's not really Napoleon Caesar —"

"Nelson Hargreaves," I finish off, smiling. "I kind of figured that. So tell me — what does the B stand for?"

He looks at me, surprised.

"I saw your e-mail address, remember?"

Now it's his turn to smile. Scrunching up his nose, he winces with shame. "Bryan. With a Y."

"Bryan with a Y?" I giggle. "Damn, and I thought the name Napoleon was really sexy."

"What? Are you telling me you don't find me sexy any more?" He pretends to look affronted.

"Hmmm, I'm not sure," I murmur. "I think I might have to do a bit more investigative reporting . . ." And slipping my hands up the back of his T-shirt and on to bare skin, I tilt my face up to his and he bends down and kisses me.

# Epilogue

"How's that looking, miss?"

The two workmen standing on ladders shout down to me, their thick Queens' accents resonating loudly through the city hum. Standing below them on the sidewalk, I crick my neck to look upwards, shading my eyes from the bright morning sunshine.

"Um . . . it's not quite straight . . . Left a bit." I yell back.

Cue lots of puffing and panting, their breath making white swirling clouds in the frosty air.

"What about now?"

I squint, cocking my head from side to side and stepping back a little away from the store. "No . . . a little higher, I think . . ."

I can tell they want to murder me. Me, the girl in the yellow coat and woollen bobble hat, sipping her mug of coffee and giving orders to two burly guys in lumber jackets, beanies and fingerless gloves, like a couple of latter-day Rocky Balboas. But seeing as I'm the one paying them, they can't. I'm the boss now.

They just grunt that bit louder to make sure of a bigger tip.

"This OK?" they holler in stereo.

I look up again. I want it to be perfect. It *has* to be perfect. I pause, my eyes sweeping over the varnished wood, the bold swirls of paint, the glint of gold against the black lettering: *Albright's*. I feel a thrilling rush of exhilaration. My new sign. Hanging over my new store. The legal papers were signed two weeks ago, but *now* it feels official. A grin breaks over my face and I feel like punching the air.

Instead, I just make do with a simple, "Perfect!"

I've been back in New York for nearly three weeks now, and I feel as if so much has happened. Well, a lot can happen in three weeks, can't it? Look how much happened during that week I spent in England.

Watching the workmen busily fixing the sign into place, I sip my coffee and smile absently to myself as my mind drifts back. I've thought a lot about that trip since I've been back, about the lessons I learned and the friends I made. And of course I've thought a lot about Mr Darcy. About what really happened back there in England over New Year.

Now I'm back in New York, back to my real life, I have to be honest, it does all *seem* a bit unreal. I mean, I was so sure back then, there was no doubt in my mind, but it's funny how things can seem different when a bit of time and space has passed. How uncertain you can become, how doubts can creep in that make you question yourself and your memories of the past. And now, looking back with hindsight, I can't help wondering, Did it really happen? Did I really meet Mr Darcy? Does he *really* exist?

I haven't seen him since he vanished that day in Lyme Park, and standing here, in the middle of SoHo, the mere thought of a fictional character somehow coming to life and turning up in a frock coat and breeches does seem pretty ridiculous. I've thought about the times we met and I guess you *can* explain them all away if you want to. Like I guess you can explain *everything* away if you try hard enough. Isn't that what sceptics do all the time? Trying to make sense of things that don't make sense by using common sense, rationality and that little big thing called coincidence . . .

In which case, maybe it *was* just a mixture of jet lag, desire and an overactive imagination that conjured up Mr Darcy at Chawton Manor. Perhaps I fainted at Winchester Cathedral and was so delirious I imagined him to be there. It could be that our moonlit boat ride on the lake was simply a dream. Our New Year's Eve horse ride a hallucination, caused by too much champagne and the rest of that *incredibly* strong joint. And our picnic at Sham Castle was just a fantasy, the result of me falling asleep, tired and upset from my argument with Spike. And, yes, it's possible that in the maze of gardens at Lyme Park, I was so lost and defeated and crying so hard that I envisaged Mr Darcy finding me. So that ultimately I was able to find *myself*.

But. And this is a big but. I'm not so sure. Part of me actually wants to believe it's true, that something magical really did happen on that trip to England and I really did get to date Mr Darcy. But I don't think I'll ever know. And I don't think it matters, does it?

Because one thing's for sure: Mr Darcy does exist. In as much as he exists in the imaginations of millions of women everywhere. Remember June, the immigration officer at Heathrow? He was real to her. And what about Rupinda, Rose, Maeve, Hilary . . . The list is endless. Right now, all over the world, someone, somewhere, is dreaming about Mr Darcy. So what if it's a fantasy. Aren't fantasies real?

"Hey, is that the new sign?"

I whirl round to see Freddy from the bakery next door loping across the cobbles towards me. He's wearing an apron and his arms are covered in a white coating of flour, all the way up to his elbows.

"It looks amazing."

I feel a huge beat of pride. "Thanks." I smile appreciatively.

"Your folks must be really proud of you."

"Yeah, they are." I nod. "They're coming down tonight with my brother. We're all going to celebrate." Happiness glows inside me. Since getting back from our respective trips, my parents and I have been making a lot more effort. OK, we'll never be best friends, but I've got plenty of friends. I don't need any more friends, I need a mom and a dad. I think admitting that to myself, and to them, was the first step for all of us.

"Wow, that's just great, Emily, really great." Freddy gives me a big, floury, after-shaved hug and then grins ruefully. "She in there?" He gestures to the store.

"You mean Stella?" I ask. "Yeah, why?" I narrow my eyes. Since getting back from England, my radar's been picking up a lot of phone calls, visits and whispered conversations between Stella and Freddy. "What's going on with you two?" I ask smiling.

"Nuthin'." He shrugs innocently, and bounds off back across the cobbles.

*Nuthin'*? Hmm. Now I'm *really* suspicious.

Watching him disappear back into the bakery, I make up my mind to quiz Stella when I go back inside. At the moment I don't want to interrupt her as she's busy in the stockroom sorting out the new orders. Which reminds me. When I got back from my trip one of the first things I did was check the new batch of *Pride and Prejudice* for blank pages, but they were perfect, every last one of them, and I know, as I personally went through them all. Plus I checked our database and there was no record of any returns. Weird, huh? I must have got the one faulty copy.

And do you want to know something else that's weird? I always kept that copy in the side pocket of my bag, but when I got home and came to unpack, I found a *different* copy. One with all the pages intact. I guess I must have lost mine, or mistakenly given it to the hotel in Bath and accidentally picked up one belonging to someone else on the tour.

Unless there's another explanation — a weird, wonderful, suspend-your-disbelief explanation — that maybe, *just maybe*, this *is* my original copy. You see, I have this theory . . .

432

There's this bit in the book when Mr Darcy leaves Netherfield in November and goes to London with the Bingleys for the winter. It's at the end of Volume I, well, actually, it's the first few lines of Volume II if I remember rightly, just after the ball. Elizabeth doesn't see him again until Easter. That's months. During that time nobody knew what he got up to, where he went, who he met. He could have done anything. Met anyone. Dated anybody.

Like, for example, a girl from New York called Emily.

Is that why the rest of the pages were blank? Because he met me? Because that day at Chawton Manor, when we were both visitors from completely different places, our two worlds collided and we somehow managed to bump into each other? I don't know how it happened, or why it happened, *but it happened*. And as a result of that trigger, a whole set of changes were set in motion . . .

At the time I didn't stop to think about what the consequences might be of me and Mr Darcy. I was too busy being swept off my feet by a man I've been dreaming about since I was twelve years old. Too caught up with living out my fantasy, and that of every other woman like me. But now, in hindsight, I have thought about it, about what would have happened if I really had fallen in love with him, if we'd somehow stayed together.

My mind begins unravelling the story at a rate of knots. Mr Darcy would never have returned to Netherfield, made the trip back to his aunt's in the hope he'd see Elizabeth, declared his undying love,

**433**

been refused and written her that letter. And Elizabeth wouldn't have had Mr Darcy coming to the rescue when her sister Lydia eloped with Wickham, she wouldn't have been able to come to her senses and realise she was wrong, and she wouldn't have been able to say yes when he asked her to marry him.

And therefore the rest of the story would never have happened. The pages would have remained for ever blank. There would have been no greatest love story of all time. No Elizabeth and Mr Darcy. No *Pride and Prejudice* as we know it. It would have ceased to exist. And it would have been all my fault. And, like the ripples produced by a stone hitting the water, the effects would have been far-reaching. The implications staggering.

Just imagine. There'd be no Colin Firth in the lake scene, no Matthew Macfadyen striding through the mist, no Mark Darcy for Bridget Jones.

At the thought of all those millions of irate Bridget Jones fans, I feel slightly sick.

But Mr Darcy did go back. Which explains why the pages aren't blank any more. He returned to his life, forgot about me and by doing so created one of the best love stories there'll ever be.

Sounds incredible?

Hell, it does. But perhaps we all need to believe something incredible once in a while. Just like I'd like to believe that the silk scarf I found outside Winchester Cathedral really *is* Mr Darcy's and not some random stranger's. I still have it. I keep it in my underwear drawer. Unfortunately it doesn't smell of that sexy cologne any more. I had to wash it after blowing my snotty nose on it and now it smells of Bounce fabric conditioner. But still, sometimes I like to take it and tie it around my neck and fantasise a little . . .

But only a little of course, and then I put it straight back in the drawer.

"Hey, Em, can you sign these delivery forms?"

Stella's holler grabs my attention and I zone back to see her standing in the store doorway, wearing her raspberry-pink cape and waving a bunch of forms at me. I smile. She hasn't taken that cape off since I gave her it. That's three weeks straight in a raspberry-pink cape. Her neighbours have taken to calling her Red Riding Hood. Not that she cares. She's in seventh heaven — or should I say Topshop heaven?

"Sure," I yell back, and draining the last of my coffee, I run across the cobbles towards her. "So," I smile, reaching her and following her inside the store, "spill the beans."

"What beans?" she asks innocently, guilt written all over her face.

"About you and Freddy," I prompt, leaning against the section of the trestle table that's right in the path of sunlight streaming through the doorway. It feels warm on my back.

"There's nothing to spill," she continues, and thrusts the forms at me. "Here, you need to sign these, boss."

I take them from her. "Don't try to butter me up by calling me boss. That's two nothings. One from you and one from Freddy." Grabbing a pen, I scribble my signature. "And two nothings make a something — it's like a double negative."

Stella purses her mouth and surveys me thoughtfully. I can tell I've really got her with the double-negative thing.

"Oh OK," she sighs, throwing her hands up in the air like a Jewish mother. "I give in. We're dating."

I look at her, a mixture of delight and disbelief. "Stella! That's fantastic! Why didn't you tell me earlier? You know I think Freddy's great. Jeez, when did this all happen?"

"When I got back from Mexico," she says, allowing herself a small smile as she remembers. "He was waiting for me when I got back and he'd made me this great cheesecake, as he knows it's my favourite, and we just stayed in, and ate too much, and chatted and —" She breaks off and shakes her hair, the tips of which she's recently dyed black. "It made me realise just how much I'd missed him while I was away. Even before Scott turned out to be such a loser, I missed him. I thought it was just 'cos we lived together, we'd gotten used to each other, but it was more than that."

Joining me in the little patch of sunlight, she turns to me. "You know, we're pretty good together," she confesses.

"Er, hello," I say indignantly. "Who's been telling you this for *months*?"

She grins sheepishly. "I know, I know, I didn't listen . . ."

"So what's it like, having sex with your husband?" I ask, elbowing her.

**436**

She blushes. "Well, at least I know he's going to respect me in the morning," she quips, and we both laugh.

We're interrupted by the phone ringing, and Stella jumps up to get it. After a moment she calls out, "It's Spike — *your boyfriend*."

Now it's my turn to blush. "Stop it," I hiss, as I rush over and snatch the receiver from her.

But I'm not really miffed, I'm only pretending. I *love* people calling Spike my boyfriend. *I* love calling him my boyfriend. I love everything *about* him being my boyfriend. Like, for example, sending him funny cards that I find in these little boutiques in SoHo, exchanging funny e-mails, chatting on the phone for hours as I lie in bed with my hot-water bottle imagining it's him and counting down the days until he's flying out to New York to visit me (it's four, I've already counted, well, actually, it's three days and twenty-two hours and about forty-five minutes), making silly doodles on the pad at work that involve writing our names, writing the word "love" and then doing that thing where you count up how many Ls, Os, Vs, Es there are and then add them together and —

OK, I'll stop now. I know that's a load of old rubbish, but I can't help it. I don't *want* to help it. Because finally, after a litany of disastrous dates, I've finally met a guy I'm crazy about and who's crazy about me. Well, *he's* definitely crazy, anyway. And it took a long time to find him, and I went a long way to find him, and it even took me dating Mr Darcy to find him, but like Jane Austen said, "*Don't be in a hurry. The right man will come at last,*" and he did.

Albeit I wasn't imagining him to be wearing a toothpaste-stained Smiths T-shirt, but then love has a habit of surprising you. Saying that, I think I've had enough surprises for one lifetime.

"Hey, you," I say, pressing the phone to my ear. "How's it going?"

"I miss you," replies Spike matter-of-factly on the other end of the line.

I get that lovely warm feeing inside. "Miss you too," I say happily, and then mouth, "Ouch," as Stella grins and elbows me in the ribs. Trust me, she has very bony elbows.

"OK, now we've got all that slushy stuff out of the way, how's the sign looking?"

"Amazing," I say proudly, using Freddy's adjective. "You'll see it soon."

"I know, I can't wait. Two whole weeks with you in New York."

My smile gets even wider. "Hey, by the way, will you manage to finish all your articles in time?" I ask him.

"Yeah, should do — I've just got a few loose ends to tie up on a couple of pieces . . ."

"What about the Mr Darcy piece?"

"Oh, didn't I tell you?"

"You finished it and the editor loved it?"

"Well, yeah, there's that," he says modestly, "and the fact that now he wants to hold it back for the Valentine's Day issue . . ."

We both groan.

438

". . . but, no, there was something else. When I came to do all the name-checks, I called up the tour company and asked to be put through to Miss Steane, and they said there was no Miss Steane at that company. That in fact they'd never heard of her. I checked the number a couple of times, but I'd definitely got the right company. Isn't that just the weirdest thing?"

"Wow, yeah," I say, puzzled.

Just then I hear someone asking Spike a question in the background, and he comes back on the line: "Hey, Em, I'm going to have to go — work stuff. Can I call you later?"

"Yeah, of course. Bye."

"Bye."

I hang up and stare at the phone for a moment, deep in thought.

"Something up?"

Stella reappears from the back carrying two mugs of fresh coffee and passes me one.

"Thanks," I murmur absently, staring at the handset a little longer, before putting it down on the counter. "He's right. That *is* really weird," I say, thinking out loud.

"What? What? Tell me what?" demands Stella, her interest now fully piqued.

"The tour guide on my trip," I explain. "Apparently no one at the company's ever heard of her."

"*Oooh*," says Stella, her eyes wide. "An imposter."

I roll my eyes sardonically. "Honestly, Stella, you watch too many crime shows."

She tuts and takes a gulp. "So who did she say she was? This tour guide?"

"Her name's Miss Steane. Hang on, I think I've got her card here somewhere." Putting down my mug, I grab my purse and rifle through my wallet. Sure enough, there's the small rectangle of cream parchment. I hand it to Stella.

"That's it? Those are her details? Just her name, no number or anything?"

To be honest, I haven't looked at it before, I just put it in my billfold, but now, looking at it, I see Stella's right.

"Huh, I guess so." I nod.

"Una J. Steane," reads Stella, tracing her finger across the black embossed calligraphy. "Well, that's obvious." She shrugs.

"Is it?" I ask. It's not being very obvious to me.

"Yeah, it's an anagram of Jane Austen."

I look at her dazedly. "What?" I whisper, my voice not seeming to work properly. "No, it can't be . . ."

"You mean you didn't work it out? Honestly, Em, you of all people . . ."

Stella continues talking but her voice fades into the background as I dive over to the bookshelves and snatch up a copy of *Persuasion*. I flick to the back cover. No, nothing. I grab *Emma*. Again nothing. What about a different publisher . . .? Spotting a hardback volume of *Pride and Prejudice*, I seize it and turn straight to the back.

Holy shit.

I'm staring at a portrait of Miss Steane, only it's Jane Austen, circa 1811. No wonder I kept thinking she looked familiar. Apart from the clothes, they're identical. Same nose, same eyes, same amused smile. Out of nowhere I suddenly remember the woman in the biography section before Christmas, the lady who bought the book about Jane Austen that I'd never seen before, who left the flyer for the tour on the counter — the resemblance is uncanny . . . My mind starts whirling. And yet they can't all be the same person — it's obviously just a coincidence with the anagram and the likeness . . .

But already I'm thinking about all the advice Miss Steane gave me about men and relationships, that strange comment she made at the lake when I saw Mr Darcy swimming and outside Winchester Cathedral when I found his scarf. Could she see him, too? And what about the ball dress? Was it from her? I suddenly remember Stella's comment. Was she some kind of fairy godmother, a matchmaker, bringing Spike and me together?

I catch myself. Oh, c'mon, Emily. No way! That's crazy!

Yeah, right, I've heard *that* before.

"Is it something I said?"

I glance up from the picture to see Stella looking at me expectantly, clutching her coffee mug to her chest. Oh, shit. I have no idea what she was just saying. I didn't hear a word.

"Oh, no . . . no," I manage composing myself. "Just noticed a few books weren't in order."

Stella relaxes her shoulders and smiles in admiration. "Jeez, you really do love this place, don't you?"

I smile as I start putting the books back on the shelves.

"So when's your boyfriend arriving? I can't wait to meet him."

"Friday," I say, feeling that familiar beat of excitement.

"So what's he like, this Spike?" She grins. "Is he like Mr Darcy?"

I pause to glance down at the copy of *Pride and Prejudice* in my hands, at the picture of Jane Austen, and it's as if Miss Steane is smiling right at me.

"No," I say, shaking my head.

And as I think about Spike, with his sloppy clothes, hot temper and crazy sense of humour, a huge smile breaks across my face.

"He's absolutely *nothing* like him."

# 2007 Mr Darcy: The Dream Date

**Mr Darcy, the dashing hero of Jane Austen's *Pride and Prejudice*, has topped a survey of men women would most like to go on a date with. Regular bloke** Spike Hargreaves, **goes on a literary tour and asks, What does Mr Darcy have that he doesn't?**

Austen's creation beat other fictional heroes, such as James Bond and Superman, in the poll, run by the Orange Prize, of more than 1,900 women. Which seems strange to me, as surely he'd spend the evening glowering at you across the restaurant table and being rude to all the waiters?

Men just don't get Mr Darcy, and how could we? For Darcy is the anti-man. He is everything a man is not and therefore women adore him. For us blokes, he's a pain in the arse. Over the years I've been compared unfavourably with him many, many times. He's the perfect gent. A sex-machine to all the chicks. He burns with sullen intensity and does so while wearing a frilly white blouse and tight breeches. And, excuse me, but no one complains about his fashion sense!

So what is it about Mr Darcy that sends women wild? What's the secret of his lasting appeal? And, more importantly, what can I learn from him?

In search of an answer, my editor "suggested" I spend a week on a Jane Austen literature tour with die-hard fans. Now, the last time I encountered Mr Darcy was when I was forced to read *Pride and Prejudice* for my English GCSE and I didn't particularly like him then. So this time round, when I found myself cancelling plans to spend New Year skiing in the Swiss Alps to visit museums in the British countryside, our relationship went from bad to worse.

Understandably, and somewhat fittingly, I was rather prejudiced when I interviewed his fans. Made worse by the simple fact that women love him. And that's not just a plain and simple "love" him, that's a Barry White "*lurve*" him.

"He's just so sexy," Rupinda Ali, a yoga instructor told me. "All that smouldering and moodiness — phwoar — I know what I'd like to do on my date with him."

Add jealousy to my list of complaints against him.

Me. A man who doesn't have a jealous bone in his body. And here I am feeling envious of a fictional character.

But it appears *that's* where I've been going wrong. Because for most women on this tour, this literary bad boy is as real to them as Santa Claus is to the under-fives. He's been their first love, and it's been an enduring love. They don't want to give him up. Through all the ups and downs of relationships, the heartbreak, the disappointment and even the happy mundaneness of marriage, Mr Darcy is always there. Brooding, dashing and full of integrity, he's tall, handsome and, a bonus here, extremely rich. He is also aloof, moody, detached and more than a little "complicated".

When it comes to women, I've learned this is a completely irresistible combination.

"He's just looking for the right woman to fix him, to unlock all his passion and allow him to love," Hilary Pringle, a retired lawyer and devoted Darcy fan informs me. "And let's be honest here, the man oozes sex appeal. Show me a woman who wouldn't want to sleep with him."

I tried, and I couldn't. Every female interviewed would, given the opportunity, jump into bed with Mr Darcy. Even Maeve Tumpane, who blushed when she said, in her soft-spoken Irish accent, she imagined he would be "the type to respect you in the morning".

Maybe this is the key to his unique appeal: he's sexy. He's also, let's face it, a bastard and although they will hate me to say this, women love bastards. Just look at Heathcliff, *Sex and the City*'s Mr Big or even Jack Nicholson's character in *Something's Gotta Give*.

Jane Austen knew this. She knew that women like a challenge and would be intrigued by "the proudest, most disagreeable man in the world". Mr Darcy was most definitely *not* a new man. Women might say they want their partners to do the dishes and help them put the duvet cover on but these are not the attributes they have sexual fantasies over.

And women wonder why we men are confused.

I did, however, learn a few things from Mr D. In keeping with these mixed messages, women might have embraced feminism, but they still adore a show of chivalry. So the next time you're tempted to bag that seat on the Tube, stand up and let the lady sit down — a few open doors, it seems, go a long way . . .

Then there's all that repressed passion. Women, it seems, *lurve* repressed passion. *Pride and Prejudice* is a whopping 350 pages long and yet Mr Darcy and Elizabeth never kiss. Which means, if you're watching the BBC adaptation, that's six hours of foreplay. Even in the film version, it's over two.

Now I'm not sure there is a man alive who can keep a woman excited for that long without so much as loosening his cravat (unless of course you're Sting. Who can ever forget his boasts of Tantric sex?), and even if you could, in today's culture, if you didn't try to kiss a woman on the first date, she wouldn't think you chivalrous, she'd accuse you of being gay.

But that's the whole point. Mr Darcy is, as Emily Albright, an attractive twenty-something New Yorker on the trip confessed, "a wonderful fantasy. The embodiment of everything hopeless romantics desire in the man of their dreams." He loves passionately. Is unimpressed by looks and clothes and charm. Is full of integrity. And, most importantly, didn't choose the prettiest girl but went for personality.

Now can you see why I want to kill him?

In short he can do no wrong. He is the perfect man. *Or is he?* As Ms Albright went on to point out on our first date, "He's not actually real — you are."

And so it seems I have the final advantage. Because although I might not be every woman's fantasy (OK, I'm not *any* woman's fantasy) and I'm certainly far from perfect, it's ultimately the real guy who gets the girl.

So stick that in your breeches and brood about it, Mr Darcy.